MR. KLEIN'S WILD RIDE
a novel by Lynn Savage

Cover art by Christian Carvajal
Cover design by Carv's Thinky Works

ISBN-10: 0-692-75902-6
ISBN-13: 978-02-692-75902-8

Printed in the USA

DISCLAIMER
Names, characters, places, and incidents featured in this publication are the product of the author's imagination or are used fictitiously. Any resemblance to actual persons (living or dead), events, institutions, or locales, without satiric intent, is coincidental.

Published by Mud Flat Press

Mud
Flat
Press

Part One: Foreplay

Chapter 1

"Adam Ryder called this morning," Sherri announced, handing me a stack of messages as I headed out the door to a lunch meeting at Shiloh's. "He says he's building the Disneyland of sex, and he wants Randall/Klein to create its Mickey Mouse." Thus began my undoing.

Sex sells. Don't I know it? Selling used to be my job. That's how I was seduced into Bliss in the first place. Remember those Corona ads with the graphics that slid over hot couples' bodies as they danced to steamy salsa music? That was me. I thought up all five of those. Remember the pizza commercials with the twenty-year-old Monica Bellucci lookalike? Her name's Vittoria Vetra. She chain-smokes and listens to hip hop. A couple of guys at Framestore created the not-so-subliminal phallus of mozzarella that swelled and burst onto her chin and lips. I'm told there were stations in the Midwest that wouldn't run the ad, but I boohooed all the way to the bank. Domino's phone orders jumped fifteen percent nationwide the week the campaign started running.

Michelle Malkin claims I wrote the line, "What happens in Vegas stays in Vegas." Don't I wish! No, a Vegas ad agency, R&R Partners, devised a similar slogan for a convention, then spent years fighting a competing claim from a lady in California who used the more familiar version on T-shirts. I did write, "I'm bored. Let's get naked and see what happens," which lured tens of thousands of red-faced visitors to Bliss Panerotic. It may have even lured you. If so, you're welcome or I'm sorry, whichever you find most appropriate.

I tell you all this, not to brag—well, perhaps a little—but to explain how I met Adam and Nicole Ryder. You've seen in the press, of course, that Adam's real name is Alex Walford. Yawn. He was smart to change it. Nicole's birth certificate lists her as Nicky Schultz. However they got started, the Ryders were now full-on moguls. The first generation of movie studio titans would've admired them unreservedly. To this day, Adam's belief in the power of his own vision is a juggernaut. The former Nicky Schultz, a prom queen at Redondo High before Justin Timberlake brought sexy back, may have expected Adam to be president or movie star (or both) someday; but until things went south, I never felt she was unhappy with her lot in life. Whatever else she may have been, Nicole Ryder was nobody's fool.

It's often said Adam is shorter than most of the women he hangs out with, but that's deceptive. He's five-eight; the guy likes tall women. Nicole's an inch over six feet, and man, is she striking. There's something about tall, un-skinny women that doesn't come across in photographs, but in person and over the phone, Nicole dominates. It doesn't matter who's standing beside her. She may never be the most classically beautiful woman in the room—that honker paraphrases Picasso—but even supermodels get out of her way. Meanwhile, there's Adam, a compact, manscaped orthodontia advertisement, Ron Blagojevich's more trustworthy frat clone, sneaking splats of Purell between every arm-clutching double handshake. Purell's slogan, by the way, is, "Imagine a touchable world." Adam had.

My lawyers tell me there are extremely true things I know about the Ryders that I'd be crazy to tell you. The word "actionable" comes up a lot. One lady, whose eyes were as dark and unblinking as a Gucci-suited shark's, promised I'd be sued out of the solar system if I blabbed. I believe her. So instead, let me dispel a few myths. Adam Ryder was not, in fact, born rich, if by rich you mean "multimillionaire." His father made a comfortable living as a sports physiologist for the New England Patriots. This freed his mom to write a children's book, *The Unfunny Monkey*, which did make cabbage—though not till after Adam got famous. No, Adam got rich the same way I did, in video. He and two college friends maxed out their credit cards to shoot the first *Ski Bunnies Xtreme*. They paid their "xtreme" amateur models in mostly lift fees and tequila shots. Adam himself is a capable skier. I've seen him glide a skateboard down a rail like a teenager.

I've heard it said he met Nicole when she auditioned for *Ski Bunnies*. Not so. He met her in college and recruited her into procuring girls for *Xtreme Ski Bunnies 2*. (The grammatical reversal in the title didn't bother anyone. Apparently sin outweighs syntax.) She's also visible in two or three club shots, sneering as she hoists her sweater to reveal the ripe lower hemispheres of two amazing natural breasts. That was the closest I ever got to seeing Nicole naked, by the way—which, given the Ryders' profession, is pretty remarkable.

If only I'd had the foresight to change my own name. But no: Gary Klein of Fortuna, California, that's me. I blew out of Stanford with a couple of national ad campaigns under my belt. I made it my driving philosophy never to think of any project as pointless or (solely) mercenary. Joe Pytka was my Kurosawa. I watched *Mad Men* as if I were studying for the bar. By the time I created that infamous tortilla chip ad with some Kardashian or other—don't forget, we actually managed to get a performance out of that illiterate French braid of silicone, and it would've been easier to elicit good acting from the chips—my agency, Randall/Klein Enterprises, was hailed as the heir apparent to GSP, the firm who brought you such modern-day classics as "Got Milk?" For whatever that's worth, right? I can tell you, it was worth quite a lot. I was the wizard of DVR-proof commercials, and I still have two CLIOs to prove it. You can hum at least three of the brain-dead jingles I made famous.

It was two or three days prior to the week Randall/Klein takes off for Christmas and New Year's. I had two assistants: Dylan, who looked like any other schmo you'd see walking down La Cienega, handled my appointments and written communications. Sherri looked like Miss November, which is what she nearly agreed to be after two years of holding suitcases on a game show. She handled the phones plus any visitor, male or female, who managed to breach my outer office defenses. Her phone voice sounded like bourbon splashed on silk. Welcome to L.A., right? Appearance is advertising, especially in southern California.

I'm not sure I knew who Adam was at the time, but Sherri did. She went to school with a girl who dry-humped a sorority sister on *Xtreme Ski Bunnies 5*, mortifying and/or titillating the entire population of Goleta, California. I guess once she reminded me who Adam was I could put a face to the name—he was usually mentioned on GNN after getting sued by someone like, say, an angry dad in Goleta, California. I'm not sure why I called him back. Business gets slow that close to the holidays. I may have imagined an exciting new cash cow. Maybe I'm just amused by the kind of people I meet in this business. I get that way sometimes. You have to, especially when you're spoon-feeding a Kardashian her seventeenth take of "Ooh, yeah." She's a Mensa candidate, that one.

I don't remember the conversation word for word. I probably had a few drinks in me from Shiloh's. But I do remember the pitch: Adam and Nicole Ryder wanted to invest the considerable fortune they'd earned as, respectively, the CEO and COO of Panerotic Entertainment, Inc.—a pile of lucre Smaug would covet—into an adult amusement park. They weren't sure where they wanted to put it. I think at that point they were leaning toward Vegas or Daytona Beach. They did know what they intended to call the joint: it was Bliss Panerotic from the moment it came to Nicole in a dream. That's right: Nicole, not Adam. In many ways Nicole was the brains of that outfit, and you can quote me if you're so inclined.

I agreed to meet the Ryders a week later at Red Medicine on Wilshire. I have a thing for Thai dumplings. Now that I'm in my thirties, I crave hot, steamy cuisine almost as often as sex. Ah, one of life's little ironies. If I were known for gastronomy, I might be judging *Top Chef* right now instead of skirting journalistic bottom feeders at the mall.

The lunch conversation I do remember, mostly because the Ryders brought pictures. I'm a visual learner. Granted, we had to keep the conversation on the down-low in a small restaurant, and I'm sure our eyes were shifting from side to side like we were in a bad spy movie, but the pitch was outstanding. The Ryders wanted to build a three-hundred-acre theme park, parking not included, in homage to the manifold joys of getting one's ashes hauled. Guests would be exclusively eighteen or older, preferably attractive, and given to, let's say, socializing.

Nicole got the idea from GNN of all places. In 2010, Argyle Greenwood interviewed a guy named Douglas Hines who built a sex robot named Roxxxy. ("After 9/11," Hines explained, "I wanted to give back.") For seven thousand dollars, you could buy a rubber mannequin—I'm oversimplifying—with a computerized voice module smart enough to carry on a rudimentary conversation and fake an orgasm, which makes her at least as bright as several of the actors I've hired. Loan me a Maserati, and I could probably pose Roxxxy on the hood and sell a billion tortilla chips. This was cutting-edge stuff a few years ago, but Nicole guessed correctly that huge strides were imminent.

I'm certainly not the first commentator to notice this, but every new media technology is quickly co-opted and made successful by porn. The printing press, first used to distribute Bibles, soon cranked out erotica. Pietro Arentino's *Postures* included engravings that depicted numerous sexual positions. Homemade nudie photos were shot to entertain and inspire Civil War soldiers. Cable TV allowed New Yorkers to watch porn at home as early as *Midnight Blue* in 1974. VHS, CD-ROM, DVD, Blu-ray, home 3-D; you name it, porn is what first made it profitable. Nicole thought Walt Disney's beloved robots and theme parks were about to go from Snow White to blue, and she believed Panerotic could make that happen.

You don't realize how big or rich Panerotic was in 2013. Panerotic Entertainment Group employed 157 people, not counting contract performers, about half the staff of Playboy Enterprises, Inc. It sucked in revenues of over a hundred and fifty million dollars a year. It left other adult companies like Vivid or Hustler in its glittery dust. The Ryders were flush with liquid capital, and they had a deal in place for millions more in financing. I could tell you from whom, but my lawyer assures us that if I do, I may as well slit my guts open with a Ginsu and wait for the vultures.

The prestigious architectural firm of Larkin Stern and Associates was already on the job. You may know LSA as the guys—Jewish guys like me, actually—who designed an all-Islamic shopping mall in Dubai. It looks like an eight-pointed star. Now they'd invested God knew how many person-hours on color renderings of a proto-Panerotic. Adam showed me designs for a plaza surrounded by casinos and swimming pools. The painted plaza was rife with tourists in skimpy swimsuits, grinning as if they were imported from a toothpaste commercial. The initial designs were smaller than the finished resort, but impressive all the same.

"Why casinos?" I asked. "I thought this was about sex."

Adam snorted and said, "It's about money. Even in the recession, casinos in Atlantic City made over a hundred million dollars a quarter in pure profit. And that's if it's snowing. Who wants to go to New Jersey in the winter? Gamblers do. If you build it, they will come."

"Oddly enough," a respectable-looking architect added, "we find the presence of casinos legitimizing in an enterprise like this. They appear more upscale, more sophisticated than a pure sex resort."

"Guys associate casinos with James Bond," Nicole said. "Women associate James Bond with seduction, glamor, intrigue."

"Yeah, it's all about pulling in the ladies," Adam agreed. "No guy wants to spend his hard-earned money at a sausage-fest. Before he'll pony up, he needs to know there's gonna be hotties in the club."

"You're gonna need more than casinos to make that happen," I replied, crossing my arms.

"That's where you come in," Nicole agreed. "This isn't about selling beer to football fans. That's easy. What we want from you is to brand us as naughty instead of pervy. We're looking for an air of adventure, like a honeymoon for people who've already gotten bored fucking each other."

"That's easier said than done."

"Vegas managed it," she countered. "Fifty-fifty last year, male to female."

"Huh."

"We're selling..." She groped for le bon mot, then sighed, "...freedom. Like a never-ending bachelorette party, only for couples. Three quarters of Vegas visitors are married. They're bored, but they don't want to take the kids to Disneyland again. They want escape, Gary. They want Panerotic."

"What they want," Adam mused, "is to feel like they're still in the game, like the parties they see in our videos could happen to them, like they'd ever be invited. Well, guess what? Now they are." He nodded at me. "You're gonna send the invitation."

"Okay, so who's your target audience? College kids? Thirtysomething parents?"

"Maybe," Nicole said, "but probably more like mid-forties, middle class. The kids can handle a babysitter for a week, so it's time for Mom and Dad to let their freak flag fly."

"Hm." I spread out the drawings. "Well, okay, no offense, guys, but the immediate problem I see is I could be looking at a casino, or a mall in Pasadena. It's *too* mainstream. Nothing about it says sex to me. And before I can sell the American public on sexy, I need to make 'em think they can live the Panerotic lifestyle. Why Vegas, by the way? Nevada's already about as sexy as it's gonna get."

The Ryders looked at each other. "Our thoughts exactly," Nicole admitted. "These are early concepts. We've been working on another direction the last few months."

"We liked Nevada blue laws," Adam explained, shrugging. "But no, not Las Vegas. Not Palm Springs. Not the desert."

"Someplace...closer," Nicole smiled. "Think more Hollywood."

"California," I mused, hoisting a Vietnamese hand roll. "You realize, of course, that L.A. is never gonna let you build Happy Sex Camp a stone's throw from Anaheim."

Adam started to say something, but Nicole cut him off. "We know. Think beaches."

I had a vision of Santa Monica Pier and Third Street Promenade, whole city blocks pulsing with tourists packed shoulder to shoulder. "If you say so." I looked at the smiling, bikini-clad resort guests in the

LSA renderings. "These don't look like forty-year-olds. That's the thing. You're selling Xtreme Ski Bunny hookups to middle-aged people who'll discover a resort full of people who look just like themselves. Talk about disappointing. Yeesh."

"We've been talking about a screening process," Nicole said. "Our clientele will likely be somewhat older than these drawings suggest, but I believe you'll find them attractive enough. Besides, the main thing we want to suggest is couples'll have more fun screwing each other in Bliss Panerotic than they would in Nebraska, a thin wall away from their kids. We'll market the resort to swingers, certainly, but the hook is that walking through the gates of Panerotic will make everyone feel like a stud or a centerfold."

"Exactly," Adam grinned, spreading his hands. "Live the Hollywood lifestyle, baby! Be a porn star for the weekend. Hell, stick around for a while. Tell people you're a billionaire real-estate tycoon. Use a fake name. What happens in Bliss Panerotic, yada yada."

"Welcome," an architect said, nodding, "to Fantasy Island."

"I'm imagining masks," I said.

"We're allowing our guests the option of an alias," Nicole replied.

"Meaning?"

"Meaning you'll register with resort management under your real name and credit card after a screening and medical check-up."

"Good."

"Then you'll pay for any purchase, including meals, with a coded ID card. The ID card can display any name you want. You can even wear a costume."

"It's like a Ren Faire for hot people," Adam said, then barked a quick laugh. "Introducing Lady Corset and, you know, Baron von Shtuppington. Whatever."

"I think what people really want," Nicole added, "is to escape from the boredom of their own sensible decisions, Gary. They want safe danger."

I chewed pad kee mow for a moment. "I can sell that," I decided. After all, I already had. I'd sold my own wife on it, not six months before.

Chapter 2

I was introduced to "the lifestyle" by a friend whose name I won't tell you, a guy from my college. He and his wife had been active swingers for about eight years, and their marriage was stronger than ever. That may seem paradoxical to you, but swingers rate themselves happier than other married couples and enjoy a far lower divorce rate to boot. My wife and I went to a pool party at his house, and it was obvious right away he had plenty of "couple friends" in their late thirties and early forties. A female guest at the party flirted with me pretty aggressively in front of my wife. That would've enraged some wives, I know, but Summer tends to be more amused than offended by such moments. After sixteen years of marriage and four years of fatherhood, I must've seemed pretty well housebroken. Anyway, when the woman saw Summer's raised eyebrows, she shifted gears and started putting moves on Summer instead.

Summer is not, strictly speaking, bisexual. She'd never had sex with a woman in 2012, not even in college. That party guest had her charms, but I doubted she was pretty enough to make Summer change her mind. The woman squeezed Summer's knee and thanked her for loaning out her husband. "I did no such thing," Summer groused, shaking her head in mild disagreement. "He's coming home with me whether he likes it or not. He's the one with the car keys and cash for the sitter."

"Fair enough," said the lady, unoffended. "Sorry for the misunderstanding." Summer caught my eye again as the woman strolled away. I shrugged wryly.

"She seemed friendly," I observed. Summer smirked but said nothing.

The encounter stuck in my head, of course, so of course I asked my frat buddy about it later via email. He seemed cagey but let on that the woman was in an open marriage.

Open marriage? I wrote back. She screws other guys?

Yep.

Lot of that going around in L.A. these days, I typed carefully.

Always has been, at least since the '50s.

I didn't reply for several minutes, and when I did I used a non-work-related email account. Are you in an open marriage? I asked him.

The answer came a minute before quitting time: *Call me tonight.*

So I did.

Gradually, over the course of two or three months, the Ryders teased out the full scope of their intentions—though not before Randall/Klein Enterprises signed a sequoia's weight in nondisclosure agreements. They even made my nominal partner sign, despite his relative invisibility in the company he helped finance.

What the Ryders wanted was Little Harbor on the southwest coast of Santa Catalina Island. There were several convincing reasons why this would never work. First, there were already thirty-seven hundred people living on Catalina, all but five hundred in the tourist town of Avalon. Second, cars are all but prohibited on the island; most residents drive golf carts. Third, while California has the most liberal legal notions about porn in the country—hence the San Fernando Valley's uncontestable primacy in the genre—there was nothing to suggest the state would welcome a sexual theme park. Most of the island, including the land the Ryders wanted and the roads and airport that serviced it, were controlled by a private nonprofit conservancy. The tide seemed to be turning against porn that year, as L.A. County tried to pass a law that required porn stars to use condoms in any film shot there.

"Yeah, yeah, yeah," Adam drawled, "we know all that. Have you seen California's checkbook lately? The governor's looking at a nineteen-billion-dollar shortfall. That takes precedence over any worries about titties on a beach, my friend."

"A topless beach, maybe. Sure. But not a brothel."

Adam looked aghast. "A brothel? Are you high? I'm not running a brothel. Nothing's gonna happen here against anybody's consent. And I do mean anybody. We're hiring dancers and actresses, not hookers." I looked down my nose at him. "Hey, what happens between two consenting adults is up to them. We ain't gonna profit from any…financial conversations that might take place. You can bet your ass on that."

"And condoms?"

"Fuck L.A. County," Adam sniffed. "We'll have condoms coming out of the walls. Safety first and all that. This isn't Rape Town USA."

I sighed. "Gary," Nicole sighed, "you're not having second thoughts, are you? We're too far down the road for a U-turn, don't you think?"

"No, I'm not having second thoughts, but I'm wondering if I might be trying to sell a project I don't completely understand. Exactly how crazy is your sexual theme park supposed to get?"

"That's up to the guests," Nicole said. "We're offering some racy entertainment and a playground. What our visitors play at is entirely between them."

"Bondage?"

"Maybe."

"Gay stuff?"

She smiled indulgently. "Sure, in that themed area. But we find most swingers keep their distance from gay men."

I knew that, but kept how I knew it to myself. "So how do you feel about this as a teaser image?" I'd already shown my preliminary concept for the debut print ad to Adam, who shrugged. Now I pushed a copy in front of Nicole. The image showed a wooden sign planted in white sand, a palm tree overhead offering minimal shade in vivid sunlight. "BLISS PANEROTIC," the sign said, pointing off to the right. A red bikini top was draped over the sign as if it'd been tossed away hurriedly. *Coming soon*, the caption read, all but winking at the reader.

"It's not bad," Nicole mused. I like the footprints running toward the beach. But you should add another pair on the other side of the big pair, and an even tinier bikini top next to the first one."

"Yowza, yowza," Adam grinned. "Now we're talkin'."

"So that's what we're selling?" I pressed. "'Come to Bliss Panerotic, you'll have a threeway on the beach?'"

"She'll have the best sex of her life on that beach, with whomever she pleases," Nicole answered, unfazed. "As long as her husband agrees. This will be a female-driven experience, just like porn and burlesque."

"You don't really believe that."

"What do you mean?"

"He thinks men'll be dragging their wives into the park kicking and screaming," Adam said. "Captain Caveman style."

Nicole regarded me thoughtfully. "Gary, how much do you know about swingers?"

"A little," I answered carefully.

"Granted," she nodded, "the man often initiates the experience. But then women turn out to be the most enthusiastic partners."

"Really," I drawled. "Yeah, that doesn't sound right to me."

"There's a party next weekend," I began, as casually as if I were discussing a damn quilting bee. "If you're interested, I mean." Summer stared at me over a cereal-bowl-sized mug of Earl Grey. She was playing the Sphinx, but I've known her too long and too closely to be fooled by her blank expression. She was thinking it through. If Summer is nothing else, she's a thorough planner. A simple question like, "What do you want for dinner?" can generate hours of cogitation.

"I don't know," she decided. "How do you feel about it?"

"Well," I said slowly, "it seems…interesting. You know. Whatever."

"You don't feel like they're cheating on each other?"

"Nah," I said, shrugging. "Not really. It's all by consent."

"You think so?"

"I mean, think about it," I ventured. "What hurts most about being cheated on? Is it the actual sex, or the fact that the asshole lied about it?" I lowered my voice on the swear word, as our daughter was eating cereal off a TV tray in the next room.

"I guess," she decided, "but it's not like I want to see some skank doing it with my husband."

"I don't want some skank, either, for the record."

"Okay, then."

"But look, we watch, you know, adult movies all the time," I said, exaggerating slightly. I watch porn all the time. She watches on special occasions. "Does it bother you to watch other people then?"

"I don't know those people. And one of them isn't my husband. It'd be different if Alexis Texas was all over *you*. Then I'd have to wonder if she's better than me. I know she's better looking."

That was true, but only because reality doesn't have body makeup, implants, and clever lighting. My wife was a cheerleader at Fortuna Union High, still a natural looker twenty years later. Snarky brunettes: only one of my weaknesses, it turns out.

"No one outshines you, dear," I said, nearly hastily enough. The corner of her wide mouth curved up in a blend of amusement and annoyance. "I guess I just think it'd be interesting to see what's going on. I don't want to participate."

"Really?"

I looked her right in the eye. "I don't think so."

"You don't think so, what?"

"I don't think I'd like to participate." And in that moment, I meant it…for the most part. I was also aware that a moment ago I hadn't meant it. A moment ago I'd been thinking of the pool party we attended. There was a woman there—not the woman who hit on Summer and me, but a Filipina named Everl, with long maroon hair draped over full breasts stuffed into a wet one-piece. I'd fantasized about Everl since then. What if she were to flirt with us? Would I still want to stand aloof and watch from afar? Then I thought about Summer, how we knew each other's tastes and turn-ons better than any stranger possibly could, and I thought it might be enough just to watch Everl tug that one-piece down over wide hips. Dreamily, Everl's sexy little belly morphed into Summer's long waist. "I don't," I repeated, even as an image of Summer gently biting a dark nipple flashed through my suddenly overclocked brain. "No. But I do want to watch. If you agree."

A moment passed.

"Let me think about it," Summer replied, then went back to her tea. The next night, she rode my lap, lost, it seemed, in her own fevered fantasies, and reached down to help herself over the edge. After she

19

came with unusual ferocity, just before I did the same, she grunted, "We should go to that party." As I gasped for air, she laughed brightly and said, "Oh, you like that, huh?" I kept silent, still foggy from climax. "I'm gonna have to keep my eye on you, mister," she warned, but the next day she listened without comment as I phoned my friend and agreed to his invitation. When she did speak, it was only to suggest a restaurant for dinner that night.

When *Xtreme Ski Bunnies X-3D* hit video shelves and pay-per-view, the influx of cash allowed the Ryders to make the conservancy an offer it couldn't afford to refuse. For a little over four million dollars and contractual promises to minimize the resort's ecological footprint, the Ryders purchased 780 acres of conservatory land, almost five times bigger than the chunk of Anaheim Walt Disney bought for his dream park. They spent tens of thousands more to secure unchallenged access to Middle Ranch Road, and thousands more than that to change the name of five miles of Middle Ranch Road to the racier Amory Way. When the Los Angeles County Supervisor ran the word "amory" through a search engine, he learned it was a man's name meaning "home strength." But any lifestyle traveler would be reminded of a word the Honorable Supervisor didn't know: *polyamory*, which swingers define as "consensual non-monogamy." To them, "Amory Way" was a blatant endorsement of the kind of sexual free-for-all I could only hint at in our marketing campaign. I can't say for sure, but if the street name wasn't Nicole Ryder's idea, I'd happily eat my own pants with A1 Sauce.

Chapter 3

My preparations began with a beach towel. As I Googled around looking for information on swingers and orgies and lifestyle parties, obsessively erasing my tracks from my browser history after each search and wondering which government agency's watch list I was now on, I kept seeing reminders to bring a clean towel. Apparently travel advice from *The Hitchhiker's Guide to the Galaxy* applies equally well to sex parties. I couldn't know how far things would go for me and Summer at my friend's shindig, but I wanted to be ready for the dirtiest possible scenario. I filled an overnight bag with two towels, friendly boxer briefs, a hairbrush, Altoids, condoms, and flavored lube because I still had most of the tube I bought for our twelfth anniversary. The morning of the big day, when my wife took our daughter to school, I snuck upstairs and rummaged through Summer's underthings like a burglar. I wasn't sure what she'd feel comfortable wearing, so I packed a fairly mundane, semi-translucent peignoir and red bra and panty set, the latter a Valentine's Day gift from her to me. Then, after considerable hesitation, I grabbed one of her toys, a pink, phallic vibrator.

I mean, how would *you* pack for an orgy? It's not like we were going to Carmel for the weekend. Just deciding which towels to pack was a minor conundrum. Were the "His" and "Hers" bath towels too cutesy? Should the towels be new or familiar? Was it best to walk in looking excited ("Hey, guys! Pants-off dance-off!") or blasé ("Oh, an orgy, whatever, no bigs")? I settled on a plain terry cloth towel for Summer and a Raiders beach towel for me. I think I wanted to seem sporty. God, that sounds imbecilic. It was!

When Summer got back, I couldn't resist showing her the bag. "Does this look like... everything?" I managed.

She held up the vibe and grinned at me crookedly. "I thought they provided these," she joked.

"No, I don't think so. You have to bring your own sex toys—"

"Dicks," she said. "I thought they provided dicks."

"Oh. Well...*those*. Right."

She pulled out her nightwear. "You want me to wear this with this?" she asked, indicating the bra and panty set together with the nightie. "What am I, a Stepford wife?"

"No," I replied. "I don't know. I didn't know which way you might want to dress."

"Me, neither," she admitted, repacking her undies. She frowned at the bag. A long moment passed. "Do you think I have nice boobs?" she asked quietly.

"Of course," I answered automatically. I'd been married for sixteen years. I knew a trap from a hacksaw.

"I mean...you always say that, but you really kind of have to, right? Seriously, though. Do you think I have nice boobs?"

"They're nice," I said. "Not huge, but nice. You have beautiful nipples. They're perky for a woman in her thirties."

"Perky," she agreed. "These boobs are perky, and they're nice. I have 'nice' boobs. Like the boobs of a 'nice' girl." I wasn't sure what she was getting at. "Mom boobs," she added, and sighed. After another reflective moment, she reached into a drawer and pulled out a pair of black, French-cut panties. She shoved these deep in our overnight bag. "There gonna be any swimming at this party?"

"I don't think so," I replied. "It's more of a cocktail party meet-and-greet type of thing."

"Meet and greet," she repeated. "Uh. Okay, then." She left the room and headed to work for a few hours. She works in a bookstore part-time. It's a nice, normal job for a nice, normal mom in nice standing in a nice neighborhood. She carries cards with her picture on them. The picture, a very nice one, was taken when she sold real estate, back before our daughter was born. "Meeting your needs since 1998," the card said nicely. There was nothing suggestive about it.

We drove our little girl to the sitter under the pretense of an ordinary date night, our overstuffed bag of lust concealed in the trunk.

Oh, you read this and pass moral judgment, but you're not truly appalled. You might tell your friends and family you are—"Can you believe what some people get up to?" you'll sneer, shaking your head in pious disapproval—but really, you're taking mental notes and wondering how you would go about packing for an orgy. You are. You're wondering what your spouse would say if you were invited to such an event. You're running through a mental search engine of neighbors, friends, and acquaintances and calculating the odds of each being a clandestine swinger. Are they happy or thrilled in a way you are not? Could you in fact be missing out? All those cars in front of your neighbor's house last Saturday night—were they participants in his fantasy football league, or guests at a torrid bacchanalia of sweat and writhing bodies? Does the pine-scented tidiness of your boss's suburban split-level mask the damning scents of orgasmic byproducts? And why weren't you invited?

"We're not planning on being out past eleven," I assured our exhaustingly Christian sitter, who accepted the news and our daughter without removing an ear bud. The other bud, which hung loose against her collarbone, blasted Pharrell Williams.

23

We drove around my friend's block three times before parking. I worried about people seeing my car, then remembered we were in our own neighborhood. Why shouldn't we be at my college friend's house? Probably a dinner party, folks would think. Maybe one of those secret suppers I heard about on the Travel Channel. Ooh, how exciting!

I was so addled that when I reached for our overnight bag, I somehow managed to lock my keys in the car. "Did you just—?" Summer began.

"Yes!" I admitted, agitated to the point of breathless falsetto. "I did. I did exactly what you think I just did. I gotta call AAA."

"Oh my God," Summer whined, rubbing her forehead. "Can't it wait till we're, like…can't it wait till after the party?"

"I need a minute!" I bleated, and called shakily for roadside assistance. Fifteen minutes later, a truck arrived and an apathetic grease monkey broke into my car for me.

"We should've taken my SUV," Summer observed pointlessly, watching the roadside mechanic's taillights pull away.

"I'm sorry, okay?" I admitted. "Do you still want to do this?"

Summer's face revealed no emotion. "We paid for the sitter. Why not?" There you go: the root of all suburban depravity. 'We might as well. We paid for the sitter.'

"We'll be fashionably late."

"I'm not expecting much in the way of fashion here, Gary. Now pull yourself together and let's go."

I haven't told you my swinger friend's name, nor where he lives or what he does for a living. I can tell you he's aggressively normal in almost every respect: he loves his average-looking wife an average amount, he has the average number of (as far as I can tell) unremittingly ordinary children, and furnished his unremarkable home in the middle-income décor of a Target ad. To simplify things, I'll refer to him and his wife as Ted and Alice. Ted, then, greeted us at the door. "Hey, Gary," he said. "What's the password?" Nervous chuckles all around. I noted with relief that my friend was fully dressed.

"You know my wife," I said, indicating Summer. She hung a few steps back on the wide porch. She looked about two seconds from bolting for the hills. "I don't know any password, though. Was that in the email?"

"I was kidding, man. No, I mean, there is a real password, but we're not being sticklers for detail, y'know? It ain't Fort Knox up in here. Hey, Summer. Dude. You look great. It is Summer, right?" She nodded slowly. "Come on in. Hey, everybody, this is Gary and Summer." *Should we be using real names? I* thought. There were about a dozen men and women milling about in the living room. Ted quickly introduced me to all of them, and I just as quickly forgot their names. I guess that answered my question. Summer was already blushing. She whispered in my ear a few seconds later that she recognized one female guest from the neighborhood jog circuit. I shrugged. What do you say? After all, the jogger was here, too. It's not like she held any higher moral ground from which to look down on us.

I surveyed Ted's unexceptional living room. It was wall-to-wall earth tones, the colors of a David Lean establishing shot of the Sahara. A TV was playing with its sound off. In the kitchen, visible through a low arch, two uncomfortable-looking men in T-shirts hovered around a table covered in potluck dishes. A bucket of Original Recipe KFC formed the centerpiece. The men looked hungry. I was, too. No one ate.

It was like I'd never been to a party of any kind before. I couldn't figure out how to behave. Summer and I stood in a corner and tried not to make eye contact

25

with anyone else. I didn't know how loudly I should speak, whether kidding around was appropriate, or why no one at this particular orgy was fucking. Weren't there supposed to be mattresses on the floor? I guess I'd pictured some sort of '70s, shag-carpeted rec room with bean bags laid out and Barry White on the hi-fi. Instead, we found ourselves riveted by the tragicomic spectacle of Homer J Simpson throttling his only-begotten son in syndication on the muted TV.

Alice breezed in from the darker, more mysterious depths of the house. She wore a floral-print baby-doll and sipped an amaretto sour. I dragged my eyes away from her copious cleavage. "I see newbies!" she announced, beaming. "You must be Gary and Summer!" We were. Alice name-checked two other couples, then snapped off the TV with no apparent hostility. "Now," she announced, "I gotta tell ya the rules. This is the front of the house. If you get nervous or weirded out, this is the safe zone, okay? People wear clothes out here. You can get something to eat, take a breather. Then there's the middle part of the house, which is the guest bedroom and bathroom. That's clothing-optional. You can fool around in there, get naked if you want to, or just watch if that's your 'thang.' Remember, no touching unless you have permission, okay? That's rule number one. No means no. Everyone got that?" We nodded obediently.

"Okay," she continued. "The backyard is kind of a middle zone, too. We have high fences and understanding neighbors, but we try not to push it. The pool is clothing-optional; most ladies like to go topless. Oh, and we do love our ladies!" she practically sang. "The hot tub's around the corner in a dim, quiet area. Please honor the no-sex rule in the Jacuzzi, okay? Also, no glasses in the pool area, please. Ted gets very aggravated about this. You can, however, get naked if you promise to behave. Personally, I like to get a little touchy-feely in the hot tub, especially after two or three

26

of these special babies." She shook her drink, already a stack of damp ice cubes. "But! The hot tub is for making out only! That's a rule! If you want to get crazy, come inside...so to speak!" We chuckled dutifully. I congratulated myself for remembering to bring towels.

"Now. The master bedroom. That is *not* clothing-optional. That is nudity-mandatory, good buddy! If you go in the back bedroom, you have to get naked. Ted'll be there most of the time. I promise you, he will go enforcer on your ass. That doesn't mean you have to fuck any specific person"—the verb sounded friendlier coming from her lips than it ever did from mine—"but you can't stand there all night and just 'oogle' our friends like a weirdo, okay?" She laughed. "That would not be cool at all. Just be cool, okay? If you want to join, ask. If you want to fuck your partner, do that. No one's gonna make you feel uncomfortable. There are condoms in dishes all over in there, but we're kinda short on lube tonight so I hope you brought your own."

She ticked through her last few instructions in rote haste. "No guys touching guys, no jizzing all over the furniture, please be respectful of other people's property, don't drink our liquor, the beer in the cooler outside is okay, keep your phone off, again, no means no. It really, truly means no. Okay? I mean that. Awesome. Now, you guys have fun! I'm gonna go for a swim!" She stepped into the kitchen long enough to set her empty glass in the sink, then scampered down the hall again. A glass door somewhere down the hall slid open and closed.

"Whew," Summer said. "That was... something."

"We didn't bring swimsuits," I muttered.

"You want to go swim?" Summer asked.

"I don't know," I admitted. I wanted to participate some way or another, but already felt the dread of impending performance anxiety.

"I don't know if I want to get naked in front of a bunch of total strangers," she admitted in a low voice.

"Would you prefer friends and family?" I asked, trying to crack a joke.

"No," she replied. "But I..." She sighed. "I don't know if this is for me. Is that okay?"

"I understand," I said automatically, bracing to lead her out the door.

"Oh, well," she said. She stared down the hall. Then, with a shrug of her shoulders: "Eh, fuck it." Having made her decision, she marched deeper into the house. I was so surprised I found myself a full room behind her as she hunted for an exit to the backyard.

The sliding glass doors were in a darkened study past the guest bedroom. The door to that bedroom was open. I didn't stick around for a lingering view of the room, but got a quick impression of women embracing on a bed. Some guys stood around, fully clothed, watching. I was relieved to see none of them masturbating; I didn't want Summer seeing anything too smutty and depressing till we were too involved to back out.

I also wanted to stand in a corner and "oogle." I wasn't sure how ready I was yet for anything else. The confusion of this was mind-blowing. For the first time in years, I felt new at sex. It was like sneaking an adolescent glance at a *Playboy* or feeling a girl up for the first time. I had zero erection, though my eyes flicked from side to side as if I'd taken speed. The utter, taboo strangeness of it all was not merely sexy but full-body thrilling. I hadn't even treated myself to a good look at any of the women in the house. My hands shook like moth wings. My heart thudded so resoundingly in my chest that I wondered how far away it was audible.

We walked outside into an atmosphere of youth, stripped to our underwear, and dove into the pool.

Not everyone in the pool area was young; far from it. There was exactly the same random collection of people you'd find at a Friday night high school football game. The guys were in shorts, mostly, and most of the women wore bikini briefs. Would you believe I relaxed into this environment quickly? It's impossible to focus on more than two breasts at a time, so my interest in any single pair diminished. There were boobs in the pool. There were vinyl rafts and duck floaties as well. The boobs were no more erotic, under those circumstances, than the inflatable ducks.

What was erotic, electrically so, was a backyard full of total strangers who might, within the next few hours, have uninhibited sex with me. Remember your first high school pool party? Remember how the image of each girl in a swimsuit, a girl you may have seen five times a week in third-period civics, was branded onto your retinas? Remember how you took every chance to memorize the scene, mentally noting the positions of nipples and freckles and camel-toe clefts? I don't know what it's like for women; maybe they're more into showing off than staring. But for me growing up, these were priceless opportunities to gain evidence as to the bodies and proclivities of my classmates. A simple game of high school water polo was as sexy as anything I did in bed later on.

Well, here I was again, stowing away images and sounds for future arousals. A woman's throaty laugh, an obviously intentional brush of my ass as I swam by, Summer's breasts bobbing on the surface as I lifted her in my arms. I didn't want to be far from her, partly, I know, because I was loath to come off as eager to stray. This had to be handled delicately. Also, I admit I was uncomfortable. Summer wasn't pulling away, so maybe she was as nervous as I was. I guess sticking to your wife like glue is the backyard orgy version of being a wallflower.

This isolationism couldn't last forever. Instead, it was only a few minutes into our swim that our hostess moved closer. Alice, not the tallest of women, was obliged to half-dogpaddle in her five-foot-deep pool, her feet bouncing lightly against the bottom. A barrel-chested, heavily bearded guy who wasn't Ted followed a pace behind her. "Hey, you guys," Alice began quietly, "have you met my good friend Kevin?"

We had not. "Kevin, hi," I said nervously, shaking his hand above water.

"Hey."

"This is Gary and Summer," Alice said. "Hello, Summer. Kevin, don't you find Summer delicious?" Alice grinned wickedly. People talk like this at parties like that. Honest.

"She's very attractive," Kevin agreed. "You're a lucky man, Gary."

"I am. This is true."

"So how long have you two been married?" Alice asked, failing to either notice or care as Kevin's hairy arm snaked around her, his fingers gently brushing her left breast. I blushed as I noticed her nipple was already plump from lazy arousal and cool water.

"Our sixteenth anniversary was three weeks ago," Summer answered. I surprised her that weekend with dinner at Spago. She surprised me with a Kindle Fire. We fucked with atypical aggression in a Santa Monica hotel room after Summer got tanked on white wine, but hadn't had sex since our return. Life intrudes, am I right?

"How'd you meet?"

"We were in high school together," I smiled.

"Oh my God," April yelped, then stage-whispered "sorry" in the direction of her nearest neighbor's house. "You don't mean?" she continued.

"Alice," Kevin chuckled, shaking his head.

"Well, I'm sorry, but I'm curious!"

"About what?" Summer asked.

"Well…if you were in high school together…I mean, you two weren't each other's…*first*, were you?"

"She's so bad," Kevin grinned.

"I'm inquisitive, that's all. Now you just hush." She rested her hand gently on Kevin's as he continued caressing her breasts.

"I was a wrestler," I said. "We did okay on the girlfriend front."

"Gary was my second," Summer volunteered. The truth is, while I'd bounced through several girlfriends, Summer was my third sex partner. I'm not sure the first two even counted due to, shall we say, timing issues. I did, however, have a fourth who wasn't Summer. To admit an irritating truth, Number Four was a source of ongoing debate in my marriage. The summer after graduation, I slept with a girl named Kellie, one of Summer's fellow cheerleaders, toward the end of an eleven-day break in our relationship. The hiatus was Summer's idea. She demanded it after learning I fantasized about other girls while jerking off. One of these girls, conveniently, was Number Four prior to the fact, though until this moment I've been wise enough never to reveal that fact to either woman. Sorry, Summer. Sorry, Kellie aka Partner Number Four.

"Well, isn't that something," Alice sighed, shaking her head in response to our woefully inadequate sexual histories. "And now here you are."

"Here we are," Summer agreed—and then, never breaking eye contact with Alice, she took off her bra, tossed it away, and stroked her own breasts unashamedly. To call this surprising would be like calling death by dysentery a bummer. My eyes must've looked like Arnold Schwarzenegger's after his Mars helmet broke in *Total Recall*.

31

My wife and I enjoyed a satisfying sex life, all things considered, but in a routine, vanilla sort of way. Blow jobs fell off years before our daughter was born, and I can't say I was any more enthusiastic than Summer in my support of the oral arts. We'd reached that point where she knew what I wanted, what she was interested in doing, and what she wanted from me. What I wanted, in turn, was a content wife, plus the freedom to fantasize about any attractive woman who wasn't Summer. Turning the lights out helped— probably her as much as me, frankly—so our bedroom got dimmer and dimmer over the years. The days of boinking each other face to face on the couch while our TV entertained itself had long since passed; and, while Summer wasn't given to pious prudishness, she also wasn't much of an exhibitionist. She didn't own a bikini. When we went to the gym, she avoided the Jacuzzi. She wrapped herself in a towel to walk from the shower in our master bath to the closet. Now here she was, breathlessly performing for a couple she'd just met.

"I like you," Alice told her. "You know that? Come play with me."

"I'm not bi," Summer whispered.

"Oh, yeah? Are you sure?"

"Pretty sure," my wife said, but then Alice waded closer and Summer didn't push her away. Kevin kept his distance, so he and I watched as Alice took my wife's shoulders, using Summer's greater height to help her float in the pool, and began kissing her gently. First her cheek, then her chin, then my wife's parted lips accepted hers, their tongues flicked together, my God— how much of this was a performance, a show to impress me and Kevin? I asked Summer later, and she rolled her eyes: "Not everything I do is for you, love o' mine." Either way, who's complaining?

Summer's B-cup tits floated below the waterline, so Alice stared at them hungrily before caressing one. "So perky," she said. "Are you as turned on as I am?"

"Perky," Summer said. "I don't know." Then she laughed in embarrassment.

"Mind if I find out?" Alice asked, but didn't wait for an answer before sliding a hand into Summer's panties. Their images merged and distorted from refraction. My heart beat so fast it was sloshing the pool. Summer whimpered from astonishment and pleasure. "Um," she managed. "Okay, so..."

Kevin glanced over at me. "Your wife, man," he said softly. "Hot."

"So is Alice." That was only half-true. Had I spied Alice on the street, maybe walking her jittery Yorkie, I wouldn't have been as impressed. But nothing is sexier than confidence, right? Availability, maybe, but the two qualities working together is an unbeatable aphrodisiac. To this day I remember each pore of Alice's body.

She broke away from making out with Summer just long enough to say, "Gary." She beckoned me closer. "I want to watch you two make love now." *Make love?* I thought. *Who talks like that?*

"Right here?" Summer asked her, flinching.

"No. Inside, in the house. Come here, baby." Alice took my hand and drew me closer still, then caressed my arm and resumed kissing Summer on the mouth. Quite a multitasker, this Alice. My cock threatened to blow the seams from my boxer briefs. Emboldened, I pressed its hardness into Summer's thigh, and she reached into my shorts and tugged me free. I was dimly aware of Kevin taking up a position on the other side of Summer and Alice, where he touched both women gently. "I want Kevin to fuck me from behind," Alice decided, "while Gary makes Summer come her fuckin' brains out on my bed. Do you want that?"

Summer trembled, overwhelmed, but then nodded. She let Alice finger her in the pool, enjoying but unwilling to initiate any harder contact. She shivered again, close to orgasm, then flinched away and waded close to me. "Let's go over there," she said, indicating a corner of the pool. When we reached it, she kissed me once, hard. "This is hot," she whispered, "but I can't. It's too much."

"You want to go?"

"I don't know...I think, maybe I...No. I'm turned on. I just...I need to not be with Alice right now."

"Okay," I said, "if that's what you want." Except really, what I wanted was more, to keep going, just keep going, keep going feverishly wherever this took us.

"I want," she breathed. "This is crazy...I want...Oh, honey, I want...Kevin. Is it wrong that I want Kevin?"

Kevin? That jolted me, partly out of jealousy but mostly surprise. She seemed oblivious of Kevin till that moment. "I want Kevin to watch us. Me and you. I want—God, what is wrong with me right now? I'm so flustered."

"I loved watching you," I told her.

"I know, it was hot, I just—she's a woman. I didn't know I'd have to be with a woman. And then there's Kevin, and he's all...I could handle watching them, you know, do it. Is that insane?"

"Do you mean that?"

"Yes, but no more than that. Just watching. I couldn't handle going any farther than that."

"Having sex," I whispered. "We knew going in there'd be sex at this thing."

"I didn't know what I wanted," she said. "I want more now, I think."

"Can we do this?" I asked her, suddenly worried. "Are we ready?"

34

She looked deep into my eyes, shivering visibly. "I want more," she told me. "Let's have more. Okay? I want more."

"Let's go inside," I managed, "and find an open bed."

"If those two join us?" she wondered.

"Then I guess we'll have...more."

"I love you, Gary. You know that?"

"I love you, too, Summer. This is...Thanks for being so brave."

She kissed my lips. "I am brave. Let's do this," she announced, then drew me from the pool.

I suppose there was no possible way it could've ended as happily as I wanted, but damn it to Hell and Ebola all the same.

Chapter 4

As much as I worried about the difficulties of publicizing what would strike most Americans as a gonorrhea ranch, I loved watching designs for the park come together. With the purchase of property around Little Harbor (now renamed "Ryder Lagoon") completed, surveyors began staking out the resort. Ferries were secured to transport visitors from Long Beach to Avalon on the eastern, L.A. side of the island till a more permanent way station could be set up in Two Harbors. Since the Conservancy was resolute in forbidding cars with internal combustion engines, a fleet of electric buses would shuttle tourists to Panerotic's east side on Middle Ranch Road. There, they'd pass through a grand entry pavilion into Zone 1, which resembled Las Vegas. Zone 1, the Strip, was the resort's central nexus, overstuffed with adult shopping, Paradise Casino, the "Sinema" multiplex porn theater, and resort infrastructure. Play some blackjack! Enjoy a sexy meal! And by all means, feel free to shop to your libido's content in our friendly adult superstore, Eros 4Ever. Valuable coupons online!

Single women would pay a mere 40 bucks a day, which included a room at the resort hotel of their choice. Couples were to be charged $60 a day plus room charges. Their room costs, of course, would be steep. Single men, gay or straight, would be expected to cough up $120 a day plus the cost of their room. Even so, it was cheaper, on average, than a full day and night at the Magic Kingdom.

Zone 2, the southeast corner of Bliss Panerotic, was comparatively small. Dubbed "Hollywood" and themed to the Golden Age of Tinseltown, it was custom designed for the BDSM crowd. (I would've loved to

36

have sat in on those concept meetings.) The Ryders fretted over this area no end. They knew there'd be an interest in dungeons, perhaps even from wealthier guests, but they didn't want mainstream patrons to be put off by the intensity of the milieu. Thus, Hollywood's decadent bondage parlors were tucked as far back from the Strip as possible. Zone 2 butted up against a state-of-the-art studio facility, slated to house all future mid-budget Panerotic shoots. Zone 2 played host to the team of designers who oversaw the outside contractors who, in turn, built and maintained Panerotic's insanely popular Internet properties.

Zone 3, "Miami," was designed with the LGBTQ community in mind. It was, in fact, the south beach of Ryder Lagoon. Given lingering homophobia among the straight swing community, this zone was to be effectively quarantined from "breeders." Thus, gay or lesbian visitors entered Miami through the Cuban-themed exterior of La Playa Hotel and Casino.

Zone 4 was the largest subdivision of the park. This tiki- and titty-strewn wonderland, "Fiji," was where lusty heterosexuality ruled. Fiji's centerpiece was a massive faux-Tahitian casino, Sanasana, where the Ryders planned to build North America's first topless water park. (Such parks exist already in a number of European nations. That will, no doubt, give some of you travel ideas.) Panerotic's gay and straight zones faced each other across the expanse of Ryder Lagoon, but clever design (and thoughtfully planted palm trees) minimized interactions between demographics. Both the northern and southern beaches offered nude swimming pools, ocean bathing, and hot tubs large enough for couples or groups.

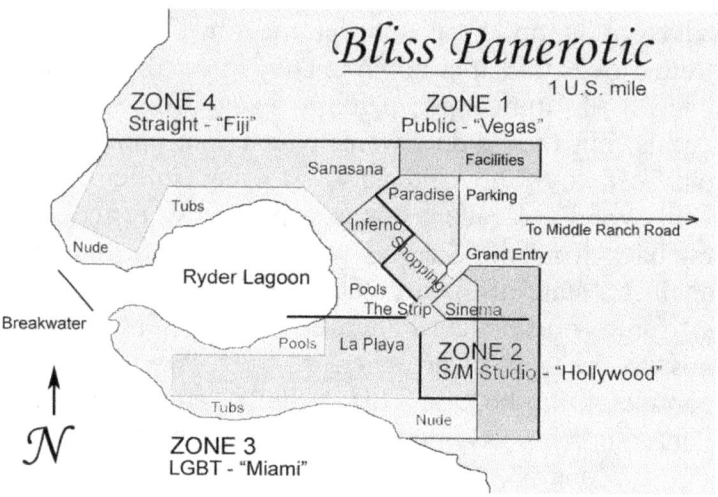

Bliss Panerotic

How, I was desperate to know, would the Ryders maintain such a resort without instituting the most virulent STD vector since the downfall of disco? Patrons would be screened by an office and clinic in the San Fernando Valley, then required to wear a button or armband embossed with a Tag square. The square could be scanned by any smartphone in direct line of sight, and included such relevant information as sexual orientation, marital status, swing category, STD history, and alter ego. Only high-level park personnel would be able to access a guest's true ID. We expected privacy concerns, but patrons were required to sign an ironclad contract allowing their stats to be posted. That way, guests could more quickly find patrons suited to their desires and expectations, and those who carried herpes, HIV, or HPV were more likely to hook up amongst themselves. I was happy to see condoms were freely available—and dirt cheap!—throughout the park.

I'm not sure why—maybe it was my budding gastronomic connoisseurship—but I was deeply concerned about the quality of food service in the park. I won't lie, I went to my fair share of strip bars in college, and nothing grossed me out faster than the juxtaposition of boobs and buffet. I'm not the kind of guy who lives for hot wings at Hooters. I like knowing my food is prepared by trained hands in an environment that doesn't call to mind a Russian mafia hangout. If I want to tip buxom dancers in boy shorts, I prefer not to be reimbursed in *E. coli*. Nothing, I felt, would kill the vibe at Bliss Panerotic faster than guests who were starving themselves from sheer terror.

I believe we can credit Food Network for the improvement in theme park cuisine over the last decade. For all its charms, Disneyland offered barely passable food service till visitors demanded more and better. As fare improved, guest complaints online and in unauthorized guidebooks gave way to effusive testimonials. Panerotic would have to serve amazing, hygienic food or complaints would be damning.

Luckily, the Ryders struck gold in the form of a restaurant consultants' office in London. The food in their park was delicious. I'll stand by that, even after everything.

Things were ramping up quickly in late 2012. One of our teams was hard at work on the Bliss Panerotic online empire. Just as Uncle Walt used his weekly TV program to rally interest in his impending Anaheim playground, we used the Internet to arouse viral enthusiasm for the Ryders' high-tech pornotopia in southern California. We hired a dozen kids from Atlanta to create a Bliss Panerotic MMOD and charged $35 a month in membership fees. The game was called *Realms of Eros*, and though it kept the real-world resort's best attractions hidden, it was wildly popular months before the park opened. The Ryders presold about four million downloads plus tens of millions later on, and it still has devoted enthusiasts now. Remember when people on Facebook pretended to be farmers or vampire slayers? It turns out what they really wanted were virtual hookups and gangbangs. No shock there, I suppose. Who the fuck wants to be a farmer? As you'll see, I myself was a regular visitor to *Realms of Eros*.

The truth is the Ryders were onto something. People couldn't wait to visit Bliss Panerotic. They wanted to *live* in Bliss Panerotic. Thanks to the Web, consumers now assumed they could maintain boring, workaday existences Monday through Friday from eight to five, then battle orcs each weekend. We all have second lives nowadays. Personally, I never got into the whole gaming thing—I never had time till recently—but I know grown men, the kind of guys who wear ties to work and clean out their gutters each spring, who juggle fantasy football teams and *Modern Warfare* campaigns and Old Republic Jedi crusades. They're PTA members who slaughter children by the dozens in online bloodbaths. I know suburban soccer moms who write and sell slashfic erotica.

A generation ago, Bliss Panerotic would've died on the vine, not due to mechanical shortcomings or insufficient technology, but because so few of us had secret identities. Folks knew they'd never get away with brazenly horny behavior. That's all changed. Do you know the organization "Christian Swingers" now claims over a million members? Most swingers identify as Christian. They go to church every Sunday morning. They sing in church choirs and send their kids to Vacation Bible School and contribute to potlucks. Then, every few weeks, they attend orgies and beg total strangers to spank their willing asses. We're all voluntarily schizo these days.

Disneyland exists to help us revel in traditional wholesomeness, and that's a wonderful thing. I admire and adore it. We can't wait to visit that vanilla-scented malt shoppe on Main Street and tell ourselves the good old days were always good. We get to wear mouse ears and pretend we love fireworks and parades and It's a Small World After All. But seriously, wouldn't you rather just bend Jessica Rabbit over one of those runaway teacups and show her how grown-ups really play patty cake? There's a hentai for every Disney princess, a porn parody of every wholesome story you can imagine.

We talk about social media, but "social" means "horny." That's why the Internet was invented, for fuck's sake. (See what I did there?) The Ethernet had virtual hookup zones before it had pictures or color. The only thing the Ryders added to its randy alt-reality was wetware. If it hadn't been them, I can promise you it would've been somebody else. Within weeks, I quit worrying about the fallout of working on such a blatantly sex-driven project and became convinced the Ryders were twenty-first-century pioneers. As my other projects wrapped up, I devoted more and more time to Bliss Panerotic. Soon it was my only campaign. I spent more hours in a makeshift office at Panerotic than at Randall/Klein.

Summer told our daughter I was working on a campaign for shoes.

The first time I saw my future bride, she was sitting across the aisle three rows in front of me on the school bus. Her hair was longer then. She wore braids over two layers of flannel. The year was 1992; grunge had come to northern California. I myself was heavily into Soundgarden. Summer was cute, but so were half the girls in school as far as I was concerned. The only reason she caught my attention at all was she was sitting next to Kellie G., a buxom cheerleader I'd lusted after since seventh grade. They were laughing and cutting up about something on TV, and I gathered Summer would be joining Kellie soon on the cheerleading squad. She was a sophomore. I was a junior.

When Summer passed cheerleading tryouts, by gyrating to a dance hit by Bell Biv DeVoe, her class schedule changed to accommodate practice. Suddenly she was in my AP government class. I caught her staring at me from a seat by the window once, but I blushed and looked away instead of meeting her eyes. Why would anyone be looking at me? Personally, I found my reflection in the window repulsive.

Sometime after that, we caught each other's eyes in the Fortuna High School gym, a dark blue cavern dating back half a century. I was sweating through wrestling practice, and she was hanging out before cheerleading practice. I got pinned by a kid twenty pounds lighter than me and trudged over to slump on the bench by her feet. "Hey," I grunted, nodding in her direction.

"You're not very good at that," she said, the first words I can remember coming out of her mouth.

"Sitting?"

"No, wrestling."

"Actually," I insisted, "I am. I'm very good. I made NCS Championships last year."

"Oh, really? How'd you do at those championships?"

I shrugged. "I got my ass handed to me by some Indian guy from Hoopa. Still, not too bad for a sophomore."

"I suppose. How're you doing this year?"

"Pretty good. That guy graduated."

"The Hoopa guy?"

"Right."

"Well, happy graduation day."

"Exactly," I said, smiling.

She snorted. "So are you gonna win now, or is this just a big ol' waste of everybody's time?"

"Is what a waste of time, wrestling?"

"Kinda," she said, and waved her hands vaguely in my direction. "This. All this…sweating and grunting and…nastiness."

"Nastiness, you say." I was mildly offended.

She grinned. "I said nastiness. Nasty."

"Some people are into this sort of thing."

"I suppose. The nastiness, or sweaty guys hugging each other on a mat?"

"Do you even like wrestling?"

"I like the smell of gymnasiums. Warm, smelly gymnasiums in the rain." It was, in fact, raining outside, that drippy, half-hearted Humboldt County rain that lasts from November to March of five years from now.

"Right. You're in my government class," I announced.

"I'm aware of that. Your name's Gary."

"Yours is Summer, right? Summer Ferguson. You seem pretty smart."

"You seem sleepy. In class, I mean. You're better now. What with all that sweaty hugging and all. Probably wakes you right up." It was true, I had a hard time staying alert in government. It was right after lunch and taught by Mr. Weeks, a gray crayon stub of a man who could drain any trace of vitality from a room with a single lethargic sentence. I usually spent that class feeling as if I'd been in shot in the ass with bear tranquilizer.

"I have a hard time caring about the ins and outs of government policy," I admitted.

"You're a bad citizen," she accused.

"I am, I suppose."

"And how else are you a bad citizen?"

"Uh, what do you mean?"

"Do you like, drink beer and stuff?"

"Mostly stuff. Sometimes beer."

"Any funny stuff?" She mimed smoking a joint.

"No. It's bad for the hugging. You?"

"I haven't yet." I was unable to tell whether she was genuinely interested or just poking me out of sheer boredom.

"Well, there's a first time for everything."

"Second time for some things."

"I'll drink to that."

43

"Wrestling, huh? Wrestling and hugging. Weird. I suppose I should ask you: do you like girls?"

"Of course I like girls."

"I don't know," she said, shrugging. "One hears rumors."

"About what?" I exploded. "About me being a…you know?"

"Yes, about you being a wrestler."

I relaxed. "Oh. Well, that's a crock. Where do people get such crazy ideas?"

"I don't know. People talk."

"You want to work on Weeks's midterm project together?" The words were out of my mouth before I was aware of formulating them. To this day I don't know how I found the courage to ask her. All I remember thinking is, she looks good in a cheerleading outfit. Her legs are super nice.

She said yes. And they're still super nice.

I want to reemphasize before we go any further that until our notorious adventures on the wild side, I never had major issues with our sex life. Sure, Summer put on a few pounds after our kid was born. That's only natural. I thickened around the middle myself. We fell into a routine, centered mostly around a three-position sequence of sex moves every second or third Tuesday—an off night for quality TV that season—but I never felt willfully deprived. We'd even made it back to the gym in recent years. If I wondered sometimes what I'd missed by never sowing my wild oats back in college, I found opportunities to watch other people do it on the Web. One of the benefits of working for the Ryders was an all-purpose password to their vast erotic smut house. Soon the Xtreme Ski Bunnies and I were on a first-name basis, at least in their immortalized MPEG-4 incarnations.

I was bored. That's not the same as a grudge. I wasn't angry at Summer. She wasn't doing anything wrong, and I had no interest in cheating on her. I worked every day next to Nicole Ryder, one of the sexiest women I ever met, and never, not once, did I try anything inappropriate with her. I never asked my incredibly desirable secretary to "stay late" or rub my shoulders. In the advertising business, where sexism was still rampant long after the *Mad Men* years, I was a model of gracious behavior. The idea of swinging infiltrated my mind, not because I wanted to commit adultery, but because I hoped to reinvigorate my otherwise unobjectionable marriage.

Which is not to say we didn't have our irritated moments. Between you, me, and the rest of the planet, I never cared much for Summer's best friend and office mate Darcy. She's built like a Weeble and smells like a Marlboro-and-vanilla-scented candle. So when Darcy came over most Saturday afternoons, braying over a seemingly endless series of blender margaritas while laughing at the looks and behavior of coworkers I'd never met, I fantasized about shoving her in the pool to determine whether she could float right-side-up. She'd wax prophetic about her phlegmy son eventually marrying my sweet little girl, and I swore familial jihad in my mind. Soon I was so fed up I'd slip out to grandiose action movies. Inevitably Summer, upon learning I'd seen a guy movie she mocked when its commercials appeared on TV, would claim an irresistible craving to see this ridiculous entertainment and, by the way, why was I so desperate to see it without her? And hey, maybe Darcy would've liked to have seen *Rage of Kickfighting IV: Fatal Bloodstain* as well, did I think about that?

There was only one thing about our happy bedroom fun time I found lacking. When Summer and I first started having sex, we were very, very young, too young it seems to me now—but I guess that's how we know we're getting old. In the moment it felt exactly right. But if I'm being completely honest—and why

45

shouldn't I at this point? I mean, what have I got to lose?—she didn't come for several years. Apparently women's internal architecture and psychological development preclude it in most cases until they're well into college, sometimes longer. It wasn't for lack of trying on my part, but I couldn't seem to push her over the metaphorical hump. If it frustrated her, she never said. I suppose she didn't know what she was missing.

But then, in her early twenties, she started coming with a vengeance. She'd climax two or three times before I slipped inside her. She had this amazing exclamation of orgasmic joy, a cross between a growl and a judo *kiai*. There was no getting around it: Summer loved getting laid in those years. To say she was multi-orgasmic was akin to saying Yao Ming is tall for an Asian dude; it's true but it doesn't convey degree. That insatiability lasted till well into her third trimester, then, gone. It never returned. And while, as I've said, we still had sex a few times a month, I was lucky if she came once per session. The yowls of animal lust were ancient history. Now as we pulled up the covers and readied for sleep, her habit was the same whether she climaxed or not: she smiled softly to herself, said, "That was nice, babe," and kissed my shoulder.

Nice? She thought our sex life was *nice*? It was nice. It was *nice*. We were such a nice couple.

Yes, but I wanted *hot*. I wanted something we hadn't felt in years: the full-bodied thrill of discovery. "Be careful what you wish for," they say, with considerable smugness, which is why no one invites careful, reasonable people to orgies.

Chapter 5

The first time I kissed Summer, back in spring of '92, I thought poets and troubadours had sold kissing short. She kissed like she was about to board a train in a movie, like my lips held immortal ambrosia, like it warded off the rigors of adulthood. My body trembled with hunger for hers. I damn near wept with desire. At that age it's hard to tell whether genuine chemistry exists or you're just desperate to get physical with anyone, but to this day, I believe we were chemically perfect for each other in those wild days of youth. She made me wait almost a year before finally allowing me inside her. Those ten months were an ecstasy of agony. When we consummated our cravings at long last—and thank God it wasn't my first time, or I'd have come in five seconds—she accepted my weight with a sigh of profound satisfaction, then kissed my shoulder and breathed, "Oh, it's good."

Most of us are scared to death about sex, men and women, till we're well into our thirties, so our sex lives happen mostly by accident. That first year wasn't anything like what I'd seen on the few VHS porno tapes I managed to sneak into my room and watch with the sound at a whisper, my parents just two walls away. Summer was on the pill for hormonal reasons, but neither of us knew enough to trust it, so I wore rubbers and often pulled out to boot. Having never seen a porno, Summer gave head like she was licking a cobra. Who cared? Just the sight of her pale naked body made my nerve endings boggle. I can still remember the first time I pulled down her panties, exposing that tuft of shiny hair (shaven vulvas being just shy of mythical in 1992), the smell of her wild ready femininity, the nakeder-than-naked warmth and wetness. My *God,*

47

what a marvel she was in my eyes. That was lust. *That was lust.*

Love is…different. Love is…well, it's a routine of duty, in a way. It's a mutual sense of responsibility. Love is nuking soup for your wife when she's hacking with flu. Love is going out in the rain at two in the morning to buy emergency tampons. Love is hair in the shower drain and picking the kid up from school and pretending no one farted in his or her sleep. It's a schedule of give and take. Yes, we were happier living in love, I think we both were, but no way was it *Fifty Shades*. That thrill of sexual discovery evaporated years ago. Every attractive woman in line with me at Starbucks was another woman I'd fantasize about the next time my wife and I had sex, and the reason Summer loved *True Blood* was her ever-ready fever for Joe Manganiello. So what? Really, so what? Happy wife, happy life, as they say, and we're entitled to whatever gets us through this anticlimactic bitch of an existence.

We never get over what makes us hottest, though, my erotica-sneaking friend. From then on, we're chasing the dragon. When Summer slipped on the negligee she bought on a whim at Victoria's Secret, what she hoped she was buying is my preference. She wanted me to prefer her to anyone else. She wanted me to crave her, forgetting any perfect-ten porn star or centerfold—not to mention all those women at Starbucks—and to lust for her more than I did any other female on the planet. But I can't. That's the truth. It's like working up a craving for the taste of a Big Mac. I know perfectly well what a Mickey D's hamburger tastes like. Cholesterol aside, I'm okay with the taste of a Big Mac. I might even choose it over Wendy's or Jack in the Box; but sorry, folks, it ain't *foie gras en croute*. Two full decades after my first time with Summer, I never daydream about sex with my wife. If she dreams about me, I'm flattered, yes, but also bewildered. I mean, it may well be that men are focused more on novelty than women are, but let's face it: no matter how much I love my favorite movie, I can't watch it two or three times a week. That dog won't hunt.

So there we were at Ted and Alice's pool party for lusty libertines, pretty Summer and I, simultaneously clinging to each other in our underwear like scared children and desperate to throw our genitalia at anyone in sight. On our way toward the master bedroom, we reentered the intermediate zone where we were allowed to watch other couples and threesomes. We held each other up, shaking with adolescent confusion, as mere feet away a chubby, determined looking black man repeatedly smashed into a white-skinned blonde woman from behind, her cries more startled, it seemed, than rapturous. We heard the smack, smack of their bodies and inhaled their blended pheromones, the musk of their sex. It was loveless and animalistic. The blonde reached below herself and clenched her own breast, then lost balance and fell forward onto the sheets. The man never slowed, ramming deeply and slapping her ass. "You know it," he grunted. "You love that black dick, don't you? Yeah. Ain't that right. Yeah, you love it."

"Fucking *shit!*" she cried into the bedding. My wife inhaled suddenly, sharply, empathically sharing the woman's orgasm.

In the next bed over, a thin woman fed her lover's cock to a woman in boy shorts. "Make him come," she ordered. "Then play with me."

"God," Summer whispered. "I can't take this. Find a bed with me now. Can we? Please?" I agreed— though I'm not sure I said so out loud, but I felt it with everything I had. We pushed deeper into the house. The lights were dim in the back bedroom. I slid my briefs off quickly, trying not to feel as if I were in a doctor's office or our bedroom or anywhere similarly mundane, then all but shoved Summer toward the scattering of bodies on Ted and Alice's bed. It may seem funny, but even then I wasn't erect, so I tried to block any view of my penis by pressing it into the mattress. Summer touched the nearest man, who muttered "Fuck, yeah" and rolled to his knees. She regarded his dick like she'd never seen one in her life, then said, "Wait." She rolled toward me. "Can we do this?" she whispered.

"I want both of us to feel good," I answered.

"Yes," she replied and kissed me, her little hand closing around me as I hardened. My entire soul was chaos in that moment, my mind awhirl, my body beyond a frontier. The next thing I knew, Summer's ass was in the air. I slid a finger in as she leaned over to take a stranger into her mouth.

I didn't know where I was, how one moment connected to the next. I swear to God, I didn't know who was whom. My cock couldn't decide from second to second whether to retreat into my body or stretch, girder-hard. "Hey, there, baby," someone said. It was Alice, her tits and belly fully exposed as she climbed into bed and straddled my hips. "I'm gonna fuck that dick ragged."

"Wait, I...wait," I said. "Wait." I felt her wet labia sliding down on me. "Wait."

"Jesus, *fuck*," Summer said, to a guy who wasn't me. "*Yes*, fucking *shit*."

I don't know what exploded in my head at that moment, but it sure wasn't the climax I'd craved. Anger? Jealousy? Loss? Did it seem my wife was kicking me aside? Perhaps I felt the enormity of that as a blast of absolute, unbearable rejection. I, too, wanted, it seems, or expected, to be preferred. Yet Summer was immersing herself in a knot of other partners. I couldn't take that. My psyche shut down. I plummeted from coherence, away from any sequence of rational thought, pushing back my intolerable emotions the only way I knew how: I ran like hell. I was out on Ted's porch in what felt like an instant. To this day I couldn't tell you how I got out from under poor Alice. I hope I didn't do her physical damage in that fugue-driven flight from her bed. She must've thought I'd gone crazy. I had.

So exactly how common is swinging, anyway? No one knows for sure. There are at least three million swingers in the States, potentially as many as sixteen million. The Kinsey Institute thinks about one out of every twenty-five married couples try it. There are over three hundred lifestyle organizations registered in NASCA, the North American Swing Club Association, not to mention clubs in Belgium, England, France, Germany, and the Netherlands. But how do we determine who's a swinger and who isn't? If a gay man and his straight wife have an arrangement, is that consensual adultery or swinging? What if a couple only tries it once or twice, or if they only watch other couples have sex over live Internet chat sessions? What if they perform for other couples but never meet them face to face?

According to writer Terry Gould and his sources, the first American swingers were World War II Air Force fighter pilots, who often lived near their wives but had the highest fatality rate in the armed services. The lifestyle broke wider in the 1960s, largely as a result of titillating ads in men's magazines. What Air Force swingers called "key parties"—though there's no evidence *The Ice Storm*'s bowl of car keys was ever an actual practice at those parties—became known in the popular press as "wife swapping." That's a deceptive term, because even then the phenomenon was hardly coercive. In recent years a "polyfidelitous," or "faithful to more than one," movement has emerged to question whether romance need always be monogamous. It's driven by women, many of whom grew up as science fiction fans. Robert Heinlein's free-love 1961 head trip *Stranger in a Strange Land* is a frequent citation, with its orgiastic cries of "Thou art God, and I am God and all that groks is God!"

That's the history. In real terms, though, each marriage is different, and each couple is different, and what works for some will never work for others. I only know what I felt all along but never let myself say till a few years ago: monogamy is both wonderful and lethally boring. It's in the nature of almost every human being to crave exhilaration, and nothing's more exhilarating than unfamiliar sexual contact. Maybe it's coded into us by religion and other conservative influences. The first time we sneak a look at forbidden sexual imagery, our physical, hormonal reaction gets welded with the dread of being caught. After that, any sex we're allowed or even encouraged to have never quite rings that bell.

There's a woman on TV who makes millions by criticizing men's romantic "pickers." She's referring, of course, to Mr. Johnson down there. Mr. Johnson could not give a fig about my religious upbringing or conventional societal notions or the proprieties of marital monogamy. Now, that's not to say my adulterous appetites couldn't be mentally overruled. I had no interest in betraying my wedding vows or my wife's trust. But lust will out; and once I questioned whether every marriage had to work a certain traditional way, the door was open to possibilities that might satisfy both my focus on the love of my life and the drive to experience new sensual frontiers. In theory, it was the best of both worlds. In theory.

In practice, here's me, Gary Klein, feeling alone on Ted's porch at one in the morning. Not all alone, though: two other guys and a tired-looking woman are out here smoking a few feet away, so I have to keep my wounded emotions in some kind of check. It wouldn't do to ruin Ted and Alice's friendly neighborhood orgy by projectile weeping. There's a window behind me, and on the other side of that window is the dark master bedroom. I hear sounds emanating from inside, too soft to horrify the neighbors, yet loud enough from where I'm standing to punch my heart with every grunt, curse, and cry. I hear my wife reveling in the sexual attention of two different men. I gather one of those men is behind her, one in front of her. She's loving every ass-smacking minute of it. It's a sound I haven't heard from her in years; she's exploding like the Fourth of July.

I hear my wife of sixteen years, a woman who comes faintly and perfunctorily with me, climaxing over and over again, panting, damn near yowling, desperate for more. I hear the mother of my sweet little girl rasping, "Yes, I'm your slut!" to a man she's never met and may never see again. She doesn't seem to have noticed I left the room. If she has, she's found way more entertaining activities to pursue than to chase me down. She likes sex with those strangers—she loves it!—more than she enjoys sex with me. Even more emasculating, I couldn't bring myself to get it on with Alice, not because she wasn't attractive in her fleshy, suburban way, but because I was too big a wuss to finish what I started. Jesus Christ. Here's my wife, squalling like a nymphomaniacal porn star between the dicks of two anonymous men, and here's me, about to cry like a sissy on the porch ten feet away. Listening. *Hiding.* Alone.

I waited till the smokers went back inside to do whatever one did in round two of an orgy. Then I took a walk around the block. The streets were quiet, as boring and predictable as any American suburb, their residents sublimely unaware of the sexual free-for-all transpiring in their midst. When I came back, I sat in the living room and watched most of an infomercial for a plastic food dehydrator that produced dehydrated, plastic-looking food. The KFC bucket on the table was still full of chicken, a cold pile of greasy MSG. I felt so low it was all I could do not to rush it and gorge myself numb. A bit later I heard laughing and showers running. My wife came out, her hair wet, her face flushed with childlike delight. "Hey!" she said, crashing onto the couch beside me and leaning into my shoulder. "Crazy night, huh? You ready?"

"For what?"

"For what? Bed, of course!" I was momentarily stunned. She wasn't finished? "Oh, man, I can't wait to crawl into bed and, like, slam into a coma!" she continued, giggling. "Whew! Man! What a workout, I'm tellin' ya."

"Yeah, it sounded like it."

"Did you have fun?"

"I did," I lied flatly, allowing myself a brief sigh, masking sorrow behind a grunt as I stood. This movement brushed Summer aside, but she failed to interpret it for what it truly was, a shove. She chattered inanities on the way to our car. I made it five blocks before bursting into tears, pulling over and weeping out the jagged remains of my heart.

"Honey! Gary! What's the matter? I thought you wanted this!"

"I did," I admitted. "I didn't know what it'd feel like."

"Well, did you at least have fun with Alice?"

"I didn't do anything with Alice."

"You did. I looked over and saw you."

"I know, but that's—she climbed onto me and I pushed her away. I couldn't do it."

"You..." She gaped helplessly. I think she knew I felt wounded by her actions, yet she was utterly confused as to how things could've spun out so wrongly. That happens a lot in marriage. "I thought...This was your idea, Gary."

"I know, I know!"

"So why are you freaking out now?"

"I thought...You know, I thought we'd be sharing it together..."

"You left!"

"I know!" I was so embarrassed and drained I couldn't express myself properly. "I wanted...I didn't know it'd be so...It was me. I couldn't handle it, Summer. I freaked out. That's all. I freaked out, okay? Jesus."

"I didn't know that, babe. I'm sorry. I should've paid more attention."

That's true, except it wasn't really true. She was in the exact situation I put her in. "I wound up on the porch," I said, laughing weakly.

"You fucked somebody on the porch?"

"No, I didn't fuck anyone!"

"At all?"

"Like, three strokes with Alice."

"Did you come?"

"No." I became humiliatingly aware I was whining. "God..." I groaned.

"So...okay, so...We'll never do this again, okay? That's fine by me. Do you hold it against me?"

"I don't know if that's...I don't know if I want to call it off yet," I said. "I'm too...I don't blame you for...doing...you know, what you did." She nodded, unsure what to say. "I know it was my idea. I know I'm being a fucking baby about it. I just...I didn't think it would go that way at all."

She nodded. "You thought you'd be the one having fun." Silence.

"No," I said, lying.

"Okay. I shouldn't have said that. You thought it'd be a two-way street."

"Exactly. I thought we'd both, you know..."

"Have fun."

"Yeah."

She shook her head, debated whether to say what she was thinking, decided against it, said it anyway. "Gary, I didn't do anything wrong."

"I know."

"I had fun."

55

"I could tell."

"And I don't feel I have anything to apologize for. This was your idea to begin with."

"I know. I didn't ask you to apologize."

"I know I must've hurt you."

"The situation hurt me," I replied. "You were having so much fun, like one big orgasm after another. More than...well, more than you ever have with me these days. Y'know?" The crux of the matter.

"Are you serious?"

"Yes. You were coming like crazy."

"Of course I was, Gary. There were two guys and...yes, it was hot. I didn't have to worry about waking up our daughter!"

"She'd sleep through anything. You know that."

"It's not the same thing. We're in the house, it's where our kid lives...It's different. You know that."

"I know, but I guess...I don't feel like it should be any different. We ought to still be rocking each other's world."

"I guess it's not that simple." She wiped her eyes and waved her hands in frustration. "At the party I didn't have to worry about what you were thinking, y'know? I could do what I wanted. I didn't have to wait for things, like, for you to do things your way, I don't know, to...to be married. I could fuck like we used to back in college, when it was fun to kind of show off to your neighbors that you were getting some. You remember?"

I smiled. "I remember that time your RA screamed at us from the hall."

"'Ooh, you go, girl!'" Summer crooned, mimicking her freshman year dorm assistant. I chuckled. "'Take ya some!'"

"It's been a long time since we went at it like that," I sighed.

"I don't think either of us wants to pay for our daughter's therapy sessions when she's a teenager."

"No." I collected myself. "Boy, you really got into it."

"I kept waiting for you to join in. I'd have hollered the same way for you, I promise. I assumed you were busy with someone else."

"Like who? Alice?"

"With anyone. I know we said we'd keep it low-key, but in that moment it didn't really seem to matter. I looked up and you were having sex with Alice. No big deal, believe it or not. I mean, I know that sounds crazy, and for a second I even started to get jealous, but then I remembered I was…you know. Doing stuff myself. Anyway. I'm sorry this messed you up so bad, babe. I didn't mean for it to wind up so awful."

"I know. You didn't do anything wrong. You really didn't. I just feel like…Shit, I don't know. It just hurt, is all. It's not fair, I get that. I just feel like you're one up on me."

"Two," she corrected, before she could catch herself. "Sorry."

"I know."

"So you think I, what, owe you one?"

"Two." She looked at me sharply. "Not really." But I did. "I don't know."

She held out her hand to shake. "Right. So never again, am I right?"

"Not for now," I answered, shaking her hand.

"You think you could try that again? It doesn't seem like that's a super idea."

"Ask me later," I said. "I can't make any major life decisions right now."

"You're right," she agreed. "Let's get some sleep." I nodded and started the car. "We'll feel better tomorrow."

But we didn't, or I didn't. It nagged me for weeks, and she didn't feel bad in the first place. She skipped around the next day like she was starring in

57

some happy-go-lucky musical. I, on the other hand, went through waves of emotion. More than anything else, I felt jealous, though not in the way you'd expect. She was stronger and braver in that moment than I had been. I suggested going to the party because I assumed I'd be a sexual Conan the Barbarian and Summer would get swept up in my manly crusade of awesomeness. How was I to know she'd be the conqueror after all? In all the years it had taken us to grow up together, I never saw anything like that primal side of her.

If you asked me prior to that night at Ted's party what the best sex I ever had was, I could name one of three or four occasions, but they would all have happened with Summer. By the time I felt I knew what I was doing in bed, she was my one and only. There was that time back in college where I did her on my most despised teacher's desk. From then on, Professor M. could give me any grade she wanted, and I'd just smile and imagine her working in the same office I'd defiled with such glee. Maybe it was that time we got crazy in a rented houseboat, or our first round of honeymoon sex down in Cabo. I suppose it's my sacred obligation to list the night we conceived our little girl, but no. Let's face it, knock-up sex is about as mechanical as injecting the cream filling into a Twinkie. I'd've had more fun gripping a *Penthouse* while ejaculating into a cup.

Now there was this. I couldn't tear the sound of Summer's orgasmic wailing from my thoughts. Near as I could tell, *that* was the best sex she ever had in *her* life, and I was just moping nearby. How to even the score? I mean, I hate to put it so bluntly or mathematically, but that was how I felt. Have you ever been cheated on? When it happens to you, you can't escape the awful feeling you've been beaten in a contest you didn't know you were playing. It doesn't matter if your "number" was way higher than hers going in. That single extra partner tips the battle in her favor. It sucks! Now here I was, losing the competition of my own marriage. Also, since technically, without meaning to, I cheated on *her* with Kellie back in high school, I couldn't even pretend I held some superior moral ground. The whole lifestyle thing was my idea, so it's basically like I begged her to one-up me…two-up me! Suck! Double suck!

To employ the most serious suburban white swear word: *unacceptable*!

I brooded over how to get back at her for days. I couldn't help it. I realize none of this makes any logical sense; I felt crazy even thinking about it. That all-consuming thirst for revenge burned out pretty quickly, thank God. But to be honest, for weeks, even months after that, any time one of Summer's female friends (other than Darcy the mad cow) came by for something as prosaic as watching a movie, I spent the whole time fantasizing about how to lure that unsuspecting friend into bed, cheat on Summer, and "even the score." In the world of physical time and space, I was a decent husband. I doubt Summer had the first clue what I was thinking. But was I lusting in my heart? You're damn right I was, every metaphorically fucking chance I could get. I resolved to make the swinger thing work in my favor, no matter what it took. By then, the ball was rolling fast and furious on Bliss Panerotic, so I doubted I'd lack for opportunities.

Chapter 6

In spring of 2013, the Ryders threw a party for investors at their *nouveau riche* palace in the Hollywood Hills. Grand View Drive is well named; it's directly behind the Chateau Marmont, a hotel most famous for hosting John Belushi's speedball suicide in Bungalow #3. I'd only been up into that tangle of cliff-hugging alleys once or twice, and even with a GPS and *Thomas Guide* it was all I could do to find the place. Honest to God, other than the glittering panorama of the Sunset Strip I can't imagine why anyone would live up there, but it's what people do when they make millions of dollars in the entertainment business. It seems moving to Orange County like all the other schmucks isn't sufficiently obnoxious.

You may think no millionaire in his or her right mind would intentionally throw his or her money and reputation behind a theme park for swingers, let alone the hardcore pornography business, but you'd be wrong. For most of porn's modern history, it was funded primarily by crime syndicate money. Yes, I'm talking Sicilian-American gentlemen with charming nicknames, loud suits, and careers in the sanitation business that didn't require them to hang around the office much. *Deep Throat*, for example, was produced by Louis "Butchie" Peraino, using money his old man "Big Tony" made as a top earner for the Colombo family. Louis's brother Joseph distributed *The Devil in Miss Jones*. Adult video was thoroughly mobbed up till well into the '90s, when FBI incursions and the plummeting value of videotapes made it wiser to look elsewhere for business opportunities. These days, the funding is more diversified and quasi-legitimate, so companies like Wicked or Vivid are run like any other small-scale production house.

As for Adam and Nicole, who started their company on credit cards and a dream, they wanted high-profile investors. Thus, they turned to musicians, athletes, and movie stars. For the most part, mainstream movie actors and directors couldn't hang the phone up fast enough when Adam called. Rappers, on the other hand, were more intrigued, as the Ryders expected. Snoop Dogg's a regular at the AVN (Adult Video News) Awards for porn performers and creators, and he produced and appeared (clothed) in two adult videos under the brand name *Doggystyle*. Rapper 50 Cent produced a series of movies called *Groupie Love*. Too $hort was more hands-on in his own adult video appearance, in *Get In Where You Fit In 1*. (You really have to hand it to whoever comes up with these titles.) DJ Yella, a founding member of N.W.A., directed hundreds of porn flicks including *Back Seat Confessions* and *Hip Hop Cheerleaders 14*. Lil Jon was in bed (not quite literally) with Vivid. You can imagine which rapper starred in the movie *Coolio & the Gang Bang*. None of these videos, incidentally, are classics, so don't rush to add them to your collection.

Anyway, I'm not a huge rap fan, but even I recognized some of the faces standing around the party. Ice-T, erstwhile pimp and bank robber in Hawaii, notorious decades ago for his song "Cop Killer," now the respectable star of a TV police procedural, sipped Diet Coke and swapped stories with two guys so tall they were probably Lakers. Summer chatted with rapper Eve, who stripped for a month when she was eighteen. I know it's rude to harp on these people's titillating pasts, but I'm doing so for a reason: we all have sex lives. Occasionally, some of us make a few bucks being sexy. Lady Gaga was a stripper. So was Courtney Love, though that's maybe not as surprising. So what? You didn't do anything in your teens or early twenties that would preclude you from being president? Well, aren't you one of Heaven's precious angels.

One of the hottest celebs eating canapés in Adam's vast auditorium of a living room was DJ Buzz Da Ramfunkshus, born Jamal Harris in the Kirkwood neighborhood of Atlanta around the time I met Summer. (Yes, I've reached that advanced age where I notice how old I was when other people were born.) Buzz did his time doing guest appearances on half a dozen more established West Coast albums, then dropped his own *Absolute Hero Part 1, The Big Banger* in May of 2011. By the Fourth of July he was the darling of iTunes, even managing to sell three million of those charming technological relics of the twentieth century, compact discs. Katy Perry gushed over him at the VMAs. You know his stuff. Your kids probably bounce around to his heartwarming numbers "Pussy Parade" and "Hit It (Like a Bitch)." In person, Harris is much less ramfunkshus, preferring to talk about high-yield treasury bonds and his new Bugatti Veyron. He eschews Polo and Cross Colours in favor of crisp Fitzgerald-fit suits. He marketed his own line of neckties through Kiton, and they're really quite dashing. I'd buy one tomorrow if I could afford it.

Okay, so maybe you don't follow the latest in hip hop. If not, and your kids are still hiding their rap adoration behind thumping ear buds, allow me to paint you a picture. DJ Buzz has the wiry build of a talented amateur kickboxer, which it turns out he is. Despite being half a foot shorter than me, I have no doubt he could whip my ass from here to Hotlanta. He's still rocking the soul patch and a dense Ice Cube afro, and he hides behind glasses so dark they could serve as space shuttle heat-absorbing tiles. He's obsessed with DC Comics and owns a rare mint copy of *Black Lightning #1* from 1977. His zest for life, fueled by millions of dollars, a harem of strippers and video vixens, and gallons of his own Buzz Fuel signature sports drink, is irresistible. What's more—and I never heard anyone else say this—he's funny, which means he's probably smart as all-get-out. He smells fantastic. My wife says it's Hugo Boss. I think it's just what unabashed wealth smells like. The man seems to glide around the room on his own private jet of charisma.

When I first met Buzz, he was chatting up Nicole and a couple of guys I imagined were lawyers. It turns out they were. One was Avi Hirschberg, who's managed to keep the Ryders out of jail in defiance of all known jurisprudence and theology. The other was Buzz's attorney, a guy whose name I've since forgotten. Behind them was a table bearing a detailed polystyrene architectural model of Bliss Panerotic. Behind that was a state-of-the-art flat-screen television displaying a 3-D computer graphic of the park. Our point of view soared east from the Pacific over the mouth of the harbor, rocketing at a virtual height of thirty feet. I'd seen this video and model before, but in showroom conditions they were hugely impressive.

"Man, I can't fuckin' believe this shit, cuz," the rapper exclaimed. "My man Adam gonna build the Disneyland of pussy on Catalina. Ain't that some shit?"

"We hope to bring you on board," Nicole purred. "You'd be the guest of honor at our opening weekend. All expenses paid, of course. You can see, and experience, what we offer for yourself."

"Oh, shit!" Buzz laughed. "You gonna get me in trouble, girl!"

"Who doesn't like a bit of trouble?" she replied.

"I don't mean to put a damper on things," the attorney-whose-name-I've-forgotten said, "but there's still no guarantee the island or county will even allow you to build it."

Adam heard that from some distance away. He immediately broke off a conversation with two sitcom actors and strode toward us. "Don't you worry about that," he sniffed. "This county needs cash more than it worries about publicity way out on the other side of Santa Catalina. If it didn't, the San Fernando Valley wouldn't still have a porn industry. We're gonna make people rich. Starting with you, Buzz. Don't tell me you don't feel me on this."

Buzz chuckled. "Oh, I feel ya, dawg. I feel ya. I know exactly what you want. You want this shit in a music video."

"Hell, yeah!" Adam agreed with a Christmas-morning grin. "To be honest, Buzz, we hadn't even thought of that angle. A video. Man! Wouldn't that be something. You and half a dozen beautiful women, strolling down the Strip like you own the place."

"And you could," Nicole agreed. "At least part of it. That's what tonight is all about. We could scrounge up anonymous money from anyone. We want you. We want investors who make us look good."

"Damn, baby," Buzz demurred, shaking his head. "You don't need to ever worry 'bout looking good. Your mama, daddy, and God got that shit covered already."

"Oh, Buzz, you smooth talker!" she laughed, stroking his arm through his silk jacket sleeve.

"Look, Buzz, bottom line," Adam said, invoking his second-favorite phrase behind *ski bunny*, "we're all gonna make a lot of money off this park. Unlike Walt Disney in '55, we're not gonna open the doors on some half-assed construction site and call it a Magic Kingdom. We're gonna get motherfuckers laid. Fuck a four-hour drive to Vegas. Hop a ferry and be in a sexual wonderland by seven o'clock Friday night. Stay the weekend. Send your penis to Fantasy Island. Or hey, this ain't about just making men happy. Women, too. Round up your BFFs and bang a total stranger in a mask. Talk about a killer bachelorette party. Damn."

"Most of all, though, we're inviting couples," Nicole corrected gently, "people who've heard about the lifestyle and want to play in a safe, welcoming, unscuzzy environment. We're keeping it classy, San Diego."

Buzz looked again at the CG simulation. Smiling animated guests, rendered by the same software that added armies of orcs to the *Lord of the Rings* movies, waved and flashed us as our virtual point of view passed. Fireworks lit up a starless southern California night. A beautiful mocha-skinned woman slid up to Buzz and nestled into his arm, sipping from a flute of Domaine Carneros. Her cleavage would've sent Gauguin into spasms of elation. "I don't know, baby," Buzz said. "What do you think 'bout all this?"

"I think it's remarkable," she said, surprising us all with a snobbish Martha Stewart accent. "I'm impressed with their business plan, and I think they've gauged the mood of the country precisely. Let's face it, the zeitgeist is craving Panerotic."

The rapper beamed. "You hear this shit?" he marveled. "MBA from Duke University, muthafucka! This here's my queen, Andréanne."

"How'd you two meet?" Nicole asked.

"On eHarmony," Andréanne replied immediately.

"It's a two-hun'ed-and-fifty-eight-question profile, man, I'm tellin' you," Buzz observed thoughtfully. "They really get to the heart of a muthafucka, ya feel me?"

By nightfall most guests at the party were at that stage of drunk where staying forever and ordering Chinese till they die sounds like a pretty damn good idea, especially since there were beautiful girls swimming nude in a pool that overlooked the neon insanity of Sunset, West Hollywood. It was the first we'd seen of any of these girls, so I can only assume Adam had them stashed in a hot chicks attic for special occasions. Two might-as-well-have-been-centerfolds and, not for nothing, a gay busboy named, I shit you not, Darth had already propositioned me, so my ego ascended to Olympus along with Adam's house. Meanwhile, Summer changed into a modest one-piece hidden behind an equally modest wrap. Modest. That had been the operative aesthetic since our night at Ted and Alice's. The jury was out on whether our relationship had fully recovered, but *modest*. We were moving ahead modestly. Go, us.

I, on the other hand, had once again neglected to bring a swimsuit, so I was content to mill around the house in relative tranquility, drunk and stoned off a hit of Buzz's extraordinary weed in Adam's state-of-the-art upstairs man cave while others whooped it up outside. I found myself drifting back to the polystyrene model. Compared to the virtual representation, it seemed charmingly old school, like something from a 1960s World Fair. With little sense of scale and no visible signage, it could've been any suburban shopping and entertainment mecca. I imagined an AMC Cineplex and Rainforest Café, with laser tag and balloons for the kids. We were talking about yanking sex out of the bedroom and acknowledging it as an everyday part of American recreational life. Why not? I wasn't a churchgoer. So why was part of me still squeamish about the project?

We're all, no matter what our religious education, brought up to believe sex and sexuality are private, like going to the bathroom or picking your nose. To be exposed at it is shameful, caught liking it even worse. I maintain my sexuality is no more extreme than most people's, no matter what Bill O'Reilly says. If you could see through walls, or more fairly if I could see you through yours, we'd find our predilections aren't all that different. I like sex with my wife, and yes, I imagine what it'd be like to bang yours. You close your eyes while having sex with your husband and imagine your son's tenth-grade English teacher, the one with the sexy sideburns and reading glasses, having his way with you on a stack of ungraded essays. We're built to be hormonal creatures. We're not merely intellects, we're also primate bodies. The Ryders were trying to build a place that made sex glamorous in a way it never really had been in America. They wanted you to believe you didn't have to be a rap star or centerfold to have thrilling, celebrity sex. They deliberately worked on your belief that underneath it all, you're a sex hero waiting to happen.

I looked at the CG fireworks going off over the beautifully rendered Bliss Panerotic and thought about the last time I'd been to a resort. I spent months trying to talk Summer into a famously sexy club in Jamaica to no avail. "Yeah," she scoffed, "like I want to get herpes on my vacation. Bugs are one thing, but come on." We went to Vegas instead. I oversaw half a dozen major campaigns that year, including those much-beloved taco chip ads, so money was rolling in faster than I knew how to spend it. Suddenly I had a 401(k) and investments in mutual funds and a college fund for our daughter. It was more responsibility than I knew how to process, more maturity than my relative youth was prepared to absorb without a fight. I wanted something frivolous. I know it was a midlife crisis. I had no delusions about luring hot young tennis players into a Corvette I was too old and creaky to drive. I just wanted to spend a bunch of money on useless entertainment, preferably something with adult appeal.

So off we went instead to the latest, most vulgarly glittery Nevada casino, the French Polynesian. What a party that was. I've never spent so much money having so little fun in my life, and that includes the night we surprised my father-in-law with his dream celebration, a night at Medieval Times. I know this sounds like a total cliché, but Summer couldn't have sex that week because she kept getting headaches. She couldn't handle the smoke in the casino proper as we passed through it on our way to and from the elevators, so she spent our whole vacation a few seconds from vomiting onto her shoes. She rallied, then got sick again the minute our five hundred dollars' worth of dinner arrived at Eric Ripert's celebrity restaurant, a dinner she took back to the hotel in a box and ignored. (The waitstaff was at least nice enough to throw a couple of chocolates in for the road. She ate those, of course. Yes, my chocolate, too.) Even more annoying, she extrapolated her menstrual cycle incorrectly, so we couldn't have sex after the second night anyway, even if her head weren't clanging off her shoulders, or if our baby girl weren't miserable from teething pain. Here's a wonderful idea: take a six-month-old to Vegas. Oh, yeah; I'm a genius that way. I came home from our vacation in desperate need of a vacation. I hadn't taken one longer than a few days since. The memory of staring out a forty-eighth floor window at young, happy libertines tanning by a tropical pool while I bounced a crying baby on my knee was too demoralizing to process.

"You all right?" a deep voice asked behind me. I turned to face a strange giant's torso.

"Never better," I said. "Man. You are tall." Booze and weed always amplify my powers of observation and insight.

"Just six-eight," the man said. "You look like a fella who's casin' his own gallows. What's the matter, the Ryders talk you into investing?" He had a kind of chicken-fried accent, the drawl that used to hail exclusively from the Texarkana region but now resides anywhere folks enjoy cheap beer and NASCAR.

"You don't think it's a good idea?"

"Bet on sex," he said, shrugging. "That's my motto. You ain't never gonna run out of opportunities."

"You must not be married," I quipped.

"Matter of fact," he said, showing me a thick titanium wedding ring and smiling. "Best eighteen years of my life."

"I'm coming up on seventeen myself," I replied, and held out my hand. "Gary Klein."

"Mr. Klein, good to meetcha. Rick Orzabal." He shook my hand in one potentially dislocating pump, like he was cocking a shotgun. He was polite enough not to use anything close to his full strength, but I got the sense he had a grip that could crush a fire hydrant.

"Orzabal," I repeated. "You're one of LSA's architects."

"Chief architect, if you don't mind a bit of immodesty. It's a big step ahead for me. This baby here," he said, indicating the polystyrene model, "is my pride and joy. The park, I mean, not just the model."

"It's a great design," I said. "Flashy. Not too flashy, though. Like...restrained." I honestly had no idea what I was talking about, and Orzabal knew it.

He chuckled. "I'm not sure how something can be both flashy and restrained, but thankee all the same."

"No, I know. I'm sorry. Fifth drink," I explained, hoisting my Long Island iced tea. "I mean...it looks like a lot of fun. That's all I want to say. Festive."

"It's gonna do for zipless fucking what Anaheim did for cartoons and kiddie rides," Orzabal boasted, his massive chest visibly puffing. The guy was truly immense, a thick middle-aged tower of a human being. The fringe around his freckled bald spot was banded into a Deadhead-style ponytail. Pale blonde eyebrows poked out over reading glasses too small for his Germanic face. He grinned behind a thick Teddy Roosevelt mustache. His hands were the size of Frisbees.

"That's not a bad line. You mind if I steal it? I'm in charge of their global ad campaign."

"Oh, yeah," he said. "I've seen that. I'm bored. Let's get naked and see what happens."

For two awkward seconds I thought he was propositioning me. Then the fog cleared and I realized he was quoting my slogan. "Oh, yessir! That's me."

"You think they'll actually let you air commercials for this place on TV?"

"Not the networks. Maybe Travel Channel. I'm dying to get somebody like Bourdain or Samantha Brown to show up, but I figure the odds aren't good."

"It's a shame HBO isn't still doing *Real Sex*. They'd be all over it."

"Yeah, and Playboy Channel's shutting us out 'cause Hugh Hefner didn't think of starting a sex resort first."

"Other than his own house, you mean."

"Exactly."

He took a swig from his beer, draining half the bottle in a single pull with no visible effect. "You seen my wife at this party?"

"Oh, uh, I guess I don't know your wife."

"You're right. Sorry. Name's Judy. She's great. The point is I did pretty well for myself. But people like to explore, y'know, go crazy, even people who are happily married. I think Ryder's gonna make Hefner look like a flash in the pan. He has a vision, this guy. He knows what people want. It's worth millions for anyone who has the balls to go there."

"I do not disagree."

"It's an amazing project. We should both be thanking our lucky stars we get to work on it."

"It's refreshing to meet a true believer," I said. "My wife thinks I'm making a deal with the Devil. She's hoping her mom never finds out I had anything to do with Bliss Panerotic or Adam Ryder."

"She here, your wife?"

"Yeah, she's out by the pool."

"Well," he said, "she must not be too bent out of shape, then, y'think?"

"No," I admitted. "She's coming round to the idea. Intrigued, I guess you could say. You from around here?"

"No, sir," Orzabal replied. "Only been in California a few years, five or six now. Got recruited from a firm in Oklahoma City."

"Oklahoma City," I repeated. "The heart of the Bible belt."

"Yeah, well," he drawled, grinning, "see, the funny thing about a belt is how quickly it can get itself unbuckled."

"I suppose."

"I'm the expert on that," he crowed. "I got my fair share of sorority zug-zug back in the day, I can tell ya. And me and the missus, we been in the lifestyle since long before we moved to sunny L.A."

"You're kidding. In Oklahoma?"

"Bet your ass, in Oklahoma. I know most of the lifestyle folks for three states around. They like fuckin' my wife." Orzabal announced this with no visible irritation or irony. "We still see 'em when we go back for a visit, hump like bandits. Good people, you bet. God-fearin', most of 'em."

"That's amazing," I said.

"Oh, yeah. Up late pokin' each other cross-eyed on Friday and Saturday nights, then back on their knees Sunday morning to praise Jesus. God love 'em. Salt of the earth."

"That's," I began, then reeled in my objections before Orzabal could take offense. "I'm still wrapping my head around that one, I have to say."

"Why, you a churchgoin' fella?"

"No. My parents almost never went to temple. I was never bar mitzvahed."

"Oh. You're one of the chosen people."

"So they tell me. I never saw much historical evidence for God being fond of us."

"Ha. Well, I was raised a good Freewill Baptist myself, praise the Lord and pass the repression. It was just how people came of age out there, leastways it was when I was growin' up. But most of us Oklahoma folks lost our virginity at church camp anyway, so it's not like we didn't know how to party. Conscience always takes a back seat to Mr. Winky down there. Yeah," he nodded, "Things get in there. Your head, I mean. Guilt. It takes a while to root it all out. Took me a hell of a long time. I'd go around and get my ashes hauled, sure, but then I'd spend plenty of mornings after worrying I was going to Hell for the sins of the flesh."

"'This one time at band camp,'" I replied.

"Oh, lemme tell ya somethin', brother, them band geeks didn't have nothin' on us fine Baptist kiddies, I can promise you that."

I shook my head, trying to expel the visual of blushing Christian teens fornicating in pup tents. "So this," I said, pointing to the model instead, "is right up your alley, then." He chuckled. "No pun intended," I added hastily.

"I guess you could say I was the right man for the job, yes. But God, no one at LSA knows about my uh…extracurricular activities. I don't need some asshole holdin' that over me. People are funny about stuff like that. Judgmental. Doesn't make much sense, now, does it?" With his Okie drawl, "doesn't" sounded more like "dudn't." "I mean, what with the Internet an' all. Shoulda realized how horny we all are by now."

"Some things we never outgrow, I guess."

"Maybe. That's sad but true."

"I know it is. I'm hitting some funny walls in my own head. I know it's all bullshit and I should just relax and go with the flow, have some fun. I'll be at Panerotic's opening weekend myself, me and my wife. I'd like to be able to, you know, live a little, right? I just…I guess I'm like you or anybody else. I was raised

72

with all those good ol' American taboos on stuff like this."

"It's funny," Orzabal mused, stroking his beard. "Hating sex is a recent invention, historically speaking. Trust me, I've done the research. You should, too. Might help you with all that marketing junk. No offense," he said quickly.

"Oh, none taken."

"But yeah, man. Hearken back to the good old days when people fucked in praise of the gods, not in fear of 'em."

"You mean, like, fertility rites?"

"'Fertility rites,'" he repeated, laughing. "Man, that's just stuffy old professor talk, y'ask me. They was *fuckin'* rites, pure and simple! I mean, farming and spring equinoxes an' all that had something to do with it, sure, but they ain't half as much fun as gettin' busy. And the gods, oh, my brother, the gods were delighted with their shameless concupiscence!" He beamed. "Not too shabby for an Oklahoma country boy, is it? I ain't as dumb as I look."

"Nicely put," I said. "It seems to me you know whereof you speak."

"I know what I know, this is true. Cave paintings, for example. There are cave paintings that show animals doin' what animals do. You mean to tell me somebody didn't get their rocks off on in those selfsame caves?"

"I imagine so."

"Tigris and Euphrates Rivers. Garden of Eden, right? Cradle o' civilization. Well, they used to have what they called 'houses of heaven,' full of what historians now call 'temple prostitutes.' Only problem is, ain't nobody found a whole hell of a lot of evidence that anybody paid these so-called prostitutes in anything other than room and board. They just liked it. That was a damn good job, man. But the Hebrews, now—your great-to-the-great-power-grandparents, you don't mind me sayin'—they wudn't too keen on such lustful activities."

"Huh."

"Herodotus said the temple fornicators of Babylon *did* get paid. But! Every woman in Babylon did it at least once! And they had to take whatever sum of money was offered, by the first guy who walked in an nailed 'em! Some women stayed for years!"

"Huh," I said again, then pointed at the model. "Hey, maybe we ought to put a pagan temple in this place."

"That ain't the worst idea I ever heard," Orzabal agreed, shrugging. "Folks like a little God with their 'God, oh my God'...'cept I wouldn't want 'em leaving Bliss Panerotic feeling guilty 'bout what they did."

"No, it's probably an idea better left on the table." We regarded the model in silence for a few more moments. "Tell me this," I said. "As a guy in the lifestyle, what would convince you to drop hundreds of dollars on a park like this? When you could pick up some strange on any weekend, I mean?"

He did me the courtesy of mulling his answer for several seconds, then replied, "Freedom, man. A place where I don't have to hide what I want, and everybody's lookin' for the same damn thing, and we don't care who knows it. Not inside the resort, anyway. No more shame. No more guilt. Oh, my brother. That'd be...paradise. Y'know? Absolute...paradise. They call a place like that a pornotopia, where everybody wants it all the time, and hot damn if they ain't all good at it. Now that is a dream I could get behind. No pun intended."

I thought about two beautiful people in a garden, making love with no guilt or embarrassment, and how their problems supposedly began when they realized they were naked. It struck me in that moment that Orzabal was right. That *was* paradise. We were none of us meant to live this way, desperate but guilty.

Chapter 7

As busy as the preceding months had been, they were nothing compared to the construction phase. I got to know Catalina Island pretty well, especially a hotel near Middle Ranch Road. Summer stayed at home with our daughter but missed no opportunity to let me know it'd be nice if I spent more time at home. I just felt I had an opportunity to watch history in the making. It was like hopping into a DeLorean and blasting back to Anaheim so I could witness firsthand the days when Disney hacked his wonderland out of an orange grove. First the land had to be graded and the cove rendered safe enough for any swimmer crazy enough to jump in it. Power lines were buried and a massive generator installed. Internet trunk lines were extended. That alone cost a fortune, but Adam was excited about launching with high-tech entertainment and community Wi-Fi from day one. Those English restaurant consultants were in and out of the Ryders' offices, browbeating Nicole into adding more kitchens. Italian engineers were hard at work designing the indoor water park. I fielded calls from national magazines and TV networks, not to mention dozens of design teams. My slogan, "I'm bored" etc., entered the international meme bank, I'm happy to say. If only there were some way to lock down royalties, I'd be a squillionaire today. I could use the money, frankly.

There were two versions of the Bliss Panerotic "interactive experience." One was a Facebook app much like any other game your friends might annoy you with, the major exception being ours boasted plenty of virtual sex. We worked a deal with Adult Friend Finder to let people meet and hook up offline if they decided to. That version was free the first few times you played it, then charged five bucks a month if you played it a lot. Guess what? People played it a lot. That was followed a few months later by a more grandiose MMOG version, a vast computer environment set on a paradise island not much at all like Santa Catalina. That was the version which included an incomplete representation of Bliss Panerotic and made exceptional use of next-gen Oculus visors to process head and eye movements into a 3-D view of a virtual environment. Turn your head, and your avatar looked in the same direction you did. The VR game also incorporated a technological breakthrough more useful for our purposes than the visors. We called it "faptics," a combination of *fap*, an Internet slang word for *masturbate*, and *haptics*. *Haptic* technology refers to any device that allows you to experience media displays by giving you the virtual sensation of touching solid objects. You've come to know our innovative, almost staggeringly lucrative, product as gLoves, a registered trademark of Tesseraction, Inc.

As I understand it, Tesseraction gLoves use a thin layer of polymers that conduct and selectively apply a weak electric charge. They've been on the drawing board for years; the real trick was getting them to simulate the feel of human skin and flesh. The sensation of hair was equally tricky but almost as important. Panerotic's contract with Tesseraction was a major coup, and even after all the fun people had at our expense, they sure couldn't wait to buy gLoves for their game rooms or offices. Don't lie: you asked for a pair for Christmas. Then you told your wife they reduce your wrist strain when you type or fill in spreadsheets. Whatever. Those aren't spreadsheets you're filling in, buddy. Be honest, man, seriously.

Did I play *Realms of Eros*? Does Donald Trump have any self-esteem? Has Paula Deen eaten pie? You could say I turned into a regular. In fact, I'm one of the few hundred people on earth who had a legitimate reason to play the game at work, not that thousands of people like you haven't done that anyway. As I said, the game's going strong. It pays the Ryders' legal fees and some of their fines. I myself have never seen a dime from it, even though I designed its fucking box and advertisements. My team built the website you downloaded it from, and I wrote its salacious slogan, "Play on, player." Give me credit. Better yet, give me cash. The slogan, delivered by a Barry White sound-alike actor named Roosevelt Price, was one of America's most downloaded ringtones in first quarter 2015. Mr. Price got a piece of that action. I did not. Have I mentioned we're living off my savings, or that I'm hoping enough of you buy this book that I can afford to send my daughter to college?

It was mid-February of 2013 when I met Cathy, or, as I knew her for several weeks, Ms. Pris. If you're a *Realms of Eros* player, bear with me while I set up the game for folks who have better things to do with their time. It opens with a "cut scene," meaning a short video, in which a fertility goddess named Gaia decrees that "from this hour hence until the end of all things, the realms of Panerotica shall offer eternal safe haven for the erotic impulse and all those who share it!" Adam, who seems to have been a Tolkien geek in his prepubescent youth, wrote that flowery, redundant line himself. It was delivered half-convincingly by a southern Californian actress trying to go legit after twenty-plus years in the porn biz. You haven't lived till you've seen a porn star emoting in a motion capture suit. The crew dressed her character in an outfit so preposterously reminiscent of a Boris Vallejo heroine that I doubt it did her mainstream career any good, but it did inspire a spike in the sales of breast implants. You're welcome, teenage boys.

Anyway, a shower of pixie dust turns a remote, sandy island into Bliss Panerotic, a haven of shameless carnality in an unspecified, crystal-blue sea. From there users could earn or buy access to the Tunnels of Pan. (You'll notice our writers weren't sticklers for mythological consistency.) The Tunnels of Pan led to various add-on environments. The first was Sinerama, a virtual backlot that paid homage to sexy cinema. The game never quite says *Casablanca*, for example, or *Barbarella*, because no one felt like braving the hassle of securing copyright permissions from every studio in L.A. Instead, Sinerama suggests those films and environments but in near-parody, with the bonus attraction that every character now behaves as if he or she were three hours into an Ecstasy trip. That dashing archaeology professor, for example, might decide to lay pipe to his coed admirers. The cartoon hottie who sings torch songs may just sit in your lap, cooing lustily as her sequined gown slips down past her shoulders. A more recent add-on hoists a space elevator to Satellite X, a zero-g bounce house for orbital sex play.

I never spent more than a few hours in any of those additional levels; I was happy just hanging around the "island." I was especially fond of a nightclub called Shag, which its clever designers gave dozens of possible looks. The floor plan was the same no matter who walked in, but its décor changed to fit each viewer's character type. When I looked around, I saw a shadowy dive for rummies, palookas and dames. Pris, on the other hand, saw a 3-D homage to the Tech Noir club from *The Terminator*. Either way, the drinks tasted like nothing. It didn't matter. We were there to go shopping.

I'd belly up to the bar, order a virtual drink with a single cyber-ice cube in it, and slip on a pair of shades as smoothly as I could. That cued the game to show me the public characteristics of everyone else in the room: their "names," orientations, and availability statuses. The game was, is, and probably always will be populated mostly by guys, but the coders made up for that by scattering artificially semi-intelligent NPCs (non-player characters) into each open room. You have the option of knowing whether any person who addresses you is an actual user or not. Clever as the programmers are, it seldom takes long to find out either way. "Mmm," a statuesque Amazon will sigh, "hel*lo*! What I wouldn't give for a ride on your big, throbbing fuck stick! Maybe we should visit Satellite X! I hear it's the latest in haptic and erotic technology, perfect for a hot stud like you!" Okay, R2-U2. Way to stifle the vibe.

Ms. Pris wasn't like that. A fantasy and sci-fi nerd in real life, Cathy modeled her avatar after the "replicant" played by Daryl Hannah in *Blade Runner*. When other players rubbed her the wrong way— sometimes literally—she'd bounce around the room like a pinball, screeching in an unsustainable pitch and basically making an off-putting spectacle of herself. I never drove her to such extremes. I clothed my virtual character in a primary-colored Dick Tracy getup. Then I offered to buy her a drink, altering my voice to sound as bored as Harrison Ford's did in her favorite movie. It was what she'd come here to find. Even so, I doubt we'd have chatted more than a minute if I hadn't been so skilled at deflecting other suitors with a clever remark. The great thing about multiplayer games is that other players have no way to kick your ass every time you mouth off. Instead, they're required to think up a witty rejoinder, a gambit they're unlikely to manage.

I'd brushed off a character in a superspy tuxedo, followed shortly thereafter by a big-breasted were-cat. Now Pris regarded me through unblinking, heavily mascaraed eyes. "I don't mean what brings you to this bar," she said patiently. "I mean, what brings you to the game?"

"I come here 'cause nothing is real," I answered, my voice pitched to rumble. "You aren't real. It's an illusion sustained by nerds who may have no frame of reference for adult sexuality. And it's perfect. A perfect mirage."

"Are you saying you're a skin job?" she asked, sidling up and sniffing my neck. "You seem real enough to me."

"Real enough to take home to mama?"

"I ain't got no mama," she sneered. "No daddy to smack my little bottom and keep me in line."

"Yeah, save it for the tourists."

"Oh, yeah? Is that how you want this to go, officer? Would you rather just read me my rights?"

"You aren't guilty of anything I can see. Yet."

"Maybe I should pick your pocket."

"You put your hand in my pocket, you might find something that shocks you."

"Trust me, officer, I'm not a woman who's easily shocked."

"I trust you're a woman. That's enough faith for me." Unless you're in the higher-cost add-ons, it's possible for any person of any gender or orientation to play any type of character, anonymously, so the Playmate you're shtupping may well be a six-foot-plus man outside the game.

"I'm a woman," she insisted. "Not this woman, maybe, but more than enough woman for the flea-bitten, booze-sopping likes of a man like you."

"At least you can tell I'm a man. Keep it up," I scoffed. "You might get to see what I look like when I'm offended. Who knows?"

She regarded me a moment longer, then stood in a single quick movement. I flinched, thinking I'd pushed too hard and she was history. "Take a look at this construction," she ordered instead, "this body. Go ahead. Take a good, long look."

"Don't mind if I do," I admitted, scanning her, not too hastily, up and down. Like Daryl Hannah in the movie, she had a tall, athletic physique in '80s hooker garb, her blonde hair the wedge of a razor-cut wig. Punks weren't normally my type, but Summer was and I was bored with what I had. It was fun to play outside my comfort zone. Still, the more a character wanted you to look at her sexual secondary characteristics, the less I was convinced I was talking to a woman. I was tired of being trawled by horny gay boys. "So what am I looking for? Nits?"

"A woman who gives a fuck how she gets off. You see one?"

"I don't know, I'm still looking."

"You've seen enough, flatfoot."

"That's what you think."

She remained standing. "I don't come here to waste a lot of time. You cool with that?"

"I don't come here to fuck around with men. Care to verify?"

"Fine." Her left hand twitched, the echo of a command her real fingers tapped out inside her gLove. A green check mark appeared next to her stats: Female √, Straight √, Seeking HetM √. That was the game's way of confirming she was really a woman who identified as heterosexual. It said nothing about her real-world biography, though, including her marital status. Like I cared. "Care to play with me?" she asked.

"Bad robot," I replied, grinning, then stood. "Your place or mine?"

"I thought we might visit the Avalon. I've been there before. It's swank enough. I'm gonna wear you out." She cocked her head. "Are you shocked?" The Avalon, named for the sleepy town on Catalina Island, was the realm's grand hotel. It represented a game area locked behind a privacy firewall so tight not even the game's programmers could see what happened inside. That wasn't for the benefit of guests alone, by the way—it excused Ryder Entertainment from liability if any angry real-world spouse came calling.

"I've forgotten what shock even feels like. Do I appear to be feeling it?"

"Who cares. We'll see precisely what you can handle, tough guy. Why don't you meet me in room"—

she consulted an invisible roster—"8418, two hours from now."

"Why two hours?"

"Real-world appointments," she said, shrugging. I found out later she was putting her youngest son, a skittish toddler, to bed. "Don't you worry. Once I've slipped into something more...less, I'll give you my fullest attention." She smiled, clearly pleased with her own performance. "Brace yourself, tec. You can handle this. Maybe." She hadn't asked me my (character) name, not that it mattered. She could call that up any time she wanted. I was going by Dash in those days, a reference to Dashiell Hammett, though of course I've changed it since. I sold that notorious handle to a prematurely wealthy financier. The proceeds covered two of my out-of-court settlements.

Like Shag, the Hotel Avalon had no objectively fixed appearance. As I walked through its lobby, I flicked past a number of options and settled on Aspen ski resort. A ripple swept across my view of the outside world, replacing the default Polynesian paradise with a snow-blanketed mountain pass. There was no check-in counter; the game servers knew whether we should be there or not. If you didn't have a confirmed appointment, meaning a date with another *Realms of Eros* user or NPC, you could summon the elevator all the livelong day for all the good it'd do you. If you got it on with an NPC, the game would automatically deduct a flat rate from your credit or debit card. The charge would appear on your bill as "FOOD MARKET, GROCERIES." Liaisons between actual users were free. One enterprising user came up with a third option: he wrote a mod that'd allow you to set up a date with a non-player character, then summon a maid and dismiss the NPC. The maids he coded, of course, were all comely nymphomaniacs. The game designers thought this was clever and never got around to fixing the hack.

As for me, I'd "bedded" a couple of NPCs without a moment of guilt, but after an aborted date with some woman costumed as a popular Xtreme Ski Bunny, this would be the first time I'd ever hooked up with a masked user. Did I really want to go through with it? I only cancelled the ski bunny date because Summer called the office to say our daughter was throwing up and could I please stop by a pharmacy on the way home, but in retrospect, I'd been glad I pulled the plug. Looking at porn is one thing. Playing a pornographic game is one step farther than looking at porn. But cybersex? That was a line I'd never shown much interest in crossing before. It seemed to fall into a category somewhere between cheating and not-cheating, a Schrödinger's one-night stand. Feeling like a dick, I put the game on pause long enough to call home and claim I'd be home an hour or two late because of last-minute print ad corrections.

"Okay," Summer said, "but don't be too late. Remember, you could barely find the coffeepot this morning. You need to get some rest." It's true, I was running out of gas. I was doing the work of three people, mostly because I enjoyed overseeing the campaign too much to delegate any part of it. But in my idiotic, paranoid head, I interpreted Summer's innocent admonishment as nagging me to drag my ass home to spend the whole night appeasing my family. Why that struck me as an unfair request, I can't remember just now.

I do remember the room, the way I arrived first and floated through it alone, my feet never touching the carpet, my hands the only part of me able to feel the thread count of the spotless sheets. The engineers tell me we'll have full-haptic body suits someday. I believe them. That luxury, however, is a long way off, so the virtual reality of *Realms of Eros* is an extremely partial reality. It touches only the eyes, ears and hands. I wanted a haze of perfume. The sexy sax music on the vintage radio was unremarkable, generic. I toggled the simulation so my view outside was moonlit, with snow tumbling past conifers in random blurs.

The room had only one door, which makes sense when you think about it. There was no reason for a closet. We could set our clothes anywhere; it's not as if they'd get wrinkled. As for a bathroom, our virtual bodies required no toilet and couldn't enjoy the sensation of running water. That was a shame. I longed to peel the clothes off Ms. Pris and slide with her into an oversized tub. At that point, I really just wanted the feel of an unfamiliar body. Sex seemed almost superfluous. I couldn't shake the feeling my behavior in the game this time around was a sin. I wondered if that would prove more appealing or deflating.

It took a few minutes longer than two hours for Pris to arrive, and I spent that time debating whether to leave. If I fled, I wouldn't even risk passing her awkwardly in the lobby, as I could simply log out of the game and vanish from its universe. So what kept me in that room despite all my doubts? How much simpler would my life have been since then if I'd lost my nerve?

Was this about getting back at Summer? Not exactly. The truth is I didn't hold that night at Ted and Alice's against her. I couldn't. It was my idea. I held it, rather, against myself. I was absolutely disgusted by my cowardice in the face of carnality. I had every intention of attending another party, but this time I'd ravish every woman in sight. Each day till then, I was living at a disadvantage. Screw that! I saw *Realms of Eros* as rehearsal time for my ultimate sexual comeback, if you'll pardon the expression.

The door opened. Pris paused in its frame. We regarded each other cautiously, she no less than me.

"Been here long?" she asked.

"Doesn't matter. Come on in."

"I'm sorry I'm late. I couldn't get on the computer. It's uh…complicated, as they say on Facebook."

"You married?" I shut my eyes, inwardly cursing myself for bringing it up.

"I uh…yes. That's…I am." She drifted into the room, her fingers sliding over the doorframe, feeling its texture. "Does that…Is that a problem?"

"I don't think so."

"Are you?"

I put my hands in my pockets, feeling clearly the gabardine at their edges. These gLoves were amazing. I don't think we realize from minute to minute how much of the real world we perceive variously through our eyes, ears and hands. I felt one g of gravity in the Avalon, of course, courtesy of non-virtual planet Earth, and much of the rest was filled in by imagination. In that moment, as far as I was concerned, I was in an opulent if sparsely furnished hotel bedroom. If Pris hadn't looked so much like a movie android, this would've been too real. I'd have shoved past her out the door. Rehearsal was one thing, but this was too drastic a leap. Instead, I answered her question. "Seventeen years. It's…good."

"Oh, yeah? Then why are you here?"

By way of stalling, I replied, "I could ask you the same question."

"You could. Except my marriage is…maybe not so good."

"I guess I," I began, then fully considered my answer. "I think my marriage is fine," I continued. "It just isn't much fun."

"Ah." She regarded the leather bands around her wrists. "I know where you're coming from there."

"When I was young," I said, "I felt so much excitement with Su—around my wife. I spent every minute I could with her. It was invigorating. Like, literally: it filled me with vigor, y'know, energy."

"I know what vigor is."

"It was like doing coke," I rambled on, "but without all that glop in your throat. Now I...don't know; it's like going to work. I don't hate my job. I kinda like it sometimes. But sometimes you need a vacation."

"Hence yours truly," she said.

"No. Hence this game, *Realms of Eros*." I looked directly into her simulated eyes. "You could've been anyone."

"Flattering," she said, smiling slightly. That smile, by the way, was added by game software that monitored her webcam and duplicated a limited repertoire of expressions.

I shrugged, conveyed also via cam. "I don't imagine I'm any different for you."

"I've been married...a few years longer than you," she said. "We met in church choir. That should tell you everything you need to know about us. Me and my husband."

"You probably fooled around in high school and convinced yourself the high you felt was love."

"Wasn't it?" she asked. "Isn't that what love is, a hormonal high? I mean, I know it boils down to something else later, but every pop song pays tribute to that adolescent rush. You can't escape it. I was only paying heed to the radio."

"They should ban marriage before the age of thirty," I mused.

"You don't mean that. You say you've enjoyed your life. It's not her fault she bores you after so many years of marriage."

"I didn't say that," I protested. "She's a wonderful person. She is. I don't think she's even boring, really. I just...it's me. I mean, that's really what it is. Things aren't new and different and exciting every day, so I get bored. That's my own problem."

"Yet here you are."

"I just want to vent what I'm feeling in a way that won't demolish my life."

"Sure, me, too," she said, "but you could've fucked an NPC. I'm an actual person. Doesn't that make things too weird?"

I sidestepped the question. "Does it feel weird for you?"

"I hate to break it to you, Dash, but this isn't my first ride on the rolly coaster."

"No?"

"You're my fourth. Fifth, if you count a guy who masturbated while I watched. Turns out the joke was on him. He took the gLove off to finish, thinking his semen would damage the electronics, so for the last bit his avatar just stood there. I did a little striptease, he made grunting noises, wham, bam, thank you, madame webcam. Then he vanished without saying goodbye."

"Classy."

"Yes, romantic. And is that how this is gonna go?" she asked. "Are you gonna do something weird, get your rocks off, and then disappear like...tears in rain? Or are we gonna get each other off?"

I was silent for a moment, then said, "I want something different. I want a surprise, some new move I don't expect, another body. I'll go home to my real life, but first I want to feel something different."

"Listen," she said. "you don't know me. I don't want to know you. I'll do what *I* need to get off. I'm here to have a fucking orgasm, two if the mood strikes me. You can feel whatever you want, but just come fuck me."

So I did. I walked toward her, found her swaying unsteadily. I think in the real world she was fond of Syrah. I couldn't smell it here, of course, but she stood with the awkward caution of a woman who'd had a few glasses.

"What's your real name?" I asked, though I'm damned if I know why.

87

"It's Pris," she said. Even through her limited range of expressions, I could tell she was looking at me strangely.

"I'm Gary."

"I don't care. I'm *Pris*," she insisted. "Just...shut up, okay?"

I nodded.

"Make this worth it," she said.

I know in most books and movies the writers walk you right up to the edge of any funny business, then look discreetly away. Well, this is not that kind of book, as you probably noticed a few chapters ago. I didn't see the point of saying I'm sex-positive, then eliding every sexual act. So believe me: I will tell you exactly how things went, both now and every time. I just have something important to throw in before I continue, and that's this: I'm not the only awful person you've ever met. Adultery statistics vary widely, but it's at least a fifth of all married men and women. If you read women's magazines, it's even higher, but experts blame those astonishing statistics ("60% of all married men! 50% of all married women!") on self-selection. In any case, there are over eight million people registered on AshleyMadison.com, a site devoted to helping adulterers meet and adulterate one another. "Life is short," the site famously observes. "Have an affair!" That's its slogan. The site pays all its bills.

As for cybersex, there's no telling how many of us engage in it now that *Realms of Eros* and its right-handful of imitators are quietly ubiquitous. Studies show most people who do it don't consider it cheating. I tend to agree: virtually feeling up an NPC shouldn't count. If I discovered Summer was spending her free time pretending to bang simulated cabana boys while I was at work, I can't say I'd lose any sleep over it. Maybe that's because there's no way she can fall in love with a collection of pixels.

In recent years, a Website called UndercoverLovers.com has registered more new female members than male. Make of that what you will, but again, I'm not the only cheater in the world—because yes, I consider my time with Pris cheating, I admit that up front—and we certainly aren't all men. There's no male monopoly on wrong.

I did not fall in love with Pris. I didn't fall in love with Cathy, either, but I'll probably never convince Summer of that. Maybe someday Summer will write her own book, and, if she tells the most accurate version of the truth she knows, maybe I'll learn more of what she thinks. She deserves that opportunity, if she avails herself of it. I've probably done a poor job thus far of representing her impression of events, but it's because I've been making them up. For all my strengths, I'm no telepath. I know only what she said.

In my mind, what happened next is a story about a man named Gary, who pretended to be a film noir gumshoe named Dash, and a woman named Ms. Pris, who looked like Daryl Hannah. Cathy, I mean actual Cathy, didn't enter the picture till later, but yes, this was an act of dishonesty. I don't believe I committed adultery per se. If a tree gets cheated on in the forest and no one's around to hear it, does it count as cheating? I tell myself these things and make these justifications knowing full well how my decisions bit me in the ass down the road, but you can see how a guy might delude himself. The warning signs were there, big as billboards.

As if you didn't know, here's what it's like to get laid in *Realms of Eros*. You can't actually feel anything, except in your hands. Typically, the experience is more like watching (and touching!) porn, which then goes into the spank bank for later recollection. You can save each encounter for later viewing from either a first- or third-person perspective. You can even, should you be this narcissistic, relive the liaison through the eyes of your conquest. It's interesting once or twice, actually, especially if you've chosen an avatar good-looking enough that you can watch yourself have sex without descending into a shame spiral.

Pris and I floated into each other's arms. The program wouldn't let our "body" volumes intersect, but it certainly felt as if they could. It's ghost sex, the immensely unsatisfying fuck of the damned. In real life, I never took my pants off. That would've been too much. In order to get her virtual clothes off, I had to talk her into removing them herself. To lay on the bed, we typed the letter *z*. I leaned forward by hitting the slash button, then typed *:P* for cunnilingus. I assure you, it felt exactly as silly as it sounds.

I don't know anything about the electronics, so it never ceases to amaze me how lifelike the haptic sensation of flesh against fingertips can be. Her avatar had a blonde landing strip of pubic hair. It seemed to sweep softly through my fingers. My tongue felt nothing as I went down on her, of course, but when I slipped a finger inside her, I felt labial resistance and moisture. Her virtual nipples stiffened instantly; I pretended to give them attention. She ran her fingers through my hair, arched her back, and murmured inarticulate hums of appreciation.

As I write this, Tesseraction is working on new peripherals. It won't be cheap, but in a few years you'll be able to buy either a haptic condom device that slips over your penis or a haptic dildo that can mimic the moves of a tongue or a penis. In this pursuit they're somewhat behind the times. For several years now, a company called RealTouch WMM has offered an "Interactive Masturbation Device" that slips over the penis and offers a variety of stimuli including heat, moisture, and rhythmic stroking, all synchronized with a pornographic video. It costs about as much as a gourmet dinner for two, which seems apropos. Tesseraction's building their own model, and I'm sure it'll offer a few minor improvements. In the meantime, if you run the right embarrassing Google search, you can probably find a way to hack *Realms of Eros* so it's compatible with RealTouch's existing haptic sleeve. In the meantime, there's always Mr. Righty and the sim's replay function.

Ladies, don't think the world of high-tech quasi-fucking has left you behind. If anything, sex toys for women have long been more realistic (if that's the right way to describe a 14-inch polyurethane dong with a vibrating head) than the equivalent accessories for men, perhaps because men are less discriminating. Or, if you and your partner wish to play together, even at a distance, there's the exciting new frontier of so-called "teledildonics." That's right, you and a close online friend can work each other over any number of ways. Consider, for example, SKDu LLC's Mojowijo family of products, which translates the motions of one device into the vibration of another. It uses Bluetooth and Skype, so whatever you do, don't call your mother by mistake while it's on. Thanksgiving dinners would not be at all comfortable from that point forward.

The moans I heard in my ear were real, but the pleasure and emotions that informed them were probably not. You'd have to ask Cathy, and I won't. I know I put on the best show I could. I asked her to stand, then grabbed her ass and hoisted her into the air. She threw her virtual legs over my virtual shoulders, and I pumped her up and down like a porn star. If I tried that in real life, of course, even with a four-foot-tall Taiwanese gymnast, I'd probably last about three or four strokes before the vertebrae exploded from my back. Occasional trips to the gym do not a power lifter make.

What I remember most about that first encounter with Pris, other than praying to God that the janitor wouldn't arrive and unlock my office door, was the faraway sound of Big Band music, as if an orchestra in the hotel ballroom were calling all couples to the dance. We were ghosts having phantom sex, our skin incorporeal, and this was a furtive intersection of lost souls. We are spirits in the material world, I thought. She pretended to come and I watched her face cycle through a series of orgasmic expressions. The command to "climax" is a repeated tapping of *j* and *k*, a holdover from chat rooms in the late 1990s. To me, its subsequent textual meaning feels all too appropriate: we're just kidding, just kidding, just kidding.

It did turn me on, though. I went home and found Summer reading in the tub. Our daughter was already asleep. Summer finished a paragraph and marked the spot before looking up. "Your dinner's on a plate in the microwave. Zankou Chicken. It's probably nasty by now."

"I know. I don't mind. Sorry I'm late."

She gazed at me cautiously. "You want to talk?" she asked.

I reached into warm water and massaged her nearest foot. "Not really. Work, y'know. It's not that exciting."

"You're working on a campaign for swinger Fantasyland. It can't be as boring as washing the dishes and half-watching *SpongeBob SquarePants*, which is how I spent *my* afternoon. That feels good," she said, acknowledging the foot rub. "You want me to rub yours?"

"Nah," I said. "Go back to your book. I'll let you read."

"You could join me," she said. "I'll make room." But I didn't. Instead, a few hours later, we had sex for the first time in a week. I lowered myself into her and shut my eyes, imagining Pris, yet another in an seventeen-year-long series of only mildly consequential infidelities. Such is marriage, in my house and yours.

Chapter 8

Bliss Panerotic construction was completely underway when Ted and Alice invited us to another party. I mentioned it as-if-casually one night while Summer was brushing her teeth in our master bathroom. I was sitting in bed looking through print ad concepts on my bedside tablet. She spoke through toothpaste suds: "I assume you told him no."

"I haven't told him anything," I said, without looking up.

She spat into the sink, rinsed, and stepped into the bedroom. She was draped in a Foo Fighters T-shirt that would've fit over a Smart Car. Our daughter had developed a habit of slipping into our room before breakfast, so Summer dressed to greet her. I got an earful every time I tried to lock the bedroom door, so instead I put on briefs. "What if she has a nightmare?" Summer would ask. "Are you gonna get up and let her in?" Until recently, neither of us had been too embarrassed about our little girl seeing us naked. Like Adam and Eve before us, however, we'd discovered sin and shame around the same time. My wife and I were back to having sex once or twice a week, and her raciest lingerie no longer hung on the bathroom door, ready for action.

"Why haven't you said anything?" she asked. "You know how miserable you were after the last time."

"Yeah, but you weren't. Maybe I overreacted."

"Ya think?" she asked, using one of her favorite expressions.

"I feel like...I don't know. It started out fun. I was having a good time in the pool."

"I'll bet you were. You haven't seen that many live boobs since your cousin's bachelor party."

"It wasn't just that," I said. "I should've been more relaxed, y'know, maybe had a few drinks."

"That's a bad idea, Gary. I've seen you drunk. You get more uptight, not less."

"Listen. Did you have a good time?"

She went back in the bathroom and brushed her hair, an evasive maneuver given that we were both getting ready for bed. "I don't even know why you'd ask me that. You know I did. It's why you got so upset."

"I got upset because I was jealous," I admitted. "I'm still jealous. Except now I'm even more jealous, because you've done it and I haven't. Look...maybe we should try it again, just stay in the same room with each other this time."

She poked her head back out. "You're serious about this."

"Maybe, yeah."

"Man," she said. "You are a piece of work."

"Yeah. Probably. But...listen, it's killing me that I wussed out like that. I'd like to at least retire a champion. Is that so weird? You want to throw a guy a bone here?"

"An odd turn of phrase, considering."

"Look. I want to show you something." I showed her my tablet, which displayed the image of a laughing couple, married or at least well-acquainted, splashing and having an ecstatically wonderful time in a pool full of similarly giddy, attractive couples. "This is what's opening an hour's ferry ride away this summer. I wouldn't mind being this couple, would you?"

"I wouldn't mind having her stomach. What does she eat, PhenFen salad?"

"He might be handsomer than me."

She swallowed half a dozen witty responses. "They do seem pretty happy," she said, smiling a bit.

"I want to be edgy like that, but clearly, I'm more of a wimp than I thought I was. I need some fucking practice. No pun intended."

"You do okay," she allowed. "I did have fun. Are you sure about this? I'm not gonna be as willing to take all the blame this time if anything goes wrong."

"I swear. I shouldn't have blamed you at all last time. It was me. I apologize, seriously."

She came over and hopped into my lap, nearly twisting my left knee out of joint. When you're a married man, of course, you're obliged to pretend such sneak attacks are painless. "Hey," I managed, an acceptable substitute for judo defenses like tossing her into the headboard, face first.

"Maybe we should get you some practice right here," she said, her nipples suddenly poking the Foo Fighters' foreheads out. Clearly she approved of my sudden sexual climate change. I set her down as gently as I could on the mattress and kissed her before she could protest. She started to say something else as I broke away, so I moved to lick her neck. "Whew," she gasped. "My."

"What kind of practice did you have in mind? Any particular skill I can work on?"

"You've got most of the basics down," she said, twisting seductively with pleasure. "Maybe it's time for a master class. I could come up with a few ideas."

"Maybe you could give Dave Grohl the night off," I said, indicating her XXXL nightshirt.

"Okay," she conceded, "but keep it in arm's reach." I helped her yank the T-shirt off, revealing a long torso, pale breasts, and two fully erect nipples. It's true, Summer doesn't have a model's abs, but she's in pretty fair shape for a woman in her thirties. I was glad we bought her that Curves membership, and I resolved to spend more time at Bally's myself.

"Maybe I should study down here," I said, kissing down her belly.

"Maybe so," she said, shivering and palming her breasts. "Hey, hand me that tablet first, will ya? I think I might've gone to high school with that guy in the picture."

"Seriously?"

"No. I still want to look at him for a minute."

Our daughter didn't bother us the next morning, which was good because I forgot to put my briefs back on before falling asleep. I don't remember whether Summer put her damn T-shirt back on. What I do remember is try as I might, no matter how much time I spent licking her secret parts or hammering away at her from the edge of the bed, I never got her to make a sound even remotely like the joyful wail she'd made at that party. I resolved to have a peak experience of my own this time around, one she'd be unable to replicate.

We arrived without incident this time, no AAA intervention required. We left our swimsuits at home but brought condoms, towels, and a small padlock for my gym bag. (I trust Ted and Alice, sure, but I never leave my wallet where just anyone can grab it.) I grabbed a flask of Sailor Jerry from the glove compartment, scanned the streets for cops, and took a fortifying swig. I offered Summer the flask; she declined. "Man. That was a hearty swallow. You okay, there, partner?" she asked.

"Million bucks," I replied. "Million bucks."

We walked up to the porch like we owned it and rang the doorbell. The door opened a crack, and Alice peeked out. "Oh, my goodness," she said. "I bet *you* don't know the password, either. There's a wave of amnesia going around."

"Is it 'horny?'" I asked.

"It is now!" she crowed. In fact, she was delighted to see us again, even me, even after that time I heaved her bodily off my person. "It was 'polymorphously perverse' when the night started, but I like yours better. It's easier to say, for one thing."

I leaned toward her. "Sorry about last time," I murmured sheepishly in her ear. "I, uh—"

"Oh, that's okay, baby doll!" she replied at full volume. "You just got a case of the scaredy-cock. Happens to the best of your species, I'm told. Seen it, actually."

"Thanks," I sniffed, then chuckled. "I'll try to do better this time."

"Will ya, now." She turned to Summer. "You think he's got it in him?"

"I think he's rarin' to go," my wife said, regarding me coolly. We moved to the kitchen and chatted with Ted and a couple of guys Summer knew from last time, one biblically. Even then, it struck me this ought to feel weird, even confrontational. I shouldn't feel comfortable engaging in small talk with a man whose dick had been five inches deep in my wife. I did, though. I'm not sure why. It felt more like we'd met on vacation. We didn't know each other well, he and I, but had an interesting experience in common. It helped that no matter what happened, I'd still be going home with my attractive wife, and he'd go home with his wife—who, it just so happened, resembled that turtle we used to draw from the back of *TV Guide*. It also helped that once again, these were among the friendliest people I'd met in L.A.

The kitchen table was still heaped with snacks no one ate, though a cooler full of beer did brisk business. We heard Alice giving her "rules for newbies" speech in the living room. Through the door, I saw two or three couples and wondered if I looked that terrified my first time around.

I made it a point to get to know a few more people before heading poolside. Over the years, I've developed a useful modus operandi for mingling, which is to pretend I'm 1980s Bill Murray. You know, been around, seen it all, that's the vibe; but I don't feel that ever-present, *1970s*-Bill-Murray compunction to amuse or impress. No, this guy, the guy I pretend to play at crowded parties, he's more of a Murray in *Ghostbusters 2*: happy to show up, friendly, not aggressively so, simply waiting for another fat check to arrive in the mail. A calls-people-"brother" kinda guy. I introduced myself as Gary but planned to say my last name was Christenberry, the name of an old high school buddy. Instead, no one asked my name, so I kept it to myself. Summer was reserved, sipping a margarita Alice placed in her hands but offering little in the way of conversation.

I leaned closer. "You doing okay?" I asked.

"Sure, just following your lead."

"Want to go out to the pool?"

"Maybe, yeah."

"We can sit in a lawn chair and watch."

"Sounds like fun." She took one more sip and set her margarita down, politely remembering not to take the glass out to the pool area. It was unseasonably warm that night, which was nice, and at least a dozen people were already naked in the pool. One middle-aged fellow appeared to have his nude quarry boxed into a corner, though she didn't give any indication of minding. Another woman came outside and stepped toward the hot tub. I watched as she wriggled out of her clothes and climbed into the Jacuzzi as regally as a mythical Greek goddess. I marveled at her self-possession, so complete it all but transcended mere sex appeal. Some people are good at getting naked. There ought to be a law to make sure they do it constantly. I suggest we name the law after Kate Winslet, but maybe that's just me.

Anyway, inspired by her example, I said "be right back" to Summer and went inside to secure my wallet and car keys in the gym bag, which I then stashed in a coat closet. I slipped into the kitchen long enough to gulp the rest of Summer's margarita, then crossed back outside. "I'm going for a swim," I told Summer. "Care to join me?"

"That was fast. You're already ready for funny business?"

"I want to start by getting *you* off this time."

"Oho." One of her eyebrows shot up. "Somebody's feeling his oats."

"Yeah, well, get your oats into the pool, and I'll feel them, too."

She shook her head wryly. "You." I shot her a jaunty salute, shucked most of my clothes with about two percent of the grace of the aforementioned Greek goddess, and lowered myself into the pool—which could've been considerably warmer, given the circumstances. (That's something to keep in mind, orgy hosts. A body gets chilled.) A short time later Summer stripped down to panties and joined me.

So what do you want to know? You want to hear how many women I slept with that night? One. I slept with one. I had sex with five, if oral counts. The fact that we're still using euphemisms like "make love" and "sleep with" for "have sex with" or "fuck" is a strong indication that whatever number I name, you'd object. If I said zero, I'd be branded a skeevy voyeur. If I said one and it wasn't my wife, I'm an adulterer. If I said two and one of them wasn't my wife, you'd say I dragged her into my depravity. Any number greater than two and I'm a pervert, pig-dog, whore.

I don't like this. Okay? I don't like you believing that your knowledge of any part of my sex life, coupled, you might say, with my utter ignorance of yours, makes you a better person than me. The sheer volume of pornography and erotica on the Internet and elsewhere in the world makes it inescapably clear we all have the same desires. At least give me credit for sidling toward mine, rather than merely fantasizing about them in a cycle of self-titilation and guilt.

As I nibbled Summer's earlobe, she rested her teeth on my shoulder as if warning me she wanted to bite but couldn't remember quite how. I think it had something to do with another trait I noticed back in high school: her teeth used to chatter when she got horny. She outgrew it after a few months or years, but in the meantime, she probably looked for ways to conceal it. No one likes having a tell. Mine, I think, was constantly rubbing my chin, worrying a cuticle, anything to move my fingertips closer to my mouth. I've probably never outgrown that old habit. Luckily, my hands were busy supporting Summer's shivering thighs, because I was hornier than a Triceratops that night.

The point is things happened. Alice was busy inside doing I know not what to whom. I was making out hardcore with Summer when she said "wow," pushed away, seemed to gather her senses, and sloshed toward the ladder. The five men and three women in the pool watched her leave, admiring her slim ass and legs. She's justly proud of those features, and I'm sure she intended our luxurious view of them. Without so much as a look back, she tugged off her panties and tossed them toward our clothes. Then she went over to the Jacuzzi and climbed in, reacting audibly to the change in water temperature.

"Hello, darlin'," someone said. A Conway Twitty fan. Terrific. Just my type.

I saw a mousy little woman in hoop earrings trying to catch my eye from across the pool. I smiled back, considered my options, and stepped toward her. If she reacted, I couldn't see well enough in the dim backyard light to tell. "I'm gonna go check out the Jacuzzi with my wife," I said quietly, "so maybe you could join us."

"Is she bi?" the woman asked. "'Cause I'm, like, super bi."

101

"I don't know," I said. Though I doubted Summer had any interest in women, I rejected this inside knowledge when it limited my own options. The night was young, so why start slamming doors now? With an attitude like that, I'd be crying on the porch again in no time.

Instead I repeated, "You should join us, see how it goes." I noticed as I moved past her toward the ladder—it's very important to not just flop out of the pool when you're watched by topless women, especially while struggling against half a boner—that Mousy Woman's areolae were, unlike Summer's, ellipsoid and brown. Different was good. This night was all about different, a break from years of the same, same, same. "Follow," I told her. She did.

I'm not sure how Summer managed to fend off the other half-dozen people in the Jacuzzi till I got there. The nearest, at Summer's immediate left, was a stocky, hairy-chested man who regarded her in much the same fashion as that with which a leopard considers an antelope. I could almost hear dinner bells ringing. I assumed he was the country music fan. "Excuse me," I harrumphed, brushing past bodies awkwardly. "Freezing husband coming through."

I cleared my throat so another guy, a thin man with silver hair and a dazed expression, slid over to clear some space at Summer's right. "Hey, your wife, man," the guy said, grinning. "Hel-lo, nurse."

"I know, right? I thank my lucky stars each morning."

"Is that what that look means?" Summer quipped. I smiled and pulled her close.

"What're we talking about?" I asked, trying to wave away some of the more chaotic pheromones.

"That new Panoramic Park, man," the guy replied. "You heard of it?"

"I'm not—Panoramic Park? What's that?" I asked. Summer elbowed me gently. I took the opportunity to look down at her breasts through softly churning water.

"It's like, out on Catalina Island, man. They're building this crazy resort. It's all like Disneyland, but with fucking! They're gonna roll out the red carpet for people in the lifestyle, man! How cool is that!"

"How'd you hear about that?" I asked, curious to see how well our marketing efforts were doing.

"I saw this link to a Web page on Reddit. It was awesome! They're gonna have waterslides and everything!"

"Ohh, you mean Bliss Panerotic," I said, intercepting another elbow jab from Summer.

"Don't let Gary fool you," Summer said. "He knows all about it."

"Oh, you just—what?" The poor guy looked puzzled. He wasn't sure whether to take offense.

"I'm the branding director for the park. I really just wanted to see which of our ads was getting out there."

"Oh, that's cool. So you do branding?" He still looked befuddled. I suspect he'd been enjoying some of California's decriminalized weed. "That's gotta hurt like a motherfucker."

"Yeah, it's…I get that a lot. It's a different kind of branding. I'm responsible for establishing the identity of the park, maintaining a relationship between company and clients. It's marketing stuff. You know."

"Oh, right. Yeah, cool. I got a cousin who does marketing, or phone sales, or some fuckin' thing, I can't remember which. You know a guy named Ricky?"

"No. Hey, let me ask you, you planning on going?"

"To where, Ricky's house?"

"No, to Bliss Panerotic. You planning a trip this summer?"

"Is that when it opens?"

"Yeah, mid-June. Big opening weekend festivities. Should be a hell of a party."

"Oh, man, that sounds cool, yeah! I'm the party *guy*, man, seriously. Yeah! Hey, thanks for the invite! Should I, like, give you my email address or what? 'Cause I been kinda between computers for a while. Fuckin' Terry, man, fuckin' Mountain Dew and shit—"

"No, everyone's invited. It's a big gala opening."

"Oh, sweet, yeah, right on…Man, your wife is hot," he repeated, then turned to Summer earnestly. "You're hot."

"She sure is," I agreed, and kissed her full on the mouth. It seemed to last a long time. My erection was back. I no longer cared. It tented my boxer briefs nearly to the surface.

"So yeah," the guy said. "You two want to switch out, or what? I brought my old lady. She gives pretty good—"

"Not just yet," I said, cutting him off again. "I think we're gonna play together for a while."

Summer looked up at me, her soft brown eyes asking if I was sure. "Let's go inside." She gazed at me a moment longer, then nodded. I stood and helped her cross the Jacuzzi.

"All right," the stoner said. "Cool. Nice talkin' to you, man. Probably see you inside."

"Nice to meet you," I agreed, my incongruous cock jabbing due east as we hastened away. After all my concerns about security and keeping our clothes and property together, my underwear was off, never to be seen again, by the time we reached the back master bedroom. I caught a dim impression of writhing bodies in dim red light and moved toward an open space on the bed. Summer slid off her panties and sat on the edge of the mattress, her wild eyes never straying from mine. I dove into her in a single plunging stroke, a cry escaping my lips. I hadn't felt this overheated in years. She was

104

so wet I barely felt friction. The sex may not have been that good, frankly, but she buried her nails in my shoulders anyway. "Go!" she grunted. "Go!"

I pushed her breastbone and she fell on the bed, her head crashing against somebody's leg. The room was moaning and grunting. The air seemed to pant. I rested Summer's ankles on my throbbing shoulders and rode her like time was running out in the world. She came in one sudden wrenching spasm, yelping and snapping her neck. It was all I could take. My hips shot forward and everything exploded. I could've been having a stroke. The room sheered sideways and down. I kept coming, pulse after pulse, my heart thudding, her hands on my ass, pulling me inside. She seemed to have subsided, but when I moved to slide out, she gasped and came again. I rested my hand on her center and she held it there, mewing and crying. I doubt if anyone in the room had enough presence of mind to stop and watch this spectacle, but they should have. We should've sold ringside seats. I coulda been a contenda.

It wasn't just that Summer and I hadn't had sex that good in years. It wasn't even that it was the best sex I'd ever had with anyone, at least as far as I could recall. It was like fucking a different woman. Her behavior, her noises, her moves, even her body felt so different it was like cheating on Summer with Summer. Afterward we slumped on the mattress and held each other, panting and sweaty, while other folks collided around us in the dimness. I regained some of my senses and saw red silk thrown over an old-fashioned lamp, a woman sucking one guy greedily as another man did her missionary style, murmuring curses. I watched two women frantically scissor while a bearded man stroked himself nearby, waiting for a path to a threesome.

Sometime later the mousy woman found us and crawled up to Summer. "I'm Fantasia," she said, as if that weren't utterly ridiculous. I wanted to say "I'm Pinocchio," but instead pulled her close and let her tongue-kiss my wife. To this day I don't know what Summer felt about that. If I had to guess, and I do, I'd say she was probably just putting on a show. She let Fantasia nibble her breasts for a moment, then pulled us all together, nudging the woman down toward my lap. I was already fully erect, as if I hadn't just unloaded in my wife, and cried out as another mouth engulfed the stiff length of my excitement. Summer stifled my gasping with her mouth, her tongue flicking mine, a kiss that took us deep into space again.

From there things got a bit edgeless. There are drugs that have the effect of dulling one's sense of hesitation: should I do this? Would that be a good idea? What exactly could go wrong? When those limits fall, we move toward anything that promises to make us feel good. I moved toward the mousy woman, who proved to be a huge fan of deep doggy style. Summer had her first black man. I know that sounds crass, but it's something she wanted to try, so she did. A while later Ted and Alice came over—I guess they'd been watching from a distance to see if I'd freak out again— and we swapped partners to fuck on the same bed. Ted gets spiritual when he comes. Alice gets really loud when you suck on her clitoris. These are things I now know about my friends. And so what? I can honestly tell you I had a great time that night. Looking back, I'm not sure what the difference was, or why it was so much easier to relax than the first time. I'm sure the booze helped, but that wasn't the ultimate reason. I think this time I was just mentally prepared to unprotect myself.

I realized an important lesson that night: there's no correlation between how a person looks and how they are in bed. My wife is attractive, but no more so than any other soccer mom speed-walking through the mall on a weekday morning. There's nothing about her appearance that screams sexpot. She doesn't dress, talk, or act like a porn star, but she can tear the roof off a joint if she puts her mind to it and thinks she can get away with it. Alice looked downright matronly, the kind of woman you'd expect to see slinging hash in a diner, but she gave head like a thousand-dollar-a-night call girl (I'm guessing). Meanwhile, you remember Kellie, that cheerleader with whom I inadvertently cheated on Summer back in high school? She could've been a *Playboy* centerfold. Maybe was—I lost touch with her after graduation, and she hadn't been in danger of setting the curve in our math and English classes. But sex with her was rather like lying face-down on a Playmate-shaped couch. It was welcoming enough, but didn't offer much in the way of helping with anything that followed. She didn't come, she made nary a peep, and I climaxed only by staring at her jiggliest features. Not a wildcat, poor Kellie. You can't judge a sex partner by his or her cover, which means an unforgettable night in the sack could be lurking behind any woman's public exterior. And how hot is that?

Then there's the unexpected pleasure of naked community. What started as an attempt to get back at Summer became something closer to a born-again conversion. I've since read *Stranger in a Strange Land*, and now I grok—understand—its merging of sexual openness with communal polyamory. It may be a temporary sensation, perhaps even completely untrue, but in that moment I felt at one with a room full of people. They became what *Stranger*'s author, Robert Heinlein, called my water brothers and sisters. It's an unforgettable sensation, unmatched by the average married person's sex life.

I never attended another party at Ted and Alice's, partly because I was about to become too well-known to show up on their doorstep and merge into the crowd. All the same, we've been friends ever since. It was Ted who encouraged me to write this all down. In fact, he and Alice are some of my only true friends in the world these days.

Unless you know how people wind up in the lifestyle, or the sheer excitement and enjoyment it offers to thousands of couples around the world, you imagine some horrible frat-party herpes exchange. There are people who try it once and never again. That's a fact. It either doesn't give them what they want, which is probably an unhealthy, narcissistic masturbation ritual, or they find they can't surrender the jealousy most of us bring to it initially. Since we were kids, our whole society has told us love can only be monogamous, and if anyone tries anything else, they did it to make you feel small. We're told true love means absolute devotion to one person, as if love were finite, as if every molecule my wife gives another person means a chintzier amount left for me. Love and fear aren't jars of jelly beans. There's no counting what either of them are. They regenerate themselves all the time. All I can truly say with absolute confidence is we have either more love than fear in our souls or vice versa, but either emotion can be nurtured and grown.

So now's a good time to say I've never loved Summer more than after that second party. I'd shared an experience with her I wouldn't have been brave enough to experience with anyone else. For all my successes in life, I never felt like much of a gambler. Part of the reason my sex life got so humdrum was I never pushed it anywhere else. Sure, I cheated on Summer with Kellie, but I was a teenager, for Christ's sake. Throw a pair of cheerleader tits at me and my brain turned to warm tapioca. That's not adventurism, it's an erection in action. Real change, the defiance of cultural mores, that's something I needed a partner to do. Summer helped me break through a ceiling in my physical and emotional life. I touched something larger that night. You can laugh if you want, but it's true. I think Summer knows it, too. Unfortunately, once we touched it, even after what came next, we didn't know how to retreat to safer ground.

Summer once told me something I'll never forget. "You were my favorite," she said. "I know mixing things up made us happy, but nothing made me happier than coming back to you." And that's the lifestyle. I wasn't in it for long, but I learned that lesson for a damn fact.

This, I'm all too sorry to say, will be a story of how one little marriage went wrong. Ain't that funny? After all's said and done, for all the glamour and special effects and titillation Bliss Panerotic offered to a slobbering mob of voyeurs, it was still about regular people, and regular people have regular-people problems. We have kids who get bullied and cars that overheat on the freeway and toothaches and mortgages and bosses we hate and average, everyday, ordinary marital blahs. I'm not Christian Grey. I don't fly around in a jet or have superhuman sexual stamina. I'm a guy, a human being—not a character, a person. As you read about what happened, I need you to do me a favor and put yourself in my shoes as if it might've happened to you, because you and I are two of a kind. You were bored enough with your mundane existence to pick this up, thumb through it, and decide you want to know what's inside. You think this book represents a chance to dip your toe into sexual extravagance without running the same risks I did. And you're right. But once you acted on the desire to know more, you and I became one and the same. You may not like that, but it's true.

What follows is the story of a man who made understandable mistakes and a woman I wish you could meet. You'd like Summer so much. She digs Billy Joel and romantic comedies and Girl Scout cookies. Her favorite author is Jennifer Egan and her favorite movie is *Love Actually*. She goes to a gym she barely tolerates three times a week to stay in shape, and no matter how many times she says she does it only for herself, I'm pretty sure she did it to make me happy, too. When her dad was alive she called him Marvin, which wasn't disrespectful because his name was Joe. She and her mom go out for Indian food at least once a month, even now that her mom gives her that disapproving look Summer calls the Glower of Doom. A few years ago, I bought one of those books that asks hundreds of questions about somebody the reader loves, a kind of test to see how well we listen. I answered all but three questions correctly, including Summer's blood type (B+) and favorite Beatle (Ringo). The only answers I didn't know were her favorite Backstreet Boy, her least favorite color, and where she spent her first vacation (it was San Francisco, not New York). But even after all that, I can't tell you what she was thinking. The great lie about a book in first person is it claims to be able to see into everyone's head. The truth is, even the best narrator can see only into his or her own head, and that's debatable. I'll make some guesses. I'll tell you what she said, best I can remember, and pretend I know what made her say it. I don't really, though. I can't. You pays your money and takes your chances, says I. It's the best I can do.

My sex life with Summer was now at an all-time frenzy. We got in the habit of going out to the garage and fucking in the back of the SUV, just so we wouldn't wake our daughter and traumatize her for life. We reacquainted ourselves with the multiple joys of oral sex, tied each other up sometimes, even booked a Malibu hotel once just so we could debauch it over a sweaty three-day weekend. I found myself fantasizing about my own wife at work. She sent me a picture of her naked in the tub once, and I ducked out of a meeting early to spend quality time in my office's private restroom. I talked Summer into logging onto *Realms of Eros* once, though she found it so ridiculous we aborted the experiment before anything could happen. But did any of that stop me from hooking up online? Of course not. I'd been looking at Internet porn for decades, and I saw this as basically the same. Over the next few months, I banged I-don't-know-how-many NPCs, then replayed the sessions in my mind as I pleasured my wife and myself. As for Pris...

This is hard to admit, but I met up with her several times, online I mean, and that wasn't the worst of my offenses. She and I began texting one another. At first she just messaged me to ask when I'd be free for another session. Then we started kidding around, just small talk, really—but small talk is different when you've heard a woman come from what you did to her online. I mean, yes, it was Daryl Hannah's face and body, but that wasn't Daryl Hannah moaning into the microphone. It was Cathy. It wasn't even her virtual self, it was Cathy, her real voice, in real time, doing to herself what I wished I could do for her. I can't tell you how many times I lost myself in fantasies about Cathy, whom I still imagined as a tall, Nordic blonde, joining Summer and me in the sack.

Over time, Pris began messaging me with little bits of nothing—you know, sick at home, how's your day going, did you catch the finale of *Orphan Black*, that sort of thing. I suspected that wasn't a great idea but did nothing to stop it. Finally one day I asked her how much she really looked like Darryl Hannah. Wouldn't you like to know, she asked. A little, she said. We're both evil robots bent on crushing mankind, she quipped. I answered, maybe it's time I got a look at the real you. Long pause. Then she sent me a single image, of her left hand sort of covering her left breast. No nipple, no areola, just a sense of its lightly freckled dimensions. In an instant I was harder than quantum mechanics. I studied every microscopic detail of that picture, from the strands of blonde hair just visible at her shoulder to three letters of a calligraphic tattoo (CES—maybe "PISCES?") at her wrist. From those minor details I extrapolated an entire woman. Perhaps tellingly, I pictured her as a kind of almost-Summer: same height, same general body type (albeit two cup sizes larger), same weight in bed, a porn-y doppelganger. I imagined myself spinning her, bending her, ramming her, fucking her, kissing her…yes, even kissing her. I did. To my everlasting embarrassment, I did.

I read once that prostitutes never kiss their clients. I wouldn't know, because paying for sex is one line I haven't crossed, but it sounds right. Sex is fucking, but kissing—so intimate. Yet such was the adultery I imagined for myself. Yes, I acknowledge right now I was cheating on my wife. Only online, you say, and to some of you perhaps that's a mitigating factor, but I know what I was feeling. I went too far, not once but several times, for months in a row. I was unfaithful to Summer. I broke faith. I'm an asshole. I knew it as it was happening. I make no attempt to justify it now. Do I apologize? Yes. Does it matter? No. Some files can't be deleted.

Yes, I sent her a picture of my dick. I guess it's one of those adolescent rituals, like keg stands or growing an awful beard, that all men get around to eventually. I don't remember why I did it, exactly. She certainly never asked me to. I don't remember her expressing any particular gratitude for it. If I was hoping to encourage her to send me a new picture of herself, it didn't work in the short term. Over a month later, though, and not for any particular reason I can recall, she sent me half a dozen body pics around four in the afternoon. Yep, there's me, ducking out of another meeting to lock myself into the bathroom. Ye gods.

I never directly expressed a desire to see her offline. To be honest, I'm not sure I felt any such desire. I liked her better as a semi-nonfictional character. In my mind, I called her Cathy or Pris interchangeably, because to me, they were one and the same. As our online relationship progressed, her character lost a few inches in height, then assumed a less future-noir hairstyle. Emboldened by my interest (and, for all I know, that of any number of other men), she was nudging her virtual representation closer to her physical self. After all, it's more fun to be complimented for how you look in real life than for your taste in 1980s science fiction movies.

I told her I worked for the real Bliss Panerotic. I told her I'd be at opening weekend. I told her my wife and I were swingers; in fact, I may have implied we'd been swingers for years. I may have told her she'd have fun at the park. I may have implied her fun would be something of a physical nature involving someone whose *Realms of Eros* avatar wore a yellow fedora. In short, I may have shot myself enthusiastically right in the foot, perhaps even reloaded and fired again. The rest was probably inevitable. I'd become a soulless god of the machine, forging thunderbolts to punish my own hubris.

I think my life was pretty perfect for a while, I must say. Now here's me, Gary Klein, noted moron, doing everything he could to fuck that up.

Part Two: Intercourse

Chapter 9

It took Walt Disney a year and $17 million—adjusted for inflation, about nine times that amount—to build his debut incarnation of the Magic Kingdom, and almost nothing worked the way he'd hoped. He couldn't get the Rivers of America to hold water till his Imagineers dug down to the Anaheim clay. Acres of orange trees had to be removed. The two largest TV networks turned down his proposal for a show that'd basically be a weekly infomercial for his theme park. Lacking champagne, the engineers christened Captain Nemo's submarines with bottles of Corona. When Disneyland opened on Sunday, 17 July 1955, California was in the middle of a 110-degree heat wave, but local plumbers were on strike so most of the fountains were dry. Women's high heels got caught in sludgy patches of asphalt that had only been laid the night before. Of the 28,000 guests who streamed through Disneyland's gates that day, most came in using counterfeit tickets. Within a few months, the park attracted hundreds of feral cats. They're still there; park officials keep them around to kill mice. Tell me that's not the makings of a great Pixar movie.

What I'm saying is even the best engineers in the world run into unexpected problems building fantasylands. Our park would be no exception. Just getting the roads in shape took months, on an island that doesn't allow cars. We had to build our own electric bus system from Avalon, but the island refused to let us put Bliss graphics on the sides. It took weeks to figure out how to convey to our passengers where we'd be taking them if they boarded.

The Ryders hired four different engineering firms. Two worked on the indoor water park and three rides: a dark ride called the Tunnel of Lust and an indoor coaster called Climax, both in Sanasana; plus a boat ride, Viva la Revolución, in La Playa. Another worked exclusively on park facilities: the power plant, water and sewage (a nightmare, by the way), fiber optics for a state-of-the-art intranet, automation facility, laundry, and so on. The fourth company, a Philadelphia firm with a solid track record in casinos, built the hotels and almost everything else. In meeting after meeting, the Ryders and I gloated over increasingly polished computer models that were far more exciting than the rudimentary version encoded in *Realms of Eros*.

Before you ask, we were deeply concerned about safety codes. Our restaurants, for example, passed every inspection with flying colors. I remember Nicole sighing reverently as she told me about a taste-testing demo she attended in London. She'd heard Japanese tourists loved visiting Hawaii and suspected we'd get more than a few in L.A., so with that in mind, she made sure to include a high-end sushi restaurant. We celebrated her hiring of a renowned Nipponese *itamae*, Keiji Hayasaka, with a Sapporo-soaked visit to Kiriko Sushi. Hayasaka-san grudgingly acknowledged the quality of L.A.'s albacore sashimi but promised he could do better things with it. I believed him.

By now we'd achieved a kind of omnipresence in the national media. As I predicted, once our first wave of marketing hit, the major news media staged most of our second wave for free. Fox News hated us so much they couldn't stop railing against us, but every time Bill O'Reilly or Megyn Kelly decried our latter-day Sodom-in-progress, we sold several thousand more advance tickets. *Time* very nearly put us on the cover, then ran a cautiously disapproving overview next to an article about the "growth" of alternative sexual lifestyles in America. Until you read quite far into that article, you'd think the Ryders all but invented non-monogamy. Simply put, after all that free chatter, the

117

first few weeks' worth of tickets were sold out completely before the park's superstructure took shape. Adam fretted we'd set the price point too low. I reminded him he could count on auxiliary windfalls from food, merch, and parking, not to mention the millions already coming in from sales of the game.

It was early in the process when someone first raised the specter of terrorism. We knew we were advocating a lifestyle that was deeply offensive to conservatives and religious fundamentalists. The phrases "Bliss Panerotic" and "Sodom and Gomorrah" went together a little too well, and we feared someone declaring godly vengeance in the form of a bomb. That led to a couple of paranoid months in which Adam went over every aspect of the park with a panel of security experts, scary guys who probably knew a dozen ways to kill me with a paper clip. That led to a round of revisions, some expensively significant, but I'm sure the Ryders slept better at night knowing al Qaeda wouldn't be razing their cash cow.

Those were unforgettable times. I don't think I've ever been so giddy in my life, but it got to be more bowling pins than I could juggle. My office set up a couple of TV shoots, and we hired a well-regarded TV director to produce a half-hour travel promo and half a dozen commercials. The ads would range in salaciousness from "suitable for Grandma" to "eat your heart out, Caligula." I think my staff at Randall/Klein thought I'd gone off the deep end. My assistant Sherri asked me casually one day if she needed to worry that she was about to be employed by a porn company. My partners expressed dismay, not only that their name was attached to such a controversial project, but that I was spending almost every waking minute on it.

I set up accounts on all the major swing sites— there are a lot of them—to institute viral marketing campaigns. I made Bliss Panerotic sound like the single greatest legitimizing moment in the history of alternate sexual lifestyles since the advent of gay marriage, and to be honest, it probably was. People were registering for tickets and game membership as triads and quads. We treated swingers as progressives, not perverts, and they responded by the thousands.

One night Summer and I were slumped on the couch, our daughter asleep between us, her head on Summer's lap. She'd fallen asleep during an unbearable movie about a princess who was imported from Orange County. My wife and I were both too exhausted to carry our own little princess upstairs, too settled to wake her up. Now we were tuned to Zimmern's latest show on the Travel Channel. About halfway through, it tossed to a commercial, and there in living color was the main gate of Bliss Panerotic. I grinned. I couldn't help it. It was the first time I'd seen one of our national ads in situ. This gate was a model; our actual gate was still a pair of flags on either side of a gravel road. "Are you ready," a suave announcer asked, "for something a little...different?" The eighth-scale portal cracked open, and fiery orange light spilled from inside. "*Coming* this summer, a theme park exclusively for adventurous adults!" The subtle emphasis on the verb was no coincidence. Tanned, naked feet ran toward a clear, inviting beach. (To be honest, that footage was shot in Santa Monica.) "It's time to recharge your relationship, in an unforgettable playground for your *hottest* lifestyle. At Bliss Panerotic, we want to bring out your *wild* side!" This was followed by a feline yowl and an attractive heterosexual couple clinking daiquiri glasses. Flames wiped from that shot into graphics advertising our location, website, and opening date: Friday, June 12, 2015, a mere three months away. I had a feeling construction would come down to the wire, but I couldn't wait to see a crowd of thousands streaming into the park.

Anyway, you've seen our marketing campaign. I checked this morning, and the YouTube hits are still mounting, even now. Within days of first airing there were parody versions on Funny or Die! and Tawdry Soup. Let 'em laugh, I thought. No such thing as bad publicity. The Onion ran a popular piece under the title "Ask a Venereal Disease," in which herpes expressed excitement about running amok in the park. Jon Stewart instituted a whole series of sketches called "'Twas the Night Before Crotchmas." My wife was particularly amused by his opening verse:

"'Twas the night before Crotchmas
We were itching for sex
No ingredient was missing
Not even Valtrex…"

Stewart's guest, Stephen Colbert, promised to write the definitive chapter about our efforts in his new travel guide, *I Got Genital Warts and So Were You*. Very funny, I thought. Just say Bliss Panerotic again. Say it! Any publicity is good publicity. And he did! By my calculations, Colbert and other late-night comedians were responsible for at least two thousand advance ticket sales the next day.

In May I began spending much of my time on the site. Our intranet was on site and active, so I could do most of my job from Catalina. It was the first time I ran into Rick Orzabal since that party at the Ryders', so he and I split a hoagie and a six-pack of beer one sunny afternoon in Avalon. I hadn't finished half my half a sandwich before he started eyeing it. Big eater, that guy. I gave him the remaining quarter and opened another beer instead. "So what're you looking forward to most?" I asked. "About the park, I mean."

"Well," he said, "Judy and I have been playing that game, *Realms of Eros*, you ever play that?"

"I helped design the webpage," I replied, dodging deftly.

"Oh, cool, so you know. Man, that game is the tits! I haven't had this much fun playing a game since the early days of *Doom*. Plus you get to fuck actual people. Well, sort of. The gLoves, that new visor, man, they're amazing. You really feel like you're knockin' one out with these people. But now that we've had a chance to meet a bunch of people online, we're looking forward to seein' 'em for real. Prob'ly hookin' up, too."

"So your wife," I said, gazing out at the ocean, "she's as into this stuff as you are?"

"Hell, yeah, she is. Has to talk me into it some weekends. I'm too fuckin' tired from work. You know how it goes."

"Oh. Well," I said, "I probably don't. Summer doesn't even play *Realms of Eros*. She doesn't mind trying new things, but I think I've usually been the driving force."

"Yeah, that's the way it used to be for us, too. Then Judy figured out how bi she is. Man, that lady! She'd rather lick pussy'n ice cream. Some days I get to feelin' like I'm just an accessory to her crimes." He chortled. "Hey, don't drink all that beer, ya lush." I took another swig, saluting him with the bottle. "Thing about Judy is," he said, scratching his salted-blonde beard, "she don't mind bein' the center of attention, now. That just ain't a problem for her at all, know what I mean? And swingin', man, when you're a woman as hot as she is—you seen my wife?"

"Was she with you at the party? I think I might've seen her in passing."

"Yeah, well, here. Take a better look." He dug out his oversized wallet and flipped it open to a photo. I braced myself, expecting she'd be nude in the pic. She wasn't. Instead, I found myself looking at a snapshot of Rick in a suit, standing next to and towering over a Japanese-American woman in a glittering evening dress. He was right. Judy could've been a retired supermodel, with boyish but perfectly coiffed hair, feline epicanthic folds, perfectly straight white teeth, and a small bust as perky and pointy as a cartoon mouse's nose.

"Damn," I exclaimed. "Holy shit. You're okay with letting that out of the house?"

"Are you kidding? I'd trust that woman with my life. She's a hell of a lot smarter'n I am, that's for damn sure."

"Yeah, but...no, I mean...you let other guys fuck her?"

"Ain't my place to say. It's her pussy."

"Yeah, but..." I said again. After all, hadn't I let other men fuck my own wife? Was Judy that much hotter than Summer? Well, yes—sorry, honey—but that's not the point. Judy was hot enough that not only would other men stare at her and chomp at the bit to get into her knickers, it seemed to me they'd go out of their way to steal her from Rick. I like Rick, but he'd be the first to agree he's no Matthew McConaughey. If anything, he looks as if somebody shot that walrus-looking guy from the Mythbusters with a *Dig Dug* gun. "No offense, but how'd you get her?"

"What, you don't think my good looks were enough?"

"I'm not sure George Clooney's good looks would be enough."

"Well, I'm not without my charms. But hey, I don't know what it was, honestly. Her daddy owned a coupla real estate offices in Shawnee, so she had a little money. Coulda gone to any college she wanted, but she dug her folks so she stuck around Oklahoma. We met at Oklahoma State. I was a Kap-Sig, she was a Chi-O. I started mackin' on her pretty hard at a party once, and we hooked up maybe three or four times. She liked to date around. Hadn't started fuckin' girls yet. But y'know, we never really dated, just had sex. Her roommate used to screech at us through the wall to shut up. Judy can get pretty worked up. One time Paula yelled—that was her roommate's name, Paula—she goes, 'You leave that poor fratboy's dick alone!' Ha! She sure didn't, though. She rode me like Megan Fox

122

rides a motorbike, y'know? I mean, *damn*." I looked at her picture again, saving a mental map of her body for later, then handed the wallet back to Rick. "Anyway," he continued. "Graduation comes and goes, I start workin' for a company outta Wichita, Kansas. Hated every last jackhole I worked with. Had an apartment there in Wichita, but I was only in it a few nights a week. I kept coming back into the City—that's what we Okies call Oklahoma City, makes no sense, I know—and crashing on people's couches so I'd have someone to party with. I ran into Judy one night at a honkytonk bar on the west side. Man, that girl could cut a fuckin' rug, I mean bidness! Holy shit, she made the two-step look like a threeway, I'll tell ya what."

"This was when, like, what year?"

"Oh, late '90s. They was still playin' Garth Brooks at the time, so whatever year that was. Anyhow, I sure did like that ol' gal. I mean *liked* her, not just liked fuckin' her, though I sure did my share of that, too. If the cab of my old F-15 could talk, boy, it'd pant, I ain't a-kiddin'. She's a little bitty ol' thing, an' I used to turn her around and—well, never mind. Just reminiscin'. The point is we hit it off. I got to talkin' to her daddy one day, and we got along, too. He's this total character, man, *funny* an' sharp as a tack. I could see where Judy got it. But her mom, now—she did not like the cut o' my gibberish one bit. She saw me in my three-day-old laundry, sleepin' on some frat brother's couch, and prob'ly figured me for a lifelong demonstration of how to be a failure. I gotta tell ya, it lit a fire under my ass. I started applying to firms in Oklahoma. Thing about it is, I didn't want to just apply, I wanted to blow their doors off. So I started workin' on projects all on my own. Designed a coupla shopping malls, an orthopedic surgeon's office, helped out with the Bricktown renovations—I was all over the place. And it worked. Got me hired at Sims & Associates. I started makin' some pretty serious money. Me and Judy got married on her birthday. Best weddin' I ever saw. The whole thing was done up in silk—red and white, y'know, the Japanese colors o' luck. Buncha fancy calligraphy. Oh, man, it was amazing. And the food? Hot damn, man! You like sushi?"

"I do, as a matter of fact. Funny you should ask. D'you know they're opening a sushi restaurant here in the park?"

"No shit? Well, makes sense I guess. Pussy and raw fish, they do go together." I glared at him as I finished my beer. "Oh, come on," he laughed. "Don't even try to act like you wudn't thinkin' it."

"I wudn't," I said truthfully. "In fact, I'm now starting to rethink that whole sushi idea."

He laughed. "Well," he said, shrugging and finishing the last of our beers, "all I got to say is, between Japanese pussy and Japanese food, you can call this *gaijin* a convert."

Maybe it was how many times he'd used the word *pussy* in one conversation, but I started thinking about how rarely I'd heard the words *dick* or *cock* around Panerotic, given how important horny men would be to keeping Bliss's bills paid. "Let me ask you something," I said. "You say your wife's bi."

"Yessir."

"You're not."

"No!" he said, straightening quickly.

"Okay. Me, neither. But I wonder why we leave that out of the equation."

"Whaddya mean?"

"Well, look. We just assume every woman who shows up here is into chicks. And we're okay with that."

"We love it."

"We do love it. Yes. And we're opening up a whole area of the park for gay men. Which is hilarious, because the Ryders know less about gay life than they do about astrophysics."

"Right."

"But there's nothing in the park for real lesbians, honestly—not bi women, I mean nothing-but lesbians—and there's nothing for bisexual men."

"Well," Rick said, "where I grew up, in small-town Oklahoma, it didn't do for a fella to say he was thataway. Now, this was twentieth-century bullshit, ya follow? We wudn't quite so enlightened back in them days."

"Same in California," I admitted. "Maybe a little more progressive, but not much."

"Okay. So the only way a fella was ever gonna come out as light in his loafers, you'll pardon the expression, was if he was full-on gay. I mean, he didn't have no choice. He wudn't ever gonna get with some girl, and he couldn't help what he was. Not that, you know, they's anything wrong with it, the fact is that fella was gay. If he was bi, he just learned how to suppress one side an' act on t'other. Now that's just how it seemed to me at the time; I could be talkin' outta my ass here. But the only gay guys I knew growin' up was guys who just didn't have any choice but to come out: they was gay an' we may as well deal with it. So I don't know, I guess I just grew up thinkin' they wudn't any such thing as a bisexual man. Now I know better. But these things take time to work their way out into the world, y'un'erstand what I'm sayin'? An' ol' Adam, he still hasn't caught up with the vast majority of it. Maybe none of us have. I mean, maybe someday every sex party'll have just as many bi guys as bi women, but for now, it seems to me they just pick one orientation and stick with it. Again, I could be fulla shit, but that's my take on it."

"So what if you were at a party, y'know, an orgy, and some guy asked if he could suck you off?"

"Well," Rick hummed, trying to look like he was thinking the question through but clearly bothered it was even being asked. Old fears and habits die hard. "I cain't say as that's ever come up."

"You've never seen any male-male fellatio at a party?"

"No. I mean, maybe I just don't go to those kinds o' parties."

"Maybe."

"Although again, it seems to me that'd probably just be a party fulla gay dudes. Say, why're you askin' me this?"

"Relax, chief. I'm not coming onto you."

"I know."

"I'm just saying, I think it's funny that we have this whole group of enlightened, rule-breaking people, the kind of people who aren't buying into conventional ideas like the benefits of absolute monogamy or God's hatred of human sexuality—the kind of people who tend to vote for gay marriage and other aspects of equality—but their get-togethers are closed to gay men, even bi men. It doesn't seem like anything that should bother us."

"Huh," Rick harrumphed. "Well, that reminds me, an' maybe this'll shed some light on what you're sayin', but I read this book by Mary Roach called *Bonk*. You heard o' her? Oh, brother, I'm a big fan o' hers. She could make a science enthusiast outta anyone. Anyway, she was talkin' about how men and women respond to sexual stimuli, okay? So here's the deal. Hook a dude up to sensors, right, so you can monitor all his life signs: sweating, heavy breathing, faster pulse, all o' that. I'm talkin' about some regular ol' straight dude. Then you show him some male-female porn. He sees that man and woman fuckin', he starts to get horny his own self. Right? Stands to reason. You show him two women gettin' it on, he gets just as excited. Okay. Works every time. But you show him two men playin' lightsaber fight, an' suddenly he couldn't care less. It's not that he's offended. He may be jus' as liberal as

Barry Obama at a Dave Matthews concert. He may have voted for gay marriage just last week. But will his body respond? Not one bit. He may as well be watchin' two buffalos head-butt each other for all the blood it's sendin' down to Papi Chulo there. Straight men simply do not get off watchin' two gay dudes have at it."

"Uh-huh?"

"Do you?"

"I do not."

"Me neither. I gotta tell ya, though, I was raised poon-hound Republican by the grace o' God, but even I'm inclined to let them homosexually-inclined folks get married and whatnot. Kinda starts to feel defensive when ya worry about 'em too much, y'know what I'm sayin'?"

"Sure."

"Okay, so for heterosexual man, wiener plus wiener equals zero erection. That's a fact. It's biology. But things're different when you slap all them sensors on a woman. Let's say she's straight as Chuck Norris. I mean seriously, you couldn't get this woman to eat pussy if it was covered in ranch dressing and cancer vaccine."

"You really love the sound of that word, don't you?"

"What, vaccine?" he said, grinning.

"No, pussy."

"Hell, yeah, I do! Kinda rolls off the tongue, you don't mind the expression! Seems kinda chauvinist piggy to be opposed to pussy, don't ya think?"

"I interrupted you," I said. "You were saying."

"Right. You distracted me with—anyway. The point is, you show almost any woman straight porn, her nipples get hard, she starts pantin', her pussy gets wet, all the standard biological stuff. Straight porn makes straight women horny, even if they're politically opposed to it for some Godforsaken, chowder-headed reason. But you show her two men goin' at it, she gets

127

just as aroused. It's a fact. Show her lesbian porn, and as long as someone's having a good time in that video, she gets wet for that, too. Her nipples go ping, all the standard responses apply. Dudn't matter to her. This struck researchers, needless to say, as somewhat surprising. So they showed these women nature videos of two monkeys humping. An' guess what? They got just as aroused! I'm talkin' downstairs, now, mind you, not upstairs. Intellectually, they didn't know they was turned on. But south of the beltline, everything was cookin' like it was Freaky Town, U.S. of America."

"Interesting."

"So my point is, we tend to fill these rooms, I mean sex parties now, with things we know are gonna turn us on. Everything turns women on, so we don't have to worry too much about that. Those women are way hornier'n we ever gave 'em credit for. You could probably show 'em a monster truck runnin' over a pickup an' they'd get funny ideas. They're easy! But men, now, we're a little bit tougher to get into the mood, shall we say. It's counterintuitive, I know. But you think about your average straight man. When he grabs his junk an' starts tuggin', or even when he's fantasizin' about the neighbor while he's busy layin' pipe to his wife, there's a fairly narrow range o' scenarios playin' in his head. He's got his old standbys: hot for teacher, soccer mom next door, barely legal babysitter...I mean, maybe I'm missin' one or two, but that's basically it. So if you're plannin' on throwin' an orgy, you want to make sure you've got some soccer moms, some girl-on-girl action, plenty o' Victoria's Secret. Everything else is counterproductive. You throw one gay guy into the mix, and that party goes straight to hell. It's not nobody's fault, mind you, it's just how us poor straight dudes are wired. We need our usual suspects to keep things erect and operational."

"So is that why the Ryders kept the gay and straight areas of the park so segregated?"

"Well, it ain't as bad as all that, honestly. There'll be a lot of crossover in the Strip areas. I think Adam was even plannin' to show some gay porn movies at the Sinema, though he'll have to make it obvious how gay they are without turnin' off the homophobes. We do have some o' those in the lifestyle community, y'know; it takes all kinds, even morons. Have to walk a careful line there."

"There's something about Adam Ryder trying to program gay movies for his porn theater that makes me all warm and snuggly inside."

"Oh, brother, you ain't a-kiddin'! D'you know he had to hire gay-people experts to work on his park?"

"Where exactly does one find a gay-person expert?"

"Well, I'm tempted to say any street corner in West Hollywood, but I'll hold back. No, he did his research, and found this consulting company called Kendall-McManes outta Charlotte, North Carolina, of all places, that does what it calls GLBT consulting. Basically, they tell you how to talk gay people into buying your product, but also how to make sure your hiring practices are up to snuff, that you're respectful of domestic partnerships and gay spouses, hell, even that you're makin' the trans folks feel at home. I ain't a-kiddin'. These guys are a big deal now. Companies are startin' to figure out they's money to be made on the other side o' the dance floor, if you get what I'm sayin'. Times bein' what they are, even conservative companies can't afford to leave all that sweet, sweet gay money on the table."

"Ergo, gay consulting."

"You bet. I don't know how deep in bed they are with Panerotic just now, you'll pardon the expression again, but it's a lot. I mean, you think about this, now. Let's say you decide to mosey on over to the Miami side of Bliss Panerotic an' have a look around when this park opens. What do you expect to see?"

129

"Um, gay stuff, clearly."

"Okay, but what exactly does that entail?"

"Um…well, it's…uh…" I searched my brain for appropriate stagecraft. "I guess I honestly have no idea."

"Okay, neither do I, amigo, but stretch your imagination."

"Probably…well…I mean, it's Miami, right? So it's probably got a lot of Cuban or Latin-American flair."

"Right!" Rick announced, stabbing a finger toward my chest. "Flair. You said it. That's a good word for it: flair. Keep a-goin'."

"Okay, well, there's probably a lot of neon, like a late '80s discotheque."

"Uh-huh."

"I'm guessing a lot of fake palm trees and shit."

"Okay. Wow, you're good at this. You ever dabble?" I opened my mouth. "Nah, I'm jus' funnin' ya!" Rick chortled, playfully punching my arm with enough force to shatter a car window. "An' yes, by the way, that's pretty much the size of it, accordin' to every interior design I've seen so far. For some reason gay and Cuban go together like Lucy and Ricky. But now imagine you're an actual, honest-to-God gay dude, and you're walkin' into Miami for the first time. You know Adam and Nicole Ryder own the place, and you know they made their livin' off college-girl titties. You know they's straight through an' through, an' you figure they just invited you here for your hard-earned cash. Not to put too fine a point on it, you think they have nothing but disdain for you and your long-maligned orientation, okay? You're disinclined, how's that for a vocabulary word, to believe they's open-minded about you and yours. Now, take a look around. All that neon, all them fake plastic trees, what do you see?"

I realized immediately what he meant. "I see pandering."

"Exactly! Condescension. A shallow, empty gesture to the gay community, with nothin' but filthy lucre in mind. And that screams lawsuit, awright? Discrimination in business. This is sensitive stuff. That's why them big-shot consultants were so important."

"So maybe what Panerotic needs is a credible gay spokesperson."

Rick snorted. "Well, I don't disagree, but good luck gettin' Mr. Neil Patrick Harris to endorse a sexy theme park. Maybe Ricky Martin or one o' them there Indie-go Girls is available."

"I see your point, but I'm gonna talk to the Ryders about buying some more ad time on Bravo."

"Sure, get the word out. Let your freak flag fly, man. Free to be you an' me. Whatever gets ya round the bend."

Rick and I strolled the lot through a sea of construction and colored flags. The place was crawling with landscapers, busily sweating in the spring sun. People tend not to think much about the plants they see at a theme park, but I can tell you they're the product of considerable thought and effort. You need trees to block undesirable views without thrusting their roots into your expensive foundations. The gardens have to be laid in such a way that something is growing all year long. Most of the weeding and other maintenance tasks will be conducted overnight, so they need to be designed to be accessible quickly. Tropical plants are great, but you have to select and buy pots and planters that fit into the surrounding motif. Hanging plants are good, especially for colorful flowers that brighten the scene and can be cared for with relative ease. Many pesticides are out; cooling misters are in. It's a whole world of design I knew nothing about, and going by the dismay on the Ryders' faces when the bills started coming in, they were just as clueless about it as I was.

I'm pretty sure landscaping cost something on the order of thirty percent over budget estimates. Sure was pretty, though!

Rick told me an amusing story from the early days of the Magic Kingdom. Disney's Anaheim park was built on land previously covered in orange trees. The Imagineers walked around the site carefully tying ribbons of various colors around the trees to differentiate those they intended to keep from those they wanted cut down. Unfortunately, every tree was mown over, because the guy driving the bulldozer turned out to be colorblind.

Like Disney, however, the Ryders had been smart enough to hire a retired military officer, a U.S. Air Force Senior Master Sergeant, to oversee construction. I met the guy a few times and found him as charismatic as a Mercury astronaut and memorably intimidating. He performed his services under the agreement that he would never be identified by name. We knew him only as "Mr. James Black." Adam called him Sarge once, and by once I mean *once*. "Were you ever in the armed services, Mr. Ryder?" the officer asked him.

"I'm afraid not," Adam replied, "but, you know, kudos to anyone who can—"

"Then I'm not your officer, Mr. Ryder," Black interrupted, "so please abide by our contractual agreement and refer to me as Mr. Black in public, Jim in private. That way I won't have to beat you senseless in full view of your employees. Are we clear on that, sir?"

"Uh, yessir, of course," Adam stammered, his eyes wide. For once his clammy skin seemed bereft of the benefits of spray tanning. "Sorry…uh, Jim. Mr. Black. I didn't mean to offend."

"I'm not offended. What matters here is clarity. We won't have this problem again. Are we agreed?"

"Holy shit," Adam muttered. "Yes, we're agreed. I mean geez, take a—" He probably started to say "chill pill" or words to that effect, but one glimpse of Black's unblinking iron stare changed his mind. "Yeah. We're agreed. Whatever's clever, man. Listen, I'm gonna...be in my office," he finished lamely, then slunk away.

In mid-May I had the honor of escorting a reporter from a Canadian news organization around the site and talking her through its E-ticket attractions. We even granted her one of the first rides on its most expensive such feature, the Tunnel of Lust, once she agreed not to harp too much on the fact that it was a six-minute track ride with no completed scenery along the way. Why did we give her such singular access? Because the reporter in question was Victoria Sinclair, the lead anchor for over a decade of a remarkable program called *The Naked News*. If you're somehow unfamiliar with this marvel of narrow newscasting, it's a subscription web site with a team of attractive people, all female since 2007, reading a variety of informative items while casually doffing their clothes. It airs daily out of Toronto and enjoys several million hits a month. Ms. Sinclair is charming, intelligent, attractive, and conducted our interview in nothing but a G-string, baby. It's a tribute to my maturity and professionalism that the *Naked News* cameras never caught me looking anywhere but directly into Ms. Sinclair's eyes. (They may, however, have caught me blinking in delight whenever she pronounced *out* as "oot.")

So technically, *The Naked News* planned to interview Adam and Nicole Ryder. Then something awful happened: a twenty-four-year-old woman in Fort Smith, Arkansas, tried to commit suicide by ingesting an entire bottle of Xanax. Luckily, she survived—it turns out most antidepressants are surprisingly nonlethal—but she did blame her chronic depression on her earlier appearance in *Xtreme Ski Bunnies 4*. According to the young woman, she suffered so much mental anguish in the five years since her fifteen minutes of fame that her life now seemed hostile and pointless. I don't doubt the severity or misery of her depression. I feel deeply sympathetic toward her family and friends. I believe it bears noting, however, that later court documents revealed she'd been sexually abused by a cousin for years, date-raped twice, and voluntarily performed in a hardcore scene two years after she stripped with a friend for Adam's fourquel. My point is, out of all the people who took advantage of her over the years, she (or her attorneys) blamed the folks with the most money.

For the record, I don't think the Ryders were responsible in any significant way for that young woman's actions, but preparing for the trial kept them anxiously frantic just when they were deepest in the pile of tasks needed to open their theme park on time. It was also the subject of many a negative salvo against the perverts on Catalina Island. "Is this the kind of fun and frivolity we can expect from the Ryders' so-called 'Bliss' Gomorrah?" they were asking on Fox News. "A poor little innocent girl, raped on camera and doomed to a life of depression and misery? Does that seem blissful to you?"

Thankfully, that story hadn't broken when Ms. Sinclair and her crew of easygoing Canucks arrived in Avalon. They were disappointed to learn I'd be acting as media rep instead of the telegenic, name-branded Ryders, but I promised to make the trip worthwhile. I handled myself well, all things considered, and the episode inspired a rapid surge in Canadian ticket orders. I impressed the Ryders so much with my off-the-cuff interview skills that they appointed me their unofficial go-to guy for media interviews and pull quotes. In essence, I became the third mouth of Bliss Panerotic.

Would that help my career? As you very well know, in the long run it most certainly did not.

By that point, I'd grown comfortable talking to women in various states of undress, and it helped that Sinclair treated it as just another day at the office. What struck me quickly, however, was her physical resemblance to my wife. They had the same brunette hair, the same hazel eyes and graceful cheekbones, same tall carriage and poise. She even had my wife's butt, I can report from direct (if surreptitious) observation. She was slimmer around the waist than Summer, but that's to be expected; my wife's career doesn't require her to get naked in front of millions of strangers each day, so she doesn't exactly push herself to superheroine extremes at the gym. Talking to Sinclair was like talking to a *Realms of Eros* avatar version of Summer. In a strange way, I found myself hot for the idealized version of my own wife. Of course, try telling Summer that! When I told her about the interview on a phone call that night, she acted as if I'd bent or even broken our vows.

"I thought we decided we'd only fool around together!" she complained, in a tone that seemed, I have to say, rather like whining.

"I wasn't fooling around," I protested. "I was doing my job, which is talking up Bliss Panerotic."

"Yeah, to some topless Canadian on a sex ride."

"Is it really the ride that has you steamed?"

"Don't be funny. You know why I'm angry."

"No, I honestly don't. She was topless because she works for *Naked News*. That's her shtick. I'm surprised she didn't take off her G-string."

"Well, thank God for small favors. Really small, by the sound of it. And oh, what a sad day for you, Mr. Interview Big Shot on his hot date with a boob model and her camera crew, lord of the manor."

"Sweetheart, you're blowing this way out of proportion."

"Don't 'sweetheart' me. Is this how it's gonna be now, my husband the face of a porn park? Is that where we're headed?" Aha! So that was her problem. She was worried I'd be more visible in my role than we expected. "Is that who I am now: Mrs. Porno, the Bliss Panerotic widow?"

I reassured her, but boy, ain't it funny how things work out sometimes? And by funny, I mean the opposite of funny. I mean shitty.

Chapter 10

As I mentioned above, what Victoria Sinclair saw and recorded that day was all too evidently a work in progress. Our ride vehicle drifted past concrete walls, bare wood platforms, and dim electric light stands. When the actual story was posted online ten days later, Sinclair's producers used a greenscreen to composite her over our computer-generated previsualization video. The bulk of our interview was conducted in the lobby of Sanasana, which was chosen because it was the impressive design feature nearest to completion. If the rides were still unfinished on opening weekend, that'd suck, all right, but we'd be damned if we'd greet our first onslaught of patrons before our ATM party of a casino was finished.

The Ryders dealt with the Arkansas crisis by accepting GNN's invitation to appear on Argyle Greenwood's classy news interview program. He records his highbrow talk show at GNN's tower on Sunset. The Ryders refused a proffered limo in favor of driving themselves to Hollywood. Greenwood wasted little time before referring to the suicide attempt, an event he called a tragedy no less than three times in twelve minutes. Adam presented himself as concerned and compassionate, Nicole slightly less so. "To be honest," Adam said, "I don't know the poor woman, but my heart goes out to her. I wasn't on set that day. Her video was shot by a cameraman we hired for the weekend. We've never had any dealings with her whatsoever, other than to sign the check she earned by volunteering to appear in one of our videos. That's the extent of it, honestly, though of course I'm glad to hear she's all right."

"As a woman," Greenwood asked Nicole, "do you feel a greater sense of responsibility or empathy for these girls?"

"Well," Nicole said, visibly correcting an immediate frown, "first of all, it's not 'these girls,' it's one woman. Second, it's become clear this young woman had any number of issues; and really, a video most people have long since forgotten about was probably the least of them. I'm not wise enough or psychic enough to know why anyone would try to commit suicide, but I have to believe it's the result of problems that have gone on for years."

"And you don't think *Xtreme Ski Bunnies* was one of her problems that led to this tragedy?" Greenwood asked.

"Again, I don't know."

"She looked beautiful in the video," Adam said, then immediately looked at his wife.

"I'm not—" Greenwood began, before Nicole hastily cut him off.

"She had nothing to be ashamed of, if that's what you're implying," she said. "She had a beautiful figure, and she showed it. Millions of women have done that on Spring Breaks all over the world. People flash each other all the time. This is no different. I don't think the answer to understanding this young woman's depression is necessarily a display of sexual beauty. That's too easy a scapegoat, especially since everyone does it to some extent. You're wearing makeup right now, Argyle, as am I. We all want to look attractive for each other."

"Literally hundreds of women have appeared in our videos over the years," Adam said, rallying. "Out of all those women, exactly one person tried to commit suicide. That's less than one percent. I mean, I'm not good at math, but it is. It's less than half of one percent. So if you were to say, look at women who were, I don't know, employed in the fast food industry—if a higher

138

percentage of them tried to kill themselves, would you blame depression or the hamburger? I mean, let's be serious."

"So you feel you have no responsibility for what happened."

"My opinion?" Adam asked. "I see no reason to believe we bear any responsibility."

"None whatsoever," Nicole agreed.

"Okay," Greenwood tried again, "but history is replete with women who killed themselves or attempted to kill themselves after working in the porn industry."

"Is it?" Nicole asked. "I can think of one: Savannah, and she was wasted on alcohol and had just suffered a major head injury. How many can you name?"

"I can't think of any," Adam said, saving Greenwood the trouble.

"Well, let's talk about this new case. Do you think it helped this young woman's depression?"

"What do you mean?"

"To be in this video. If she was depressed, do you think that experience helped her or hurt her?"

"How would I know?" Nicole asked. "I know when I look good I get a major ego rush. She looked good in that video. For all you or I know, it made her whole year to be in it, to have that much attention lavished on her. Okay, so now it's years later and apparently she's sorry she made that decision, but that's rewriting history to an extent. You can't have it both ways."

Apparently, some producer on *AG360* found a list and whispered into Greenwood's earpiece. "There have been other porn actors who've killed themselves," he insisted belatedly. "Shauna Grant, Jon Dough. Several others."

"I'm not familiar with those cases," Nicole said blithely.

"Yeah, we tend to focus on the here and now," Adam agreed.

"This tragedy," Greenwood said, "it's not the sort of thing you want to have happen when you're about to open a crazy sex resort."

Nicole and Adam looked at each other in frustration. "See, that's—" Nicole began.

"Yeah," Adam said, "it's like—"

"I mean, where to begin?" Nicole said, raising her hands to the heavens.

"It's not some crazy sex resort," Adam insisted.

"Let's just start from the beginning," Nicole said. "You keep saying tragedy. That young woman is alive. Her suicide attempt didn't work. From what I hear, she's going to be fine, and she's, you know, at least now she's getting some help. I'm not saying it's a great thing, what happened, but I don't think it rises to the level of a tragedy." Greenwood opened his mouth to speak, but Nicole plowed ahead. "Second, we can't control the timing. We're aware of that. Stuff happens, right? It's sort of out of our hands. What I do know is, third, we're opening an adult theme park, the first of its kind anywhere on earth. We want to concentrate on how sex is healthy and good and revitalizing and magical, and then people want to turn it into this life-draining sickness. One has nothing to do with the other. We're here to celebrate human sexuality, not wallow in depression and sleazy…whatever."

"Can you see why people might worry about a theme park devoted to sex?" Greenwood said, then grinned. "I mean, the disease vectors alone."

"No, that's just it," Nicole said.

"Argyle," Adam said pointedly, "you're not being fair. You know we're going out of our way to make sure people are tested before they come to the park. If they do have herpes or HPV or any other STD, they have to clearly indicate that in their avatar stats. That's a fact. If we find out they've lied, they'll be escorted from the park and never allowed back in. Now, listen, Nicole and I have been to one of those sex resorts you're talking about, in Jamaica. There were people having sex all around us, in the pool, you name it, and I never saw a condom once. That's unhealthy. But as of right now, that's where sex-positive people have to go to spend their vacation around people with the same healthy interest. What we're offering with Bliss Panerotic is the opposite of that."

"That's true," Nicole said. "We're not hiding from anything. If you carry the virus for herpes, fine. That doesn't make you an awful person, it means you got careless a time or two. Big deal. All we ask is you tell the truth about it like a grown-up. Then everyone stays safe and protected. Okay? This is going to be a condom-friendly environment. We want people to have an amazing time. Believe me, no one will come away from Panerotic feeling gloomy about sex or themselves."

"Does this park include a strip bar?"

"It does," Nicole said.

"Does it have a porn theater?"

"Absolutely."

"Argyle, Argyle," Adam cut in. "Tell the truth now. Have you seen one of our movies in the last few years?"

"I have not."

"Well, then—"

"I have seen those incessant ads for *Xtreme Ski Bunnies* late at night."

"That's the old Panerotic," Adam said, quickly waving the reference away. "It's a holdover. It's how we made our bones, and that's well and good, but we're bigger and better now."

"It really is a much more legitimate enterprise than most people think," Nicole added.

"You're talking about your erotic movie business?"

141

"Yes," Adam said. "It's an indie film studio, just like any of the mainstream boutique houses in Hollywood or West Hollywood. We shoot on the same digital cameras they use to shoot mainstream independent features. We hire people who aren't just good at, you know, having sex. They actually act and write and direct and all the stuff you expect from a legiti—you know, from a mainstream movie."

"One of our cinematographers has an Emmy," Nicole noted. "This guy's the real deal."

"Look at Heidi Licious," Adam continued.

"Heidi who?" Greenwood asked, startled.

"Heidi Licious. She's one of our feature performers. Now, she's somebody who took drama classes in college. She's an actual actor who just happens to love having sex with hot guys and hot women on camera. And now she's appearing on *Howard Stern* and *Tosh.0* and other mainstream entertainment shows—"

"I'm not sure Howard Stern counts as mainstream," Greenwood demurred.

"The guy judges *America's Got Talent*! Literally millions of people listen to his radio show, so yes, I would argue that he is. And Heidi goes on there and yes, of course Howard wants to talk about the porn business, but she also talks about acting and how she wants to be in thrillers and, like, Judd Apatow comedies and stuff. And we encourage that. We're making stars at Panerotic, real stars who can hold their own with anyone in the so-called legitimate movie business. And we're able to do that because we don't view sexuality as anything to be ashamed of."

"That's right," Nicole agreed.

"Something we should hide in the closet," Adam continued. Greenwood raised a single eyebrow.

"Sexuality is not a liability," Nicole avowed. "Not anymore. Not to us! This is the twenty-first century, Argyle. We don't have to go around demonizing sex as if it weren't something everyone does. It's a healthy, magical part of our psychological makeup. We should revel in it, not shove it in the back room so our neighbors won't see."

"So what happens when you run into those neighbors at Bliss Panerotic?" Greenwood asked, tilting his head again in a gesture of TV curiosity.

"What do you mean?" Adam asked.

"Well, let's say you and the missus bought tickets for a weekend at Bliss Panerotic. Then you show up and your kid's third-grade teacher is there. Wouldn't that get a little awkward?"

"If she looks good, invite her to the party," Adam crowed.

"Or if *he* looks good," Nicole threw in, grinning. "We don't want to be sexist."

"And you think that won't seem weird at the next PTA meeting?"

"Argyle, look at it this way," Nicole said. "Would it freak you out if you ran into someone you knew at an ice cream parlor?"

"No."

"Well, why not? I mean, ice cream is fattening and sugary and makes you gassy. I mean, there's all these things that can go wrong with ice cream."

"Well, but I think the benefits of eating ice cream outweigh the risks, in moder—"

"Exactly! And that's how people feel about sex, too, which is why the human race still exists. Just like eating ice cream, having sex is a treat for the senses. It makes you feel good. It makes you happy. It's good for your ego, and unlike ice cream, it's incredible exercise. If you put on a condom and go about it like a grown-up with half a brain, the benefits outweigh the risks. So no, we don't see any reason to treat sex any differently from any other fun thing you can do with your body, whether it's eating ice cream, canoeing on a lake, or going to the gym so you look good for a news camera."

143

"Hey, now," Greenwood said, smiling.

"Bliss Panerotic is for couples who are proud to be sexy," Adam announced, repeating a line from one of my commercials.

"So what do you say to people who ask," Greenwood began, employing that time-tested journalistic method of posing a question without taking any responsibility for asking it, "'Sex is sacred; sex is for procreation or for married couples only?'"

"Argyle," Nicole said, smiling, "correct me if I'm wrong, but aren't you involved in a relationship that goes outside Biblical norms?" She was referring, of course, to Greenwood's longtime significant other, a male attorney from upstate New York.

"Hey, now, this isn't about me."

"Maybe not, but you see my point. I mean, however people may feel about God or the Bible, and trust me, I'm a good Christian girl myself, but that doesn't mean I adhere to every last word the Bible says about sex. My feeling is, we've pretty much gotten past that in our culture these days, don't you think so?"

"I'm not sure. You don't consider the Bible an authority on sexual matters?"

"No, no more than any other fornicator does. And that's most of us, right? I had sex before marriage. I had sex before I met Adam. He had sex before he met me. We're human beings. We didn't worry about lightning bolts from heaven when we were doing it then, so I don't see the point of getting all worked up about it now."

"I suppose the point is people feel it means the difference between God's approval and disapproval."

"Well, listen, we're told God disapproves of gay people," Nicole said. "I don't buy it. I get a strong sense the church still disapproves of female priests, and we don't all agree on that. I think God loves those who love. Yeah. I really do. It's as simple as that. So am I saying we should all go out there and treat each other

144

like crap just to get our rocks off? No, of course not; I think we have to be respectful. But I don't think God sits up there and logs all our, you know, infractions on a chart."

"What about you?" Greenwood asked Adam.

Ryder raised his hands in defeat. "I'm not a, you know, Bible scholar. I don't lose too much sleep about that stuff, to be honest. I just want people to have fun. Everything that happens, in our movies or in Bliss Panerotic, is consensual, y'know? That's the key. It's just two or more consenting adults. I don't judge that. If you do, fine, but don't come layin' all your hang-ups on my doorstep. I didn't invent this stuff. I'm just, we're just providing a playground, y'know? It's a fun place to play. And it's gonna be huge, Argyle, you know it is. Sex is coming out of the closet, not just gay sex but every type of sex. And I'm tellin' ya right now, it is never goin' back."

As May raced into June, I found myself sleeping about four hours a night. There simply wasn't enough time to get everything done. I hired two more assistants out of my own pockets to keep them off the Randall/Klein books. My partners and associates were making it very clear they'd had enough of my singular attention to one client, especially a client who was about to open a controversial sex park. One by one, the major news networks floated the story of Bliss Panerotic to see whether people were offended enough to spend hours a day waiting for each salacious new item, and, one by one, they discovered the story was ratings gold. Fox News, of course, lambasted the Ryders on moral grounds, accusing them of all but injecting chlamydia into Californians' water supply. MSNBC opposed the park on feminist grounds; they even found a guest willing to reiterate Andrea Dworkin's old claim that all pornography is rape. The guest went on to insist any woman who visited Bliss

Panerotic, even on her own dime and of her own free will, was actually being coerced into doing so by a patriarchal system; ergo, rape again. GNN took a more restrained tack, in which news readers tracked each phase of construction while making not-so-subtle faces at the utter baseness of it all. As grateful as I was for the unpaid publicity, it curled my hands into fists. I have nothing but contempt for the lot of them. They spray their pseudo "outrage" at a gullible public like a toreador flailing his red silken cape at a bleeding bull.

With all that pent-up aggression, it stands to reason I found one more opportunity to visit Pris in *Realms of Eros*, busy as I was. Why her? I mean, honestly, the whole point of the game is to e-bang as many partners as you can, right? It's all about digital notches in a virtual bedpost. Yet I kept going back. I've had months to think about it, and it strikes me that the main reason I did that was adrenaline. It felt wrong, more wrong than chatting up bots or total strangers, and that's what made it feel right. I was desperate for the cheap, awful zing of transgression. On TV, a midlife crisis takes the form of a gray-haired guy buying a convertible he can't afford to impress a twenty-year-old blonde he can't keep, but that's not how it is in real life. In messy real life, we tend not to opt for clean, extravagantly idiotic breaks. We go for small stupid: we tiptoe past the line of what we know we can get away with, solely to energize our system with the charge of having done so. I've never had an actual affair. I never did, no matter what you might think. I had everything but. Sound familiar? President Clinton did not, I repeat, did not have sex with that woman. By his own self-delusional definition, he had everything but. Because everything but is the new nothing! I was presidential, damn it! But yes, I did cheat on my wife, as I've admitted before. What's the difference between cheating and having an affair? I guess it's a virtual

146

Darryl Hannah wig. That's the best rationalization I can offer.

So here's me, Gary Klein, happily married man, father of one, employer of five, ejaculating into a condom from the intensity of a virtual sex act in a nonexistent hot-sheets hotel made of pixelated nothing. On my way up to the room I picked up a tall brunette bot and customized her to look more like Summer, then set up a threeway with it and Pris. Twisted, right? The Summerbot said nothing, merely stroked herself as I rutted into Pris from behind. It felt like real sex only to the extent that the condom I wore was pre-lubricated. I never told Pris the bot resembled my wife. For all I know, she reconfigured her own view of the room to make the Summerbot look like Ryan Gosling. I don't know why I wanted Summer in the room, other than it made me feel guilty; and damn, was that hot.

After Pris and I, by which I mean Cathy and I, came a couple of times each, I dismissed the bot and held Pris while she talked. I mean, what the inexplicable fuck, am I right? What kind of nonsense is that? Who bangs the Barbie-doll avatar of a woman he met in a digital sex game, then lays around and talks for an hour like a love-drunk college student? I should've ended it after the orgasms. They were the fun part, the part that never got me into trouble.

That's when I learned Cathy was separated from her husband, a staunch Tea Party Republican who worked for a chain of while-you-wait oil change garages. He was the kind of guy, she said, who's probably addicted to Internet porn but has actual sex with all the lights off. She cheated on him once, five years before in Scottsdale, Arizona, but he had no idea and she'd all but forgotten the other dude's name. Cathy was a mother of two who worked part time for a smartphone company with offices in Glendale. I found her on Facebook but didn't friend-request her. (She probably found me, too, but I'd already switched all my settings to private.) I looked at pictures of her with her kids, eating fried chicken legs at Busch Gardens, and laughing with friends. She looked nothing like Summer. In fact, she wouldn't have been my type had I met her outside the game. I marveled yet again at the disconnect between people's public personae and their sexual selves.

Here was a woman you wouldn't give a second look in the grocery store, not even if she were bending over mist-bedewed melons with suggestive abandon. It wasn't that she was unattractive. It was, rather, that she looked chronically unhappy, like someone who'd be difficult to live with more often than not. The other dads probably saw her on Parent-Teacher Night and thought, *I bet I know why her husband checked out.* But he hadn't. She had. Between the two of them, Cathy was the more sexually voracious and experimental. She offered to bring a woman home from the bar one night to share with him, and he looked at her like she'd offered to bathe him in wet hamburger meat. What drove Cathy and her husband apart wasn't frigidity. It wasn't even sex. It was simply that they'd forgotten how to talk to each other as if they hadn't just met at an office function no one wanted to attend. They didn't care enough about each other to hate each other enough to get fully divorced. Their teenage son blamed his father for their troubles. Their preschool-aged son wet the bed. Their dog Max reserved judgment.

I told her a bit about myself but fudged some details. To this day, Cathy probably thinks my wife's name is Shannon. (I was flashing on Shannon Doherty, one of my dozens of adolescent celebrity crushes, when I blurted the fake name.) I told her I worked in advertising and intimated I was working on the campaign for Bliss Panerotic. I never told her I was running it; but again, I did say my wife and I would be at the grand opening.

"You're lucky," she said, gazing at me from her glossy, pale avatar face. "I could never get the hubby to go to a place like that." I have an instinctive flinch reaction, by the way, to any use of the word *hubby*, so I hope the *Realms of Eros* face recognition processors didn't pick that up.

"Yeah, but you're as free as a bird now."

"I'm still trying to figure out what 'separated' means," she said. "I know it means we're physically apart. But mentally? Emotionally? Forever? I don't know. It's too much. The boys miss him. I miss him, but I also hope I never see him again. Life doesn't let you have everything at once."

"You haven't been with anyone but him since the separation?"

"Says the man who just lured me into a threesome."

"No, not much luring. A virtual threesome. Virtual, please."

"It'd still get me stoned in many countries."

"Be that as it may. You haven't—"

"No, Detective Dash. Stop grilling the femme fatale. I've been locked in my room like a spinster for months. Just me and my computer and haptic gloves and a Kindle full of sci-fi erotica."

"Sci-fi erotica? I didn't know they—"

"Lauren Dane. Laurann Dohner. This is big-time stuff, man. You should try it. Makes *Fifty Shades of Grey* look like a *Sweet Valley High* book."

"I understood some of what you just said."

"Oh, shut up. That erotica crap is what I've had instead of a husband. What's he's been up to, I have no idea."

"Probably nothing."

"Probably nothing. That's right. Just a 4G Web connection and the ol' five-knuckle shuffle. Now, can we please talk about something other than my failing domestic arrangement?"

"Yes. And the timing could be better, but I'm probably not gonna see you for a while."

"Why's that?" she asked, with considerably less disapproval than I might've hoped—which is strange, because I was seriously thinking about moving on to a whole new *Realms of Eros* partner altogether, maybe bots only. I'm not saying I felt guilty. I felt...anxious, that's all.

"I've got this grand opening coming up. I'll be stuck on Catalina most of June. I gotta pay more attention to my home life. My family's starting to forget what I look like."

"I could send them a JPEG."

"Hey. Don't even joke."

"Wocka wocka," she said, then frowned. "I'm gonna miss you, shamus."

"You mean that?"

"Yeah, I kinda do. You're fun to bounce around on."

"Life should only be so simple."

"What do you mean?"

What *did* I mean? "I guess...I've been wondering why one person isn't enough, y'know?"

"You mean marriage."

"I mean love. Because yes, I do love my wife. I don't always understand her. Hell, there are mornings I don't even like her. She spends hours in the bathroom, my God, Pris, you wouldn't believe it. And lately she's been erasing my Dodger games off the DVR—never mind. That's neither here nor there. The point is, you marry someone because they make you feel good and you think you can do something good for them. You like having sex with 'em and they give every impression of liking it with you. I mean, how different does it feel, moving from one partner to another? Pussy's pussy, as a friend of mine would say."

"Ah, you silver-tongued devil."

150

"No, but you know what I mean. It's not like one woman feels like 'eh' and another woman feels like 'wait, I had no idea they did that!' It's vagina. And a penis. Okay, yes, I mean, there are differences in size or whatever, but basically it's the same act. But the second we get something going with one partner we like, we can't wait to test-drive every other vagina in town. It makes no sense."

"Well, I think women are wired a bit differently in that regard."

"Do you really? Then why are you buying all that space smut?"

"Sci-fi erotica, thank you very much. And printed erotica's about how we feel about ourselves."

"And shirtless men."

"And shirtless men, yes. But mostly it's…you know, we want every man to want us, the more the merrier. That doesn't mean we're going to act on it. When you were single, did you screw around because you wanted to dip your toe in every stream, or did you do it to make yourself feel better about you and your own attractiveness, your accomplishments as a man?"

"God, I don't even remember anymore," I lied. I hadn't spent much time single. But I thought about my single or formerly-single friends, and she was probably right. I got the feeling they felt a greater sense of worth and manly power the more recently they'd gotten laid. No one likes to feel unfuckable. Once we're married, in fact, no one likes to feel he or she couldn't get someone else.

"If your husband came back right now, tonight, and said, 'I'm ready to change, just tell me what you want me to fix,' what would you tell him?"

She lay silent for a moment. "I wouldn't know where to start," she said finally. "It isn't like there's anything majorly wrong with him. He's good to the kids, he makes a decent living, he treats me with respect. So he likes porn, big deal, I'm dressed up as a robot to rub one out with a guy I barely know. Who am I to judge?"

"So what's the problem?"

After another long beat, she said, "He quit trying to be special. When we were younger, y'know, he bought into all that cultural bullshit about how we're rock-star astronauts or whatever, and one day some TV producer was gonna knock on our door and tell us it was time to come out and be super rich and famous now. It was awesome! He had this band with his friends—God, they were terrible. Terrible! It was like Nickelback's tour bus had crashed into the Dave Matthews Band, and this band was the fluid that leaked out of the crash. Called themselves—oh God, what was it? The Monsters? The Munsters? Something like that. Anyway, they sucked. But I used to sit in his oily garage and listen to 'em pound away for hours. I felt drunk watching 'em fill themselves full of hot air and talk about, I don't know, their first tour of Europe or something. They believed they were special. When I was with him, I felt like a badass. God, my mom hated him! Used to call him 'the grease stain.' Now he's the father of her grandkid. She can't say enough good about him. Says he's 'Mr. Responsible' and I'm banana boats for letting him walk out the door. I don't think he's picked up a guitar in fifteen years."

"And you? Have you kept the magic alive?"

"Ha, what do you think?" she snorted. "He comes home, I don't even bother cooking dinner anymore. 'Get a pizza,' he says. I make him eat Canadian bacon; he doesn't bother putting up a fight. He fucking hates Canadian bacon! Grow some balls, man."

"I know you make an effort in the sack."

"More for me than for him, I have to say." She sighed heavily. "He came over to see the kids last week, I asked him to stick around and watch a movie with me and my oldest. *Superbad.* You seen it?"

"Sure."

"So halfway through the movie, my tough teenager gets weirded out watching jokes about boners with his parents, so he drifts off to go miniature golfing with his friends. My little one just wants to throw popcorn all over the frickin' place, so we put him to bed. Now James and I are parked on our butts with about two hundred yards of couch between us, and we both already saw the movie when it first came out anyway. So I says, hey, movie lover, care to run upstairs to the snack bar? And he goes, 'What?' like he can't even muster up the kindness to pretend that wasn't the stupidest line ever. I'm like, oh, never mind. Forget it. You missed your shot. And he could've had me right there and then. He could've boned me on the couch. I knew he wanted to. Had an erection you could've hung mailbags on. But when push comes to shove, he didn't see the point of taking off his shoes. He'd already been down that road, know what I mean? He'd mapped the territory, so why climb the same mountain twice?"

"Yeah, but still," I wondered, "why pass up an opportunity that easy?"

"Hey, who you callin' easy?"

I ignored that. "I don't know what they tell you women on *Oprah*, but most of us men get propositioned like that about once every decade."

"Well, first of all, *Oprah*'s been off the air for like forever. You should talk to your wife about the important stuff in life. Second, I mean—what a jackass, right? Seriously! I'd'a jumped on him like a fat kid on cupcakes, just to show him what he was missing. But nooooo. When it comes right down to brass tacks, he'd rather look cool and act like he's past it all just to make some ridiculous point, I don't know, show me he'd won. I had to ask for sex, so I lost and he won. Or something. God, you men are so dumb."

"I can't argue with that."

"So what about you? Wifey still treating you right in the ol' boudoir department?"

Remember what I said about *hubby*? That goes double for *wifey*. "Oh, I really shouldn't talk about—"

"Gimme a break, man. Jesus. I been spilling my guts for an hour here. Throw an F.B. a bone already." F.B.: *fuck buddy*. Is that what Pris and I were? Did a couple of times "together" in a video game even qualify? Christ, was I cheating on Summer for real? Nope! Because we weren't really fucking, remember? I'm not horrible! And I'll stand by that, even though I didn't correct Pris's mischaracterization, so I guess that's one more prick point against me.

Instead I said, "You really want to know about my wife?"

"Sure, why not?"

"I've been thinking about her a lot lately. It's funny, I feel like I've known her forever, but she still finds ways to surprise me. I should like that, but...I used to think it was wonderful, y'know, that I'd never plumb the depths of this woman. Life would be an ongoing adventure from now until our great mutual sunset. Now I'm not so sure. Now I'm wondering how you can live with someone, Christ, eighteen years, and not know what's going on in her head."

"You probably have some idea."

"No, I mean—okay, I'll give you an example. The other day we're talking on the phone about something our daughter said. Apparently my daughter thinks I'm working for Disneyland. I don't know where she got that idea. I didn't tell her anything about Bliss Panerotic, she just got the wrong idea. Thinks I'm building spinning teacups or something. Evidently she doesn't get that I'm in advertising, but whatever. That's kids. She just thinks I do whatever's needed. Which is sweet, right?"

"Adorable."

"Anyway, so she asks my wife why I haven't taken her to go live at Disneyland with Minnie and Mickey. And my wife says they don't have school in Disneyland, so we have to keep her in Sherman Oaks so she can go to school with her friends. And then I say, well hey, maybe that's not such a super idea, blaming the fact that we don't live in Disneyland on our daughter's education. I don't want her to grow up resenting her teachers and school and all that. And my wife goes, like, *nothin'*, radio silent. I mean, there's a silence on that phone like we're inside a monastery. So I go, what're you thinking? And she slaps back, 'Nothing," without even thinking about it. Except of course I'm not buying that, because—"

"The old dreaded 'nothing.'"

"Exactly. This ain't my first week of married life, okay? I know 'nothing' pretty much always means 'something I don't want to talk to you about.'"

"Smart man."

"Well, I try. So I say, no, really, what're you stewing about? And then of course it's 'why do you always think I'm stewing' and all that bullshit. Which is all an obvious smoke screen, like, 'Deploy chaff!' I mean, really, you must think we're all brain-dead or something."

"Hey, leave me out of this. Besides, if the shoe fits."

"I was using the generic 'you.'"

"The gender 'you.'"

"Right. Whatever. And I think to myself, 'Self, if you really did know this woman as well as you think, you could predict where this discussion is going.' And because I'm all paranoid now, I assume she's gonna bitch about how much time I'm spending away and maybe if I have a problem with how she talks to her kid, I should try it myself and all that."

"Which is probably exactly what she was thinking."

155

"Thanks. Except nope, she fooled you, too!" I exclaimed. "Turns out she was hoping we could take our daughter to Disneyland for her birthday, but then she remembered her birthday's on a Thursday this year and the weekend after that we'd already told some friends from up north they could come stay with us, so now she's wondering if we should just be wonderful people and spring for Disneyland tickets for our friends *and* our kid, and how much would that cost and could they all fit into our SUV? And maybe we should see about getting a room at the Candy Cane Inn so our daughter could take a nap in the afternoon and go straight to bed after the fireworks that night, except no 'cause let's face it, they're probably booked two years in advance, and besides, could our daughter even fit on all the rides yet? Oh, and maybe we should try to watch *Cars* soon so she'll know who that truck with the dental problem is. And of course all this flashes through her head in about two thirds of a second, so she figures why bore me with a bunch of unrelated nonsense. Oh, and by the way, maybe I *should* start spending some time at home while we're on the subject. Then we're off on that after all. I'd created my own fight. So go, me! Or so she says. Who can tell?"

"You don't think she was looking for any excuse to gripe about it?"

"About my time away from home? Yeah, maybe. I don't know. She's usually pretty direct. But it's stuff like that that makes me wonder how well I really do know her. We're supposedly best friends—we *are* best friends, no one else is even close—but I couldn't tell you if my life depended on it whether she's truly happy about her life. Or with me."

"You think she figures you're cheating on her?"

"She probably wonders."

"That'd make me a rhymes-with-bitch, too. So what's she do for a living? She ever out of the house for long stretches of time?"

156

"Nah, she works part time for Barnes & Noble, not that we need the money. I'm…Y'know, I'm in good shape, knock on wood. Have been for years. We have savings and a college fund and life insurance and all that good shit, so the money my wife makes goes mostly into clothes and stuff for the kid. That's her fun. She's all about mommy-daughter time. They like to go to the Stand, y'know, eat turkey dogs and go to the movies on Saturdays. I mean, they're tight like that. It's cute. But I wonder sometimes whether my daughter knows my wife better than I do. I mean, my wife's existence has become almost entirely about being a mother. I realize this sounds ridiculously selfish, but I miss the days when she looked like she was happiest around me, not our kid."

"That just comes with the territory, man. You knew that when you knocked her up."

"Yeah, I know."

"So you don't ever invite yourself along for turkey dogs and popcorn?"

"I got the distinct feeling it's a girls-only club. No daddies allowed in the tree house."

"Aww. A certain detective feels left out." She reached over and nudged me virtually in the ribs, not that I felt any contact.

"Aw, Jesus, why am I telling you this?"

"Don't be like that. I'm interested. Honest Injun."

"'Honest Injun?' Who says that? What century are you from?"

"Uhh, *Blade Runner*, hello. I'm from 2019, dude, *duh*. Don't you watch movies? Or don't they have those in Dick Tracy World?"

"I'm from film noir, thank you very much. I'm Fred MacMurray."

"From *My Three Sons*?"

"No, from *Double Indemnity*. Who's the movie buff now?"

157

"I didn't think he had a hat in that movie."

"Black fedora. Well…at least it was black in black and white. Never mind that. The point is, I shouldn't be whining about my marriage to a woman I met in a sex game."

"Try to think of me as a bot. Your secrets are safe with me."

"You *are* a bot."

"I meant a real bot—no, I mean, a non-player bot, not me pretending to be Daryl Hannah pretending to be a robot. Geez, now I'm confusing myself. The point is who would I tell? I'm never gonna meet this woman. You can say anything you want. The psychiatrist is in, only five cents."

"Well," I began, then didn't know what else to say. My disorganized thoughts coalesced on a memory from a few years ago. "I remember one night, our daughter couldn't sleep. She was just a baby then. We took turns trying to bounce her to sleep on our knees while playing the only board game we owned, which was Trivial Pursuit. And I've always been pretty good at that game. Used to hit local trivia nights in bars when I was in college. Somehow, though, I'd never played it with my wife. Isn't that weird? Cranium, sure. We used to play that with"—I almost botched her fake name again—"Shannon's brothers and sister. But we'd never played the one game for grown-ups we owned that wasn't on PlayStation 2. So we started playing the game, and I mean, she beat the holy *shit* outta me. I barely got a wedge in my pie. She's skipping all over the board answering question after question, like, these epic ten-minute turns. She knows science and technology, popular culture, NCAA basketball, you name it. I had no idea she was so knowledgeable. I knew she was smart, but how did she cram all that junk in her head and I never noticed her doing it?"

"I assume she reads a lot. She works at a bookstore."

"Yeah, she's always got something going on her Kindle, plus she likes to watch all those science and history channels. I come home, the DVR's all full-up with *Mythbusters* and *Nova* and all that shit, but somehow I never made the connection: oh, *duh*, that plus that equals my wife's a genius. I mean, all this time, to tell you the truth, I kinda thought I was smarter than her. You believe that? Not that I ever thought she was stupid, just...I don't know. I never noticed her paying such close attention to the world. Ha! Goes to show what I know. Turns out I was the village idiot all along."

"So she's wondering why you can't just do your work from home after five. You can't blame her for that."

"I don't blame her for anything."

"So why can't you work from home?"

I shrugged, a gesture the software probably did recognize and reproduce. "I love the park," I admitted.

"Oh, yeah?"

"Yeah, it's like...I get what they're going for. They want to be as openly proud and joyful about sex as those whack-a-mole Christians are about their creepy Jesus theme park in Florida."

"Oh, you're talking about, uh, 'Bible Land'— what is it?"

"Holy Land Experience. Yeah. Crucifying Christ daily since 2001."

"Lord."

"Exactly. And by the way, there used to be another one, called Holy Land U.S.A., in Connecticut. I'm turning into kind of a theme park expert these days. Can you tell?"

"I can see that."

"The place closed down in the mid-'80s, but then a few years ago, some douchebag teenager strangled, raped, and murdered another teenager at the foot of a giant cross on the property. Happy times, right? So yeah, I'll stack Panerotic up against Holy Land U.S.A. and its batcrappery any day of the week."

"You don't think it'll be dangerous?"

"What do you mean?"

"You don't think men'll get out of hand and date-rape women?"

"I don't know. I sure hope not. It'd be the undoing of the park. But I know a couple of swingers, and believe me, those women can take care of themselves."

"They shouldn't have to."

"No," I acknowledged, "but I gather there'll be at least as much security as you'd find at any strip bar."

"So this is the first sexual theme park ever?" she asked. "In the world?"

"Pretty much," I replied. "There's a kind of erotic sculpture garden in Korea called Love Land—oh, and they have another one full of giant statues of penises. You think I'm kidding, but I'm not. They tried to open one in China, but it pretty much died on the vine. So it's that and a couple of museums, but that's it. The Ryders are pioneers."

"You sound like a new convert."

"Maybe," I admitted. "Maybe I am. Maybe I believe my own ad copy. But honestly, why should this blow anyone's mind? How much time a day do people spend on the Internet? And obviously one of the key attractions is porn. People love that stuff. They can't get enough of it."

"Women can."

"Maybe, but did you know the fastest-selling paperback novel of all time is *Fifty Shades of Grey*? They've sold tens of millions of those things, and they're terrible!"

"I don't know. I read one. I thought it was kind of fun. It was different."

"And that's just it. People want something different. They've stopped paying for porn, 'cause they

160

can get it for free. The Ryders realized that, so they protected their livelihood by segueing into something different. They took an aspect of life people have hidden behind closed doors out of fear of embarrassing themselves and said, 'Wait a minute. What are we so ashamed of? Let's have fun with this.' I think it's about time."

"Well, okay, then. You've talked me into it. Where do I sign?"

"You better hurry," I said. "Tickets are selling fast."

"James'd have a heart attack if he found out I left the kids with him so I could spend a weekend slutting it up at Screw Central."

"I'm not hearing the downside," I quipped.

"Oh, leave him alone," she said, swatting me again. "James is okay, just not okay for me. And Shannon, is she gonna be okay with this? You make her sound kinda conventional. Prudish, even."

"Do I? I guess I do. She's not, though. She's…" I trailed off, looking for the right word. "She's a mom. She grew into that. She accepted it. Now it's hard for her to act all frisky again, 'cause she's too used to putting on a mature face in front of the kid."

"Maybe," Pris said. "But do you even know that, though? You said before you don't really get her. Are you just guessing about what she's thinking? Maybe she really hates the whole concept of Bliss Panerotic. Maybe she doesn't want to go but she's afraid to say no to you this late in the game. Maybe she's all about it and doesn't want to give you the satisfaction. I mean, what if she's some total nympho?"

"I'm pretty sure she's just like everyone else," I said weakly.

"There is no just like everyone else! We're all different, man. It changes from day to day, especially for women. She could be all blasé-blasé today and like, some total porn star tomorrow. You don't know!

Maybe she's a beast and you just can't handle the idea!"

I laughed. "Okay, with all due respect, you don't know her. That's kind of funny of you to even say that."

"What, that she likes sex? Are you telling me she doesn't?"

"No, she likes sex fine, she's just not insane about it."

"Insane like you, y'mean?"

"No, I'm not...I mean...she's pretty normal."

"You don't know what normal is, man. Normal is, like, an illusion."

"Okay, I've said too much."

"I'm just saying, man, you're gonna learn a lot about her on this trip. I hope you're ready to handle it. People are crazy, man. You may have unleashed the tiger."

I laughed again. "I should probably go."

"Fucking *be* like that," she snapped, sitting up. "I'm trying to open your mind. You can take it or leave it. I've learned a lot about myself since I had kids and had to start processing my life as a grown-up. People change, and they don't tell anybody 'cause it happens so slow they can't even figure out how they've evolved. Your sweet little turkey-dog, PTA wifey might be freakier than you ever imagined. Freakier than you ever wanted her to be. And here you are looking for freaky behavior from me, when she's been begging for wild cock at home."

"Settle down," I protested.

"She might be ready for change and you can't handle it. That's what happened to me."

"Okay," I said. "I'm sorry that happened. I'll watch out."

"You're a fucker, man," she said. "You should, like, *abre los* fuckin' *ojos*, okay? Open your eyes. Deal with that."

162

I said little after that; I was clearly in over my head. Instead I jumped into my virtual pants and logged out of the game, never to cyber-bang "Ms. Pris" again. I don't know if she'd talk to me now. I haven't tried. I've refrained from logging onto *Realms of Eros*, period, since last summer. My lawyer says I'd be calling down the wrath of the gods at each keystroke.

Since that conversation I've had multiple occasions to talk to Summer at wearying length about our notorious sex life, by which I mean experiences that happened both inside and outside the park. We've exchanged emails, some cordial, most not, about what happened and how we might process it and move on with our lives. I've kept all those emails, and some of them run into the thousands of words. So please believe me when I say I've tried like hell to dig my way into Summer's deep, wounded heart and find out what everything meant to her and God help me, after all this time I'm still no closer to knowing a damn thing. I think all she knows how to do now is to nestle deep into her burrow and hibernate. Her emotions are still playing dead.

Chapter 11

On the morning of Thursday, June eleventh, my wife and I woke up at our usual time, six a.m. Ordinarily I'd hop into the shower first, before Summer even made it downstairs for a bowl of Cream of Wheat with our daughter, because I'd have to run off to work. This day was different. This morning, she beat me out of bed, and I heard her pour a hot bath while our clock radio sang to itself. I didn't hear our little girl moving around downstairs, but that was okay; we had time to let her sleep in till she was roused by summer sunlight knifing through her window blinds. I thought about slipping into the bathroom and joining my wife in the tub, but then I realized I wouldn't fit and she'd probably locked the door anyway. Life is so unromantic sometimes.

Instead, I took my phone off the charger and started skimming through emails. Just responding to messages marked "CRITICAL" or "PLEASE RESPOND ASAP" or "HOLY SHIT!" took a full fifteen minutes. With the grand opening a mere day away, my existence had become one long emergency. The inevitable end result, of course, is I was light-years past caring about any of it. We'd flung tens of thousands of dollars into last minute ad buys that targeted L.A., San Diego, and San Francisco. I had four major phone interviews lined up for that afternoon, including one with *Playboy* and another with the *New York Times*. God help me, I thought. What if I get them confused?

I was in a good mood and offered to take my family to IHOP on the way to Summer's sister's place. We ate French toast and pigs in a blanket and somehow our adorable little girl managed to insert whipped cream into her ear. We sang along to the *Frozen* soundtrack, one of her favorites, and she was still in a good mood when we arrived in Manhattan Beach. She loves spending weekends with her aunt and uncle, largely because they let her stay up into the wee hours of the morning playing *Kingdom Hearts III* and *Lego Star Wars: New Republic*. But hey: look at me not criticizing. I guess it's safe to say I'm no one's idea of a model parent at this point myself.

Summer sniffled a little as we got in the SUV but blamed it on smog and overcast.

I put on my seatbelt but didn't start the car. "What's the matter?" she said. "I'm fine, really. I promise."

"I know," I assured her. "I'll miss her, too. That's not—"

"Yeah, but you're not as used to seeing her as I am," she chided.

"Listen," I announced, and sighed deeply. I took a deep breath, then worked my way into a speech I'd been working on for days. "I know. You're right. Okay? I admit that. I haven't been around very much, and I—I can't say I had any way around that, but I wish I'd had more time to spend. After this weekend, a lot of this insanity will fall off my shoulders and onto someone else's. I think for the next few months I can even be home for dinner more often than not."

"Well...that'll be good."

"I know. It's something I miss. You may not know that, but it is."

"I've been worried about you. You've been working yourself into an early grave."

"Hon...I want you to know I didn't mean for things to get this out of control." She nodded slowly. "I think...you wonder if I had to be away all that time, and I did. It's certainly not because I'm upset with you or my life or...Y'know, I'm not out there banging my secretary or anything."

165

"I never imagined you were."

"Good. I want...Look, honey, I've been thinking about this a lot and I feel bad for being away so much. I've put a great deal of strain on you and our marriage and while I do think it'll all be worthwhile in the end, I can see why you thought I was flying off the rails. Most women don't have to put up with schedules like I've had the last few months."

"No, that's probably true."

"I...listen," I said again. "I want you to think of this weekend as a crazy second honeymoon. No holds barred, okay?"

"No holes?" she said, jokily flinching backward against the car door.

"No, I meant...holds...I mean we don't have to worry about how much it costs. The checks have been coming in from the Bliss campaign and we're doing just fine. Let's go and have a ball. No pun intended," I finished hastily.

"Even our first honeymoon was weird," she remembered, grinning. "You spent half the week locked in the bathroom, cursing the *camarónes del diablo.*"

"Yeah, but the first part of the week was pretty good, before I ingested the meanest stomach bug in Cabo San Lucas."

"I knew we were in trouble when you barfed in your hat on the way back from Mandala."

"God, I'd forgotten about that! I loved that hat."

"You sure didn't act like it."

"No, I sure didn't. You've stuck with me through a lot of crazy shit, Summer. You're one in a million. I want you to know that I see that. You're the best friend I ever had, and I still can't get over how lucky I am to have met you." As I spoke, I reached into my jeans pocket, from which I withdrew a box from Zales. She looked at it, looked up at me with huge manga eyes, and reached over to take the box.

166

She popped it open, saw the carbon crystals inside, and said, "Gary, they're beautiful." And they were. I nodded at the two-karat stud earrings and said, "A little something to brighten your eyes for the weekend. You deserve it."

She looked back at me and shook her head, bemused. "Sometimes," she said, "I forget how much I love you."

Looking back, it was all too prophetic.

We drove to San Pedro, Adele purring on the CD player, Summer occasionally reaching up to fondle her new earrings happily. Her mood waned a bit when she saw how much we'd have to pay for parking in addition to the already hefty fare for the Catalina Express ferry to Avalon. (Its Two Harbors leg actually gets you closer to the park, but our hotel was in Avalon.) We bought tickets for the 11:45, then strolled around Harbor Village, licking oversized ice cream cones like teenagers.

The ferry took an hour and fifteen minutes, during which time Summer paged through magazines on her Kindle and I attempted every puzzle in the *L.A. Times*. I looked over at her, admiring her lanky figure and chic sunglasses. I was such a lucky man. To have that woman on my arm—it made no sense why I'd ever need another. And yet, there we were.

"What?" she said, looking up.

I shook my head, smiling. "You'll be the hottest woman there."

"I doubt that," she said, but couldn't hide her grin as she returned her gaze to *Entertainment Weekly*. I'd already seen a mockup of the print edition that week, as its cover featured a painting of Bliss Panerotic. SEX COMES OF AGE, the headline read. Sea gulls screeched and wheeled outside as the overcast finally burned off. It was June in southern California, the world smelled like coffee and sea salt, and all was perfect. I shut my eyes and breathed it in.

The dedicated Panerotic ferry was in dry dock one last day, as its paint finished drying and inspectors gave its three repurposed boats one more hard round of scrutiny. We pulled into Avalon at one, Summer called her sister to make sure our daughter was settling in— she was already three levels deep in a dance game—and we sat for lunch at Café Metropole. How we were still hungry by that point I don't know, but we polished off a gyro and crab salad sandwich in minutes. It was that kind of day.

As we sat in our patio chairs, bloated as Orson Welles in a Paul Masson commercial, Summer rubbed suntan lotion on her neck, arms, and legs. She massaged the lotion under her mid-thigh shorts. Oh, the sight of it, honest to God. "Let me ask you something," she said, oblivious to my prurient interest.

"Sure."

"The Ryders want you there for opening weekend. But do they really want you participating in opening weekend?"

"What do you mean?"

"You don't think they'll look askance at you hopping naked into the hot tub?"

"They just want me to look like I'm having a fabulous time. I don't think they care if I walk around with a pelican on my head. As long as I handle the press junket tomorrow afternoon with some measure of professionalism, I can do whatever I want the whole rest of the weekend."

"Okay," she drawled. "Just seems weird."

"You don't think Barnes & Noble wants you to know a lot about books?"

"Of course they do."

"Well, the Ryders want me to know a lot about gettin' it on."

She sighed. "You do okay."

"Just okay?"

"B-plus."

"I'm gonna tickle you right here in front of everyone."

"Try it," she said, completely unimpressed. "I'll smack the shawarma outta you right here in front of God and everybody."

"I submit," I laughed. "Uncle." We polished off our drinks and walked over to the hotel that served as the staff and employee gateway to Bliss Panerotic. The food and booze had thrown a soothing blanket over my opening jitters, but I was warm with excitement. This was it! At noon the next day, Panerotic would open its metaphorical arms wide to the slavering masses...and their wallets.

When we arrived, the hotel's lobby was overrun with confused first-day Panerotic cast and crew, so its pale, sweaty desk staffers were running around like they were dodging frantic bulls at Pamplona. Judging by the tweaked-out looks on their faces, it seemed clear they believed they were in imminent danger of catching airborne STDs. They were dealing with a motley crowd. It included an overwhelmingly Latina army of housekeeping workers, most of them probably undocumented; a trio of Italian water park consultants, only one of whom spoke English; two dozen members of DJ Buzz Da Ramfunkshus's posse (though not the rapper himself); and there, towering over the assembly in a dirty gray PGA cap, was my buddy Rick Orzabal. "Thunderball!" I yelled, invoking his high-school linebacker nickname.

His head whipped in my direction. "Sushi Boy!" he cried back. We cut our way through the crowd. He seemed positively giddy, his right arm around a petite woman I recognized as his wife, Judy, plus his right around an auburn-haired woman I'd never seen. "This

169

your special lady?" he all but hollered, nodding at Summer.

"Summer Klein, Richard Orzabal. Roland Orzabal, Summer Klein."

"Call me Rick. Damn, amigo, she is one fine piece of ass!" It was like he'd just offered an update from his broker at E.F. Hutton: in an instant, the decibel level in the lobby dropped from buffalo stampede to mid-Thursday airport.

"Rick!" Judy exclaimed, laughing.

"Uh, thanks?" my wife managed.

"Oh, hey, I'm sorry. I forget where I am sometimes. That was me being effing retarded. Which I'm also not s'posed to say these days, 'retarded' I mean, but at least I didn't say '*fucking* retarded.' Jesus, shut me up."

"You have gotta start keeping this guy on a leash," the redhead said. "I know where you can buy one."

"Ah, where are my manners," Rick stammered, "but I guess we've already explored that conundrum. This is my wife, Judy Orzabal-Saga."

"Pleased to meet you," Summer said.

"I've heard wonderful things," I said, shaking Judy's delicate hand.

"Yeah, I shudder to think," she acknowledged, elbowing Rick.

"Nothing but the facts, baby girl, the exceptional facts. And this is Davee Jones, who's here as a writer for the *Dallas Observer*."

"And for fun," Davee said, her eyes glinting. "I mostly write sub-dom erotica. This is like a honeymoon in Vegas for me." She looked around anxiously. "My husband is around here somewhere, prob'ly climbing the walls for a Starbucks." Her voice carried a slight Midwestern twang, as did, surprisingly enough, that of Judy. I found myself openly admiring their figures. The

Panerotic mindset had already kicked in. More ominously, Summer noticed me ogling.

"Forgive my husband's eyeballs," she said. "They have a way of getting ahead of his brain."

"That is true," I said, blushing. "Sorry about that. You're both very...well. I'm gonna um, change the subject now. Anyhow. This is my better half, Summer Klein. Certainly my better-behaved half."

"Not that it's a high bar to leap," she groused. Then Judy got me off the hook by complimenting my wife's new earrings. "A gift from Gary," Summer admitted. "I guess that buys him a certain degree of latitude."

"He buys me a coupla diamonds," Judy drawled, "he can stare at anything he wants."

"Keep those diamonds in the family, Gar'," Rick advised. "It's about to get crazy up in here. Little Miss Judy and I are here to party like it's 1999, my friend. Summer, I've heard a lotta good things. You're a brave woman for comin' out here. This weekend's gonna be epic."

"Is everyone in this place a swinger?" Summer wondered.

"Oh, hell, no," Rick answered. "Most of these people are park staff. They're as vanilla as angel food cake. Ha! They're in for a rude awakening. My wife and I been doin' this for a long time, but we're the exception in this room."

"And you?" Summer asked Davee. "I'm sorry, is that a rude question?"

"Different lifestyle," Davee said. "Padded handcuffs, a little light bondage, that sort of thing. We're here to check out the Hollywood area."

"You'll have to tell me how that is," I said. "I haven't spent much time in that wing of the park. Not really my scene. 'No pain, no pain' and all that."

"Chicken."

"I keep hoping to talk Davee and her lamer half into partying with us," Rick said, hugging her shoulder.

"Nah, you'd break me in half, ya big lug."

"If you didn't break him in half first," Judy said. "I know how you get down, girl."

"This is so—" Summer began, then took a moment to decide whether she wanted to continue. Judy nodded encouragement. "I'm sorry, this is just so unusual for me. People talking to each other so…openly, about…things. Happening. To body parts. And people. I mean, Gary's had months to get used to this. I'm still pushing against my own boundaries."

"You were probably raised super-Christian," Judy said.

"No, not at all. I don't know if we ever set foot in a church, other than weddings and funerals, till I was almost out of high school. Then my sister and I only went out of curiosity. My best friend was Catholic and I wanted to see how it'd feel going to church in that beautiful cathedral. Turns out it didn't do much for me. I just think I inherited a lot of America's taboos, maybe. I can step outside it sometimes, but it's hard until something clicks. Usually it's that third drink kicking in."

"Gary and I were talking about that," Rick said. "You might see some stuff this weekend that's gonna blow your mind. But y'know, it's like gettin' on a roller coaster for the first time, ain't it? I remember standing in that line—I think I was prob'ly twelve or thirteen years old—and I thought you'd have to be crazier'n a shithouse sociopath to get on that thing. My dad had to drag me the whole way. Called me a damn sissy for bein' so nervous. It just seems so dangerous, like there's no way you wouldn't just fly out of the car and go sailing over the amusement park. Then when our car started goin' up that big chain lift, oh, sweet Marie. I thought for sure we was all gonna die. You 'member your first time?" he asked his wife.

172

"Vividly," she said. "It was at Marriott's Great America in San Francisco. I'm pretty sure it's a Six Flags now. Anyhow, looking back, it probably wasn't even that scary a ride. I think it had two whole loops. I was thirteen, though. I was sure I was gonna pee my pants. Then I did, of course. Had to go on a water ride afterward to cover it up."

Rick laughed. "Yeah, but then...y'know, ya go over that first rise and ya go sailin' down...and your limits change. Y'know what I mean? Your world gets more exciting. You realize you can handle the scare of it and get past it to what's awesome. You've been to a couple o' parties, right?"

"Sex parties? Yes."

"You have a good time?"

"I did. Much better than I expected to, honestly."

"Well, there ya go. It's like you're already cruisin' down that first big hill. It only gets better from here."

"I've had orgasms that lasted till I was tired of having them," Judy said, smiling and closing her eyes.

"Okay, but...there, see?" Summer protested. "That's what I'm talking about. I'm not used to talking about my orgasms in a hotel lobby." Judging by the weird reactions of staffers as they passed, they weren't used to overhearing it.

"Think of it as dancing," Judy said. "Sometimes you get dipped, sometimes you don't. But it's always an amazing way to express yourself by using your body in a dialogue with someone else's. Or, you know, maybe lots of someone elses. It's just dancing. It moves you. It makes you feel free. You're unlimited." She laughed. "I guess I'm sounding like some kind of maniacal hippie right now. 'Here, have a brochure.'"

Summer gazed at her for a moment. "You sound happy," she decided.

"I am." She hugged Rick tighter. "We are. We both are."

"Man, you two are in for something unforgettable," Rick repeated, and he was right—because I don't think we were there more than five more minutes before we heard a sudden crash of broken glass. A woman screamed, loudly. The milling crowd around us transformed into a school of panicked fish. They wheeled away from the noise in unison, then lunged toward it when the urge to escape was overcome by the need to rubberneck.

"What the hell is this?" a stocky man I didn't know demanded, lifting a heavy, brick-shaped object high enough for most of us to see over the fray. In fact, the brick-shaped object was a brick, painted black and stamped with a gold cross.

"Oh, my God," someone shouted. No pun intended, I suspect.

"Is that a Bible?" someone else wanted to know.

"It's a brick—" the first guy said angrily, but was interrupted by an enormous burst of thumping and smashing. We really did back away from the front windows then, wondering if we were about to get shot. Hotel clerks vanished behind the desk. Wedges of glass shot through the air, piercing nearby clothes and skin. We were lucky no one was seriously injured. A heavy vehicle—I was told later it was a stolen hotel courtesy van—peeled out of the turnaround and onto the street. All in all, about two dozen bricks were thrown against the hotel walls or through its wide glass windows. The damages ran into the thousands of dollars, and two young women who had the misfortune of standing near the windows were taken to Catalina Island's small medical center. Between them they took about a dozen stitches but were ready for work the next morning. They were in food service, so I doubt they received any insurance from the park's bewildering management

174

structure. We were all freaked out by what happened, and it started the weekend on a discordant note.

In the last few months we'd received bizarre, even threatening messages from the Westboro Baptist wingnuts, so in the chaos of the moment I assumed that lunatic "church" was behind the attack. Come to find out, the guilty parties were a group of teenagers associated with a fundamentalist church near the USC campus. In any case, they used full-sized bricks, each of which weighed about five pounds, and I hope those kids get finger rot from their cheap-as-shit chastity promise rings. Summer was crying, people were dabbing each other's cuts with Kleenex and strips of the morning newspaper, and Rick just kept muttering "you sons o' bitches."

I remember Judy staying calm through the whole event. "I guess I tend to forget how dangerous and mean-spirited so-called *moral* people can be," she said, a sheen of moisture in her eye.

My keenest memory of the event was Rick staring irately at a simple gold cross on a brick that'd just been thrown at innocent people. "You okay?" I asked.

"Yeah," he said, gritting his teeth. "I just got it."

"Got what? The brick?"

"No, I got *it*."

"What do you mean?" I asked.

"They were throwin' the Book at us," he explained. Cultists. Say what you will about 'em, at least they have the same obnoxious sense of humor as the Deity they claim to represent. Maybe that's worth something, but I doubt it.

Adam and Nicole showed up just as the ambulances were leaving and the hotel staff was looking for something to cover the broken windows. The hotel phones were ringing off the hook. I fielded three calls in rapid succession from news agencies who wanted a comment on the attack. I called my contact at GNN and left a statement on her voicemail, then turned my phone off. When I turned it back on two hours later, I had dozens of messages but deleted them all without listening.

We were scared, an adrenaline terror that lasted for hours. Nicole hugged everyone she could and promised to pay more attention to park security. After Adam and I commenced sending everyone off to their staff rooms in the Miami area of the park, he and I and seven or eight high-level staffers convened to discuss how we could do exactly that. The immediate answer, I'm sorry to say, was there wasn't much we could do on short notice. We were opening the park the next day, which limited our options considerably. Had things gone differently, I'm confident the Ryders would've followed through on their pledge to keep the wackos outside. Even our baseline park security probably could've done the job of keeping the college kids and their goddamn bricks out, but this was a wake-up call. We'd been so worried about al Qaeda or ISIS, it was as if we'd never seriously considered the possibility that some Christian fundamentalist wacko would come at us in an attempt to impose the tenets of Old Testament morality.

We weren't the first park to deal with this. In the months after 9/11, Disney Parks spent tens of millions on heightened security. (Of course, we didn't have tens of millions, so we spent what we could.) In late 2001, a team of law enforcement folks converged on a Jacksonville theme park called Adventure Landing to drill terrorism response strategies. Government experts ran simulations to see what would happen if a maniac unleashed smallpox in a well-attended theme park. The results were chilling: thousands of dead tourists, tens of thousands infected. Why are park owners so paranoid? Amusement parks have been the target of insane behavior in the past. They're like whack-a-loon catnip.

In August of 1970, members of the anti-Vietnam-War Youth International Party, or "Yippies," stormed and captured Fort Wilderness on Disneyland's Tom Sawyer Island. They took down the period-appropriate fifteen-star American flag and hoisted a Viet Cong banner in its place. The park had to close early, thirty thousand paying customers were sent packing, and the Yippies turned rowdy. Not coincidentally, it was the twenty-fifth anniversary of the atomic blast over Hiroshima, Japan. Reports differ on whether anyone was injured, but thirty-two people were arrested.

In March of 1981, a guy in his twenties accused another guy of touching his girlfriend. There was intense disagreement about this, which ended when the first guy stabbed the second to death. Nothing exceptional about that scenario, except it happened inside the Magic Kingdom. The assailant ditched the weapon in the moat around Sleeping Beauty's Castle. He later contended his victim lunged into the knife, a claim which apparently didn't fly with the jury so he got eight years to life. It may surprise you to learn Disneyland itself was found negligent to the tune of six hundred grand. What made park managers in any way responsible? They didn't call for paramedics. Rumor has it that for many years Disney had a policy of hustling injured people out of the park in unmarked vans, all so promotional materials for the park could claim no one had ever been declared dead within its gates.

A few hours after the afternoon salvo of bricks, Summer and I recovered sufficiently to hop into a little red golf cart, part of the Panerotic fleet, and drive the three and a half miles to the wrought iron gates of Bliss Panerotic. The cart was tagged with three linked valentine hearts, a trademarked symbol of the park. We'd lifted a branding idea from Disney's Imagineers, who concealed three-lobed mouse-ear icons throughout their resorts, and added hundreds of linked valentines to our own properties. If you were the first to find a trio of "Wild Hearts" in *Realms of Eros*, you earned a free month of play. If you found one in the actual park, well, you kept it to your damn self, because who wanted to admit they both attended the gala opening *and* had nothing better to do than look for valentine graphics?

When Summer first saw the size and scale of the complex around a bend in the road, she said, "Impressive." A minute later, as we drove up to the main gate, she asked, "Should I be wearing protection?" I let security scan my coded wallet card, and the rococo gates swung wide.

"You folks have a wonderful time," the guard said, oblivious to the fact that nothing exciting would happen till the following morning.

It is true, however, that we were hit with a sugar-cookie blast of warm vanilla air within seconds. Again, this was something we stole from the folks at Walt Disney's Theme Parks division, which uses ye olde malt shoppe on Main Street U.S.A. to pump the smell of ice cream and waffle cones into grateful consumer nostrils. Now, it may seem counterintuitive to use a scent so inexorably associated with baked goods, which would seem to remind one of Grandma's kitchen. It was a calculated risk. We didn't want the park to reek of danger and skank from the get-go, we wanted it to smell *nice*. You know: friendly. We were hoping to convey feelings of safety and cleanliness, affection and comfort. "Hey, smell that!" Summer exclaimed, relaxing visibly. But it wasn't the sole reason we chose vanilla. It turns out both men and women find dessert smells far more arousing than perfume or cologne. (Besides, we had a feeling our most enthusiastic visitors would bring in plenty of those muskier smells on their own.) Elsewhere in the park, we set up kiosks to bake and sell little shareable banana-nut-bread loaves, which have an odor that's highly provocative to women's senses. We also took advantage of our southern California locale to justify a number of freshly-squeezed orange juice stands—not just because the markup on orange juice is nothing short of a mugging, but also because the bright, clean aroma of citrus is go-go juice for feminine arousal.

Summer leaned into my shoulder. "This is beautiful, Gary. You people have done something amazing here. I can't say I expected it, but it's true."

One of the first things she saw was the gorgeous Art Deco façade of Sinema Theater rising thirty feet into the blue evening sky, tapering slightly along the way to look taller still. (Nearly every theme park design these days uses forced perspective to exaggerate dimensions. Guess where they got that idea, folks? Yep, Uncle Walt's Imagineers.) This wasn't your weird uncle's porno theater, reeking of squalor and bodily fluids. No, this was a place you'd pay top dollar to see the summer's most rabidly anticipated Marvel popcorn movie, except that wasn't the standard bill of fare here. The movie playing that opening weekend was called *Erotic Getaway*, and starred Heidi Licious, Alan Granite, Stephanie Lix, Morgan Velvet, and *AVN* "Up-and-Cummer" Allison Brady. The one-sheet poster advertising the "film" was professionally done and quite the equal of anything you're likely to see outside your local cineplex. If you didn't know better, you'd swear you were looking at the poster for a breezy Judd Apatow comedy. That was intentional. Again, the idea was to treat sex as if it were just another mainstream treat, like a day in the Magic Kingdom or a milkshake from 31 Flavors.

I'm not ashamed to say I've watched *Erotic Getaway* several times now, though I'm sorrier to say I've always watched it alone. It deserves to be seen.

179

Half a dozen mainstream critics reviewed it as if it were a mainstream film, so it has a score on RottenTomatoes.com. (At time of writing it's at 57%, but hey, what do you want? That's not too shabby for porn.) I think it's fair to say the script, or let's call it a scenario, includes three or four genuinely funny bits of dialogue. The plot, such as it isn't, revolves around three young couples who meet for, you guessed it, an erotic getaway at a cabin near a postcard-perfect California lake. Had there been an *Erotic Getaway II*, it would've taken our randy protagonists and four of their looser-pantied friends to Bliss Panerotic. Sadly, however, the *EG* franchise was tainted by events soon to follow, so the storyline ended pretty much exactly as you expect. I've never had the pleasure of meeting Ms. Lix, but I can tell you the scent of pine in the air makes her especially fun to be around.

I'd seen Heidi Licious a time or two before on the Internet. No, I wasn't watching her work for the cinematography or witty banter. I was watching because it's fun to watch porn clips for free on the Internet, and porn starring Heidi Licious is especially engaging. I mention this specifically because she was booked as a guest of honor, if that's the right word, opening weekend. I won't lie; I was looking forward to meeting her.

A gentle sea breeze ruffled Summer's hair as we parked outside the theater and walked around. I knew from experience that the tickle of an afternoon breeze could focus into chilling shoves on cool nights, despite the angled vector of the Strip. We were planning to use portable foliage as windbreaks and deploy dozens of outdoor heaters. It wouldn't do to have people's clothes flying off for the wrong reasons, not even outside a glorified porn theater or strip bar.

The area opposite the Sinema offered a variety of female-friendly snack stands, handmade jewelry purveyors, and adult shopping emporia. Summer and I had spent a few hours in "grown-up" stores over the years, including the bizarre Hollywood staple called Hustler Coffee. (You walk in and it looks like a chrome-ier version of Starbucks. Turn a corner, and it's butt plugs as far as the eye can see. I mean huge, lethal, rubber contraptions that look like traffic cones. Try not to fart; it'd sound like Louie Armstrong playing the megaphone. If overpriced lattes make you gassy, Hustler Coffee may not be the place for you. But I digress.) We usually walked out buying nothing more than a couple of cheap tubes of lube. Eros 4Ever was different. It made shopping for sex toys feel like a trip to IKEA, minus the Swedish meatballs, of course.

I sure do love Swedish meatballs.

Anyway, the store was closed till the next day, but it was full of attractive young men and women stocking shelves and giggling over ludicrous items in Panerotic's pansexual inventory. There was a chocolatier right there in the store, plus comfortable places to sit and enjoy a snack or confer with Eros 4Ever's uninhibited, knowledgeable sales clerks. One woman, surely no older than twenty, saw my wife wryly hoisting a vibrator with the heft and high-tech intricacy of a lightsaber and extolled its virtues as if it could revitalize the industry of enhanced masturbation, you'll pardon the expression, singlehandedly. "Besides," she chirped, "you'll never have to worry about it getting lost in there."

"In there? Please! I couldn't lose this thing in a hoarder's garage," Summer yelped. "What does it do, your taxes? Do I have to learn JavaScript to use it?"

"No," the saleswoman laughed, winking, then added, "Just Braille."

"Are you telling me you've actually used this— no, don't tell me. It's none of my business. I don't want to know."

"Sure you do," the sales clerk said. "My name is Amber, and yes, I have used this. Several times, in fact.

Well! Not this particular one! But this model. You get it."

"I never get it like *this*," my wife said, and glanced at my non-vibrating crotch.

"Hey!" I protested.

"Honey, please," Summer said. "No woman gets it like this from any man. Unless you have three speeds and a self-deploying kickstand, you've got nothing on this apparatus, I promise."

"This thing got a female equivalent?" I asked our sales clerk, Amber. "Or do the sex toys just get it on with each other like Greek gods in the break room? 'Cause I'd totally watch that. I mean, it'd beat that battle robot TV show all to hell."

"Do you play *Realms of Eros*?" Amber asked.

"Uh, well, I'm familiar with the concept," I said, blushing a bit myself now.

"Oh, don't be nervous. I play it myself, all the time." *Please don't be somebody I know from the game, please don't be somebody I know...* "I was just thinking there are input-output devices you might enjoy, too, y'know? A lot of our tech-savvy male customers swear by them. They're basically cock sleeves, but with all types of sensors and massagers built in. Some of them are pretty rad. Even lubricants, but you have to be careful 'cause you don't want that stuff getting inside the electronics. But yeah, they say it's like fucking the sweetest, tightest pussy in the world."

"Oh...wow," I said, my vocabulary reduced to two syllables.

"You just said that," Summer said, blushing toward infrared. "Right here. Right out loud."

"Oh, I'm sorry," Amber said, looking confused. "I wasn't trying to offend you. I just think it's crazy we can't talk about vaginas like the amazing gift from the goddess they are. I'm a hundred percent bisexual myself. Do you enjoy women?"

"I'm…uh…wrapping my head around that," Summer managed.

"Either one of you got a birthday coming up? This vibe'd make an amazing gift."

As it happened, Summer's birthday was less than a month away, but I was already planning to buy her flowers and dinner at Providence. Boring, I know. "Anniversary," I said instead.

"Oh, how many years?"

"Coming up on nineteen," Summer said, "unless I leave him for RoboCock here."

Amber burst into delighted laughter. "I love that! RoboCock. Wow. Nineteen years. Man, you two must be doin' something right. What's your secret?"

"Total honesty," I couldn't believe I heard myself saying.

"A spirit of adventure," Summer decided, then looked around. "Apparently."

Amber showed us around the rest of the establishment, which felt more like a high-end department store than even the best suburban vibe-and-porn shop. Once she got over her blushing fit, I believe even Summer was duly impressed. It really did attempt to mainstream the experience of buying stuff to make your sex life better, a concept which, when you think about it, seems long overdue.

Amber excused herself to go stock the lingerie section, which featured Panerotic's signature line, FunMentionables: "Party wear for today's uninhibited woman." Summer was pleased to see the featured model was Apple Angel, a Midwestern pinup "girl" who was not only pushing forty but also an unapologetic size 14. (Her actual-human-sized waist was offset considerably by a staggering duo of 42Fs.) "There," Summer said, "now, see? Why can't more lingerie models look like that? We don't all want to look like Pixie Stix." For a second I thought she was

183

referring to a porn star, then realized she meant the cylinders of kiddie-cocaine candy.

I decided it was wisest not to comment on Summer's near-absolute lack of resemblance to Apple Angel—she's both thinner and, shall we say, sleeker around the thorax—nodding instead at the wisdom of Eros 4Ever's laudable gender politics. Mostly I wondered if Angel took the gig for a lifetime supply of free, burlesque-ready underwear. Bras, especially in her size—those can't be cheap.

We paused in front of a glossy poster featuring Ms. Angel in the kind of outfit *Playboy* centerfold models save for special occasions, like Vegas show openings and job interviews with Hef. "What would you do if I came strutting in one night wearing something like that?" Summer asked.

I looked at her. "Is this a trick question?"

"Come on, don't be like that." I wasn't sure how I was being. "Would you just attack me right there?" Aha, so this was getting her imagination in gear. Nothing bad or unpromising about that!

"I think you'd probably make it as far as the nearest flat surface," I mused. "Hopefully it'd be something padded. And sturdy."

"Now we're talking," she said, beaming. "Correct answer, babe."

"And what about that?" I said, pointing at a nearby display of banana hammocks with cute cartoon elephant heads that wrapped around a man's—

"Yeah, not my favorite," she laughed. "But hey, you want to try that firefighter's costume on, I'm game to get rescued."

"Sheesh," I said, glaring at the price tag. "It'd be cheaper to burn our actual house down. Is the fire truck included?"

We returned to the Strip. Two doors down was the swanky exterior of Luxe, Panerotic's version of

184

your friendly neighborhood topless bar. It may seem strange to devote floor space to a strip club now that the Internet is a delivery system for on-demand nudity, but this version took advantage of the nationwide craze for what folks call "new burlesque." The Ryders paid generous consultation fees to an L.A. troupe called the Velvet Hammer in a quest for a strip bar that women could enjoy just as much as their straight, male, significant others. No one was in the club tonight, but it was obvious that an attempt had been made to evoke the classic Hollywood nightclubs of the '30s and '40s. There was even a marbled band shell for a sextet of real instrument players in tuxedos. I heard rumors Lady Gaga'd reserved one or more VIP booths for Luxe's extra-special opening weekend production, *Badass Belles*, but those turned out to be unfounded. To the best of my knowledge, she was never in the park, though I wouldn't be surprised if she were approached by the Ryders with special intensity.

One of the bartenders noticed my staff cart and took time out from washing glasses to ask if my "better half" and I would like a drink on the house. We declined, as I was eager to show Summer the rest of the resort.

Who gets a chance like that? I mean, honestly? How many people get to stroll through a theme park devoid of paying customers, on their own, going wherever they want, with no one interested in shooing them away? Imagine driving your flux-capacitor-equipped DeLorean to Saturday, July 16, 1955, the night before Disney's six-thousand-guest, invitation-only preview gala. Imagine you had the park to yourself that hot summer night—except you wouldn't, even then, because the Golden Horseshoe Saloon was open for a corporate sponsors' dinner. Three nights before that, Disney and his wife enjoyed a full performance of the Golden Horseshoe Revue to celebrate their thirtieth wedding anniversary. People don't get to wander free in empty theme parks, especially not humble brand management directors. After everything that happened, I still look back on that quiet and, dare I say it, romantic night with a great deal of affection. It was a lot more fun and exciting than even the most non-food-poisoned nights of our honeymoon.

We finished browsing the Strip right about the time the sun disappeared behind the horizon. Within minutes, the crisp white light of a waning crescent moon lit the plaza. The breeze remained calm and sensuously warm. Behind us was a Gothic alley that led into the S&M dungeon areas. To our left was the pastel Floridian façade of the gay quarter; the insistent bray of Cuban horns drifted over the stucco wall. Directly ahead of us was a clean, sandy path to the renamed Ryder Lagoon. Permanent cabanas held hot tubs built for two, three, or twenty. An Olympic size pool was filled but covered, its lifeguard towers unmanned.

Can you believe the Ryders trucked in extra sand? It seems strange for California, I know, but it had the dual effect of both widening and whitening the beach. This made for better tanning and cleaner views to the blue-water cove. It was no Waikiki, but again: we had it to ourselves. "Care to go for a swim?" I said, untucking my shirt.

"Are you serious?" Summer asked, grinning.

"Why not? By this time tomorrow, this beach is gonna be full of bare-ass people of all sizes, ages and descriptions flapping their way to the water for a skinny dip and God knows what else. Right now it's just us. When are we gonna have an opportunity like this again?"

"You're out of your mind," she said, but didn't automatically dismiss it.

I know I've told you my wife is beautiful, but I don't think I've told you (or her) as often as I should. My wife is as lovely to me now as the day I slipped a ring on her finger at a Dodgers game in 1996. I'd be lying if I said she hasn't aged a day, but she sure hasn't aged decades. I tell you all this now because as my wife smiled at me, tucking her shoulder-length hair back behind her ear for the hundredth time that hour, wondering if she should throw caution to the wind along with her undies, I felt so enraptured by her I could drop to my unworthy knees in the sand. What was I doing looking for anyone else in a goddamn video game, or even in this ludicrous park? That's what I was asking myself just then. I remember it like it was yesterday.

After a few seconds of deliberation, Summer took off her blouse and strode toward the water, her freshly browned skin (she'd been hitting the tanning salon in nervous anticipation) goose-bumping around a lacy black bra I'd never seen before. I watched her stroll away, her long legs so mesmerizing, shoes kicking up fantails of sand. I let my eyes linger over her still-shapely ass, then followed the line of her back up to her thin neck. Ah, so lovely. She looked back over her shoulder, feigning more shyness than she obviously felt. "You gonna join me or what?"

I said, "Maybe I got a better idea."

"Oh, yeah? What's that?"

"Well, I just realized that water out there is probably colder than it looks."

"Oh. I hadn't thought of that. The hot tubs aren't on, though."

"I know. They're filling 'em tomorrow morning. That's not what I was planning."

"Okay, well, talk to me, cowboy."

"I was gonna show you around the rides and stuff, but maybe it'd be more fun to wait till they're full of happy tourists."

"Happy or horny?"

"Probably both. And I doubt either of us are hungry, even if I could find a restaurant with anyone available to serve us."

"I couldn't eat another bite," Summer said.

"Hm. Well...then maybe I'd better just use this pass to one of the high-roller suites in Sanasana."

"Ooh!" Summer breathed, lighting up. "Luxury accommodations? I could get behind that!"

"I could get behind you."

She jerked back in surprise at that, then stepped into my still-clad chest. "I could handle that, too." She laughed, shook her head, and looked straight into my eyes. (We're within two inches of the same height. She's tall, I'm not.) "You should probably kiss me right now."

"I should?"

"Yeah."

"Right now, you say?"

"Right *now*." So I did.

Sanasana was a vast complex almost a mile long and bracketed to wrap around the circular lagoon. It was themed to resemble the finest tropical resort hotels, though it also held a casino, the water park, four restaurants, a boudoir photographer, and plenty we never got around to seeing. Much of its ground floor was the park's themed casino, so we bought a bottle of champagne at the nearest casino bar and took that up seven floors to our suite. If it wasn't the best place to stay in the park, it was second only to the Ryders' personal suite and office around the corner. It was designed by the same company that handled the Vdara in Vegas, so it had the same tactile, clean appearance as the rooms in that all-suite hotel.

Summer was gobsmacked. "This is the most beautiful room I've ever seen in my life!" she gasped. "It's like they plucked it out of my dreams. Is that an edgeless pool?" It was, looking out over the bay from a broad white balcony. "Where is the bathroom? I gotta see this. The toilet must be made out of diamonds or something."

I followed her in. "Nope, just porcelain. I think it has Japanese controls, though. It'll probably sing you an aria if you ask it nicely."

"I might. Oh, my God, this freakin' shower! Look at this! You could host a full-sized wedding reception in here!"

"I would go to that reception."

"I'll bet you would! Holy crap, Gary, I can't get over this. And they really don't mind if we stay here?"

"Not tonight," I said, "but just for tonight. Tomorrow I'd have to drop four grand a night on it just like anybody else. Well...anybody who has four thousand a night. But yeah, the Ryders know how hard I've been working."

"So do I, love. I thought this day would never come, and you'd just drop dead of exhaustion out here on the island before I ever saw you again."

"Oh, it hasn't been that bad, has it?"

"Gary...it has. And you are going to give me the night of my life tonight, because it has been *horrible*. We haven't seen you. Your daughter's all but forgotten what you look like."

"Yeah, I know," I sighed, "That's probably true. But hey...how 'bout this shower?" It really was something. Imagine a stone grotto with padded seats. Now add a gleaming apparatus to simulate driving rain throughout, then another to bathe you horizontally, then another that felt like gentle mist. I'd pay cash money just to sit in any of those showers, let alone all three or the rest of the room. Within minutes we were naked and wet and going over each other every way we knew how. She climaxed so loudly and unreservedly that I lost all control of my body. It was like *Clan of the Cave Bear* in there. I was out of my mind with lust for my own wife, and Jesus, it felt good.

Which is not to say we didn't spend plenty of time in that bed. I'm not sure what the damn thing was stuffed with—cherub carcasses? Amazon tits? The point is, not only did we have three hours of Olympic-caliber married sex on it, we slept like Jesus owed us a favor. Just before that, a little after two in the morning, Summer and I stood naked on the balcony, looking down from our celestial nest onto a wonderland of carnal delights. If this was satanic temptation, it worked. I had, once and for all, officially crossed over to the Dark Side. And good riddance to virtue!

Most likely, you've never had an experience quite like that. Think back on your wedding reception, gazing down from your table at family and friends who felt more like your loyal subjects. Now amp that up by a factor of ten to the holy fuckbutter. We felt like superheroes.

In 2012, a study at the University of Canterbury in New Zealand found that while religion and kids do make people happier, they're bested by alcohol (aka "partying") and, most of all, sex. Now, maybe that's just how they roll in Middle-earth, but I don't think so. I think it's bigger than endorphins, too. It's about feeling wanted. What could possibly feel better than that? Last week a Starbucks clerk with the bumps of two nipple rings poking out her uniform flirted with me, and it wasn't just the requisite smiley face to talk me into buying their overpriced biscotti, either. No, she was doing her best to make it clear she found me attractive. I went from zero to I-could-die-now in no seconds flat. Then, of course, she saw my debit card and realized who I was. She looked up and got as far as, "Hey, aren't you that guy who—" before I cut her off.

"Never mind," I said. "And hold the biscotti."

Even housekeeping left us alone, so we didn't drag our superhero asses out of bed till almost ten a.m. Then I spent half an hour watching GNN's pre-coverage of the opening from the roiling nirvana of a perfectly calibrated Jacuzzi. Summer called for room service, and though they weren't up to speed yet, she did sweet-talk them into sending up a box of French pastry. I didn't bother getting out of the tub, and it turned me on no end to see my wife answering the door in her laciest underwear. The delivery guy's eyes nearly vacated his skull. You'd better get used to that, I thought. You're gonna see a hell of a lot more once this job kicks into gear.

My wife ate half a Danish in a gulp, then slipped into my lap. "You're blocking the TV," I said into her high, tan-lined breasts. They smelled of sandalwood and chlorine.

"Is that all you can think of right now?" she sighed.

"No," I admitted, "but I probably need to get downstairs, and if you keep this up, that's never gonna happen."

"Do you love me?" she asked.

"All the time," I replied.

"Then why don't you turn off that TV and wear me out," she purred.

Okay, so maybe I did have her one more time before we got dressed. It was that kind of morning.

Part Three: Penetration

Chapter 12

As Summer and I rode down in what amounted to our own private elevator, we held each other close and shared little secret honeymoon smiles. I'd deliberately left my phone off all night, but when we arrived in the lobby I turned it on to find it all but exploding with frantic messages. I flicked through as fast as I could. Most were from Adam, wondering a.) did we like the room, b.) did we…you know…*like* the room, and c.) why the hell wasn't I downstairs for the six a.m. press event? I thought, *What six a.m. press event?* I didn't sweat it too much, though, because as it turned out, the Ryders were so busy they'd forgotten to inform me or, indeed, several angry reporters of the event until five in the morning.

I kissed Summer, who wandered off in search of breakfast, then headed over to the main gate. I heard the thunder of uncontrolled humanity and slipped outside into a forest of suits and tight skirts. Adam was there, beside himself, standing uncomfortably on a makeshift platform surrounded by hundreds of reporters, bloggers, *Daily Show* correspondents, and other talking heads. I worked my way through the jostling, telegenic crowd to shout in his ear. "You been up all night?"

"Haven't you?" he shot back. "Don't lie to me, pal, I've been in that suite. Now what do we do with all this?"

I wracked my brain. "Make 'em interview each other? Nice suit," I added, stalling.

"Thanks! I had it tailored," he yelled. "Makes my dick look enormous."

In spite of myself, I looked down. He was right. How do they do that? Unimportant. "Here's a thought," I announced, then turned to the crowd. Instantly a constellation of cameras and camera phones swung in my direction. "Ladies and gentlemen," I hollered, "mostly gentlemen. Heh. I see a few ladies out there. Hi. My name is Gary Klein, and I'm the brand management director for Bliss Panerotic. You uh...I know you all have a lot of questions, and I wish we could give you an advance tour of the park, but the fact is we just don't have time now. If you look over there, you'll see the first electric buses starting to arrive from Avalon. We're expecting about twelve thousand overjoyed guests today. The park is completely sold out."

"Yeah!" Adam yelled, pumping his fist into the air. I was lying, by the way. We were at eighty percent capacity. Not too shabby, though, for a Friday, when it's harder to lock down a babysitter for the kids.

"As you can see, we have our hands full. It's amazing to watch how L.A. and, in fact, the rest of the country is responding to our innovative theme park. We look forward to giving them a big, amazing wet dream of a weekend they'll remember for the rest of their lives." Yes, I really did say that. I was tired. "So, in the interest of saving time, I wonder if you'd all just help me out with something. By a show of hands, how many of you are here to make fun of us?"

This induced a startled beat, followed by a chuckling wave of self-conscious uncertainty. "No, seriously, it's okay," I encouraged, "you can tell the truth. How many of you are here just to crack a few jokes at our expense?" The *Daily Show* folks shot their hands up; in fact, they looked happy to do so. Some others, including two or three name-brand reporters I recognized, slowly raised their hands as well. "Okay," I said. "That's fine. I don't mind that. Sex is funny. I know. I've seen it. But let me try a couple of other quick questions. How many of you here, by show of hands—how many of you have ever been rock stars?"

No hands went up.

"No one? Really? By show of hands, have any of you ever had a personal encounter with Jesus?"

The reporters laughed, but their hands all stayed parked at their sides.

"Well, that's bizarre. So how many of you have been truly, deeply in love? I mean, valentine hearts in a cloud, romantic comedy, 'you're my soulmate forever' kinda love?" About a quarter raised their hands sheepishly. "Ah, that's better. Good for you."

"Where's he going with this?" I heard Adam mutter to his chief of operations.

"Now," I said, arriving at my point with a smile. "How many of you, and don't be embarrassed, now— how many of you have ever had mind-blowing sex?"

The vast majority of the crowd thrust their hands into the air like they were pointing at Superman. People chortled and nodded at each other nervously. It took a while for their laughter and self-congratulatory jubilation to die down.

"Well, there ya go," I said. "That's a great American dream that is actually attainable. You can have terrific sex. Ain't nobody gonna come along and declare you a rock star, and you're prob'ly never gonna be president, but you can have a great time with another human being in bed. Or a Jacuzzi. Or a Burger King bathroom, I suppose. I heard that once in a song." Reporters my age or older laughed and reminisced about Digital Underground. We bonded.

"At Bliss Panerotic, we are here today," I said, "to celebrate gettin' busy. And you can crack jokes, make fun all day long, but the fact is, about once a year you get terrific eyeball mileage out of some court story that fascinates us only because it's about sex. You run ads—I know, I've planned some of them—that feature the beauty of people's bodies and the association of lust with the happiness of buying and enjoying a product. That's not some kind of closely-guarded secret. The joy of sex is one of the greatest, most attainable joys of life.

You can call it a gift from God, or the goddess, or evolution's way of saying you might want to try and reproduce here. It doesn't matter. The point is we're tired of acting like sex is something to be ashamed of. We love sex. We," and I indicated Adam, who gazed at me as if he'd never met me before, "love sex. So do you. So do your significant others. They love sex with you. And this is all about making that happen." Hands shot up. "Yes!" I crowed, forestalling any argument. "And in new and exciting ways. This isn't the nineteenth century, folks. We don't have to pretend we only know the missionary position with all the lights off and a hole in the sheet."

That was when I spotted Nicole Ryder calmly stepping around the side of a generator that had been set up last night to help the media cover the opening. It would be insufficient to say merely that she looked fantastic. The truth is she looked like a million boners. Slit skirt up to here, cleavage down to there, and solid use of fabric in between. How she made that look professional I'll never know. She looked like Satan's realtor. Cameras shot in her direction as if her torso held a giant electromagnet. "Good morning, gentlemen," she purred, accepting their adoration with the casual assuredness of a born monarch. "Ladies. You all feeling sexy today?"

"Woo!" someone yelled.

I took this opportunity to lean over to Adam again. "You want to say something?"

"I don't think so," he said. "You're doing fine on your own."

I nodded. I had an even better idea. "Nicole Ryder, ladies and gentlemen. Ms. Ryder, would you care to come over and say a few words?" She considered this, nodded, and strode through the crowd like she was on her way to ascend a Cape Canaveral launch tower. I nudged Adam, who reached over just in time to behave like a proper gentleman by extending his hand and helping her onto the platform.

I realized I was staring at Nicole's tits and hoped the cameras hadn't noticed. Luckily, they were all trained on her.

"Good morning," she said again. "Well. This is quite a turnout. I don't have much to say, except...Y'know, I was raised Mormon." I admit, I hadn't known that. "It's true. I was LDS until I was, oh, eighteen or nineteen. I grew past it, no offense to anyone who's still a member. But the fact is I was raised to learn exactly how and when to say no. I just never learned how to say yes. I had to learn how to say yes to what *I* wanted, not what other people—let's be honest, mostly men—wanted me to do. And that's a difficult thing for young women. We're never told we can think about what *we* want, only what's expected of us. I don't know, maybe men go through that, too. But unlike men, I didn't know what my body wanted or how to go about finding it for myself. I had to learn. I was lucky. I never went through the problems many young women go through while learning how to satisfy their own sexuality. I never got pregnant. I wasn't date-raped. I was lucky enough to come of age at a time when if I wanted to learn about sex, there were safe, relatively informative ways of doing so. But the last thing I learned, and maybe I'm still learning, was how to enjoy myself rather than always devoting myself to giving joy. And that's what this park is all about for me. It's about taking ownership—of my body, my sexual desires, my sexual life. Of sharing happiness with my husband, but also being honest about what gets me off in this world. And that is powerful. It's not empowerment, it's the presumption of power. The *taking* of power. It's me owning my power. And this place is going to change women's lives. I mean that, truly. A lot of very talented people worked on this park, and it belongs to them, too. But as for me and my

198

contribution, this is my gift to every young woman who comes of age after me. It's my way of saying, this is your body. You own it. It belongs to you. And you can find your own pleasure however you want. " The crowd of cynics had gone reverently silent. She looked out over the crowd. "Some of you don't understand this," she said. "But you will. It'll happen. The world is changing. This is our time now. Women's time. And whatever you may think of Bliss Panerotic, this park was made primarily for them."

Bit by bit, person by person, all the women in the crowd started hooting and clapping. Only then, as men realized they were coming off as closed-minded assholes, did they see the benefit of nodding, applauding, and shrugging away an opportunity to ask humiliating questions.

So you tell me: was there anything shameful or funny about what Nicole said?

By eleven a throng of visitors had assembled in a noisy but celebratory mass outside the wall, and buses and other transports were still cruising into our bland-looking, four-level parking structure. Dozens of ticket takers and other park personnel massed just inside the gates to deal with the onslaught. Not to put too fine a point on it, they were hot. I don't mean baking in the sun kind of hot; it wasn't terribly warm. I mean *hot*. We never officially discriminated with regard to looks, of course, but come on. First impressions do count. The attendants were mostly young California women, aged 18 to 25, incredibly beautiful and given to flirting. Did guests stand a chance of hooking up with them? I doubt it, but wouldn't be surprised either way. Let's just say the hiring software was unopposed to seeing strip bars or Hooters on those applicants' résumés.

We'd been able to get most of the casino up and running, along with all but two of the restaurants, in time for opening fanfare. Most of our ticket sales were prepaid online, so we already knew this would be a staggeringly successful day for us. A few last-minute visitors clustered around the ticket kiosks some distance away. A lot of our guests were ready for cosplay; I spotted a Sailor Moon, an Edward Cullen, a Bettie Page, and two Klingons in movie-quality regalia among their forward ranks. I heard the digital snaps as guests took camera phone pictures of each other and the gate. I've since spent long afternoons looking through those photos, from *Time* to the tabloids to Facebook memes, and I've realized our main gate looked like nothing so much as the entrance to Willy Wonka's chocolate factory in the original, 1971 movie version. I suppose there were worse associations we could've made than a candy-coated paradise for kids run by a serial-killer-slash-probable-pedophile, but not much. I'm surprised I didn't notice the resemblance at the time.

Summer found me in the crowd, and we split a twelve-dollar turkey sandwich that should've cost six. Theme parks, right? You're paying for the ambience, not just the deli meat. We were both starving after our night of hardcore exercise, but a proper lunch could wait. The real insanity was about to begin.

Just inside the gate, artfully staggered to allow unimpeded pedestrian traffic, was a forest of video screens under red protective canopies. The screens showed the kind of not-quite-pornographic images familiar to admirers of my TV ad campaigns. Bodies slid against and around other perfect bodies: a hip, a graceful shoulder, a meticulously man-scaped six-pack, full lips parting away from a wet tongue, strong hands tugging auburn tresses. Lusty voices sang opera. Delibes's "Flower Duet" from *Lakmé* trailed off into the hiss of a summer thunderstorm before the audio faded entirely. If you listened closely, the last sound you might've heard was a woman uninhibitedly enjoying herself—or was that your imagination playing tricks on you? (Hint: it was not.) The mob sensed the big moment was at hand, and the plaza fell utterly silent. After a brief pause, a smoky contralto purred from PA speakers.

"Welcome," the voice said, oozing lust and self-delight, "to Bliss Panerotic, the wonderland your body's been craving. But first, we want to ask: are you ready to get...sexy?" The packed crowd went absolutely bonkers. "All right, then. Are you sure you can handle this?" Again with the mayhem. "Then get ready to have your mind...blown." A cheap joke, I grant you, but everyone laughed. "The park will be opening in just a few minutes. We ask that you please enter the park in an orderly fashion. Remember, there's plenty of excitement and pleasure to go round, and we'll be open all...night...long." That wasn't strictly true, of course. Most attractions would close by eleven; but, as in Vegas, the casinos, bars, and hotels would run twenty-four/seven. The hot tubs remained open (and busily occupied) till at least three a.m.

For the record, that silky contralto, which we used in a number of commercials, belonged to actress Paulette Holman, a former soap ingénue who now specializes in books on CD. I looked her up on Facebook a few months ago, and she surprised me by accepting my friend request. Of course, she also made me promise to tell you who she is. Apparently any résumé credit helps if you're an actor trying to break out of the pack in L.A., even if that credit is a cheesy pre-opening gate announcement for Bliss Panerotic. And honestly, who am I to judge?

"As you go through one of our main security gate scanners, a park attendant will process your ticket," Holman's sex voice continued. "Remember, if you've paid for a certain number of days but remain in the park longer than that agreed-upon term, your card will automatically be charged for the additional time. Each Panerotic day officially begins at noon, so each one-day pass is worth exactly twenty-four hours. You should also have been issued a personal scan Tag bracelet, which displays your relationship status and other vital information. If so, please make sure you're wearing that bracelet now. If not, a new one may be issued at any time for a nominal fee. Just check in with the Security Center inside the Sinema theater complex. Every visitor, even masked guests, must display the bracelet prominently at all times. That includes in the pools or hot tubs. Don't worry, the bracelet and scan pin are fully waterproof. You may remove the bracelet once inside your room, but do keep it close, to be ready should any safety concerns arise." In other words, in case you go bughouse and a large, aggressive man with a buzz cut has to kick down your door to keep you from murdering your date for the evening. These are things we had to worry about.

"As always here at Bliss Panerotic, no means no and yes means...yes, please!" Holman continued, her voice all but fizzing into steam. "Now. We hope you're ready, 'cause it's time to get this party started. Are you excited?" The crowd went nuts again. "Hey, how 'bout you, sexy ladies—are you ready to get...wild?" Our female guests hit that unified "woo" chord programmed into them sometime around junior high. A musical fanfare rose to a crescendo. "Then it's time to get...it...on! So please, come inside us...right...*now!*" And with that, the mechanized gates of Bliss Panerotic spread wide.

I honestly don't know if I've felt such a lightning blast of excitement and, dare I say, pride since the morning my beautiful daughter was born. That's the truth. Of course, I worry as I write that, because I know someday—hopefully decades from now, when she's married and has kids and moral choices of her own—she'll read this and be justifiably appalled by the comparison, but in that moment it felt as if I'd sired another baby. *I did this*, I thought, for moments allowing myself the ego-gasm that comes from ignoring every other person's contribution to any major accomplishment. *This park is my baby*, I thought. And yes, I know that sounds ludicrous now, but my desires were woven into its design. It had elements of my personality, because I was there from the beginning. Hundreds of us came together in an orgy of art, social change, and technology that lasted years before culminating in this joyous climax. My DNA was in Bliss Panerotic; and, as I watched the flood of guests stream inside, I couldn't wait to show off everything we'd made.

Summer leaned in to murmur into my ear. "The world just changed," she said. "You guys changed it."

I turned to look at her. "You think so?"

She shrugged, then leaned in again. "This would never have been okay before. You made it okay. Sex is fun, and you made it acceptable for people to say so in public."

I smiled, intensely pleased with myself. I mean, sure, public admiration for carnality predated Bliss Panerotic, but who was I to argue with Summer's perspective on history? That'd be obnoxious.

Believe it or not, there were rules in Panerotic. You couldn't just bang someone against the wall outside Sinema—but believe me, people tried. Park security officers roamed the grounds, beefy hands clutching high-tech Taser batons. These officers' uniforms were carefully designed to look so inherently intimidating that people wouldn't confuse them for the "stripper cops" they might see in Luxe. In fact, our park security guys looked more like SWAT officers, which some may have been in former lives, and none were shorter than six-two. There were no firearms allowed in Panerotic, even on our guys, but our guys were total badasses without them. If you were a visitor who decided to get pushy, that lasted about five seconds before some hulk of a dude in a crisp khaki uniform came and not-so-gently escorted you to a holding tank belowground. Once you were there, you stayed till Security got tired of looking at your dumb ass, at which point you were firmly escorted to the parking lot, never to return. We had a similarly restrictive policy about drugs. If we found them on you, even if you swore they weren't yours or had a medical card or claimed they were part of your religion, you promptly received a one-way ticket out of the park. Weekend over, permanently.

Having said that, park guests could wear whatever the hell they wanted, including nothing at all, so long as their bracelet was readily visible. Summer and I wore blue and gold VIP bracelets. She was dressed for a Catalina summer in sun dress and faux-designer shades; I wore a blue two-piece suit from Men's Wearhouse and a smile I'd had whitened the week before.

I spent the next three hours doing one interview after another, blah blah empowerment, blah blah sexual freedom, blah blah contraceptives. The faces were starting to run together, but I know I talked to a guy from *Playboy* and a woman from E! Entertainment. I distinctly remember the woman from E! kept trying to slip a fifty-dollar bill into my hand so I'd feed her an exclusive interview with DJ Buzz da Ramfunkshus. "Jesus Christ," I told her, "fifty bucks doesn't even buy you his Twitter handle. How long have you been in this business?" I left her stammering and turned to the next judgmental face. I kept the fifty, of course.

It probably wouldn't hurt our reputation to have a few celebrities hanging around, but the reverse was untrue so those celebrities slipped quietly through the VIP entrance south of Zone 2. I can't tell you the name of every well-known person who graced the utility corridor beneath Hollywood that weekend, but some are a matter of public record. Buzz was there, of course, along with three or four of his Gat House posse. Heidi

Licious, Nina Hartley, Cody Rockets, and other name-brand porn performers signed autographs outside the Sinema, where they were treated like mainstream movie stars by hordes of adoring fans. By all accounts including his own blog, Mr. Rockets added something on the order of two dozen notches to his belt that weekend, including one as he waited in line for an iced latte. How he managed that even in Bliss Panerotic I'll never know, but well played, sir. Good to the last drop, indeed.

We sold tickets to professional athletes from the NFL, NBA, NL West, and WWE, though I can't say for sure how many of these gentlemen actually attended. I know for a fact we played host to a former judge from one of those TV singing shows, though she spent all her time in Luxe and dropped thousands of dollars on bottles of Cristal she never drank.

A celebrity chef raised eyebrows in Sanasana when she and a well-endowed guest made so much noise they could be heard down the hall. (Keep in mind, that was one noisy hall by nine o'clock.) TMZ claimed to possess a recording taken from outside the chef's hotel door but never posted it. Should you ask, I'd declare myself highly suspicious. I do, however, have it on excellent authority that one popular TV comedian received hummers from three different women during a 4:15 screening of *Erotic Getaway*. Apparently his fans were driven to a starfucking frenzy after two of the picture's leads re-enacted their big scene in real time in front of the screen, a la *Rocky Horror Picture Show*. Perhaps I've mentioned our singularly generous policy on public displays of affection? Now, heaven knows, anything goes.

By six p.m. my work for the day was effectively done. I checked my phone and waded through forty more messages, including congratulations from Victoria Sinclair and a death wish from a Southern-drawled gentleman named "Tommy Ray." How he got my number is beyond me, but he promised to shove a fist up my ass till I came. I'm assuming that was meant as a threat, though he announced it with considerable glee.

I phoned Summer, who, it turns out, had spent the last hour moving our stuff to a different hotel room. The high-roller suites were all booked by paying customers that night, so we were downgraded to ordinary prole status. (Third floor: hardware, personal items, ladies' lingerie.) "I'm finished here," I said, "and exhausted. You hungry?"

"Starving," she said. "Where do you want to go?"

"How 'bout sushi?"

She thought about it, then said, "Nah, I need something substantial. I've been looking through the visitors' guide in the room, and I'm kind of intrigued by one of the restaurants in Sanasana."

"Oh, yeah? Which one?" Like I didn't know.

"You heard of this place called Sensurround?"

"I had a feeling that'd be the one you'd pick."

"It's kinda pricey, but..."

"Tell you what, I'll put it on my tab. I can pay 'em back next month in radio spots."

"That might take you a while," she admitted. "This is like Spago meets Cirque du Soleil."

"I know the place you're talking about. We tried to get the L.A. Times food critic to review it, but she wouldn't take us seriously. It's dinner theatre, right, except everyone gets naked?"

"I don't know about that, but the commercial on the park information channel says it 'brings new meaning to sexy desserts.'"

"I know how you love those."

"Who doesn't love a good sexy dessert?"

"What's the dress code at this place?" I asked.

"Same as anywhere else in the park," she replied. "It's whatever you want."

"Not so, my dear, not so. The sushi place demands suit and tie, knee-length dresses, and formal behavior. The chef told me if he sees anyone going at it on a table he's closing up for good."

"Well...sure. Hygiene. I see his point. But no, we can wear whatever to this Sensurround place. It's funky. I was hoping you'd stay in that suit, actually. It gets me kinda excited."

"Does it now? I like how you're getting into the swing of this place."

"No pun intended."

I chuckled. "That's actually true. I did not intend a pun. But yeah, it's nice to see you...I don't know..."

"Throwing caution to the wind?"

"Yeah. We could use a good stress break."

"I feel safe here," she said, "and that helps. Plus, oh my God, did you throw down like a Jedi master last night or what?"

"I have to say, I felt pretty good about my level of performance."

"That time you went down on me at the foot of the bed..."

"That amazing bed."

"That amazing bed!" she agreed, laughing. "I should've written down the brand name. My God, that mattress was a gift from baby Jesus."

"How's the bed in our new room?"

"More like ours at home," she sighed. "Not that it's ever stopped us before."

"Care for an afternoon delight before dinner?"

"No, I'm starving. Now get your ass over here and pick me up for dinner before I waste away to nothing."

As I've said, the quality of theme park restaurant food has skyrocketed over the last few decades. We've become a foodie nation. Theme park designers started touting the quality of their culinary offerings and the critical praise heaped thereon. Bliss Panerotic boasted several laudable restaurants. By far the best were Katana—the sushi restaurant helmed by Chef Hayasaka—and Sensurround, our dinner theater. A team of designers and circus directors from Prague put it together in a mad rush over the last five weeks of park construction. In terms of décor, it was meant to evoke the Moulin Rouge, but even an architectural imbecile like me could tell it took stylistic liberties with the period. The menu was rooted in Escoffier's classic French cuisine, but he would've been floored by the desserts.

We were shown to our tables by a woman who looked like the nineteen-year-old offspring of Jennifer Lawrence and Wonder Woman. Our servers, guys who almost made the cut at the floor show in Zone 3 Miami, resembled seminude superheroes. I don't know if I've seen such a dense population of über-hotties anywhere else, and I've been to Skybar. Then the food arrived: *tartare de bœuf*, goat cheese with herbs and floral honey, a zingy *niçoise* salad with yellowfin tuna. There were moments when I neglected to breathe. In fact, believe it or not, there were moments when I couldn't pay attention to the live entertainment, hypnotic though it was. The first act, a curvaceous opera singer in a gown that looked as if it'd been sewn out of silk, lace, and optimism, regaled us with "Mon Cœur S'ouvre à Ta Voix" from Saint-Saëns's *Samson et Delila*. (Don't be too impressed. I had to look it up on my phone, earning disdainful looks from the snobs at the next table over.) "My heart opens to your voice," the diva sang, her voice husky with insistent emotion, "like the flowers open to the kisses of the dawn." A voluptuous tear slid down my wife's cheek. "Ah, respond to my tenderness! Fill me with ecstasy!" I got a little choked up, too, but that was mostly because of the fragrant dish of *escargots à la Bourguignonne* that had just arrived.

It's a credit to how wonderful those savory devils smelled that my wife ate snails for the first time in her life, declaring them "not even gross."

The mezzo-soprano gave way to a pair of dancers, who prowled around the room in a slithering Argentine tango. Summer loves all those celebrity dance shows, so this was right up her alley. She fired optical come-ons at the male dancer over the top of a glass of Willamette Valley Pinot Noir the size of a softball. With every sip, her breathing slowed, and her hand climbed higher up my leg between bites.

If you've ever witnessed *Zumanity* in Vegas, you know there's a fine line between sexy and tacky. I felt Panerotic's show remained on the highfalutin side of eroticism most of the time. I particularly admired its restraint in costuming. Rather than send each performer out nude, the producers cast people with world-class bodies and looks, and then clad them in second-skin outfits you wanted to run your fingertips—hell, your face—over. But even that bit of modesty fell by the wayside when the aerialists took the stage. Clad in thongs and hair ribbons, a pair of lithe dancers, one skinny and Asian, the other curvy and black, slid around and through each other twenty feet in the air. Had they fallen, they probably would've escaped with a broken limb or two, but it wasn't the danger that made the act sexy. It was the exertion. Those women were working up there, laser-focused on each other, sweaty, gasping, animal, primal. My wife's fingers brushed against the tent stake of my erection just in time to find it achieving the solidity of an iron bar. She gasped, her eyes meeting mine sidelong over her almost-empty goblet of wine.

I nearly fainted with lust. My mind was flooded with a vision of taking her there on the table, her ass knocking snails and beef tartare aside as I swept up her sundress and plunged myself into her feminine well. The image hit me like a drug trip, wild and

209

overwhelming. My vision of the outside world swam. I thought for a moment I'd been roofied; but no, I was merely feeling sensual need at its highest, wracked with it, on shimmering fire with it. I turned away and drained my scotch and soda.

We went straight from small-plate appetizers "suitable for sharing" to a lovely gratin of Gruyère and fennel served with perfect roast beef. Meanwhile, a Joan Jett and the Blackhearts cover band stalked out for "Crimson and Clover." People were dancing in the aisles, and there was quite a lot of kissing and caressing. "Glad you're feelin' all sweet on each other now," the lead singer said, peeling her T-shirt off, "'cause here come the desserts." She launched into a sweaty, lust-soaked cover, stripped to the waist, of "Stay" by Shakespear's Sister; meanwhile, impeccable slices of gateau arrived. Dancers tumbled around and over each other on stage. The alcohol hit me in another hot rush, and I leaned over and commenced making out with my better half like a teenager in daddy's car on prom night. I'm not sure when or even if the check arrived; they may have simply charged it to my card. All I know is, the bill came to just under five hundred bucks, and the evening was worth every penny.

When Summer and I left the restaurant a few minutes after nine, we were changed human beings. We were flushed, excited, younger, full of butter and pepper and round Oregon wine, our tongues soaked in honey and black cherry juice, our fingers laced, our hearts in overdrive. The string of Summer's dress hung down her arm, her shoulder tanned and excruciatingly lovely. My wife. I slid my hand around her waist and buried my lips in her neck. Her breath hastened. "I'm so turned on right now," she breathed, heedless of passersby. "I just want to take you back to the room and destroy you."

"This place," I said, "it's like we've been showered in pheromones. My God, what's that perfume you're wearing? It's making me insane."

"I don't know," she said. "A woman in the bathroom sprayed it on me at Sensurround. It's probably illegal."

"It should be," I said. "Jesus, Mary, and Joseph. Listen, before we go back to the room, and trust me, we are going back to the room, I want to check out the beach."

"Oooh," my wife replied. "I like where that's going. Let's be bad tonight, honey. I need it." Her wish was my demand.

We walked past an artificial arroyo full of grotto-like pools, where men and women tangled in a haze of pastel-lit mist. Laughter filled the air, along with a few grunts and moans. The arroyos were designed so casual passersby couldn't see under overhanging rock ledges, but it was easy to imagine what was transpiring there. The reference to Hefner's notorious grotto was intentional, though I daresay ours were larger. Nearby vanilla atomizers labored to compete with the reek of chlorine, ultimately failing. I won't say those pools would win any sanitary prizes, but at least whatever microorganisms went into them died upon contact. "Human stew," my wife sighed, shrugging.

A lot of work goes into making theme parks even prettier at night than they are in the sun, and that was doubly true for our up-all-night variety of resort. The dance club, Inferno, led the eye toward the faux-Tahitian expanse of Sanasana on our right, palm trees rustling in the breeze. Over a ten-foot-high wall to our left, disco lights pulsed against the Cuban façade of La Playa. Maybe this is my outdated prejudice talking, but if the straight areas of Bliss Panerotic were out of control, imagine the mayhem in Zone 3. The mind

211

balks. In any case, there were a few female-female couples strolling the beach, hand in hand, and I don't remember anyone complaining. Most of us were too damn busy with our own pursuits to care.

Swimsuits were encouraged here in the pools and hot tubs closest to the casinos' main entries. Farther out around the circular bowl of the lagoon, all bets were off. Either way, there was plenty of skin on display in the moonlight; and while our patrons weren't as nubile and lithe as the models in our promotional materials, at least they seemed happy. The moon shimmered against gentle waves lapping in from the Pacific. Electric campfires flickered, smoke-free. A few brave souls ventured, sans swimwear, into the ocean but found it too chilly for comfort. Better to join fellow nudity enthusiasts in the Jacuzzis and mingle as befitted the carefree milieu. Imagine Eden. Now add gambling and Wi-Fi.

Of course, this is not to say everything went perfectly that first day or night. No, far from it. One burly guest barfed up $220 worth of sushi in the nude pool just west of La Playa, inspiring another inebriated patron to sock him quite emphatically in the mouth. A couple had athletic sex on one of our golf carts, doing permanent structural damage to it if not to themselves. A hacker in San Rafael managed to, pardon the expression, penetrate our park security and swap our guests' posted sexual orientations for twelve and a half minutes, resulting in considerable confusion and embarrassment. A fight broke out after someone lost ten thousand dollars on a single poker hand in Sanasana, culminating in the permanent eviction of four paying guests. The health department left message after message, demanding to know what the hell we were planning to do about our incomplete inspection process. That lasted till Nicole got on the phone and pointedly, vividly reminded them they had no actual jurisdiction over Panerotic property anyway. While that was legally

212

true, it left us open to charges of running an STD wildlife preserve. I heard rumors of airborne HPV in the pool mist, which is absolute nonsense. For the most part, claims of rampant venereal disease were unfounded, though I doubt anyone in our delectable restaurants took his or her chances on the five-second rule. All in all, I'd say we maintained at least as high a standard of cleanliness and safety as your average cruise ship, though I concede that sets the bar low.

If you were there, though, you remember what it was like. Whatever may have befallen us over the next thirty hours, that first, idyllic night was nirvana for most of us. I'd like to think it foretold a world in which sex, even sex between two or more unmarried adults, is completely legitimized, set free from its shameful reputation. I looked around and saw couples, and a fair number of triads, being kind to each other. The Ryders' dream had been achieved: we'd stepped outside the bonds of puritanical judgment, treating love and sex and friendship, no matter how new, as intermingled. It was paradise regained, and it worked. For the most part, that first night, it worked.

"Look at this," Summer said, gazing out at the beach. "It's like summer camp all over again, a high school make-out party."

"We never got invited to those," I pointed out.

"That's because we were already together. There was no point in hooking us up."

"Still," I said, "no one likes to feel left out. Come on. Let's go crash this party. You game?"

"Surprisingly, yes," she replied.

I should tell you that to use the phrase "hot tub," or to misapply the brand name Jacuzzi, for what they had at Bliss Panerotic is misleading. Those are just the terms we all used. To be more accurate, the hot tubs were grottos unto themselves, heated to a perfect hundred and four degrees Fahrenheit, lightly roiling, surrounded by music speakers and aroma dispensers. That first night, the scent was juicy orange. While that wasn't as much of an aphrodisiac as the engineers intended, it did keep everyone awake and alert as they spent multiple hours in the soothing hot water. It also did a great job of cutting through the welcome chlorination. The speakers played '90s slow-jam R&B: Toni Braxton, Janet Jackson, Mariah Carey. Summer sang along under her breath, slightly but consistently off-key.

There were lockers for stowing our clothes, coded to our ID bracelets. (Locker rentals were assessed by the hour, of course, and the fee was automatically deducted from our credit cards.) You could certainly buy a swimsuit of almost any conceivable level of modesty at Eros 4Ever, but few visitors did. Instead, we just stripped down to our undies or, before long and nearly to a person, our Friday flesh tones. I saw bodies of every size, ethnicity, and weight class. Two attractive young women helped a gnarled young man—I'm not sure what his disorder was, but it was significant—out of a wheelchair and into the tub, where he promptly used his hands to bring one of them to a shuddering orgasm. She laughed delightedly at the attention of dozens of spectators, happy to perform.

There were padded areas half-submerged in the water. You can imagine what those were for. But you didn't have to imagine long; they were in near constant use by nine o'clock.

The tubs twisted around corners, under rock overhangs and warm waterfalls. It was gorgeous. As we walked farther away from the Strip, much like the floor plan in Ted and Alice's super-swingin' party pad, the tubs got progressively more uninhibited and orgiastic. We moved through two or three in a row, settling on a tub large enough for a dozen people in which soft swap was the order of the game. In other words, it was look, maybe even touch, but dance with only the person what brung ya. That was fine by me and Summer. She sat in my lap, her right hand lazily tugging at my lap as I teased her firm nipples at the waterline. As we played, we half-watched two handsome (if middle-aged) men caress a young blonde woman we could barely see through the tangle. One of them slid what may have been the entire blade of his hand into her, and she gasped and bit into his shoulder.

"Touch me," my wife said. I reached for her center, but my arms weren't long enough. Instead she turned and kissed me, scissoring my upper leg and working herself into a panting fever. "I'm gonna do you now," she announced heatedly in my ear, then did so, easing her body down onto me in full view of the other trio. At some point an African-American couple slid into the tub near us, and the woman leaned on the edge of the pool so her companion could lap at her with abandon.

"You motherfucker," the black woman said. "Yeah. You get that wet pussy."

Is this turning you on? Are you blushing in a coffee shop somewhere, hoping no one notices what's on your e-reader? 'Cause it sure as hell did it for me. Having sex in public here with these people was like haute cuisine after years of McDonald's. Not that I'm opposed to an eight-piece McNuggets, mind you, but there's eating and then there's *dining*. I felt like an absolute sexual god, and I'm pretty sure the feeling was shared by everyone in sight. We were all the stars of our own *Erotic Getaway* sequel.

In fact—"Hey, I know her," I muttered, as the blonde woman in front of us turned to take one of her companions unabashedly into her mouth.

"Who, her?" my wife whispered, nodding toward the blonde.

"Yeah," I murmured into Summer's ear, "we saw her on that movie poster on our way in. That's Heidi Licious."

"Hiding what?" she started to ask, in entirely too audible a volume.

I made a shush face, then nibbled at Summer's left breast. She gasped and clutched my hair. "You're amazing," I told her a few moments later. "But that"—I leaned close again—"is Heidi Licious, the porn star who's in that flick they're showing out front."

"Oh, that—at the Sinema, right? What was it called?"

Erotic Getaway."

"Right. Have I seen that before?"

"Not with me," I answered, then wondered if she'd seen it without me. No fair!

"I want you to fuck me while she watches," Summer said, and I was stunned yet again to find this was the woman I married, the woman who makes mediocre casseroles for her family while drinking cheap-ass Australian Shiraz, the woman who likes shopping for hand-knitted scarves on Etsy. It was like meeting her alter ego, the Amazing Sex-Woman, for the first time—and I could not get enough of it. This was my *wife*. I was married to a heretofore unknown Aphrodite.

At some point in the middle of giddily ravishing Summer missionary style, an activity slowed by the water in this soft, padded area, I suddenly became aware that a hand which wasn't mine was rubbing Summer's clitoris. My wife had her head thrown back, half-swooning from the heat, enjoying the ride, so I noticed this rather personal intrusion before she did. I looked up the length of a thin, tan arm to find Heidi Licious, her slightly fanglike teeth visible through a wicked grin, enthusiastically pleasuring my wife as I pounded away. This scenario was more than I could take, and I came like someone had poked me in the prostate.

(Was I wearing a condom? No. I confess I was not. I was deep inside my very own wife at the time, but yes, praise be to chlorination all the same.)

"Oh, he likes that," Heidi growled, and my wife looked up suddenly. "He likes it when I help."

"You," Summer said.

"Relax, honey," the porn star said. "Let a master get this done. I know exactly what I'm doing." After a few reluctant moments, Summer lay back, overwhelmed. Her body rolled through a slow, subtle orgasm, which she came down from in a sighing exhalation.

We lay there numbly for several minutes, drained, dehydrated, muzzily spent.

It turns out porn star Heidi Licious, contrary to any reasonable expectation, had elected not to have actual, penetrative sex in the hot tub that night, confining her activities to public foreplay instead. (Even the most gifted professionals need a break, after all.) Instead, she curled up in the arm of one of the middle-aged gentlemen who'd accompanied her, a thin bearded man with graying hair and a Navy-style eagle tattoo on his chest. The other fellow wandered off to parts and pursuits more lascivious. The black couple drifted into a pool farther into the warren of hot tubs.

"I guess I should probably say I know who you are," I told Heidi, addressing her quietly.

"Oh, yeah?" she said, tapping the side of the tub restlessly. "Jesus, man, I wish I could smoke here. Fuck." As with everywhere else in California, 'smoking here' was relegated to out-of-the-way exile areas far from the pools.

"You're Heidi Licious. We saw your movie poster coming into the park."

"Yeah, that's me. You seen that movie yet? Have you watched me get fucked?"

"No, we uh, no, not yet," I said, taken aback.

"Eh, doesn't matter," she laughed. "Does it, Mike." She patted her companion on the leg. He chuckled, barely paying attention, half asleep.

I leaned against Summer, drowsy myself. "This is Summer. My wife."

"Hi there, Summer. I liked making you come."

"I uh," Summer said, "yeah. I. You know I. Liked. That. As well. Thanks."

"What's your name, cowboy?" Heidi asked, nodding her slightly cleft chin at me.

"Gary Kl—um…Gary. Sorry. Still getting used to the…you know, the vibe here."

"Yeah, it's different, that's for sure. Even for me." She hooked a thumb at her partner. "This is Mike. He's my suitcase pimp."

"Your what?" I managed.

"My suitcase pimp." She looked at Mike. "They don't know what a suitcase pimp is. Course they don't. Why would they?" Mike just smiled, his eyes closed. "I do porn, okay? You know that. Well, Mike here's my boyfriend, so he gets to lug around all my makeup and shit when I go on the set or do photos or whatever. Plus I gotta fly around all over the fuckin' place doin' strip shows."

"I didn't realize you did that, too."

"Oh, yeah. We all do that. It's killer fuckin' money, y'know? Hard work, though. Enh. Pays the bills. Dunnit, Mike?" Mike's lethargic smile never wavered.

"Do you," Summer began, then tried another conversational gambit. "Is that fun, that line of work?"

"Line of work!" Heidi snorted. "Listen to her! 'Line of work.' Like I'm a fuckin', I don't know, like, notary public or somethin'. Yeah, I guess it's all right. You meet a lot of cool motherfuckers. I get paid to

218

come, y'know? Ya can't beat that with a hammer. I get to fuck all these hot guys and sexy-ass bitches and this loser here gets to watch me. Don't you, Mike?" No change in facial expression from Mike.

"Are you okay with that?" Summer asked him.

Mike still didn't answer; just kept right on smiling. "Mike likes all of it, man," Heidi said. "He likes the money. He likes the pussy. He likes fuckin' parties, and drugs...It's all good. He gets to fuck anybody he wants—that's our thing. I mean, what the fuck am I gonna say about it? We have fun, me and Mike. You guys come here like this is fuckin', you know, Disneyland, right? But we live like this, or sorta like this, all the time. Not this nice, maybe, but you know what I mean. All bets are off, man, fuckin'...you want that shit, you go fuckin' out there and get it. That's our whole thing."

"Don't you worry about, I don't know," Summer started to ask.

"Crotch rot?" Heidi laughed.

"Yeah. I mean...no, I...yes, I mean...Yes. You gotta be careful."

Heidi shrugged. "You don't know, man, we use condoms, like, most of the time. Except on movie shoots, of course. And here. Some parties. Okay, so maybe not *most* of the time. But we do get tested, like, *all* the time. Every month. A lot of people don't know that, but it's true. Here in California? I gotta go in every thirty days for a blood test. That's just, like, life in the porn biz. I make this guy go at least every couple of months. Plus I'm fixed. He's got a vasectomy. We're good, man. No little rugrats here. You're safe with us."

"I work for the park," I said. "Did Adam invite you?"

"Adam who?"

"Adam Ryder."

"Oh!" she laughed. "That motherfucker! The guy who signed my fuckin' check!"

"Yeah. They paid you to come here?"

"Nah, they paid my way in. Plus he paid me a shitload for that *Erotic Getaway* thing. He found out I did some, like, theatre in high school and just about shat a kitten. He couldn't make out that contract fast enough, man! Says he wants real actors in his movies, like I'm Meryl Streep or some shit. Tried to claim I went to college. Now I gotta tell everybody I majored in nursing. Holy shit, I hope nobody ever has a fuckin' heart attack in front'a me, I'd prolly lose my shit. Anyways, I just live up the road, in fuckin' Pedro. Mike wanted to come to this place so I said sure. We were s'posed to have, like, a big red carpet thing for the movie, but I guess that fell through. It's pretty good, though. The movie? A lot better than my usual fuck flick, I gotta tell ya. Kinda funny, I thought. You should see it."

"I will," I said. "*We* will." Summer looked at me and shrugged.

"You two crack me up," Heidi said. "'Specially you. Little Miss Suzy Homemaker." She regarded Summer cagily. "You ever thought about doin' porn, honey? You could totally be the hot MILF. Teach the young girl the ways of the Force and shit."

Summer replied carefully, not wanting to offend. "I uh...I'm not sure I'd be any good at that line of—I mean, doing what you do. For a living."

Heidi elbowed Mike. "She fuckin' kills me. She's tryin' to be all mannerly and shit. 'And what do *you* do for a living?' Ha! Like it's a fuckin' tea party. Gimme a break, man. Everybody fucks. And everybody *gets* fucked. Some of us just get paid a shitload of money to do it. This guy probably doesn't pay you shit, am I right? It's like '*unh*, blow my load and go make me a sandwich.' Am I right?"

"Hey, now," I objected.

"Nah, he's all right," Summer said, nuzzling me. "He's good-lookin', plus he knows what he's doing in the sack."

"And what do you do?" Heidi asked. "'For a living,' I mean."

"Oh, I work part-time at a bookstore."

"Oh, okay, and like—is that supposed to pay the fuckin' bills? In L.A.? Come on. You two live around here?"

"Yeah," I said.

"Prolly got a nice house, right, two-car garage, HBO, all that shit?"

"We do," Summer acknowledged.

"Okay, so lemme get this straight. You pay for all that stuff workin' part-time at a bookstore? I mean, wow. Are the books made out of, like, gold or fuckin' diamonds and shit?" Heidi asked, laughing.

"No," Summer said. "Gary makes enough for both of us. He works in advertising."

"Oh, okay," Heidi chuckled. "Advertising. I get it. So he makes the money. And you get to fuck! Am I right? You get them titties all up in his face and you're like, I'm gonna fuck his fuckin' ass off! Is that right?"

Summer stammered helplessly. "What are you—no! We've been married for almost nineteen years. This is just a getaway for us."

"Oh, okay. Great," Heidi said. "I know how it is, girl. You got tired of fuckin' this guy around two years into the shit, but damn, it's good to be married and have a nice house and fuckin'…kids…You got kids?"

"I don't want to talk about—" Summer started.

"Those little fuckers ain't cheap! My sister's got three of 'em, man, each one cuter than fuck, but those little bastards go through money like, whoa, holy shit! She fuckin' hasn't had a vacation in, like, ten years! But her husband only works for, like, some roofing company. And she still has to fuck him every night and pretend like she wants to. I know how it is."

"You're being awfully personal," Summer groused. "I mean, I know that sounds funny given where we are, but—"

"'Given where we are,'" Heidi quoted. "I just watched your husband play bury the baloney in your hooha, my friend."

"I don't think you understand," Summer said, blushing.

"Oh, I understand, trust me. I seen things you wouldn't fuckin' believe. I started modeling straight outta high school, a'right? I mean I hadn't even graduated yet before I was shovin' my way in front of a camera. But I couldn't get on with any of the big agencies in town, so then I started modeling wherever I could. Art modeling, that kinda shit. College boys tryin' to hide their hard-ons while they drew me naked. It was cool. I did okay with some of that. Then some guy recruits me, like, shootin' bra shots for underwear companies that weren't Vicky C's, if you know what I mean. But it paid pretty good. I got nice tits, man, what can I say. It's the fuckin' truth. Thirty-six C's, all-natural, perky as fuck. So next thing you know I'm making thousands of dollars, and my face is startin' to get out there. So I made sure it wound up, like, close to fuckin' trays of cocaine, right? That's just how I rolled back then. Party, party. And I shouldn't have to worry about money these days, I did so fuckin' good—but five minutes later, it seems like, my fuckin' phone is ringin' off the hook 'cause I keep forgettin' to pay all my bills. Then it suddenly dawns on me that I *can't* pay the bills, on account o' I ain't got any money. After all that, I'm flat fuckin' broke. So of course things went south. I been on billboards, man, and I've slept under 'em, that's the truth. I seen every fuckin' thing."

"So how did you wind up in porn?" I asked.

"Oh, you know, some guy at one of my old contacts knew a guy who knew a guy in the business. It was eight hunnert bucks for a couple hours' work, man. I owed two months back on my rent. So it was either that or start hooking, and who needs that shit. But it turns out I liked it. Seriously. It's fun to get this much attention, man. The money's good, I get to travel. People see me at conventions and lose their fuckin' minds. So I'll say it again: everybody fucks, and everybody gets fucked. I just like to get paid for it, that's all, man, personally. You do it however you want, though. It's all good, sister. It's all good."

"I'm not judging you, honestly," Summer said.

"We're not in any position to," I agreed. "I helped market this park. I've probably written you a check for something myself, somewhere along the line. So I'm part of this life same as you are."

"Well...it ain't quite the same, is it?" Heidi laughed.

"No, I suppose not."

"That's the thing: I just keep fuckin', and the money keeps comin'. It's crazy. Ain't that right," she said, nudging Mike, who gave every indication of sleeping where he sat. His smile, however, was fully intact. Apparently, life had been good to ol' Mike.

"Do you make enough money to save?" Summer asked.

"I do when I quit nozzlin' up coke," Heidi said. "But fuck, I fuckin' love that shit, man! Goddamn, it's hard to say no sometimes. But yeah, I'm tryin' to be a good girl. Relatively speakin'." She nodded her chin at Summer. "You ever do any drugs? A little coke, a little weed? Take the edge off? Fuckin' put it back on?"

"No. I smoked pot once in college," Summer said.

"Oh, well, look who's in the Bad Girls' Club," Heidi sneered.

"Leave her alone," I said. "We've got a kid now. It's different."

"I guess, but it doesn't sound like you two were ever in trouble. So you don't smoke, either?"

"Not in months. You gotta set a good example when you're a parent."

"Like comin' here?" Heidi said, spreading her arms.

"You make a good point," I admitted. "Except I don't feel guilty. Not for this. I'm just here to have fun with my wife. Besides, our daughter's in good hands. She's got a great mom." I hugged Summer's shoulders; she smiled a bit automatically.

"Yeah, I'm just messin' with ya, man. Mike and I fuck everything, like we're gonna criticize your shit and whatnot. Rock on, my brother. That's what I say. Rock the mother-fuck *on*." Then she leaned back, relaxing in the roiling heat and orange-scented steam.

A short time later it soaked through my consciousness that I needed a restroom. "You're gonna leave me here?" Summer complained. "I could get molested at any minute."

"By her," I joked, indicating Heidi, who was tucked into the crook of Mike's arm and apparently dead to the world. "I got the feeling you didn't mind that."

"What're you talking about?"

"When she was feeling you up. You took it in stride."

"Oh, so you're jealous now, is that it?"

"No, not at all. You want to get a handy from a world-renowned porn star, you go right ahead. Not Mike, though. He looks too happy. Guys like that are probably up to something."

"He is. He's a suitcase pimp, weren't you listening?"

"I gotta pee," I said. "That's all I know." *Funny,* I thought. *Even in an adult theme park, I still use the grade-school euphemism* pee. Some things never change. We carry around the brains of our much younger selves, tucked within a porous outer shell composed of all the things we flatter ourselves to believe we've learned and internalized since then.

"When you find the bathroom, come back and let me know where it is," Summer said, closing her eyes and leaning back. "I'll be up to my eyeballs by then."

"Classy," I laughed. "That's the stuff."

I girded my loins in a towel and heaved out of the tub, then carefully navigated a thin concrete strip around the pool to find my way out of the faux-stone grotto. That took some time; it was misty and I was disoriented from the heat. I looked around for a public restroom, finally locating one about fifty yards away. Without a park map, it was hard to find such amenities, and I realized the architects had done a poor job of marking them. I made a mental note to bring this up to Adam next time I saw him, as it wouldn't do to have guests give up and simply pee in the pools. It'd happen, though. Folks are disgusting that way—careless with their bodily fluids, you might say.

At least Panerotic's restrooms were clean. Happily, no one was using them for sex, as there were plenty of far more inviting places to do so in the immediate vicinity. I washed my hands all the same. Cleanliness, they say, is next to godliness, and I knew exactly where my hands had been the last two hours.

I was leaving the restroom when I passed her going into the ladies' room. It was Cathy. I'd never seen her in person before, not even on Skype or other video applications, but I knew instantly and completely it was her. I stopped cold in my tracks, then took another step, my body debating between flight or play dead.

She was fully dressed and seemed completely unsurprised to see me vacillating in a towel at Bliss Panerotic. "Wait here," she said. "I'll be out in a minute. I gotta whiz like a Russian racehorse." And then, having delivered that biological report, she proceeded into the restroom, humming lightly.

I considered bolting for the safety of the tubs. What the hell, right? I had no idea she'd be there at Panerotic. That's the God's honest truth. I may have hinted she should come, but I didn't think she'd really do it. Now here she was, Cathy I-Won't-Say-Her-Last-Name, aka Ms. Pris the Valkyrie sex avatar, here in real life—or at least as close to that as a sexual theme park could get.

I don't know why I stayed. For the life of me, I honestly don't. I suppose I was, as they say, caught up in the moment, a melodramatic rapture victim. I was in the middle of a crazy story and wanted to see how it'd end.

I was standing in the exact same spot when she exited the restroom. "I wonder where that expression came from," she mused. "The Russian racehorse, I mean. Some czar must've owned a racehorse who really liked to urinate. Just did it everywhere. I wonder about that sometimes, y'know? Expressions. Like, 'there's more'n one way to skin a cat!' I mean—okay, but honestly, like, how many ways do you need? How many cats do you plan to skin in your life, y'know what I mean?"

"What're you doing here?" I blurted, skipping rudely past her preliminary banter.

"I had to pee," she said.

"No, I mean, at Bl—"

"I know what you meant. I was kidding. I came to meet you."

"Meet me here? Now?"

"Where else? You'd rather I showed up at your high school reunion? 'Hey, how's it goin', I'm Cathy, care to dance the hokey-pokey?'"

"I didn't—I had no idea you were coming."

"I know. And believe it or not, I didn't come here *just* for you. I'm a separated woman, remember? I thought I better drop this red-hot vajayjay on something before I change my mind and go back to his worthless ass. Can't have that. Turns out I was right. This place is outrageous. A girl could get banged here like a duck at a shooting gallery if she weren't careful. You know they have theme park rides devoted to fucking? That's insane. These people are goddamn committed. Oh, but I guess you're one of 'em, aren't you? Randy bastard. You look good in a towel, by the way. Am I babbling? I feel like I'm running at the mouth. I might be kinda nervous."

"You came out here to see me? Why didn't you just look me up on *Realms of Eros*?"

"We've done that, remember? We've been down that road. Besides, I thought it'd be fun, y'know? It's like that guy jumping out of the supply closet. You remember that joke? 'Supplies!' You heard that one? I love that joke. Okay, so I really do feel like I'm babbling now. It's verbal diarrhea. Sorry about that."

"I'm sorry, I'm just—I really am trying to process this. You know I'm married, right? It's not like anything crazy can happen."

"No, I know. Except—I kinda got the impression you and she were swingers, right? Like, ring-a-ding-ding?"

"'Ring-a-ding-ding?' Who the hell says that? Are you for real?"

"Hey," she said, miffed. "I think Sinatra said that. Not a bad role model, ya ask me. That motherfucker got things done. Of course I'm real. I got feelings, y'know."

227

"No, I—you're right. I'm sorry. It's…Cathy. Look. My wife and I are not swingers. I mean—I don't think we are. Not really. We've tried it a couple of times. Sometimes we liked it, sometimes we didn't, so I don't know if that's who we are or just something we played around with. But either way, there's *no* way my wife is gonna be cool with me seeing you."

"You mean here, or in the game?"

"Probably both!" I exclaimed, before I could think.

"Then you probably shouldn't have been playing that, should you?" She regarded me pitilessly. "I mean, when you think about it, it's not like I had to hunt you down, is it, Gary? Or should I say 'Dash?' Are we not on a first-name basis now? How's this work? 'Cause my memory is your avatar was sitting there in Shag, waiting to pick someone up and hop to it. By which I mean the sex. Which…you did. Right? I mean, that did happen, right? I'm not having a stroke or anything else I should worry about?"

"No, it did happen. And yes, I did meet you there several times. But really, I just thought of it as a game."

"Oh, did you, now?"

"No," I moaned, "I'm sorry, that came out wrong. I just…I didn't expect it to cross over into real life. I'm not trying to have an affair here. I'm in love with my wife."

"Oh," she replied, unimpressed. "Well, that's sweet. But sorry, that's not how you made it sound, ever. The way you described it, she was about as exciting as baseball in winter. Or is she displaying previously unseen levels of freakiness now that you're here in porno paradise?"

"Well, yes, actually, she is, but that's not the point. My point is, if you came out here looking for some kind of real-world activity, I'm afraid I have to disappoint you."

"Oh, well, that's lovely, now, isn't it, m'sieur. No, I didn't come out here expecting anything, except a warm reception and maybe a hug. I know you have your own life. Jesus, I'm not some crazy-ass stalker. I'm a separated woman who lives an hour away and for God's sake, why the fuck shouldn't I come out here and try to nab a little strange on my weekend? Who have I got to answer to? I'm a big girl now; I don't have a curfew or nothin'. The nerve of you, Gary. You got quite a little ego on you, y'know that? Anybody ever told you you kinda think you're the shit?"

"No, I—you're right. Sorry. I shouldn't have assumed anything."

"You're damn right you shouldn't. This is supposed to be fun."

"I know. I get that. My wife and I are here, okay? And it's good, y'know? We're having a really great time here, first terrific vacation we've had in years. I've been working so hard, on this park more than anything—well, in place of everything, to be honest—so we haven't seen much of each other these last few months."

"Oh, so is that why you were boning me in *Eros*? Just a tide-me-over wank spank?"

"No, it was...look. I don't know why I do half the things I do, okay?" I gripped my towel nervously. I noticed her wrist tattoo did in fact say "PISCES," and her right wrist had another tattoo of two fish. One for each son, I imagined. "Cathy, look. I'm sorry if I gave you any indication that you and I should come out here and...pick things up in real life. That was never my intention."

"I know, but you weren't exactly discouraging, either. You can admit to that, right?"

"I...can admit to that, yes. And it is nice to see you."

"I can see how delighted you are." I flinched, then quickly glanced down at my crotch to make sure she wasn't speaking literally. Nope, still flaccid. It probably would be for hours at this high-stress, humiliating rate. Cathy sighed. "Look. I'm gonna go hit the casino, maybe drink myself into a stupor. Then I'm gonna find some good-lookin' single dude, maybe not single, who gives a rat's ass at this point, and work him over like the harlot-in-training I am. Is that okay with you?"

"Of course. I—you know, do whatever you want. Have some fun. I'm sorry this got weird."

"I'm gonna leave my bracelet in public mode," she said. "You can find me when you're able to spare a few minutes and shoot the breeze. We can meet for coffee. Or, if that's too sexually charged, I guess you can watch me lose my soon-to-be-ex-husband's money on the slot machines. It'll be scintillating."

"I do want to talk to you," I said. "I just want to be wearing pants at the time."

"Ha! Why start now?" she asked. "We're old friends, you and me and those cute sexy knees of yours. Gimme a buzz, Gary. Play your cards right, maybe I'll let you get me into a towel, too. It's a buyer's market out here."

"I'll look you up," I said. "I promise. Tomorrow, probably. Tomorrow morning. I'll see you. Looking forward to it." I was already backing away, subconsciously pushing her away with open palms.

"What a treat this has been," Cathy declared, frowning. "You better watch out. A girl could get used to such royal treatment."

I nearly ran back to Summer in the hot tubs. I had no intention of messaging Cathy, in the morning or any time ever again. Sad to say, I quickly put her out of my mind. After all, there were strangers fucking the paint off each other not five feet away, and some of them were awfully attractive. I had other things, and people, to do.

Chapter 13

Our skin was about to slough off after three hours in and around the hot tubs, so I led Summer back to our room. We didn't have sex that night, just held each other and watched a *Daily Show* rerun. I used to be a real fan of that show...not so much anymore. They've really milked what feels like an unfair amount of comic nectar out of me and my salacious travails.

We held hands under the sheets, Summer and I. How 'bout that? Pretty sweet, don't you think? I sure do. She's a good woman, Summer. I love her, as I should've all along. She fell asleep curled like a cat in the crook of my arm.

I dreamed that night. I remember it vividly, as it's one of a handful of times I've engaged in lucid dreaming. You know about that, right? If you ever realize in the middle of a dream that it's only that, a dream, the realization usually jolts you clear out of it. But if you do by some chance remain therein, you develop superhuman powers. You can will other characters, or your own virtual body, into doing almost anything. Gravity's an illusion—raise your arms and float away like the last son of Krypton. Or, if you're in a more lascivious frame of mind, walk up to the most beautiful person around, tear his or her clothes off, and go crazy. You can have your way with anyone you want. It's your world. Be a god in it.

In this particular dream, the landscape of Bliss Panerotic invaded my office. A ride full of tourists shot across the hall into the Randall/Klein conference room. I wandered into the lobby, where my staff was answering phones from the comfort of a rock-walled Jacuzzi. I took off my suit and slipped into the tub, then bent my favorite assistant over the edge, tore her clothing aside like wet tissue, and rammed myself deeply inside of her. She reacted as if nothing especially remarkable had happened. In fact, she never changed facial expressions. (Sherri, if you're reading this, it meant nothing, especially to you.) As for me, I felt sexually ravenous, yet the act itself was frictionless and ultimately unsatisfying.

Having explored Sherri's body, or at least my mental extrapolation thereof, I decided to find someone equally gorgeous to ravish. I departed my office and strolled out onto La Cienega. Dozens of pedestrians turned in my direction like penguins regarding a documentarian. They were all Summer, and their eyes were all sharply accusatory. I shot awake and couldn't catch my breath. I stared out the window at a parking garage and scrubby hills; we'd been downgraded from one of the best suites in southern California to a functional room on the inland side of the park. *I want to make things right*, I thought. *I want to deserve this wonderful woman I've found.*

I came back to bed, kissed Summer on the shoulder, and rolled into four hours of undisturbed sleep.

I woke to the tarmac howl of Summer drying her hair a thin wall away in the bathroom. "Good morning, babe," I yawned. She didn't hear me, or didn't respond. I glanced at my phone: Saturday, June 13, 8:14 a.m. I scrolled through a dozen overnight email messages, sending only a few cursory replies. I was on vacation, damn it, and today would be the best day of my life. I resolved to *carpe* the shit out of this *diem*, grab it by the scruff of its neck and shake it till gold doubloons rained at my feet. I even tried the bathroom door, hoping to slip in with my wife and distract her before breakfast. Sadly, the door was locked. Instead, I turned on the room's minuscule TV and watched GNN inform its worldwide audience, disappointedly it seemed to me, that free-loving amity had not devolved into serial rape and disaster inside Bliss Panerotic on opening night.

"We saw reports of numerous sexual assaults on Twitter," the reporter intoned glumly, "but we've been unable to substantiate those reports. In fact, on closer inspection, it seems few if any of those Twitter accounts actually belong to people who have visited the park. So for now, the world watches and waits, as this grand experiment in taboo behavior continues."

Waits for what? I thought angrily. *Why would anyone want this to fail? Wouldn't it be more fun if it succeeds?* Ah, but such is the fate of moral dreamers in this world: never valued in mainstream society, embraced only by those with one foot in the future already.

We headed downstairs for a light breakfast, croissants and good coffee. Summer made fun of the way I pronounced "croissants." I made fun of her for ordering a cappuccino and then putting cream and sweetener in it. We made fun of each other for dressing like absolute tourists. I was in cargo pants and a summery button-up shirt; she a light sweater over a cream-colored sundress. The sweater covered lightly-sunburnt shoulders. She smelled like coconut oil and comfort.

It was overcast that morning, but the coffee warmed us up as we sat at an outdoor table and listened to the waves. "I should've dressed for this," Summer said. "My whole body's one big goose bump."

"I assure you it is not," I said. "Besides, this'll all burn off by noon. You know how L.A. weather is. It's gonna be perfect."

"What do you have to do for the Ryders today?"

"Nothing, really. I blew off some emails this morning, and I have a short interview with somebody

233

from MSNBC at one. Other than that, I'm on vacay. Let's get cray-cray."

Summer laughed. "Why are you talking like that?"

"I don't know. I'm trying to get down with the lingo, stay youthful."

"I'm pretty sure no one says cray-cray except on bad sitcoms."

"Oh, really? So no one'll L-M-A-O if I say it?"

"You," she laughed, "are one disturbed individual."

"It's true," I said. "I am a work in progress."

We finished our breakfast and strolled through Eros 4Ever again. The store was full of shoppers looking for ways to get even cray-crayzier than last night. (Summer's right. That sounds weird. I'll stop now.) The park seemed to be one enormous walk of shame this morning, minus most of the shame. People were quiet and docile, drifting without speaking, content with each other. Good sex'll calm you that way.

I noticed a lot of gay couples had ventured into the mostly-straight area. No one cared. It gave me hope.

I texted Adam and asked if we were still on for MSNBC at one, hoping we weren't. He texted me back immediately: *Yeah get there libral asses out here if u can!* Not a great speller, that Adam, but you have to admire his enthusiasm. I told him Summer and I were having a great time and MSNBC would love this place. They're progressive, I reminded him, a bunch of Ivy League Democrats. They'll be all over this, perceive it as sticking it to the establishment. *Just make sure they no were not sexest*, he replied. He said he and Nicole were still in bed, so I guess they were happy with how things were going so far. I got a quick mental image of Nicole riding Adam and wondered how that'd be. Hot, I imagined. Summer asked what I was thinking, and I came up with some bullshit about how Heidi Licious thought we were square and I could live with that. "You were smiling," Summer said. Mea culpa. "You're very handsome, you know that?" I hugged my wife to thank her for the compliment.

"We look good together," I said.

I'm an eight out of ten by L.A. standards, but yes, I do clean up nice.

We decided to spend the morning in Sanasana. The hotel façade seemed muted this morning, its neon lights retired until dusk. The casino area was surprisingly full. One-armed bandits gulped money right and left. The ambient music strove for late-night-cable-TV slutty but settled for cheesy. The bar was doing brisk business in mimosas and bloody Marys. A line of groggy tourists shuffled down a long hall toward the breakfast buffet: only $14.99 for all the made-to-order omelets you could stomach. The Lucky Buffet may not have attracted the best-looking subculture in the park, but hey, those folks knew a great bargain when they saw one.

Summer excused herself as we passed a public restroom. While I waited, I got curious and activated the Bliss Panerotic app so I could read Cathy's stats and location. Ms. Pris was still in her room, several floors up. (For legal reasons, location info was left deliberately vague on the program once visitors climbed above ground level. Park security could locate anyone at any time, but my access to such information was restricted.) Her in-park avatar was a tomboyish elf. *Ms. Pris*, the stats read, *bi-curious, age 30s, separated, interested in men and women, currently unavailable.* Hm, I thought. Maybe she enticed someone up to her room last night after all. Good for her.

Except perhaps I was just a bit jealous? No, I think not, though I was curious what sex in real life with Cathy would be like. I mean honestly, who could blame me after how things had gone in the game? She was fun in there. Was I jealous, though? No. I had no reason to be. So that guy upstairs, whoever he was, knew something I didn't. Big deal. It wasn't like I had any claim on her. She came out here to see me, so what? I blew her off, she got busy with somebody else. These things happen. It was nothing to get irked about.

"Come on," I said, irked, when Summer exited the bathroom. "Geez, that coffee goes right through you sometimes."

"I guess so. Is something the matter?"

"No, it's fine. Don't be weird. Let's go check out the rides."

"Who's being weird?"

"I—nothing. I was just saying don't be, that's all. It's no big deal, seriously. I just slept on my neck funny. Sorry." I stretched my neck elaborately and, as it happened, needlessly. There was nothing the matter with my neck.

"You want me to rub it?"

"No, I'm good."

"Are you sure you're up for an amusement park ride? I may have worn you out already."

"I'm always up for an amusement park ride. Come on, it'll work out the kinks."

"No pun intended." Summer squeezed my hand. She was being so nice, and I chided myself for looking Cathy up in the first place. It was none of my business where Cathy was or what she was doing. Whom she was doing. I rolled my neck and accepted an ibuprofen I didn't need from Summer, washing it down with a midmorning screwdriver.

I probably could've gotten out of paying for the Tunnel of Lust ride by flashing my staff pass, but if we'd tried to cut past the line of surly guests, we might've been lynched. As often happens with new rides, this one was having mechanical issues and stopped working at the slightest provocation. The folks running it looked as if they would've been happier staffing an Ebola ward. Since there were only two rides in Sanasana and neither was cheap, the designers sought to give visitors their money's worth by making each line part of the attraction. Again, we embraced the philosophy of Disney Theme Parks, where the arduous ordeal you or I call a line is retitled the "pre-show" or "scene one."

An attendant who looked like she might've been planning suicide kept an eye on us as we shuffled back and forth, back and forth. Keep in mind, people were wearing whatever the fuck they wanted, so about a sixth of the guests were showing off body parts they wouldn't and couldn't have displayed in any other park. The overall effect was less sexy than surreal, and I'm not sure I ever got used to it in daylight.

Overhead screens flashed vintage erotica: French postcards, Tijuana bibles, stereopticon pinups. "You may be aware," a warm baritone announced, "that erotic art is not a recent invention. Perhaps you've found items like these in your grandparents' attic and wondered what those old so-and-sos got up to." We chuckled, our boredom slightly alleviated. The attendants ignored the screens, having already heard this monologue dozens of times by now.

"But these are by no means the earliest works of erotic art. Why, some of the earliest artworks known to archaeologists are little statues like this one, the Venus of Willendorf, and it's easy to see what the sculptor found most interesting about his subject." Indeed, the statuette had breasts about the size of her head. They sagged over a spherical belly, which in turn led the eye toward a prominent mons. "Apparently," the voice-over quipped, "the men of 23,000 B.C. were into BBWs." A black couple nearby chuckled appreciatively. She wore shorts and an inconsequential bikini top and looked much like the statue. He stood five-four in a leopard-print thong.

"The ancient Greeks and Romans were fond of erotic art, both homo- and heterosexual. This would later prove embarrassing to Victorian prudes, who idolized those ancient cultures till explicit paintings and sculptures were discovered in the ruins of Pompeii." One such sculpture flashed on the screen: a marble satyr determinedly fucking a goat. That was startling enough, but the goat was on its back in the missionary position. It looked sleepy-eyed, as if it'd been roofied. "You can see," the announcer noted, "why this got their attention." The soundtrack helpfully included a *baa*. "In fact, pieces like this one were locked away in a cabinet for almost a century."

Next up was a ceramic sculpture as graphic as *Erotic Getaway*. "Here's a piece from the Moche of ancient Peru. It was sculpted around the time the New Testament was written, and it depicts a young woman deep-throating what must've been one very grateful warrior." The guy's dick was the size of his forearm, and his hands covered his mouth in a gesture of amazement. The woman's anus and vagina gaped open, as did, for understandable reasons, her eyes.

"Get it, girl!" the black woman cheered, which initiated a new round of giggles between her and her lightweight companion. Others around her joined in.

"You've probably heard of the Indian *Kama Sutra*, which was written and illustrated around the same time. It's a sex manual reputed to have been inspired by the couplings of gods. This position is known as the Longbow."

"Hm," Summer said. "I may have to talk you into trying that one out later."

"Apparently the gods didn't throw out their backs," I noted.

"The Japanese word for erotic art is *shunga*," the voice-over continued, "and it was popular in all levels of society by the sixteenth century. This example is called *Prelude to Desire*, by Utamaro in 1799, and it looks like the prelude to limping." Indeed, the gentleman in the colorful print once again sported a phallus the size of a police flashlight. That caused female guests around us to groan, laugh, and kid each other. It was impossible to read the expression of the woman in the print, as it was hidden behind her lover's head, but I gathered she was bracing for impact.

"Meanwhile, in Europe, the aristocracy was busily collecting erotic art, including this piece by Titian. It's called *Venus and an Organist and a Little Dog*, and the organist seems intent on tickling the ivories." A pudgy, nude woman lounged brazenly on a bed, the aforementioned pup by her side. A fully-dressed organist sat at the woman's feet; but although the fingers of his left hand hovered over a keyboard, he'd turned completely around to stare at her crotch. "You can see why this era was dubbed the Age of Discovery." The soundtrack added light piano music, along with a coquettish squeal of delight. "Here's *Jupiter et Junon*, by Agostino Carracci, around 1595." A heavily muscled Jove hoisted his lovely sister/wife into bed, visibly parting her labia with his mortal-sized prick. She seemed, if not impressed, then at least DTF.

The image shifted to another, more familiar painting, then zoomed into lurid detail. "Look closely at the center panel of this well-known triptych from the year 1490, *The Garden of Earthly Delights* by Hieronymus Bosch, and you'll see people engaged in all sorts of interesting pastimes. This panel represents the many temptations of the flesh." A young man appeared to be planting roses in another person's anus; it was impossible to determine the recipient's gender or, for that matter, opinion of the gift.

"The word *pornography* hails from ancient Greece, where it meant 'writing or art about prostitutes.' The English novel *Fanny Hill* was considered pornographic in 1748. Most European countries banned all forms of porn until well into the

239

twentieth century. Even so, the first French adult films appeared in the 1890s. This film, *Le Coucher de la Mariée*, starred stripper Louise Willy." On the screen, a waspwaisted, curly-haired brunette helped the lady of the house prepare for her bath. "By the 1920s, underground stag films were produced by the dozens in France and America. Often, these films were shown in brothels, but Austrian theaters hosted men-only movie nights called *Herrenabende*. By the 1950s, traveling salesmen moonlighted as porn distributors. In 1969, a Swedish film, *I Am Curious (Yellow)*, threw the doors wide open, and the early 1970s saw the release of such classic escapades as *Deep Throat*, *Behind the Green Door*, and *The Devil in Miss Jones*."

A curly-haired woman who could've been a realtor sat opposite a blonde devil. "Filled... engulfed...consumed by lust," she moaned. It was Georgina Spelvin, the former chorus girl who starred in *The Devil in Miss Jones* at age 37.

"Pornographic videos came home with the advent of cable and the VCR in the '70s and '80s. The rest is history," the announcer concluded, "except it may surprise you to know that some of the most respected artists of the last few centuries have dabbled in Eros. Hokusai may have been the finest, most famous artist in Japan, but even he enjoyed a bit of *shunga*. This is *The Dream of the Fisherman's Wife*." My wife gasped. The image was startling: it showed a nude woman being kissed orally and vaginally by two red octopi. "This print is something of a comic strip," the announcer continues. "It includes printed dialogue."

"Finally I have you in my grasp!" a male voice, presumably the larger octopus, crowed. "Your bobo is ripe and full. How wonderful! To suck and suck and suck some more. After we do it masterfully, I'll lead you to the Dragon Palace of the Sea God and envelop you!"

A woman with a slight Japanese accent replied, "You despicable octopus! Your sucking at the mouth of my womb makes me gasp! Aah! Yes... it's...there! With the sucker, the sucker! Inside. Wiggle, wiggle. Oooh! Ooh, good. Ooh, good! There! *There!*"

Summer looked at me and fanned herself wryly. I stifled a laugh.

"Jeff Koons painted and sculpted himself in sex scenes with his wife, a famous porn star named La Cicciolina. Born Ilona Staller in Hungary, she continued to shoot hardcore even after she was elected to the parliament of Italy in 1987." In a painting so naturalistic it looked like a *Penthouse* photo, Koons ejaculated onto the ass of his bottle-blonde sex goddess. "The paintings are from a series called *Made in Heaven*. Picasso himself created hundreds of erotic artworks, including this piece, in which the master depicts himself as a minotaur ravishing his mistress, Dora Maar."

"Y'ever get the feeling," Summer asked, "these guys really just wanted to hang out with a bunch of naked models and brag about how big their dicks were?"

"Which brings us up to the present day," the announcer continued, "when erotic art often goes by another name: mainstream advertising." Dozens of print ads flashed by in rapid succession, including one for the Burger King Super Seven Incher, another for PETA, teenage Brooke Shields in her Calvins, a Budweiser bathing beauty, Abercrombie & Fitch, Nikon, Dolce & Gabbana—soon the images switched so fast they were all but subliminal. I did, however, catch a print version of my Kardashian tortilla chip ad.

"Hey!" I yelled. "Did you see that? They used my taco chip ad! I hope they remembered to pay someone for it. Hopefully me."

My wife snorted. "I wouldn't count on it. Something tells me neither what's-her-face Kardashian nor Brooke Shields have any idea they're being featured in the line at a sex ride."

And with that we reached the loading area for the Tunnel of Lust, which sounded like a boat ride but wasn't. Instead, it applied the same general idea as the Haunted Mansion in Disneyland. If you've never been to the Magic Kingdom, here's how it works: you board a two-person vehicle (called a "doom buggy" in Disney parlance), which spins you into a programmed pattern as it progresses round the show building on a looped conveyor belt. In our version, the ride vehicle was built to resemble a foreshortened view of a luxurious bed, draped in velveteen red and wrapped in a padded, ornate headboard to limit its riders' peripheral vision. Disney's Haunted Mansion track is 960 feet long, with a ride length of seven and a half minutes. Ours wasn't quite that ambitious; it traveled 740 feet in a little over six minutes. It was clearly overpriced at twelve bucks a passenger. Still, it beat the smelly crap out of any other amusement park sex ride you've ever been on, so there.

I suppose I could simply prevail upon you to search for handheld point-of-view ride videos on YouTube, as they were uploaded within hours of the park opening. (Thanks a lot, grateful tourists.) Luckily, though, the ride was so dark the videos aren't very good. Instead I'll talk you through it, using the audio from one of those smartphone videos to refresh my aging memory.

Our morose attendant, who looked about two and a half minutes past eighteen, wore a naughty teacher outfit so lushly cheesecake you could all but lob tennis balls into her cleavage. Seriously, if this girl was old enough to have earned a college degree and a teaching certificate, then I'm Patton Oswalt. (I promise you: I am not Patton Oswalt.)

"Welcome to the Tunnel of Lust," our attendant recited, making no effort to sound any less robotic than the animatronics we'd encounter on the ride. *Poor kid.*

Does your dad know you work here? I thought, a sure sign age was finally catching up with me. "This is a dark ride, so please keep your hands and arms inside the vehicle at all times. It's up to you and your date to decide how handsy you're allowed to be *inside* the bed while you're riding it. We're about to launch you on a sensual tour of the history of sex, so get ready for your lesson. Pay attention, or we might have to keep you after school." She handed us each a pair of 3-D glasses. "Please wait to put these on until after you've climbed into bed. Enjoy the ride." She hit a button, and the speakers emitted a panther yowl and whip crack. We rushed onto the conveyor belt, matched speeds with our appointed ride vehicle, and hopped aboard.

Much like its Disney equivalent, the car slid past stage sets augmented with robotic figures. It also embraced the Universal Studios innovation of including 3-D, high-definition movie screens and interactive stage effects. "Hi, everybody," said a smoky female voice from speakers near our ears. "I'm Dani Fiero, featured performer and director for Panerotic Pictures. Together, you and I will take a sexy trip back in time to meet our horniest human ancestors. Then we'll trip the light fantastic through the course of human history, catching glimpses of our rich sexual past along the way."

The ride also had optional Spanish or Japanese language soundtracks, which the attendant could engage at the push of a button as a car left the loading zone.

"So lean back," Fiero purred, "put on your birth-control glasses, and get ready to rock. We're traveling back in time some three hundred thousand years." As we entered the ride track proper, the cars swiveled forty-five degrees to face a wide video screen. The screen showed a long, glowing tunnel, which seemed to extend deep into interstellar space, launching us into a temporal portal. This was accompanied by surround sound effects, water mist, and laser strobes.

"Neat!" Summer exclaimed.

"For many years, children were taught we humans descended from one unwed couple in a garden. It's a charming story, made especially memorable by casual nudity. Nothing spices up a myth like some naked-time sex appeal!" Two animatronic figures, an idealized Adam and Eve, stood nervously in the shadow of an exotic fruit tree. They made comic blushing faces and attempted to cover their naughty bits from our sight. A smiling serpent reared nearby, grinning and hissing at their obvious dismay. I was interested to note that the figures looked Middle Eastern, and the fruit tree appeared to bear, not apples, but pomegranates. Someone put some thought into this.

Our ride vehicles slid past the Edenic scene into a puff of colored mist. The background seemed to jump-cut to prehistoric Africa, courtesy of another 3-D screen. "Nowadays, we know the history of human beings goes back a lot farther than ancient people believed. In novels like *The Clan of the Cave Bear*, science-fiction author Jean Auel popularized the idea that early humans had sex only in the rear entry position common among other large mammals. But why? Even in the Stone Age, humans likely had sex in any number of positions. Besides, in a largely matriarchal society, women called many of the shots." Now, here was something you wouldn't see in Disney's New Orleans Square: a lifelike robotic caveman (and –woman) orgy. Half a dozen naked humans went at it on furs strewn around a smoky campfire. Yes, one couple enjoyed a rowdy round of doggy-style, but another got after it in the missionary position, the cavewoman's ankles astride her lover's beard and grin. The third woman fellated her partner as he fingered her amply pubed crotch. They looked happy—and contemporarily human. This was *Homo sapiens*, our direct genetic forebears, and they seemed to have a yen for knocking boots. In fact, as we passed a rock outcropping, a fourth

244

couple grunted in the missionary position, but the man in this couple looked slightly more brutish.

"This *Homo sapiens* woman is enjoying a vigorous dalliance with a stud from a species quite similar to her own. His species is called *Homo neanderthalensis*." Fiero pronounced "thal" as "tall." (Again, she must've been directed by a devotee of current anthropology and German phonetics. *Homo neanderthalensis* was discovered in a cave near Düsseldorf, so the current trend is to pronounce it with a hard German *th*. Thanks, Discovery Channel!) "We now believe early humans interbred with several other closely-related species, as a few percent of modern human DNA are really Neanderthal DNA. But hey, who doesn't like a little bit of strange every now and again?"

We passed into a room with Egyptian décor. A temple prostitute, draped loosely in a blue, beaded wrap, moaned as she ground on a younger man's lap. "While Islam and the Torah emphasized sex for procreation, ancient Egyptians believed unmarried people were free to have as much guiltless sex as they liked. They had numerous methods of contraception, some more effective than others." Among those methods, apparently, was crocodile dung, which I suspect worked primarily by deterrence. "Egyptian mythology," Fiero continued, "is full to bursting with lusty sex stories. They even attached dildos to their mummies after death, as they believed hot sex continued in the afterlife."

"Tut, Tut," my wife quipped, and I snorted. Another screen smoothed the transition between animatronic stages.

"Sadly," Fiero sighed, "the time-honored Roman orgies probably had more to do with food and wine than group fornication. It was the Greeks who enjoyed the most varied sex lives. They loved Eros in all its forms and had no concept of 'age of consent.'

245

They worshipped the phallus—who doesn't?—and their ruling god, Zeus, was said to rape both women and men for kicks. The goddess Leda transformed herself into a swan to avoid his royal advances, but even that didn't work." We were treated to a computer animation in which a marble-statue-like figure of Zeus ogled a decidedly flustered looking swan. "Nice try, Leda." A man snickered lustily on the soundtrack, followed by the trumpet of an oversexed waterfowl. A view of Mount Olympus was occluded by mist.

"So with all these cultures happily boffing their brains out," Fiero continued, "you're probably asking, 'How and when did Western culture come to the conclusion that sex is sinful and dirty? Where do these crazy taboos come from?'" The mist cloud parted, and we found ourselves in a candlelit stone chamber. A man in a hooded *stola* scribbled away in Latin on a ragged sheet of papyrus. "This is Augustine of Hippo, the fourth-century saint who popularized the idea that righteous people should resist their own physical desires. He believed women and physical lust were distracting forces that seduced men away from God's love. All this despite the fact that the Good Book itself can get rather steamy."

We rounded a corner, and on a grassy hillside outside Augustine's rustic church in Egypt, a young couple made out in the shade of a sycamore tree. Her Coptic tunic was open; his hands cupped firm breasts with dark nipples as she moaned into his kiss. A baritone voice quoted from the Song of Songs, chapter 7: "Your stature is like that of the palm, and your breasts like clusters of fruit. I said, 'I will climb the palm tree; I will take hold of its fruit.' May your breasts be like clusters of grapes on the vine, the fragrance of your breath like apples, and your mouth like the best wine."

"But the pleasures of sex were discouraged throughout the Judeo-Christian world," Fiero continued, "until Victorian doctors argued whether women should even be allowed to have orgasms. In the 1880s, Dr. Joseph Granville graciously invented the vibrator to help finish off so-called 'hysterical' women in his office." A screen showed an intrigued Dr. Granville and his black, metallic device—which looked about as sensual as an industrial belt sander—noisily going to town on a bucking English rose, her bustle and petticoat in wanton disarray.

"Relax," Dr. Granville urged, his beard neatly trimmed but his bowtie askew. "I promise this will not hurt a bit." His patient expelled another whoop of release.

"With the twentieth century," Fiero said, "came a systematic, less judgmental form of sex research, thanks in large part to women like Clelia Mosher and Katharine Bement Davis. The Kinsey Report of 1948 was followed quickly by the work of Masters and Johnson, who studied female sexual responses as they would any normal anatomical function."

A 3-D screen lit up with a supernova of sexual imagery, from Bettie Page pinups to Burt Reynolds hairily reclining in *Cosmo* to Linda Lovelace earning her alter ego to Dothraki couplings on *Game of Thrones*. "So here we are in a new millennium, still torn between ancient taboos and the call of the wild. It looks like you've decided to let your freak flag fly, and good for you! But what about the future? Is it possible we're on the verge of a whole new sexual frontier?"

We drifted around a corner. Our car spun toward a lacy boudoir, where what looked like a trio of centerfolds lounged in unmistakably carnal poses. "Meet our high-tech trio of commercially available sex robots," Fiero announced. The blonde on the left is Susie Sexbot, who runs on batteries and gyrates when she's touched. She's powered by a handheld remote control, and you can rent her *and* her android stud, Harry Harddrive, for parties. Her Asian friend in the

247

middle is Honey Doll, who moans and groans thanks to her onboard MP3 player. Then there's Eve, from a California startup called Pygmalion Industries. We've come full circle, folks. At Panerotic, we're partnering with Pygmalion to introduce Eve and androids like her to the full consumer market in a few years. In the meantime, we plan to make several dozen 'shebots' available for private appointments. So what can Eve do? Say hello to the hot people, Eve."

The underwear-model-shaped robot turned her head and looked directly at us as a spotlight shone on her from above. She wore a silk teddy, and her auburn hair swept back from a lightly freckled forehead. Her eyes were moist enough to resemble real eyes, her skin inviting rather than rubbery. Full lips parted. Eve bid us good morning in a calm contralto. "Well, hello! What would you like me to do for you today?" she asked. "I'm up for anything. You name it, I want it. I can see you're a couple. Gary and Summer. Boy, would I ever like to play with you two sometime. Maybe next year? Just as soon as I work out a few...personal kinks."

Here's the thing: I watched the techies install Eve a week before we opened. I knew her limitations. She wasn't freestanding, any more than those two other glorified sex dolls were, and she didn't always respond to user queries in ways that made sense. In fact, her Wi-Fi kept glitching, so if she weren't connected to the wall by a firewire cable hidden behind her, she wouldn't know us from a bowl of petunias. Even so, she was stunning in action. Computer animators talk about the "uncanny valley," that weird level of realism synthetic figures can achieve that almost, but not quite, convinces us we're looking at actual humans. In some ways, that almost-alive quality is more disturbing than not-even-close. I got none of that from Eve, though, at least in these carefully posed and lit conditions. If I didn't know better, I'd think I was looking at a real, live, willing, preposterously attractive California girl.

(After all, many of our real women in southern California are somewhat bionic.) She left all but the most advanced animatronic figures in Disney parks in her bonerific dust.

I've heard it said a significant fraction of the world's sex tourism industry will employ the services of sex robots by 2050, but found that notion ludicrous...till I saw Eve. If it's true prostitution is the world's oldest business—and I rather think hunting and gathering snuck in there ahead of it, but be that as it may—surely the shame of paying for sex is almost as ancient? There's no sense of accomplishment in handing someone fifty bucks and pleading for a rub-and-tug. It's no credit to anyone's charisma or physical attractiveness. Also, if a john has even the most rudimentary conscience, surely he (or she) feels some sympathy for the plight of those reduced to selling personal space invasion. Ah, but now here comes Eve! And Roxxxy! And Susie Sexbot! And Harry Harddrive! If IBM can make a computer that beats human champions on *Jeopardy!*—and it already has—then surely some money-hungry tech startup can devise a machine that responds to sexual contact as a human would?

Was Eve that machine? Probably not, at least not that first demo model. But while Pygmalion Industries is no longer in the Panerotic theme park supply business, it's still merrily tinkering with android designs. As I write this, Eve's next-gen sorority sister is due to hit the high-end international consumer market in less than eighteen months. Her project name is Galatea, she speaks seven languages, and her nethers can work on your junk in ways no vagina could ever reproduce. She gives hours of oral sex, in the unlikely event hours should be necessary, that should qualify for an Olympic medal if not the Nobel Peace Prize. I can't afford her; nor, very likely, can you. Rest assured, though, hundreds of Galateas will soon be slurping away on the grateful genitalia of billionaires in Tokyo, San Francisco, Dubai, Kuala Lumpur...A more affordable model will join her in bedrooms around the world less than a decade later. Time marches, and bounces, ever on.

Before long, it'll be passé for men to marry men and women to marry women, as it should be. But will the next controversy be a human being's right to marry a machine? Will humans fall in love and/or lust with artificial intelligences? We already live in a world where kids seem unable to go longer than an hour without checking their smartphones. We love our cars and plasma TVs and tablet computers and phones, but will we ever *love* love them? When idiots try to put the genie of sexual freedom back in its bottle, they insist it'll lead to perverts hooking up with children and animals. Pat Robertson asked whether a 2009 anti-hate-crime bill might make it okay for "weird" people "to have sex with ducks." (I wish I were kidding. I'm not. Look it up.) But as loopy as that slippery-slope mentality might be, it's true that freedom inspires greater freedom. If I admit I dabbled in orgies, and you're free to marry a person of your own sex, then surely human-android sex and love are up for grabs?

The question Fiero asked on that ride, about when and why we otherwise intelligent Western folks decided sex was repulsive and shameful and shouldn't be discussed without chaperones and near-fatal blushing, is an important one. But here's an even better one, at least from where I'm sitting: why am I still so worried about what you think of my experiences? Why do I hesitate before I write details of my sex life you'll find more amusing than shocking? Why do I allow the constant mockery of talk show hosts and disingenuous news anchors to rattle me? Is it because I'm ashamed of myself? If that's the case, why? I went on a sexy vacation with my wife. That's all it was. We experimented, we *played* together, as we had for years before that. God willing, we'll do it again, though that seems less and less probable with each passing day.

When I tell people I'm writing this account, they ask, "Sheesh, don't you want to move on? If I were you, I'd never bring it up again." But I read memoir after memoir of folks doing every kind of drug, stealing, pimping, acting horribly to loved ones, and we take it all in stride. It's only when others reveal sexual quirks that we titter like morons.

Our bed-car spun one last time, to face forward as it returned to the loading area. Fiero reminded us to check for loose belongings, then bid us a sexy day at Bliss Panerotic. "Make it a day you'll never forget," she exhorted. In retrospect, Dani Fiero, mission accomplished.

My wife and I hopped out, faces flushed. We held hands as we threaded a crowd of equally aroused tourists.

"That was…interesting," Summer remarked.

"Yeah. Kinda makes you think, doesn't it?" I *was* thinking. I still am.

"About what in particular?"

"About how weird it feels to be in a sexual theme park, when every other kind of human fun is A-OK."

"Aren't the Ryders worried about including all that Bible stuff? You know, making fun of it."

"They weren't making fun of it. They're dismissing it."

"Okay, exactly. That's just what I mean. Like, if terrorists or Christian weirdos are already eyeing the park, won't that just make 'em more likely to attack?"

"I hope not. But no, I don't think so. Those people never attack for a reason. They attack because they start to feel dumb. And rather than admit they might believe a dumb thing, they distract themselves by attacking other people."

"You think Christians are dumb?"

251

"No," I said, "of course not. I think believing the world's less than a million years old is dumb. I think believing sex is always bad is dumb. It's like saying God's perfect and He gave us something we'll truly enjoy—in fact, we need it to thrive and reproduce—but oh, by the way, you go to Hell if you do it. I'd like to think we've outgrown that crap. But yeah, maybe we haven't. I don't know. Maybe someday we'll be watching this place on the news as it goes up in flames, wondering how Adam and Nicole could be so stupid as to taunt the bear. Either way, the wingnuts are bound to hate this place. It seems to me we might as well go all the way." I chuckled. "Besides, naked sex robots."

"Naked sex robots," she agreed. "But why sex? It's so arbitrary. It's like if someone decided to make dancing a sin. Or kissing. Or eating steak unless it's medium well."

"I'm pretty sure those used to be sins."

"Still are, prob'ly, somewhere," she acknowledged. "People are weird. I'm having fun here. I don't feel like we're doing anything bad by coming here, do you?"

"No. But I bet you never told your sister where we were going for the weekend."

"Hell, no, I didn't. I told her we were going to Vegas."

"'Cause that's better somehow."

"Normal people go to Vegas. Not here."

"Aren't we normal people?"

"I don't know. I kinda wonder sometimes, especially after that last party. Gary, I mean it! Maybe we aren't normal. Maybe we're weird."

"Does that bother you?" I asked.

"I don't know. I never thought being normal was one of my major priorities in life, but I've spent so many years doing only normal things." She shook her head rapidly to clear confusing thoughts. "It makes my head hurt. Screw that. I just want to have fun."

"Are we having fun now?"

"Yes, we are!" she decided, beaming. "This is a good vacation. Bizarro, but good." We drifted through the casino toward Climax, the indoor roller coaster.

"I miss spending time with you."

"You do?"

"I sure do."

"Then why don't we ever do stuff like this? You know, go to Vegas or Paris for real? We can afford it."

"Yeah. Especially now. I took some of the money I made from this Panerotic gig and invested it in the park. Now that's it's open, I think we are gonna make a tidy chunk of change on this place. I mean, look at these people, "I said. "They're having the time of their lives. Ten years from now, nobody'll think this is weird. It'll be like Vegas or Hedonism II, something cool married people do to have fun and shake off their day jobs."

"You think?"

"Absolutely. It'll be like we bought stock in Disneyland in 1954. We'll retire in Tahiti."

"I can live with that."

"Me, too. Just you and me, babe. We're gonna be sitting on a beach with a couple of fruity umbrella drinks, living off our insane pile of sexual theme park money. People are gonna wish they were us, and that is a true fact."

"Well, how 'bout that," she decided. "Aren't you the most brilliant husband ever?"

"I do what I can," I replied modestly.

It was 10:47 a.m. Pacific time. Outside, the overcast burned off quickly: a perfect summer day off the southern California coast.

Chapter 14

Climax was a Wild Mouse roller coaster, an off-the-shelf ride inside a custom-built environment. It raced through twenty-three hundred feet of track in about eighty seconds. The Ryders bought the coaster cheap, then had it reassembled inside the casino. Ride engineers deployed sound and video projection systems around it so as we hurtled down the track, sexy images were projected past us in the opposite direction to make the car seem even faster. It was like whizzing past a drive-in movie at freeway speed, assuming the drive-in showed lurid striptease videos. These shifted to full-on porn as the ride came to its, you guessed it, climax. Meanwhile, a woman's lustful moans rose over a wah-wah guitar on a soundtrack that blasted us from speakers behind our head. It was inspired by Space Mountain but felt more like Disney's Aerosmith coaster in Orlando. It was fun, and if you wanted, you could even ride it naked. Some did. We did not.

Legend has it Uncle Walt had a strict policy banning rock 'n' roll in his amusement parks while he was still alive. In fact, even after he died, the parks refused to allow facial hair or skirts without hose until the twenty-first century. I wondered what Walt would've made of this ride. I'm not sure what I made of it.

By the time we worked our way through the long line, I was worried about getting off the coaster in time for my one o'clock interview. Luckily, we finished the ride about a quarter to one. "Tell you what," I said. "Why don't you go find a restaurant you like? I'll go upstairs and primp for my interview, then meet you for lunch after I finish."

"Sounds good," she said.

"No sushi, though," I warned. "That ride has me feeling a little oogy."

Summer kissed me almost chastely on the cheek. "No sushi, I promise. Handsome devil." Then she strolled down the hall. It was the last time I saw her smiling in my direction.

I ran up to our room and changed for the interview. I skimmed through my emails as I headed downstairs: aha. The reporter from MSNBC was named Chastity Paulsen. (I should've taken her first name as an omen and run for the ferry.) She arrived with a cameraman named Roy something who said fewer than a dozen words and regarded Paulsen with terror in his eyes. I think she punched him when no one was looking. She stood five-two in heels and had a voice so loud and confident it could've knocked down sequoias. I was taken back immediately by its intensity, and I found myself stammering like an idiot. I met her near the main gate, which had been relatively quiet since a fresh crowd of tourists stampeded through it an hour before.

"I thought I was s'posed to be talkin' to the Ryders," she blared, "but instead they send you, no offense! So why is that? They're too busy to talk to a goddamn national news organization?"

"Yeah, well," I said, "they uh, you know, they're on vacation, so—"

"Some vacation! A coupla thousand perverts swappin' bodily fluids on a breakwater. Big deal! They could spare fifteen minutes, I'm sure."

"I uh, well, I'm fully empowered to—"

"I know, I know, don't get your panties in a bunch. Jesus, you're lookin' at me like I got peanut M & M's shootin' outta my nose! Okay, let's get this over with. Tell me again who you are? And don't forget to spell it like I'm goddamn retarded."

"I'm, uh, Gary—"

"Not yet, for fuck's sake! Did I say start? Jesus! I need you to listen, okay? Things'll go a hell of a lot smoother if you pay attention to all the words that come out of my mouth." She over-enunciated the last few words as if I were from a country with a name that was ninety percent consonants. "Roy needs time to set up. You're dealin' with two hardcore professionals here. You got this, Roy?" Roy grunted. "'Course you do. This fella's a pro. Not like some people. I'm just sayin'. Not even a press tent set up. It's like two hunnerd fuckin' degrees out here. I got sweat stains like those doctors on *M*A*S*H*. Which was s'posed to be what, Roy, Korea? Hey, Gary, was it s'posed to be Korea? Looks like Griffith Park to me. Never mind. Roy'll make me look good. Frame me out, Roy. You know how we do. So anyway, what? You were sayin'? What, it's Jerry or something?"

"Huh? Who is?"

"Your name, brother man. Do you know it?"

"Oh, sorry. It's Gary, Gary Klein."

"Which is spelled how, exactly? Remember how I tol' ya to spell it?" I spelled it. She repeated it carefully, then launched into more of her rat-a-tat patter. I caught every other word. If it was designed to knock me off balance, it worked like a charm.

"Could you repeat the question?"

She sighed in one quick, impatient exhalation. "I said, 'Will there be any official comment on the attack Thursday night?'"

"You mean the one in Avalon?"

"Yes, you remember. When somebody hit ya upside the head wit' a brick."

"No, I, well. I'm not an official, so I can't really have an offi—"

"Does your company, Panerotic, have any response to the act of domestic terrorism you witnessed on Thursday?"

"My company is—what? Domestic terrorism? No, it was only some kids."

"Yeah, well, so was the Boston Marathon bombing."

"Okay, but no one was seriously injured. It was a minor blip in what turned out to be, you know, an extraordinary weekend."

"And your position with the company is?"

"My position?"

"Your job."

"Oh, well, that's temporary, really. I'm their acting brand management director, but I doubt that'll las—"

"Brand manager? *Acting?* What the hell does that even mean? Why the fuck am I talking to *you*?" she exclaimed, clearly annoyed by what she considered the second-class treatment of a journalist.

"My wife and I are here on vacation."

"Ohh, that's funny. And she was okay with this?"

"Yeah, we're both having a great time. Okay with what, though, specifically?"

"Excuse me?"

"I mean, why would she be bothered?"

Paulsen chortled. "Holy shit, look around, man! It's herpes and cocoa butter as far as the eye can see!"

"That's not true. I mean, I haven't seen any kind of park overview, but if somebody has an STD they're required to show it on their visitor stats. I haven't seen much of that at all, certainly no more than—This is the same question we always get, and I swear to you, it's an empty concern."

"So we're supposed to just take your word for it."

"You can do whatever you want, I guess, but what makes you think the incidence of herpes would be any higher here than in an L.A. singles bar?"

"Exactly," she said. "That's why I meet all my prospective fellas in church."

"Okay." I shook my head to dispel my astonishment at Paulsen's apparently heartfelt answer, and that's when I saw her coming toward me.

Cathy. *Shit.*

Not a-fucking-gain, I thought. *Any time but now!* I tossed a nod in Cathy's direction, attempting simultaneously to greet and ward her off. It didn't work. She parked directly behind Roy's left shoulder, arms crossed, and watched me being interviewed. My concentration, already drifting, caught an ocean breeze and vanished altogether.

I realized Paulsen had asked me another question, of which I caught maybe a phoneme. "I'm sorry, could you repeat that?"

"You okay, there, buddy? I ain't keeping you from anything important, am I?"

"No, it's—I saw someone I knew. What did you—?"

"Funny you should mention that," Paulsen interrupted. "What do you do if you run into somebody you know here? That's got to be a kick in the ol' funky junk, huh?"

"No, I—well. I do have friends here, aside from my wife. People I met in the course of working with Adam and Nicole Ryder. We're uh, well, we're, you know, it's exciting to work as a team on an important and uh, innovative, thing. Experience. Park."

"Are you havin' a breakdown?" Paulsen laughed. "Should I call 911? Hey, man up, buddy! What kinda manager *are* you?"

"I ask myself that every—nothing. Look, sorry. I just got off a roller coaster, so my stomach is still doing loop-de-loops, plus I'm probably a little tired."

"Yeah, well, we ain't rescheduling this interview, I can tell you that right fuckin' now. This is airing tonight, so maybe you oughta take a minute and pull your shit together, huh? 'Cause frankly, and I ain't sayin' this to be mean, but right now you kinda look like you ain't got both feet in the pool, there, friend."

"I—you're right. Sorry. Gimme a second, okay? I kinda need to deal with this other…person." Paulsen watched as I brushed past Roy (who grunted) toward Cathy.

"That your wife?" Paulsen hollered after me.

"No," I yelled back. "One second! One! I'll be right back."

"You betcha, Red Ryder. Take all the time you need," Paulsen hollered. "It ain't like I'm standin' around here pickin' my nose in Satan's sandbox for a routine interview like I'm some kinda asshole or nothin'."

"Nice tie," Cathy said, by way of hello.

"Thanks." She was wearing cargo shorts and a white Scissor Sisters concert tee over a neon-pink bikini top. Not the sexiest ensemble, perhaps, but the temperature was expected to climb into the high eighties that afternoon. She was ready for beach action. "I like your hair that way."

"Yeah, my hair's exactly the way it was last night." Probably. "So am I getting Alzheimer's, or did you miss an appointment this morning?"

"An appointment?"

"I thought you were planning to look me up for coffee."

"No, I, well, I thought I might, but then my wife and I got busy."

"When you say 'got busy,' do you mean you had sex, or that you and Shannon had other engagements?"

"The latter. We went on the roller coaster and that Tunnel of Lust ride."

"Well, that sounds fun."

"It was."

"Which is why," she said, "I waited so I could go on that with you."

"Uhh, that's weird."

"It is? What's so weird about it? Who wants to go on a ride like that by herself?"

"I—I can see that. Listen—"

"You want to be careful who you're calling a weirdo, buddy. I mean, last I checked, you and I were kinda into the same stuff, y'know what I mean?"

"I know. Look, what I mean is, it's weird that you keep hunting me down as if we were—"

She started. "Hunting you down? I mean—"

"—a couple." I locked eyes with her and put my hand on her shoulder. "Because we're not." She stared back at me, her skin flushed. "You know that, right?"

"I think," she said, after a beat, "you have me confused with someone else. Maybe that weirdo astronaut chick who put on Depends and chased a married man halfway across the country. That's not what's going on here. You know that, right?"

"I think you're taking things a little more seriously than they deserve."

"Oh, you do? Is that your expert opinion, Dr. Freud? You think an affair is something I oughta just laugh off, like I do it every day of the week? Is that how you think this should go?"

"'Affair?'" I blurted. "Who said anything about an affair?" I wanted to look back at Paulsen and Roy, make sure they were minding their own beeswax.

Unfortunately, Cathy's eyes chose that moment to start welling up with tears. "Well, what do you call it?"

"We were playing a game!"

"Some game! Y'know, women are different. We have feelings, okay? It isn't just wham, bam, thank you, ma'am for us."

"I know. I just thought, you know, it's *Realms of Eros*. Who takes that any kind of seriously?"

"Me, for one."

"But it's a video game! I might as easily have been fucking a bot! Jerking off with one! Whatever!" You may have seen all this, of course, heavily bleeped, on the comedy or news program of your choice.

"Wait," she said, raising her hands and backing away a step, "wait, wait. Wait. Let me get this straight. You're saying all I am is a jerkoff partner? So doesn't that kinda make me, like, not a whole person?"

"Come on, Cathy!"

"Oh, excuse me, I forgot I had a name there! Because forgive me if I'm, you know, misunderstanding your analysis of the situation, but apparently I was just Ms. Pris, a sexbot, something you used to wipe your dick on."

"No, that's not—!"

"Because excuse me if I'm wrong, but don't they call that a what, a sex *object*? A thing? Were you objectifying me, *Dash*?"

"Could you please keep your voice down?"

"No, I think everyone should hear this. I mean, there you are, lookin' all fancy with your tie and slacks, standing up on, what is this, MSNBC? Being all professional and representing the business community and whatnot. Well, good for you, dude, except some of us have actual lives tied up in this thing. I mean, that may not be what's important to you, but I don't appreciate being treated like a game on the Internet."

"I didn't mean I was—"

"I'm a person, okay? And I don't give a shit what MSNBC thinks or how long that dwarf in the heels has to wait, I need some insight on what's goin' on here."

"Jesus, Cathy, what're you hoping to find out?"

She glared back at me. "For starters, I want to know if you ever had any intention of looking me up here, in real life, like a *person*."

"I didn't even know you were here till last night."

"Okay, but once you did know."

I shook my head, helpless. "I wasn't—"

"Did you plan to look me up? Or just hang me out to dry like a used jizz rag?"

"Holy—look. I don't have time to talk this through with you now."

"So make time."

"I don't know where to begin." I should've begun, of course, by checking on Paulsen and Roy.

"Put your thinking cap on and talk to me, Gary, or I'll go tell that bitch from MSNBC an erotic anecdote that'll French-braid her hair."

"Oh, my God! Look, chill out, okay? I never had any intention of being unkind to you, but you're starting to piss me off."

"Oh, I'm pissing *you* off? That's hilarious."

"My wife," I said, selecting a topic I wouldn't have chosen had I known Roy was videotaping me.

"What about her?"

"She is *here*. In this park. As my date. And we're having an amazing time. I'm so crazy about her I could put it in skywriting."

"Yeah, well, hallelujah for true love. So why did you start something with me?"

"For the same reason I go online and look for porn: variety. I'm a man. I like seeing different faces and hearing different voices when I have sex or masturbate. It makes things more exciting. Don't you?"

"This ain't about me."

"And *Realms of Eros* was one way I had of doing that. Another was porn. It's no big deal, I swear to God."

"So I was right. You did just use me to jerk off. Or to get off with your wife. I bet she'd love the shit outta that."

"Basically yes. I used you. I did. I'm sorry if that hurts you. But come on! You were using me, too. You know you were."

"Gary, I'm losing my husband. Okay? You know that. It's an absolutely insane time for me. And yes, maybe I did just log onto the game for a couple of kicks. But things got serious. You know they did. Just...don't fucking lie to me about that, okay? I will lose my goddamn composure. We talked. I got to know you. We had a relationship, Gary. You can't pretend we didn't."

A relationship? Did we? But that's cuckoo for Cocoa Puffs. Right? The poor woman was out of her mind, yes?

Right?

I got dizzy. I thought I got dizzy. The planet was moving.

"Cathy..." It was, though. *The planet was moving.*

"What the fuck?" Cathy wondered, expressing my own thoughts precisely.

Chapter 15

Imagine the world as a fat, round fish swimming in space. Picture its scales sliding past each other, each scale preciously thin, opalescent. The earth's crust is likewise fragmented and fragile. Some have compared this outer rind, the "lithosphere," to an eggshell, but the shell of a hen's egg is three times thicker, relatively speaking, than the crust to which we cling for our lives. Jagged tectonic scales of rock slide over and around each other, smashing each other to pieces in super slow-mo. Each plate carries the momentum of quadrillions of tons of stone at the breakneck rate of three inches a year; less than thrilling, perhaps, but faster than the growth rate of human fingernails. This crawl drags on over millions of years. Some plates are able to slide over or under, bending as far as ninety degrees to drop out of each other's way. Others—like the Pacific Plate, which carries four trillion tons of seawater, plus broad slivers of California and New Zealand—can only grind raggedly against each other over the course of millennia. The circular boundary of the Pacific Plate is Ground Zero for three quarters of the world's volcanoes and nine out of ten of its earthquakes, hence its common, all too literal nickname: the Ring of Fire...

—Edward Hayes, *Pornotopia: The Bliss Panerotic Debacle*

The Catalina Fault runs along the southern coast of Santa Catalina Island. It's where two relatively minor tectonic plates meet beneath the sea. Southeast of the island, it crashes into the San Pedro Basin Fault and the San Diego Trough Fault at a subterranean three-way intersection, but that wasn't our problem. The problem was the S-turn the fissure made less than five miles from shore. That geologic feature is called a restraining double bend, and very likely, you've never heard of such a thing. I certainly hadn't. But I heard its results now, awesomely loud, as the ground fell away beneath my feet. It throbbed like hugely-amped speaker distortion. The earth groaned and rumbled, apocalyptically enraged.

I've lived in California my whole life, so I damn sure know the woozy feel of an earthquake when I'm in one. I can't say I've ever gotten used to sudden tremors, of course, but I've never found them any more disturbing than, say, a Wild Mouse ride. This was different. I knew it within moments.

There are aspects of physics we've come to rely on, foremost among those being gravity and the permanent there-ness of earth. Down stays down, the ground pulls our feet, and we're shielded from the whiz of our planet zipping and twirling through the Milky Way Galaxy for hundreds of miles every second. When that protection is suddenly yanked clean away, we're reminded we live at the mercy of gargantuan forces beyond our control. It demolishes order. We find our brains jolted into primal, even nonverbal states. It's like being cast from reason into Hell.

Cathy and I were thrown to our knees. I grabbed her and tugged her into a desperate embrace as she screamed. Roy sat cross-legged not far away; he seemed interested, sure, but not terribly impressed. I wonder now if he's one of those people like Kristen Stewart who has only one facial expression. Paulsen cried, "Shit, holy balls, mother fuck!" then regained sufficient control of herself to narrate the event for Roy's camera. I tuned her out. A moan of inarticulate panic lowed from my throat.

Some quakes begin with a lurch of unfathomable power. The Northridge quake of 1994 started like that, though I was in Fortuna at the time. I

265

was, however, a toddler when a 7.2 earthquake hit one morning in Humboldt County. My parents recall being physically tossed into the air. Their bed skated across the floor like a Roomba, and six drivers were injured when an overpass collapsed on Highway 101. This quake, the Catalina monster, felt more like being on a 747, plunging through a deep well of turbulence. We plummeted, then bottomed out and rolled to the side. It was awful. We were on a bucking planet. It wanted us off.

The earthquake that unzipped the Catalina Fault that afternoon measured 7.8 on the Richter scale. It doesn't sound too much worse than the Humboldt quake, does it? Seven-two, seven-eight—what's the difference? But it *was* worse, a whole lot worse, because the Richter scale is different from standard incremental scales like thermometers or radio knobs. It's logarithmic. I'm no math genius, but apparently that means the Catalina quake was four times more intense than the temblor my parents and I lived through in northern California. And, as I mentioned, they still like to tell stories about that early morning wake-up call.

I was terrified out of my ever-loving mind. The earthquake seemed to last hours, but dozens of home videos posted to YouTube confirm it lasted less than forty seconds. I heard terrifying creaks all around us as Panerotic's earthquake-proof casinos—which, luckily, conformed to L.A.'s rigorous construction codes—slid back and forth on rollers within their foundations. I heard the piercing chord of hundreds of men and women screaming. Alarms yodeled from the few dozen vans parked outside the main gate. Glass shattered and rained down the Strip in glittering squalls. A man who had somehow miraculously stayed on his feet was suddenly dashed to the ground so hard his arm snapped, blood spraying for yards. He screamed like a girl. I stared in morbid fascination at exposed flesh and bones.

We heard neon bulbs exploding in loud pops; the Sinema marquee warped and flexed.

"This isn't real, it isn't real!" Cathy cried. She threw her arms around my neck and yelped as the ground danced beneath us.

"It's okay," I said, lying. "It's fine. It's okay. I've got you, babe. Cathy, we're fine."

Just when I thought the quake was dwindling, another heavy wave rolled through the asphalt. Glass shattered past the corner to our right. I turned my head in time to watch an optical ripple slide along the windows of Eros 4Ever before they, too, gave way. I believed at first a woman's body toppled through them, but it was only a mannequin in pricey lingerie. The roar subsided gradually. I staggered to my feet. My body felt sore. I had wrenched my back falling, then worsened the ache by clenching all my muscles at once from sheer terror. Cathy's leg bore a nasty, bloody scrape from her fall to the pavement. She wept as I helped her stand up.

"It hurts," she whimpered.

"I have to go find her," I told myself.

"Is it over?" Cathy asked. "Are we okay? Is everyone alive?"

"I don't know," I admitted.

"The buildings are standing. An earthquake. Was that an earthquake?"

"A big one."

"My kids," she cried, her voice catching.

"Mine, too. I need to go back into Sanasana. Can you walk?"

"I'm so scared." Her voice shivered.

"Come with me."

"Help!" the man with the broken arm screeched. "I'll be right back," I yelled, then ignored him. I'm ashamed of that now, but my mind wasn't working. Instead, I helped Cathy limp forward. We rounded the bend in the promenade, and the beachside area of the park spread before us. It had been tossed in all directions, demolished, undone. The only saving grace was of course there were no children; the scene was ghastly enough without little bodies. Men and women clumped together in terrified groups and regarded each other's wounds with uncomprehending eyes. A large African-American man lay face-down, unmoving, at the foot of a hedge. Dozens fled the casinos toward the safety, they assumed, of open beach. I slumped at the prospect of fighting crowds of escapees to look for my wife. Maybe I'd stand here and wait a minute, see if she'd come out.

A sales clerk fell as she escaped Eros 4Ever and was all but trampled by a stream of panicked tourists. A burly security guard rushed over to help her. She ignored him, despite what appeared to be a three-inch gash on her cheek, and looked out to sea with exhausted, hopeless eyes. Semiconsciously, I turned in that direction as well. There was something else wrong. When I saw what she was looking at a second or two later, my mind balked at a sight in defiance of logic. *What the hell?*

The lagoon was half-empty now. I saw the gray line of a short granite breakwater at its far end. Beyond that...

When tectonic plates crash at a restraining bend, they don't just grate against each other. One hoists the other up or down, in a phenomenon called seafloor uplift. As the plate rises, it pushes a column of water above it. That creates a ripple of millions of gallons of water, and it spreads in all directions at the speed of a passenger jet.

The tsunami reared with no more sound than any other wave. A ribbon of white foam a foot off the surface roiled against the rock wall, swelled over it, and once again flooded the lagoon. I turned to run but found Paulsen and Roy close behind us, directly in our path.

"It's coming!" I yelled. There was screaming behind me, a yelp of aggrieved disbelief.

"Oh my God," Cathy said.

"Is that—?" Paulsen asked. "Are we—?"

"Huh," Roy grunted, backing away.

I don't know why I did this. I honestly don't. It made sense at the time, but never since. I pulled Cathy to my chest and tucked her against me, my chin in her hair. The lagoon flooded its banks. A hissing tower of foam was launched into the air on all sides.

I felt more than heard Cathy crying. The tsunami surge rolled up the beach and kept coming, faster than any Olympic sprinter could run. "My God, Gary, no."

"This is it," I said. "Sorry. I love you."

That is what I said. The tsunami hit my legs like a bison. The rest I can't remember at all.

Part Four: Afterglow

Chapter 16

You can see why this isn't so goddamn funny to me.

It's not the height of a tsunami that matters; it's the weight. For every cubic foot that washes ashore, add another sixty pounds of impact at thirty miles an hour. The waves—there were five—tossed our bodies down the Strip as if we were rag dolls. If we hadn't slammed against the main gate or some other obstacle, we would've kept going for miles. Cathy's left leg was fractured and badly infected. I suffered two broken ribs, a shattered ulna and, as you know, worse.

I had dozens of friends in Bliss Panerotic that afternoon. Some you've met; most you haven't. I thought it best not to write about those victims who were wounded more deeply than I. I certainly haven't written about those who, I weep to say, are no longer with us. A man named Emerson, for example, an outdoor operations manager, died when the waves dashed his body against a faux-stone enclosure near the hot tub grottos. He passed in the arms of his girlfriend, a pharmacist from Torrance, a trauma she relives in nightmares at least once a week. He and I became close over the preceding six months, and I miss him even more than I would've expected. His wife maintains his Facebook page as an online memorial. I visit it often to catch up on what others have written, though I never comment. My name and picture would only distract, and his family deserves better.

Rick Orzabal and Judy Orzabal-Saga were ordering lunch when the quake hit, in a fast food joint that looked like but wasn't a Subway. (Subway had the foresight to cancel its park franchise a month before opening. Well-played, sandwich artists.) Judy was uninjured, but Rick fell down heavily and aggravated a football injury in his right knee. He still gives me shit about it, but at least we stayed friends. He makes me laugh, which in turn keeps me sane. He and Judy are talking about returning to the Midwest, but I'm selfishly hoping they'll change their minds and stay.

Jamal Harris, aka DJ Buzz da Ramfunkshus, was partying in one of Sanasana's high-roller suites with two producers, a hype man, six video models, and a porn star I won't name. He and his wife barely noticed the quake—now that's a party—but his posse watched the tsunami pass from their balcony. I'm told he was deeply upset by what happened at Bliss Panerotic and plans to write a three-part epic about it for his next album. I wish him and his newlywed wife, Andréanne, much success.

Chef Hayasaka bounced back from a mild heart attack, and he and his famed New York eatery received a third Michelin star late last year. If you're hungry for sushi, you could do a lot worse. Just don't tell him Gary Klein sent you. To tell you the truth, I'm not sure he was ever that fond of me, and he hates being reminded of the money he lost on Katana.

Heidi Licious and her boyfriend-slash-suitcase-pimp Mike left the park early Saturday morning. They were in Avalon shopping that afternoon and escaped serious injury. When Panerotic declared bankruptcy, thus rendering her contract null and void, she starred in a feature called *Shattered Bliss* for a rival company based in the San Fernando Valley. I've seen a trailer for it—yes, porn flicks have trailers now—but not the actual movie. I'll probably watch it someday, as I was enticed by her character's hilariously inappropriate line about the disaster: "I sure hope those horny-ass bitches can float!" Well-played, Heidi. Rock on, am I right? Rock the mother-fuck on.

Sixteen minutes after the tsunami swept ashore in Bliss Panerotic, it hammered the ports of San Pedro and Long Beach, but folks there had time to prepare so were able to escape the scene on foot. There were injuries and property damage all over southern California, and thirty-eight people were killed. Sadly, seventeen of those deaths were in Bliss Panerotic. I know it's customary to blame the Ryders for all those deaths, but it wasn't their fault. How could it be? As Pat Robertson said two days later, it was "an act of God." Of course, he immediately added, "you'd better believe, friends, that God is not mocked."

Chastity Paulsen and, one assumes, Roy, were back at work the next day. She was live on-air for much of that week and wore a hideous contusion on her face as a correspondent's war wound. Her status at MSNBC improved dramatically, but her on-camera bellow has not. To me she still sounds like Rita Moreno yelling, "HEY, YOU GUYS!" on *The Electric Company*, but I admit I'm probably bitter.

Adam and Nicole Ryder were uninjured by the quake and tsunami, though she cut her arm badly hours later while aiding in rescue attempts. She was given eight stitches by medics on site. She and Adam were subsequently the focus of two class-action suits and dozens of independent suits, most of which they won. A few judges felt they could've done more to establish earthquake safety procedures or to help the survivors, but Californians generally understand there's only so much you can do. We hadn't had time to get ready for anything that enormous. It's part of the reason disasters come early in project histories, I suppose, though coincidence is always a bitch. The *Titanic* scraped an iceberg after four days of service, LZ 129 *Hindenburg* went down in flames at the start of its second season, *Apollo 1* burned three men alive in a pre-launch test, and we caught a similarly unbeatable hand. It wasn't the lawsuits that did the Ryders in. It was seawater. Cleaning and repairing the beach areas and casinos took more money than Panerotic Entertainment Group had, and Zone 3, the LGBT zone, never felt new or inviting again. The odors of dampness and desperation lingered. For that and so many other reasons, attendance was never the same.

I went back to the office and worked on our other accounts, but the big fish kept swimming away. After two excruciating months my partners asked politely whether I might consider severing our relationship. I couldn't blame them. We went our separate ways: them to the middle of the pack where it's safe, me to what Springsteen called the darkness on the edge of town. I made a few shekels doing anonymous consulting work, but between Randall/Klein slimming down to become Randall & Associates and other whopping life changes, my once-secure fortune is vanishing fast.

There were those who suggested, some jokingly, some not, that the waves were a spanking from All-Smitey God, a Noah's deluge in narrowcast miniature, unleashed to eradicate one particular colony of leprous licentiousness. Personally, I think the Big Voyeur Upstairs must have better things to do, but I'll leave you to choose your own comforting chicken soup of theology.

Adam and Nicole struggled to keep their park in business, then labored even more frantically to sell it. Buyers wanted nothing to do with the place. By September the writing was on the wall. Both the Ryders and Panerotic Entertainment Group, Inc. declared Chapter 11 bankruptcy on January 8, 2016. I haven't seen the Ryders in person since opening day, but we did exchange a few cordial emails over the next few months. They were asked to comment for this book but politely declined, then immediately severed any form of communication. I haven't heard from them since.

I was taken to Avalon Medical Center, where I regained consciousness later that night. Because we were found pressed against the main gate, Cathy and I were among the first victims removed. Summer on the other hand was badly concussed but received capable treatment on the spot, by medics who choppered in from L.A. We didn't see each other for several days. My phone was completely waterlogged, but I was able to save it by burying it in grains of dry rice overnight. There were too many messages to deal with. Nothing from Summer, though: she forgot her phone in her rush to get out of the park. For sixteen hours I had no idea whether she was alive or dead. It was the longest night of my life. From patients' rooms around me, I heard TVs playing and replaying footage from the quake in mainland L.A. The Panerotic story, or any news from Catalina Island, was slower to break.

Cathy called and left a message from her hospital phone, but I didn't know the number so I skipped it for hours. When I heard the message, I stared at the wall, completely helpless, for several minutes. "This isn't over," Cathy vowed, her voice slurred from a soothing cloud of painkillers. "I gotta talk to you, buddy. This is serious, dude. You're not gonna use this fuckin' tidal wave shit as an excuse to get out of talkin' to me, okay? So don't even think about it. You watched out for me today and I appreciate that. I'm not gonna forget it. But we are in love with each other, Gary. We shouldn't, like, pretend it's just one of those things. We should finish this, okay? Get together. We should make this all right." *But it isn't*, I thought, *and you can't. It's my job to do that, and you aren't the way I wanted to do it...plus you might be as crazy as snow in July.*

It's what I thought then, anyway. I've since learned to be kinder to sad, lonely people in crisis.

How Chastity Paulsen and her cameraman saved that video I'll never know. She called three times that afternoon looking for a comment or, if I were well enough, an interview. I didn't respond. In fact, I've never responded. They salvaged the data somehow and aired it the next day, with my name prominently displayed as "GARY KLEIN, PANEROTIC SPOKESMAN." They ran Roy's astonishing footage in a package that also included my grandiose comments the day before at the grand opening. You know: "We look forward to giving them a big, amazing wet dream of a weekend they'll remember for the rest of their lives." The contrast between my polished self and me dealing with Cathy as the world flew out from under our feet a day later made for truly unforgettable television. Believe me, I know. I had boasted myself into a class-five poop monsoon.

By the time Summer was released and able to track me down, I was staying in a budget hotel away from the shore. The video ran several times, but she hadn't seen it, only heard about it. I knew it was a matter of time, though; as God is my witness, I really wasn't trying to hide a damn thing. I was thrilled, in fact, to see her alive and in one piece. I was also rattled and unable to finesse the situation as I would've preferred. "That woman," Summer said, "what's her name?"

"It's Cathy. I knew her as Pris."

"The news is calling her Cathy. I haven't heard anything about Pris. Who's Pris?"

"It's all the same person. Before that, I mean, I knew her as Pris."

"So how do you know her?"

"It's a long story—"

"Did you honestly tell her you were in love with her?"

"No," I replied, because a.) I hadn't seen the footage yet, either, and b.) I'd forgotten I said any such thing.

"Don't lie to me, Gary. I mean that. You know how important this is."

"I know that. Honest, I grabbed her to keep her safe from the quake. That was it. That was all there was to it."

"So how do you know her?"

"I met her in a video game."

"How did—Gary, that doesn't make any sense."

"*Realms of Eros*," I explained. "We were chatting in *Realms of Eros*."

"You mean that sex game online?"

"Yeah. It was like we were chatting. That's the whole thing. I'd never even seen her in person till Friday night."

"I was with you Friday night."

"I know, but I saw her at the park."

"You did? When was this?"

"When I went to the bathroom. You were still in the Jacuzzi."

"Did you sleep with her?"

"No! I never had sex with her. Honest."

"Gary, I don't know what to believe. You say she came all the way out to the park to see you, but you never really met her before that?"

"Yeah. She lives in L.A. It wasn't that far. She and her husband are going through, like, a thing. She's probably really messed up right now."

"And she's married?"

"She was. Is. Separated. They're probably gonna get a divorce. Is she okay? Does anyone know?"

"You don't need to be asking questions about any other woman right now, Gary. It's me you need to worry about. Let me do the asking, okay? Is that fair?"

"Yes. Of course it is. Sorry. You're right. What do you want to know?"

"I want to know if you ever had sex with that woman."

"No. We only had sex in the game."

"Uh, excuse me?"

278

"It's a game. You have sex with each other. In the game."

"I don't consider that a game, Gary."

"No, it's like...playing. It's just...stupid. Y'know? It doesn't mean a fuckin' thing. It's like those games people play on Facebook. It doesn't mean you're a farmer."

"If the chickens show up, and you tell the world you love them on national TV, it does."

"I don't think I really said that. I wouldn't. Why would I say that?"

"I don't know, Gary. Why would you?"

"Where'd you see this video, anyway?"

"My mom and sister both called. They're running it twice an hour on MSNBC. It must be incredibly popular; it's all I keep hearing about. Earthquake, tsunami, and now your crazy sex drama. It's the fucking trifecta."

I asked her how our daughter was. "She's fine now. I was able to reach her this morning. She thought we were dead. Have you called her?"

I hadn't. I was in a bad place. "I will," I said, "as soon as we're done here. I promise."

"You better." She looked at me as if I were dead, or a monster, or something in between. A serial killer. A wolfman. A toad. "This isn't over, Gary. We're not even close to finished talking about this." And it wasn't, and we weren't, but I don't have the heart to tell you anything more about those awful, pointless conversations. It went on and on, but all I can say is we never got anywhere close to what really went wrong.

Once we saw the video, even I couldn't tell her how I felt. I didn't know what I was feeling, for one thing. When I thought I knew, which was rarely, she wouldn't believe me. "Liars lie," she said. "Cheaters cheat. If you'll lie once, you'll lie again. And if you can't be trusted one night, I don't know why I should believe you the next."

What she called cheating, we used to call playing. She'd rewritten that marital history in her head. She did as much of that playing as I did, and she seemed to enjoy it every bit as much. But what the hell, right? I still insist those experiences weren't where we went wrong. I don't know what my biggest mistake was, but it wasn't those parties at Ted's, and it wasn't what I did at Bliss Panerotic. It was Cathy—except really, it wasn't. It was me. Stupid me. Fucking *me*.

I was unfaithful to Summer, though not the way she or you probably believe. I was unfaithful in that I stopped putting her first. Even if we'd allowed ourselves to become weekend swingers, I still should've put my wife first. I have much to apologize for, but that was my greatest offense and the one I regret most profoundly and constantly.

We've been taught to expect stories in which good-looking people have hot, titillating sex, then get punished for lustful behavior. This isn't one of those stories. I wasn't punished for sex with my wife or with anyone else. I was punished for withdrawing my preference for a woman who richly deserved it. I was selfish. I was wrong. I was wrong.

Of course, I never spoke to Cathy again. She divorced her husband, quit her job, and moved back with her parents in Colorado Springs. She and her husband have joint custody of their sons, and all of them treat her like a whore and a failure. At least that's what she told me in a long email I received two months later. I deleted it and never replied. I'm sorry, Cathy. Truly I am. I hope you find someone who makes your world lovely again. You've been through as much nastiness as I have. When it happens to women, they call it slut-shaming. When it happens to men—I'm not sure there'll ever be a fair name for that. I guess they mostly just call it a joke. Man up, Gary Klein! Can't you handle a joke?

See, there was something about that video that stuck in people's minds. As the nighttime comedy shows wrestled with questions of how soon to crack wise about the quake or what kinds of jokes they could tell, Cathy and I made for an awfully convenient punch line. Neither of us had been killed or even permanently injured, and we weren't out of the country like the Ryders—they fled to parts unknown till early 2016—and my God, we flew directly into camera like we were in an epic visual effects shot from some Roland Emmerich disaster flick. How cool was that? Oh, I know, folks. I get it.

The thing is, Summer didn't think it was funny, either. I forgot her in the moment of the quake, but you comedians forget about her every time you show that fucking clip. You forget she was stuck at home crying, or that our daughter had to ask her why Daddy was hugging that woman. I wonder how you'd feel knowing Summer's coworkers repeat your hilarious comedy routines, their laughs fading each time she appears round the corner. I don't blame you for forgetting I'm a human being; I blame you like crazy for taking my stupid mistakes out on her.

When she filed for divorce, I cried for two hours. Then, when I reread the documents and understood she had no intentions of keeping me away from our daughter any longer than seemed reasonable under the circumstances, I signed those dry white pages and returned them to her lawyer the next day. It's not that I wanted my marriage to end; not at all. Never that. I just didn't have the heart to drag it out. We still see each other often, but only for pickups and drop-offs. I try to talk, but she changes the subject and always has somewhere to be. We never fight. It isn't our way. We never finished that talk the way she wanted. And I don't kid myself: this book isn't a great way of finishing anything. It's just the best way I know of earning a living now and telling my side of the story. I'm not especially proud of what I have to say. I guess it is what it is. But it isn't what it wasn't, despite the jokes or anything you've heard on TV.

There are people, my parents among them, who wish I'd never heard of Bliss Panerotic in the first place. But no matter how many times I take the fall for a park full of people, the worst thing that happened there, to me at least, was losing the only woman I ever loved and the best friend I've made in my whole pitiful life. A book about my experiences in what Conan O'Brien insists on calling "Titsneyland" probably won't help, but I did want to tell my side of the story. I can take a joke as well as the next guy, but there's more to this debacle than you've heard on any news channel—especially on MSNBC.

I wonder what would've happened if I'd never suggested attending that party at Ted's? I damn sure wonder what my life would be like if I'd caught the flu and sat out that weekend on Catalina Island. When I lie awake at night, though, pondering those alternate universe scenarios, what I long for most is my wife's soft, snoring presence beside me. Losing everything is about as fucking awful as it's cracked up to be.

I will not try to justify my actions. You can make of them exactly what you will. I do hope, however, that as you've worked though this account you've realized there were all kinds of people at Bliss Panerotic. There were doctors and lawyers and grade school teachers. There were atheists and Protestants and even Catholics, though I'm not sure how they got around the whole contraception thing. We didn't look like stereotypical 1970s porn stars. (I do think that guy on *SNL* does a pretty good impression of me; I just never had anywhere near that much chest hair.) What Jon Stewart calls "Sure-Ass-ic Park" was nobler than some squalid little den of iniquity. It wasn't a germ-soaked resurrection of Plato's Retreat, it was a Magic Kingdom for grown-ups. There were thousands of people who believed it could've been exactly what it wanted to be: a sexual Eden. There were months when I believed in that dream of a pornotopia. In some ways I believe in it now.

My wounds haven't healed—not the deepest, most agonizing hurts, anyway. My mind and spirit are definitely not right. But for all that, it wasn't Panerotic that led me astray. God knows it wasn't Cathy or Heidi Licious or any other woman, whether real or imagined. It was something in my own dissatisfaction. And that is always what it seems I come back to: dissatisfaction. Insufficiency. A need where none existed, a need I felt my whole life. So when I close my eyes at night, I wonder why I had such sweet love, *knew* I had it, yet I still wanted more, ever more—more variety, more passion, more adventure, more youth. Was that my own special sin, or do you feel it, too?

Are you in love? Is it enough? Are you happy, or is bliss out there somewhere, still waiting on some imaginary horizon? Am I alone in this, or are you just like me?

References

A.M. America. Anchor Alia Murray. GNN, New York. 12 June 2015.

Bird, P. "An Updated Digital Model of Plate Boundaries." *Geochemistry, Geophysics, Geosystems* 4 (2003): 1027.

Brain, Marshall. "July 17 1955: Disneyland Opens in Anaheim Calif. [sic]" *HowStuffWorks.com*. 1 July 2007 <http://adventure.howstuffworks.com/disneylandopens.htm>.

Brook, Kip. "UC Researching Happiness, Pleasure and Engagement." University of Canterbury 12 Nov. 2012. <http://www.comsdev.canterbury.ac.nz/rss/news/?feed=news&articleId=614>.

Carvajal, Christian. "Pilgrims in Pornland." *Western Zeitgeist* Sep. 2015:42-49.

"June 15, 2015." *The Daily Show*. Host Jon Stewart. Comedy Central, New York.

Easton, Dossie, and Janet Hardy. *The Ethical Slut: A Guide to Infinite Sexual Possibilities*. Emeryville: Greenery Press, 1997.

Erotic Getaway. Dir. Dani Fiero. Perf. Heidi Licious, Allison Brady, Alan Granite. Panerotic Entertainment Group, 2015.

Gould, Terry. *The Lifestyle: A Look at the Erotic Rites of Swingers*. Buffalo: Firefly Books, 2000.

Hayes, Edward. *Pornotopia: The Bliss Panerotic Debacle*. Olympia: Fear Nought Publications, 2016.

Heater, Brian. "Roxxxy the 'Sex Robot' Debuts at AVN Porn Show." *PC Magazine*. Online. 9 Jan. 2010.

Hines, Douglas. Interview with Argyle Greenwood. *AG360*. GNN, Los Angeles. 10 Nov. 2012.

Jabali-Nash, Naimah. "Chloe Ottman Murdered at Holy
     Land USA by Friend, Say Police." *CBS News
     Online*. 19 July 2010.
     <http://www.cbsnews.com/
     8301-504083_162-20010911-504083.html>.
Johnson, Peter. [sic] "Pornography Drives Technology:
     Why *Not* to Censor the Internet." Indiana
     University Maurer School of Law. *Federal
     Communications Law Journal* 217 (1996): 49.
Klein, Gary. Interview with host Trevor Noah. *The
     Daily Show*. Comedy Central, New York. 24
     Feb. 2016.
---. Interview with host Victoria Sinclair. *The Naked
     News*. 22 May 2015
     <http://www.NakedNews.com>.
Koenig, David. *Mouse Tales: A Behind-the-Ears Look
     at Disneyland*. Irvine: Bonaventure Press, 1995.
---. *More Mouse Tales: A Closer Peek Backstage at
     Disneyland*. Irvine: Bonaventure Press, 1999.
Levy, Donna K. "Surge in Domino's Sales." *Adweek* 5
     Aug. 2013. *Adweek Online*.
     <http://www.adweek.com/adfreak/
     surge-in-dominos-sales1518662>.
Lovgren, Stefan. "'Sexy' Smells Different for Gay,
     Straight Men, Study Says." *National
     Geographic News* 10 May 2005.
     <http://news.nationalgeographic.com/news/
     2005/05/0510_050510_gayscent.html>.
Marcus, Steven. *The Other Victorians: A Study of
     Sexuality and Pornography in Mid Nineteenth-
     Century England*. New York: Basic Books,
     1966. 266.
Marling, Karal Ann. *Designing Disney's Theme Parks:
     The Architecture of Reassurance*. New York:
     Flammarion, 1997.
Meese, Edwin, ed. *Attorney General's Commission on
     Pornography: Final Report*, 1986.

Mieszkowski, Katharine. Interview with Mary Roach. *Salon.com*. 4 Apr. 2008. <http://www.salon.com/2008/04/04/mary_roach/>.

Noreen Finley vs. Adam and Nicole Ryder, Sebastian County District Court, Fort Smith District. Still in process at time of publication.

R&R Partners, Inc. vs. Dorothy L. Tovar and Adrenaline Sports, U.S. District Court, District of Nevada, case # 3:04-cv-00145-LRH-PAL, terminated 10 Aug. 2006.

Rayner, Richard. "Back in the Swing." *New York Times Magazine*. Online. 9 Apr. 2000. Rayner cites a study by Edgar Butler, a professor at the University of California Riverside.

Roach, Mary. *Bonk: the Curious Coupling of Science and Sex*. New York: Norton, 2008.

Robertson, Pat. Media Matters et al. 30 Apr. 2009. <http://mediamatters.org/video/2009/pat-robertson-asks-whether-the-hate-crimes-bill/149707>.

Rockets, Cody. "Hot Coffee." The Rocket Man Blog. 12 June 2015. <http://crtherocketman.com/blog/hot-coffee.htm>.

Ryder, Adam and Nicole. Interview with Argyle Greenwood. *AG360*. GNN, Los Angeles. 19 May 2015.

Ryder Harrison, Evelyn. *The Unfunny Monkey*. New York: HarperCollins. 2012.

Savage, Lynn. "The Notorious Gary K." *L.A. Weekly* 18 June 2015: 18+.

Ski Bunnies Xtreme (and series). Ryder, Adam. Panerotic Entertainment Group, 2010+.

Steinman, Alessa. "The Softcore CEO." *Cosmopolitan* May 2014: 102+.

TMFDeej. "Imagine a Touchable World." *The Motley Fool*. Online. 28 Apr. 2009. <http://caps.fool.com/Blogs/imagine-a-touchable-world/186751>.

Williams, Jalinda. "Suicide Attempt Linked to Nude Video." *Southwest Times Record* (Fort Smith, AR) 14 May 2015, early ed.: A1+.

Yeoman, Ian, and Michelle Mars. "Robots, Men and Sex Tourism." *Futures* 44.4 (2012): 365-71.

Acknowledgments

Gary wishes to thank Summer Ennis Klein for twenty wonderful years together. He's indebted to his extended family, especially "Alice," "Ted," and the Orzabals, for repeatedly coming to his emotional rescue during the darkest months of his life. It's been a long way back, and he shudders to think where he might've gone without them. He asks that you please continue to support disaster relief groups like the American Red Cross, who were there when the earth rebelled and oceans rose and who didn't go home till Summer and so many other innocent people were safe.

The author (and writing partner Christian Carvajal) would also like to thank Summer Klein. She met with us one afternoon deep into our second draft and verified certain details while scoffing at others. Suffice it to say she's less than overjoyed by the publication of this book, but accepts Gary's need to defend himself. She asks that you please respect her and her daughter's privacy by leaving them well enough alone. Her maiden name has been changed in this book.

Lynn is grateful to Marcie Colvin and James P. Monaghan at *Western Zeitgeist* for permission to reprint certain materials and for access to their research database. If we made any factual errors, these should not be held against our editors, publishers, or the hardworking troupers at *WZ*. Stay in print, guys. We need you.

This book owes a great deal to Ned Hayes, who helped us turn a mediocre "final" draft into a much-improved submission copy.

About Christian Carvajal

Christian Carvajal, known to his friends and family as "Carv," is a full-time writer in Olympia, Washington. His article in *Western Zeitgeist* was a pivotal source for this larger work, and he served as Lynn's writing assistant through publication. He thanks his wife, Amanda Stevens, for a life full of bliss and adventures both foreign and domestic; and dedicates this account to his father, Frank Carvajal, who adopted a path that works. Thanks also to Apple Angel, Trina Archer, Davee Jones, "Emma," Rick P., Smack and G., V.C., and all the other pioneers who've been willing to talk to us, on or off the record, about their excursions in Bliss Panerotic.

To learn more about the authors, visit Carv's Thinky Blog at http://www.ChristianCarvajal.com. There you can read some of Carv's earlier works, including screenplays, short stories, a free adaptation of *Hamlet*, and an agnostic's guide to *Rereading the Bible*. Be sure to check out his first published novel, *Lightfall*, a satirical account of the Apocalypse as seen from a churchy college town in Oklahoma.

You can also follow Carv on Twitter (where he's @carvwriter), via his author page on Facebook, or by emailing him at carv@ChristianCarvajal.com.

www.ingramcontent.com/pod-product-compliance
Lightning Source LLC
Chambersburg PA
CBHW062133170626
46813CB00002B/683